# BULLSHIT

## ETC

(Sea stories 1970s – 2000s)

# BULLSHIT

# ETC

by

G. BURTON

First Published 2017

# INTRODUCTION

With apologies in advance to Conrad, Melville and other giants of the genre, I offer here my own attempt at a collection of sea stories.

# CONTENTS

## NOW THIS AIN'T NO BULLSHIT.................1

## LESSONS FROM A LIFE AT SEA.............82

## JUNGLE RUN..........................................100

## MORE LESSONS......................................214

## FWE.........................................................222

# NOW THIS AIN'T NO BULLSHIT

Now this ain't no bullshit. Great opening line for a story, don't you think? Well, I think it is. And do you know where it comes from? It's from this old seaman's joke where they ask: What's the difference between a fairy tale and a sea story? And the answer is that a fairy tale begins, "Once upon a time," while a sea story begins, "Now this ain't no bullshit." Course there's stronger ways to tell that joke, but since you never know who might read this story, I figured I better just use the word bullshit. I don't want to offend anybody, you understand.

No, the only thing I want to do is write a book and make some money, that's all. Cause I been thinking for a long time that I should give up going to sea and become a writer, but there's just one little problem with that plan, and that's the fact that I got no talent. No talent and damned little self-discipline. So instead of writing, I been shipping out all these years, just thinking about writing but not doing it. And it wasn't till the other day when I ran into this guy I sailed with a long time ago that I finally came up with a way to actually write a story.

Cause as it turns out, this guy's got a hell of a memory, and between his memory and my tape-recorder... Hey wait a minute, this is no good. This isn't the way you write a book. So maybe I should start all over again and tell you this story in a writer-type way, okay?

So here goes: The story starts out with me running into

this guy. Ken. A guy I sailed with a long time ago on the *Arkansas*, this beat up old C-4. Or maybe the story really starts earlier that morning when I'm taking my morning bath or shower or whatever you call it when you splash yourself with water out of a bowl like they do here in Thailand. Cause the first time I splash myself, I get this real intense flashback to this night aboard the *Arkansas* when I was out on bow lookout and I got hit by one of the strongest rain-squalls I ever ran into. I don't know why, but I didn't have my rain gear with me that night, and I got hit by this squall where it rained so hard I felt like I was standing under a waterfall or something. I could barely breathe because there was so much water coming down, and I had to grab onto something to keep the force of the rain from knocking me over. The squall didn't last long, only a few minutes, but it sure did soak me all the way through.

So anyway I have this flashback to the *Arkansas* that morning, almost like a premonition or something, like I know I'm gonna run into somebody I sailed with on that ship. And sure enough, when I go to have breakfast at this hotel down on Sukhumvit, I run into Ken.

Oh, I forgot to mention that all this is taking place in Bangkok. That's where I been staying the last few months, first at the Federal Hotel where I always stay when I'm in Bangkok, but lately at this bar-girl's house in a place called Soi Pompak. Her place is pretty far out Sukhumvit and way off the main road, right along the edge of the *klong* (that's the Thai word for canal) that runs parallel to Sukhumvit. It's a pretty long walk from her place to the area around the Federal, but I need the exercise so I make the walk most every morning. Walk clear down to the hotel where I can get myself a real breakfast instead of just rice.

So I walk into this coffee shop and right away this guy

recognizes me. He yells out, "Hey Dave. Dave Berger," and I go over to him. I know the guy looks familiar, but I just can't place him till he tells me his name and says that we sailed together on the *Arkansas*. So now I know who he is and I ask him how he recognized me so quick. I mean it's been fifteen, damn near twenty years since we sailed together. That's a long time. And we were both awful young back then. We both changed a lot. But he says he's got a good memory, and boy he sure is right there.

Anyway we get to talking, and it turns out that he remembers everybody on that ship—and I do mean everybody—and he remembers everything that happened and everything that anybody said. He's got like a photographic memory or something. And I'm so amazed at how much he remembers that it's a long time before I get around to asking him what he's doing here in Bangkok. He tells me he's here as a tourist, him and his wife, and when I ask him where his wife is, he says she's out shopping and he's supposed to go meet her in a little while. So I say, why don't you go get her and bring her back here and then we can all walk around together after I finish my breakfast. And he says okay and takes off.

When he's gone, though, I start having second thoughts about spending the day hanging out with him. Or I don't mean with him, but with his wife. Cause you see, I'm not really sure how to act around women like that. Wives and stuff. I'm always afraid I'm gonna do something wrong or say something I shouldn't. I mean, you can't talk to them the way you talk to whores or anything like that. And I don't hardly ever talk to women except for bar-girls over in this part of the world. And with bar-girls you don't have to worry too much about what you say. They probably heard worse before.

Course that's only if they speak English at all. Cause

this one I'm with now, Pou, doesn't speak a bit of English. All she can say is "good," "no good," and "make love," and that's as much conversation as we ever have. I know a few words in Thai, mostly about eating or buying stuff, so the only time we ever talk to each other is at mealtime. But what the hell. I'm not with Pou for the conversation. I'm with her for her body. And if I want conversation, I can always go talk to a tourist in some bar.

Pou works in a bar on Soi Cowboy, which is the area where I hang out lately, ever since they tore down all those waterfront places out in Klong Toey. The Mosquito Bar and all the rest of them. Yeah, Klong Toey used to be my area. I always used to hang out there and I knew everybody, all the regulars and all the locals. Mama-san in the Venus Bar was a good friend of mine. She knew what type of girls I liked, and she always used to take care of me, if you know what I mean. But containerships killed off that area. They took away all the good-paying seamen customers with their fast turn-around and their flags-of-convenience, so the Thais finally tore down that whole block of bars. And now there's nothing left but a parking lot where they used to be. Just a parking lot. I mean it's hard to believe, but that whole world is gone. That whole little Bangkok waterfront world where I used to spend so much time. It's gone. It's nothing anymore. It's nothing but a parking lot and a fading memory.

But I should get back to my story, shouldn't I? Klong Toey used to be a great place for seamen, but now it's gone and talking about it's not gonna bring it back.

So anyway I'm sitting eating my breakfast, and after awhile Ken comes back with his wife. Suzanne. She turns out to be a damn good-looking woman. Real classy. Be a complete knockout if her nose was just a little bit smaller. And not only is she pretty, but she's also real nice and friendly. She says she's always wanted to meet someone from the *Arkansas* cause she's heard her husband talk about them and she wonders what they're really like.

We get to talking and everything's going along fine. They tell me about how they live in New Jersey and how Ken's now a bigwig with some stevedoring company he's been with for years. And when it comes my turn to talk, I tell them about how I'm still shipping out and how I'm staying with Pou in her house out on Soi Pompak. And no sooner do I tell them about Pou's place than Suzanne says why don't we go out there and get Pou to join us and have her show us around some of the Thai parts of town. So I say okay, it sounds good to me, and we all go out and get into a taxi.

Now to get to Pou's place, you gotta get out of the taxi at the end of the street, and then you climb right up onto the bank of the *klong* and walk along for a little ways till you come to this wooden walkway that leads back to the house. It's not exactly a pleasant walk cause the *klong* is so dirty and the swamp underneath the walkway smells real bad. I don't know what exactly is in that swamp, but I do know that it's thick enough that chickens can walk on it. Anyway, when we get to the walkway, I look at Suzanne and I see that she's kinda holding back. But I tell her not to worry. You can't hardly smell it at all inside the house. And she says okay, she's game, and she comes along. And then once we reach the porch, out where the big water urns are, we take off our shoes and go on inside.

But it turns out that Pou isn't home. She musta gone somewhere with Nit, the other bar-girl who lives with her. So now we start to talk about what we should do next, and while we're talking I remember the tape-recorder, and I say that I'd like to tape Ken telling the story of the *Arkansas* while we wait for Pou and Nit to come back. Ken loves the idea, but Suzanne says she's already heard the story so many times that she doesn't think she can stand hearing it again.

I can see that one of her problems is that she's not comfortable in this house, cause for one thing there's no furniture. All there is in this room where we are now is some shelves underneath the wooden ladder that leads up to the room where Pou's married sister lives with her husband. So I show her the bedroom where Pou and Nit and I sleep, and I take the mattress that's propped up against the wall and lay it down on the floor so we'll have somewhere soft to sit. And when Suzanne sees that she's not gonna have to sit on the hard, wooden floor while she listens to Ken's story, she finally agrees to stay.

So then with the three of us sitting there on that mattress, I get out the tape-recorder and plug in the little mic and I tell Ken to go ahead and tell his story. And what comes next in this book is the story Ken told us that day.

\* \* \* \* \*

–Okay, so here goes. The story of the cruise of the good ship *Arkansas*. Or whatever I should call it… That's not much of a title.

–Anyway the *Arkansas*, that old… that… that wreck. That's what it was. It was a wreck. There's no other word that adequately describes it. It was a relic, a dilapidated old relic. It was… It was like when that German seaman in Dakar asked me, "Is your ship from a museum?" It was a museum piece. It was an antique, a broken down old pile of rust that somehow—perhaps miraculously—still managed to stay afloat.

–It was an old seven hatch C-4 with a split house, one house forward between holds two and three and the other aft between six and seven. And it still had all its cargo gear, that old-fashioned type where you had a single winch for each boom so that you had to tie the topping-lift off to a cleat and you had to swing the booms by hand. It served as a bulk-carrier at the time since they'd removed all the tween decks and turned each hold into one big compartment. And at the time I went aboard, it was carrying a full load of bulk corn bound for Dakar, Senegal and Tema, Ghana. The hull was painted black and the superstructure was white, but even after being aboard for several months, I still couldn't tell you what color the decks were supposed to be since the only color you could see in them was a rusty red. And as far as the accommodations went…

—Well, the forward house was so small that it only had room for the Captain, two Mates and the Radio Operator to live, which meant that the two Third Mates—of which I was one—had to live somewhere else. And while George, the other Third Mate, had a normal room back in the after house with the Engineers and the unlicensed crew, my situation was very different. Because when I came aboard, I was led not to either of the houses but rather to an old Bosun's locker out on the main deck.

—You see, just forward of number three hold on the port side, there was a ladder leading up to the raised foredeck where the forward house and the first two holds were located. And right there beside that ladder was the door to an old locker. I was a bit hesitant about opening the door at first, but then once inside I saw that it had been converted into a room with a bed and a desk and even its own head. And as I unpacked my gear, I kept saying to myself what a strange little room it was, out there on the maindeck all by itself.

—It was equipped with a little portable air-conditioning unit, but instead of mounting it so that the unit vented outside, they had the thing sticking into the head. And that meant that all the hot air from the unit stayed right there, making that head into such an oven that it was always way over a hundred degrees in there whenever we were in hot weather. And on top of that, the unit had no run-off system for the condensation that accumulated in it, and being mounted right over the toilet, all the water would come pouring out of it and land right in my lap as I sat on the can whenever the ship took a roll out at sea.

–Oh, what a room it was. And what a first impression it made on me to come aboard and be shown into that strange little room, that room which would be my home for the next few months. I could see right then and there that this wasn't just any old ship, and I could tell that this wouldn't be any old trip. I could tell that it was going to be a memorable voyage, a truly memorable one. I mean there I was, straight out of the academy and going aboard my first ship—and my last one, too, as it turned out—and I found myself living in an old Bosun's locker out on the maindeck. Oh, what an impression! What a first impression it made!

"You say it was your last ship? You mean you never shipped out again after that?" (That's me talking.)

–No, I never did... I got married shortly afterwards and started working ashore.

(He sighs and looks over at Suzanne, but she shoots a look back at him and he gets back to his story.)

–As I was saying, that room made quite a first impression on me, but as it turned out, it was nothing compared with the second impression which I received shortly after we sailed. A second impression that... Well you see, it was like this: I came aboard in Norfolk at about eleven o'clock at night, and as I knew that the ship would be sailing for West Africa at midnight, that meant I barely had time to change my clothes and go familiarize myself with the bridge before we left. And since I was told on coming aboard that I would be on the twelve-to-four watch, I knew it would be my bridge-watch going out.

—So I went up and looked around the bridge where the Second Mate had already finished a quick gear test and left, and it wasn't long before I knew my way around. After all, it was a very simple, old-fashioned layout with only a bare minimum of equipment. There was an old hydraulic telemotor with its big wooden wheel and also an electric steering-stand with automatic pilot, and there was an engine order telegraph. This telegraph, though, wasn't like the ones found on most ships built within the last fifty years or so where you just move it to the position for the engine command you want to give. No, it was one of the old ones where you had to ring it all the way up and back every time you wanted to give a command—just like in those old movies. Yeah, it was quite an antique. And only slightly more modern were the radar and fathometer and the radio direction finder which was mounted in a corner of the chartroom.

—It didn't take me long to familiarize myself with that little bit of out-dated equipment, and I was sure I had the situation under control when the Captain came up and asked me if I had the Bell Book ready to go, ready to record our engine commands and other maneuvering information. Bell Book? I'd forgotten all about that. He didn't get mad at me, though, he just showed me where they kept it and told me to get it ready.

—That Captain wasn't much of one for getting angry. Or for that matter, he wasn't much for showing any sort of emotion. He was a slow-moving, slow-talking Greek who had almost no personality at all, and what little personality he had seemed forced and phony, like a front he was putting up for the outside world while he was actually living inside himself, in his own private little world. Yes, he seemed to prefer that world, though from the impression I got, it couldn't have been much more interesting than his public one. I can't say where that impression came from, that impression that there was as little going on inside as outside, but it must have come from somewhere... Like maybe from the fact that he always looked and acted like he was on downers, walking around with his eyelids drooping halfway closed and speaking so slowly that I was never sure whether he was slurring his words or not. Because slurred and clear pronunciation would have sounded exactly the same in that dull, slow monotone of his.

—Anyway, back to the story. I soon had the Bell Book ready, and I was once again sure I had the situation well in hand when the Pilot came aboard and we began to untie the ship. Yes, I had things under control, or at least I did until the moment came when the Captain told me to turn out the deck lights, at which point I realized that I had no idea where the switches were. The Captain grumbled slightly as he pointed them out to me, and I responded by rushing over and dowsing the lights as quick as I could. But no sooner had I done so than I suddenly found myself in a strange new environment, in a darkened bridge with which I'd only barely been familiar in the light. And what's more, I had no flashlight. Flashlight! I needed a flashlight, and it wasn't long before I remembered having seen one stuffed behind a handrail over near the small table where the Bell Book was sitting. Only trouble was, that table was clear across the bridge from where I was standing, and it took quite a bit of groping around in the dark before I was able to find my way back to the table and then find the flashlight.

—Once I had ahold of the light, though, I could definitively orient myself within my little corner of the bridge, and I soon managed to do so: flashlight in hand,

Bell Book in front of me, and with telegraph and sound-powered phone to the engineroom near at hand. And so in that way, ringing the bells I was told to ring on the telegraph and then writing them down in the Bell Book, I made it through my first undocking without further incident. And then after we had cleared the dock and gone some distance down the channel, I even felt brave enough to venture all the way to the chartroom where I could look at the chart and try to identify the buoys we were passing. And as time went by, my world expanded even further in that pitch-dark bridge, from my little niche by the telegraph to the chartroom to the radar and finally all the way out to the bridge-wings where it was easier to spot the lights of the buoys we were passing than it was from inside the wheelhouse.

—But it was just when I was feeling truly comfortable with my situation—with watching the ship heading out Chesapeake Bay toward the sea while listening to the Captain feign interest in the conversation he was holding with the Pilot, and with me moving about the bridge with ever more confidence—that suddenly all hell broke loose. Pardon my French.

—For all at once, without warning, all the lights on the entire ship went out, and at the same time the ear-shattering bell of the radio auto-alarm began blasting away, accompanied by the softer buzzing of the steering- and gyro-failure alarms. It didn't take me long to realize that we'd just lost the plant, but even after figuring that out, I still had no idea what I should do in an emergency like that. And I stood frozen in place, turning mental circles as I asked myself what to do, and watching and waiting for some sort of orders, until finally I heard the Quartermaster say something to me. But I couldn't tell what he was saying because of the noise from the auto-alarm bell, so I moved closer and asked him to repeat himself.

–"The rudder's right ten and she won't come back to midship," was what he said, and as it sounded like a pretty important piece of news to me, I went out to the wing and told the Captain what the Quartermaster had just said. The Captain got excited when he heard the news—or at least as excited as he could get, which was a rather lethargic sort of excitation—and he began calling on his walkie-talkie to the Chief Mate to get ready to drop the anchor. As the Mate didn't answer him, though, he called again and again while I stood uselessly by watching the ship curve slowly to the right, away from the channel and toward the mudbanks. The Captain tried everything he could think of to get the Mate's attention, shining his flashlight toward the bow and even cupping his hands and yelling, but nothing seemed to work as the ship turned slowly and steadily toward shallow water.

–The Captain yelled and cursed and muttered insults about the Mate, and then finally, just when he was about to give up hope of ever reaching the bow, the Mate's casual voice came over the walkie-talkie, "Did you want something, Captain?"

–"Let go the anchor! Let go the starboard anchor right away. We're going aground!"

–And soon in the now dead silent night—Sparks had silenced the auto-alarm bell while we were out on the wing and the Captain had earlier turned off the other alarms—I could hear the deep metallic rumble of the anchor chain as it went out. I could hear the chain go out and out and continue to go out, and I could hear the Chief Mate call frantically over the walkie-talkie that the brake wouldn't hold, that there was too much strain and he couldn't stop the chain.

–The Captain responded to this news with perhaps the

deepest expression of emotion of which he was capable. He clucked his tongue two or three times. But no sooner had he made his last cluck than the rumble of the anchor chain slowed dramatically and then stopped altogether. And it wasn't long before the Chief Mate's now calmer voice broke the dark silence, "Captain, we're on the mud." To which the Captain responded with yet another cluck.

–So there I was, barely two hours aboard ship and we'd already run aground in the middle of Chesapeake Bay. What a ship! What a trip! What an eloquent sign of what was to come! Do you remember that? Do you remember us running aground?

"Yeah, of course I do. Or at least I remember tying up the tug that came along and pulled us off during my watch." (That's me talking again.)

–That's right, because as it turned out, the anchor had slowed the ship down enough to where we hadn't run hard aground. And so the tug we called for assistance was able to pull us off the mud during the next high water which was sometime around dawn. And once the ship was refloated, we continued on our way as though nothing had happened.

–The Captain took a gamble and never reported the incident to the Coast Guard, and all he told them when they overheard us on the radio calling for the tug was that it was a precaution. He said that we'd lost the plant and been forced to anchor just outside the channel, but he never mentioned a word about us being on the mud. And as we were able to refloat the ship so quickly, the Coast Guard never caught on to what really happened. And so by the time I returned to the bridge for my next watch at noon that day, we were free and clear of Chesapeake Bay, well out onto the open sea and on our way to Africa.

\* \* \* \* \*

–The trip across was uneventful. We didn't hit any bad weather and we didn't have any more breakdowns. We just fell into our routine of standing watches and eating and sleeping and passing the time. But it was during that slow, uneventful passage that I got to know my shipmates, my companions in the adventure upon which I was embarking. I got to know those shipmates, those losers, those odd-balls who made up the crew of the *Arkansas*. That collection of misfits who had somehow all come together aboard that one ship.

(I think he's laying it on pretty thick here, cause while we had a couple of real strange ones on that ship, most of the guys were just a normal bunch of seamen. Guys like hundreds of em I sailed with over the years.)

–I've already mentioned the Captain and his slug-like personality. And the Chief Mate was even less interesting being that he was the total yes-man, a guy whose only trait seemed to be that he agreed with whatever the Captain had to say. But then there was the Second Mate. Do you remember the Second Mate? Old Bill Burns? Wild Bill as we used to call him?

(Right here you hear me laughing. Laughing hard cause I definitely remember the guy. I remember him crystal clear.)

–What a man! What a fool! The biggest fool of all on that ship of fools. A misfit among misfits. A weirdo in a class by himself. Oh, the things he used to say and do… And I remember how we used to sit around in the evenings and tell Second Mate stories. Stories about all the crazy things Wild Bill had done that day, because he used to do so many strange things that… But no, he's going to be the star of this story, so maybe I should save the stories about him for a little later.

–Instead I'll talk about the second biggest fool of all, a

fool who just happened to be one of the ABs on my watch. Hutchins was his name. Do you remember Hutchins? Now there was an oddball. There was a wacko, a complete and total wacko. He was... No, I shouldn't even say he. I should say they since there wasn't just one person inhabiting that guy's body. There were several people living there—four, five, six, I'm not sure how many—though the one thing I can say for sure is that each member of that group hated each and every other member.

–Poor old Hutchins. He never stopped talking to himself all day long, and his on-going one-man conversation seemed to consist of nothing but one long, continuous argument. An argument in which he argued every side. He'd confront "Mr. Green" over some money problem or over some question regarding future plans, and "Mr. Green" would answer him in a tone that soon degenerated into a simple name-calling session: you bum, you dope-fiend, you fool. And from time to time, "Jim" or "Mr. Fairmont" would intervene in the argument, though not on the side of either the one I took to be Hutchins or of "Mr. Green." No, they would each take their own sides with no one ever agreeing with anyone about anything.

–I used to listen to Hutchins argue with himself the whole time we were on watch together, every watch during the whole two hours that he was on the wheel, and I never heard him take a break. Most of his arguments were mumbled so that I couldn't tell what he was saying, but then from time to time, he would break out with a loud, clear statement: "I told you to shut up." "Man, you're about to drive me out of my mind." "You got me goin' in circles and squares and rectangles." "I oughta kick your... butt." And on and on he'd go, mumbling away and then blurting out: "This is just junk." "Keep your opinions to yourself." "You don't belong here in the first place." On and on for two straight hours.

–I understand that his arguments would begin as soon as he got up in the morning and they wouldn't end until he went to bed at night. All day every day. A lot of people were afraid of him—they always made him work alone out on deck, away from everyone else—but in the whole three months I was with him, I never saw him do anything the least bit violent. All his violence came out verbally, and all of it was directed toward "Mr. Green" or some other member of his private menagerie.

–The other AB on my watch was O'Neill, a guy who wasn't crazy like Hutchins was, but one who was just as much of an oddball in his own way. Why, just looking at him you could see that he was a bit odd given the way that his scraggly beard and his unkempt red hair made him look even more like a first cousin to an orangutan than his build and his facial features already did. And the way he used to dress. He'd always wear loud, loud shirts and short pants with rag-bag pockets sewn onto them and sandals with dark sox. And he always wore a pair of sunglasses over his regular glasses in the daytime. Not the clip-on ones or anything like that, but a full pair of sunglasses over a full pair of regular glasses.

–But as strange as he may have looked, he was one of the nicest guys I've ever met. And what a difference between the two hours I spent on watch with him and the two hours I spent listening to Hutchins argue with himself. O'Neill was a guy who would laugh and joke about anything. And no matter what happened, no matter what anyone said or did, he never got excited and he never got angry. He'd just look at what was happening around him and then he'd stand back and laugh.

–And the sea stories he used to tell! He told me so many of them in that husky voice of his, stories about himself and his sea-going family. Like there was the one about his cousin being one of only three survivors from a ship that broke up in a storm off Cape Hatteras—a ship that was a lot like the *Arkansas* by the way—and of course it was a story that he decided to tell me right when we were in rough weather during the passage home. And there were other stories as well. So many stories. Stories about all his years at sea and about his going to sea during World War II when he was still just a teenager. And I especially remember his story about the landing at Normandy where they had to drive their ship clear up to the beach and then scuttle it in order to form a breakwater. What a story that one was, and especially with the way he told it.

—Yeah, he sure was a great guy and a great watch-partner: easy-going and easy to get along with, never a fuss and never a moan. Jeez, I sure would like to run into him again. I wonder what ever happened to him.

(He looks at me like he wants an answer, but I just shrug my shoulders. I mean, the guy's probably dead by now, but I don't want to come out and say it.)

—Well anyway, there were a few other colorful types in the deck department. Like remember the Bosun? He was funny. He was this Swede who had such a strong accent, on top of which he had such a severe speech impediment that it was impossible to understand a thing he said. So each morning when he assigned the crew their jobs for the day, they'd all stand around trying to figure out what he was telling them, and then they'd just go out and do whatever they wanted since none of them had understood a word he'd said. He was funny in that way...

—And how about Possum, do you remember him? The AB that everyone called Possum? They told me he got that name because he looked like one, though to me he looked more like a weasel than he did an opossum. And not just any weasel, either, but he looked like a paranoid weasel, and he moved with the same sort of extreme nervousness as a squirrel. He was short and skinny and always unshaven, and he had the unmistakable look of a wino. And his nerves? Why I remember how when we hit a little bad weather on the trip back across the Atlantic, you could just see him falling apart. "This ain't no ship, this is a submarine." "I don't want no money, I just want to get off alive."

–And like any good wino in those days, he was death on pot-smokers, and he always used to hassle you, Dave, because you were the only guy aboard ship who had really long hair. He used to go by your room, open the door and sniff like he was checking for drugs. And then there was that night in Ghana when he was on gangway watch and you came back from shore, high as a kite. He kept asking you if you were on "cloud thirteen," and all you could do was look at him and laugh, just laugh and laugh and laugh. I was watching you two because I was on watch with Possum that night. Do you remember that?

"Yeah, I guess." (I'm lying when I say it, cause I don't remember it at all. And in fact, I just barely remember that guy Possum.)

–Oh, and there were other characters, too. Characters in the engine department and the steward's department... Why, I bet I could name all of them if I tried, all the misfits and all the more-or-less normal ones, too. I could recite the entire crew list.

"Please don't." (That's Suzanne talking for the first time.)

–No...?"

"You really remember everybody after all these years?" (That's me talking now.)

–I sure do.

"Wow, that's some memory you got there. It must be

photographic or something."

"No, it's not." (That's Suzanne again.) "His memory's nothing special. It's only when it comes to the *Arkansas* that he's got a good memory. And that's probably only because he's told the story so many times, to people at the office and people we meet. He talks about that ship so often..." (She doesn't finish the sentence, it just kinda fades out.)

—Why don't we get back to the story?

"Yeah, good idea."

—Well, there were many characters on that ship, but the people I got to know best of all were the fantail crew, the group of young guys who used to gather on the fantail in the evenings to, uh... partake of the, uh... the forbidden herb.

—Remember Sue, even you smoked pot a few times back in those days, so don't...

(Suzanne doesn't say a word, and she doesn't even give him a hard look or anything.)

—Anyway, I found out about the group on the second or third day at sea when I was walking around the decks one evening after supper and came across a couple of guys hanging out on the stern: you Dave and Pat the Day Third Engineer. You guys waved me over and offered me a toke, and then when we finished and you had to go to the bow for lookout, Pat invited me to come down and hang out in his room. And in that way we established a pattern which we were to follow for the rest of the voyage.

—Pat quickly became the ringleader of the little club that was beginning to form, and his room became our clubhouse, being not only relatively large but also being well situated, not far from the galley while still fairly isolated from other rooms so that we had a lot of privacy in there. Pat was by far the saltiest member of our group, having a few years of sea-time behind him as well as being the only one who had made the previous trip on the *Arkansas*. And it was under his leadership that the group quickly grew in size during those first days at sea as we all got to know each other aboard ship and as we began to distinguish the dopers from the boozers.

   –We were soon joined by George the eight-to-twelve Third Mate, a laid-back California dude who was fresh out of the academy and making his first trip ever, just like me, though in his case he'd just graduated from the California state academy. And close on his heals came the two messmen, Jake and Link, who were both aboard their first ship, fresh new graduates of the union school at Piney Point. They were a couple of city boys, though each was from a different city and each had a distinctly different personality. Jake was this happy-go-lucky Russian Jew from Brooklyn who made friends quickly and who loved to play the big spender when he was ashore in spite of the fact that he only made messman's wages. Link on the other hand was a tough guy type out of South Philly with a strong accent and a bad attitude, though when you got right down to it, his toughness was mostly talk. Talk that he expressed at very high volume whenever he got angry or excited.

   –And so that became our group, our little gang of dopers who would meet and hang out in Pat's room each evening, sitting around together and talking and dreaming out loud and making periodic trips to the fantail. And though at first sight we might have appeared to be a pretty motley bunch, that's not the way we saw ourselves at all. No, we thought we were downright formidable. And on top of that, we had so many dreams back then, the type of dreams that young, adventurous guys tend to have. Dreams that mostly seemed to be brought up by George but that all the rest of us would immediately sign up for: multi-million-dollar smuggling schemes and lost treasures just waiting to be found and ships that we could buy to start our own company and all the rest. Oh, there were so many different things that we talked about in those days. There were so many dreams… Do you remember them, Dave?

"Sure, I remember them. Kinda." (I mean, what does he want me to say? I know how young guys like to talk that type of garbage.)

–Well, I remember them very well… But of course they weren't the only things we discussed on those evenings. No, far from it. We used to discuss anything and everything, from girls to cars to sports to politics to just simply telling stories about our juvenile exploits or about people we'd known or about events taking place aboard ship. And when it came to events aboard ship, you must remember how our favorite stories were always the Second Mate stories, the stories about all the crazy things that the Second Mate did day after day throughout the trip.

–Good old Wild Bill, he was such a character! He was an old-timer who'd been ashore for something like ten years and was now coming out for one final fling at sea, one final childhood adventure. And a childhood adventure it truly was because of the way he was so far advanced into his second childhood that he always gave the impression of being a ten-year-old kid on a visit to Disneyland. He used to get childishly excited about anything and everything, and he would spend all his free time wandering around and getting into things, inspecting the decks or rummaging through lockers and playing with the equipment he found there. Inspecting it and repairing it whether it needed to be repaired or not.

–Each day he'd go out on his inspection tours, and each night… No, I really can't say what he did at night. The only thing I know for sure is that he didn't sleep, because I remember how all during the hot weather—which is to say during most of the trip—as I'd be going to the bridge at midnight each night, I'd find him out there on deck just outside his room. He'd be standing there wearing nothing but his underpants and smoking a cigarette while staring off into the darkness, and he'd be so lost in his thoughts as he smoked and stared at the dark horizon that he wouldn't even notice me go by. This in spite of the fact that I'd pass within a few feet of him. And if he was out there at that time of night, right in the middle of his sleeping time, that meant that he couldn't have been getting more than a couple of hours' sleep a night. So maybe it was the lack of sleep even more than the heat that made him act so weird. Because remember how he kept getting weirder and weirder as the trip went on? Well, something must have caused it, whether it was the heat or the lack of sleep or just plain senility. I really don't know what it could have been.

–One thing I can tell you for sure, though, is that none of it affected his professional ability, and that was because of the fact that he had none right from the beginning. He was such a terrible navigator! He had this old sextant that he'd bought second-hand back in the Thirties, and it was already out-of-date even then. I mean, that sextant really belonged in a museum, not aboard a ship. And when you combine that antique sextant with an incompetent navigator... Oh man, whenever he shot stars, the lines he'd get would fall all over the place in such a random way that most of the time it was impossible to even pick out a fix position. And on those rare occasions when he did come up with a good cross, the position was usually out by fifty miles or more. That is, it was out from the sun-lines that George and I were getting. And the situation got to be so bad that the Captain was finally forced to go out and shoot stars himself since it was the only way he could get a star fix

that had any relationship with our ship's actual position.
—And not only was Bill an incompetent navigator, but he was also very peculiar. Very strange right from the beginning. Like do you remember him and his coffee can? Well you see, that ship was so old that there was no head on the bridge, and since Bill had to take a sh...

(He looks over at Suzanne and then goes back to talking.)

—Since he had to move his bowels every morning at exactly six o'clock, a time that fell right in the middle of his watch, he had to find some way to answer the call of nature. So during the first few days, he called the Chief Mate to come up and relieve him each day while he went down below. But then when the Mate got mad and told him to stop calling him out, Bill had to come up with some other solution. And the one he finally chose was to bring a coffee can with him when he came up to the bridge for watch. And from that day on, at six o'clock sharp each morning, he would take that coffee can out onto the wing of the bridge and relieve himself right there, squatting over the can out on the wing.

(You can hear me laughing here, cause I remember.)

—Oh, and the way he used to eat. What a show he'd put on at each meal! I used to sit at the same table as him, so I always had a front-row seat to the spectacle. And what he would do was he'd shovel his mouth completely full of food and then force it all over into one cheek and chew on it as fast as he could. Or rather I should say that he would chew it in that way whenever he stopped talking for a few seconds, but since that hardly ever happened... Because the main thing he would do at mealtimes was to talk and expound. He'd expound on anything and everything throughout the meal, speaking in that old-time Carolina farm-boy accent of his and looking absolutely ridiculous with his shiny bald head and his wire-rimmed glasses and with one cheek bulging almost to the breaking point and with little particles of food flying out between his crooked teeth as he blabbed away... Well, it was comical. It was truly comical.

—Though you know, I wonder if some of it may not have been an act, like for instance the way he'd constantly go after that poor, meek little Radio Operator and almost intentionally crawl under the guy's skin. Because you see, Sparks couldn't stand Bill, and he was so obvious about it that even Wild Bill must have been aware of the fact. But no sooner would Sparks come into the room and sit down at our table than Bill would be going right after him in an aggressively friendly way. "Ain't that right, Sparks?" And each time he spoke, wimpy little Sparks would visibly cringe before mumbling out a reply without even looking up, evidently hoping that Bill would take the hint and leave him alone. But the tactic never did him a bit of good as Bill would keep after him, asking him question after question and making him cringe and mumble out replies over and over again. Poor little Sparks.

(He stops talking for a minute here like he's trying to decide what to say next.)

\*　　\*　　\*　　\*　　\*

—Well, enough about Bill for now and enough about the other members of the crew. What I should do is move along with the story.

—As I said before, the trip over to Africa was quiet and uneventful, or at least it was if you don't count that grounding. All I did on the crossing was to follow my routine: I stood my watches, my twelve-to-four watches, and during each watch I spent two hours listening to

Hutchins argue with himself or himselves or whatever you'd call it, and I spent the other two hours shooting the shit with... or I mean, shooting the breeze with O'Neill. And then each evening, I'd get together with the gang that gathered in Pat's room, hanging out and talking and making the occasional trip to the fantail to, uh... you know.

–Anyway, it wasn't long before we arrived at our first port which was Dakar, Senegal, and no sooner had we arrived there than the quiet life we'd been living aboard ship was turned completely upside-down. Because no sooner was the gangway down on the dock than we were invaded by a mass of humanity. Longshoremen swarmed all over the ship, filling the decks until it was almost impossible to get past them and with some of them even venturing into the passageways from time to time. They worked and ate and slept right out there on deck, and they wandered everywhere on that ship, sometimes looking for a quiet place to sleep and sometimes looking for something to steal, be it old scraps of wood or rope or empty oil drums or even some of the corn that we were carrying as cargo. And all night every night, there would be people walking around the ship checking doors in an effort to find places that weren't locked, with that little room of mine— that locker out on the maindeck all by itself—being one of their favorite targets.

–Yes, it was crazy. It was a circus going on aboard that ship, a complete circus. But you know what? There was an even bigger show taking place out on the dock, out where the corn that came off our ship was being dumped into piles that grew ever larger as time went by. And that was because there in Dakar they used clamshells to discharge the corn, clamshells that they hooked onto the ship's antiquated cargo gear and that the longshoremen used to scoop the corn out of the holds and load it onto small conveyor belts which then piled it up on the dock. And once it was on the dock, there would be a few guys working around the piles, shoveling the corn into fifty-kilo sacks and then sewing the sacks shut. But since the process on the dock was a lot slower than the process on the ship, the piles of corn grew and grew until they turned into small mountains. And the more they grew, the more tempting they became for the people wandering around the dock area.

 —I used to stand around and watch them for hours from up there on the ship whenever I was on watch, and it was never dull. There was always an endless stream of people coming by trying to steal corn, and likewise there was a constant pursuit by the guards whose job it was to prevent them from doing so. I remember one guy who tied cords around his cuffs and then filled his pants with corn, filled them so full that he could barely walk. And when the guards caught him, they lifted up his feet and shook the corn out of his pants which was their way of making him put it back. And making them put the corn back was the only thing the guards ever did to the people they caught. They made them put it back so that they could come back and try again a little later on. In the time I watched the show, though, I saw a few people get away with corn. Not very many but a few. Like I remember one well-dressed guy with a briefcase who stopped as he walked by, quickly shoveled the briefcase full of corn when no one was looking, and then continued casually on his way. And there was another guy, a big, mean-looking guy who simply refused to stop when the guard confronted him. Instead, he shot the guard such a threatening look that the guy backed down and let him go. But for every one who got away with it, there must have been hundreds who didn't. Oh, what a circus it was, what a twenty-four hour circus.

—And the circus wasn't confined to the dock area, either. No, not at all. The entire waterfront was the same. It was all a part of the same big circus. That whole waterfront was filled with rundown bars and lowdown whores... or I mean prostitutes. And there were pushy street-vendors everywhere you went. It seemed like everyone there was trying to sell you something, and not one of them would take no for an answer. They'd follow you all up and down the street saying, "What you give? What you final price?" Oh, it was terrible. And I haven't even mentioned the guys who would try to pick your pockets or steal the watch right off your wrist. What a show! Do you remember it, Dave?

"Yeah, sure." (That's me talking, of course.)

—All those hawkers and all those hookers?

"Yeah, that was a pretty wild port, all right." (And it was pretty wild, too, though I probably been to a few wilder places than that over the years.)

—Wild, that it certainly was. Dakar was wild and it was... It was terrible. It was terrible and repulsive and beautiful at the same time. Yes that's right, it was beautiful, because the truth of the matter is that I loved the place. There was always so much going on there, something happening every minute. And it seemed like the whole five days we were there was one big, long adventure. Or maybe I should say that it was a whole series of little adventures that ran one right into another. Like do you remember our first night in town? That night when we made the mistake of letting a shore-pilot show us around, because what he eventually did was he led us into some lowdown bar filled with hostile-looking Africans. And then once we were inside, he leaned over and told us that if we gave him enough money, he'd get us back out of there alive. And us? We did as we were told, though once we were safely outside, we grabbed him and turned him upside-down and

shook until the money came falling back out of his pocket.
 —And there were so many other little incidents like that. So many that I don't know which to describe next.
 (He looks over at Suzanne right here, and he sees how she's starting to move around like she's uncomfortable where she's sitting or like she's getting bored with the story, so when he starts talking again, he's got kind of a different tone.)
 —Well, I guess there's no point in discussing them all. They were just a bunch of days and nights of partying. Though maybe I should describe one more night, that night when we had our little problem in the Chez Vous. Do you remember that night, Dave?... Oh no that's right, you weren't with us that night, were you?
 —Anyway, what happened that night was that we went into the Chez Vous which was the classiest place in the waterfront area. It was the only one that had French hookers instead of Africans though that wasn't the reason we hung out there so often. And in fact, I don't think that any of us ever used the services of those French women. Or at least I know that I never did.
 (And he looks at Suzanne when he says this.)
 —No, the only reason we hung out there was because it was the cleanest and most comfortable place we knew about around there. And whenever we went in, it was to sit around and drink and nothing more. No girls and no trouble, or at least no trouble until that last night. And of course that night, we brought all the problems on ourselves, just as you'd expect with a bunch of guys like us.
 —Because what happened was that we were sitting around on the patio by the little swimming pool out behind the bar, just sitting there drinking in the calm, tropical night air when all of a sudden Pat got out of his chair and said that he felt like going for a swim. And then no sooner had

he said it than he dove into the pool with his clothes on, shoes and all. When I saw him do it, I said to myself that it seemed like a good thing to do, what with all the heat and humidity, so I stood up and did the exact same thing. I dove in and swam around for a minute or two before climbing back out. But then just as the two of us were getting out of the pool, the woman who owned the bar came charging out onto the patio, yelling and screaming at us in French. We had no idea what she was saying, of course, but from her tone of voice it was pretty obvious that she wasn't happy about what we'd just done. She went on and on, and Pat and I stood there dripping wet, giving her nothing but blank stares in reply until she finally calmed down enough to begin speaking to us in English. And what she said at that point, aside from the personal insults, was that she wanted us to pay her two thousand Francs—each—for having polluted her pool.

–Now, I don't know if we even had two thousand Francs among all of us. That was a lot of money for a bunch of cheapskates like us to be carrying around. But in any case, we had no intention of paying it to her, and that's what Pat told her in no uncertain terms. And upon hearing what he had to say, she started to scream at us in French once again, meanwhile blocking the sliding glass doorway that led back into the bar. George intervened at this point by getting right in her face and speaking a phony, made-up French, and we used the distraction to get past her. But then no sooner had we entered the bar and started toward the exit than we came upon another obstacle to our escape, because standing there in the doorway leading to the street was this huge, muscle-bound African bouncer. And we stopped the moment we saw him, none of us wanting to be the first to confront him. Instead, we decided to try talking with the French woman one more time. But unfortunately, this new conversation proved to be no more fruitful than the previous one had been. She still insisted upon us paying her two thousand Francs each, and we still insisted that we wouldn't pay. So she accused us of ruining the best bar in Dakar, and Link answered by saying stupid things about America and France in his usual loud voice. And she took the opening this gave her to switch from personal insults against us to national insults, and we answered by telling her exactly what we thought of the French, and she… Well, you get the picture.

–What eventually happened, though, was that feeling as indestructible as we were that night, we finally just said to hell with it and shoved our way past. And as luck would have it, that big bouncer turned out to be pretty passive as he let us go by without a struggle. Out into the street where we glanced about only to find that a couple of local cops were just turning the corner and coming right at us, cops who were apparently answering the call that the bar owner had made. So looking for a chance to make our getaway, we flagged down a taxi that happened to be coming down the street at the moment, and then Pat and I along with one or two others jumped inside and made our escape. Or at least we thought we made our escape. We thought so until the driver, evidently responding to whatever it was that the cops had yelled at him as we drove by, turned a corner and pulled up in front of a building a short distance away. A grey, nondescript building with several policemen milling around in front, one which we immediately recognized as being the local police station.

–Some cop on duty came up to our taxi and, after hearing what the driver had to say, he spoke to us in French. We answered him in English, though, and his only response was to wave for us to get out of the car and follow him inside. And then once inside, we began asking around if anyone spoke English only to be met with a series of blank looks or negatives. It seemed that no one in the entire station spoke English. And since none of us spoke French, we found ourselves to be at a complete impasse. But in spite of the language problem, we were all feeling cool and confident knowing just how minor the whole affair had been. Or that is we all kept our cool except Link who soon decided that he wanted to get out of there. And when the cops wouldn't let him go, he began to argue with them, telling them that he wasn't wet, he hadn't gone swimming, so they had no reason to hold him. They failed to understand what he was telling them, though, so he tried saying it louder as though that would help, louder and then louder still, but since they still had no idea what he was talking about, they stubbornly refused to let him go.

–We soon saw that we had no choice but to stand around and wait until someone showed up who could speak English. So we hung around there together, talking and making jokes to pass the time—and to help Link keep his cool—and the only incident that occurred during that time was when I lit up a cigarette only to have one of the cops come over and say something to me. I responded by offering him one but he refused, so I offered him the whole pack which he also refused. And it was only after some time and a lot of sign-language that I finally figured out that what he was telling me that there was no smoking in the station—none for the "prisoners" in any case.

–And we'd been waiting around there for an hour, maybe more, when finally some high-ranking cop who spoke English showed up, and though he didn't speak very much, at least he knew enough to be able to ask us, "Any trouble?" We answered him with, "No, no trouble." And he said, "Okay, go back to your ship." And that was it. That was the entire interrogation and the entire investigation, and it was also the final resolution of our case. There were no official statements and no red tape. We just walked out of there and headed for home. Now is that swift justice or what?

—And while our emotions had been working themselves up pretty high throughout the events at the bar and the station, that swift and painless resolution of the case sent them right through the roof. Oh man, the way we yelled and laughed out loud all the way back to the ship! We were so pumped up and so boisterous that the muggers and the hustlers and even the hawkers kept their distance. None of them were brave enough to get in our way that night.

—Man, what a night it was! And what a feeling! A feeling of... of... a feeling like we'd just pulled something off, like we'd gotten away with something. Do you remember it, Dave?

"Yeah, you guys were real rowdy when you got back to the ship." (Or at least I guess they were, cause I don't remember that night at all. I mean, if I'da been there...)

—Yeah rowdy, that we were. Rowdy and ready to party. So ready that we spent most of that night in Pat's room talking and laughing about our escapade. Oh, what a party we had that night!

(He stops talking for a minute right here like he wants me to say something, but I got no idea what to say except, Yeah, that's right, so I don't say a thing.)

—Well, all that happened on our last full night in Dakar, so we never got a chance to go back to the Chez Vous and thumb our noses at that French lady. Instead, we just quietly and discreetly disappeared. We sailed off into the sunset. Though before we headed out to sea, we stopped over at a fuel dock on the other side of the harbor. And while we were at that dock, I saw what to me was the perfect illustration of third world social injustice. Because after all those days of watching poor people being stopped by the guards and made to put back the handfuls of corn that they were trying to steal, I now saw how those very same guards—in alliance with the longshore boss—make a real haul in stolen corn.

—You see, they had previously filled and stashed fifteen or twenty bags of corn aboard the ship, and no sooner had we arrived at the fuel dock than they proceeded to haul out those bags and unload them. But since most of the guys who were stealing the corn weren't longshoremen, their efforts at using our cargo gear were comically inept. They banged booms into each other in their struggle to get the bundle of bags onto the dock, and then when they finally landed it, they dropped it so hard that a couple of bags burst open. They quickly overcame that small misfortune, though, by scooping the spilled corn up off the filthy, oil-covered dock and pouring it back into the sacks. Whoever they ended up selling it to would never know the difference. And selling it was exactly what those guys were up to. They sold it to some buyers who had driven out to the fuel dock to meet them, though before the deal could be finalized, the whole bunch of them had to stand around for what seemed like hours and haggle about the price in whatever language it was that they spoke.

—And that, my friends, was my farewell to Dakar. That was the last impression I took away with me from that wonderful, disgusting, exciting city: that little group of men—the guards and the longshore boss and the buyers—standing around on an oily dock haggling over bags of stolen corn. And when you get right down to it, I'd say that it was a very appropriate farewell. Don't you think?

\* \* \* \* \*

–Our next port was Tema, Ghana, where we were supposed to finish discharging the corn. We'd only discharged a little over half the cargo in Dakar, so we were running with slack holds...

–And I remember how at the academy they taught us about all these regulations for grain ships, like for instance how you're supposed to install shifting-boards so that the cargo can't shift on you and other things of that sort. Well, forget about it. On the *Arkansas*, we just ran with the holds half full and hoped for the best. And if by chance we'd hit bad weather on the way to Tema, that corn surely would have shifted to one side and the ship would have rolled right over—all hands lost. Luckily for us, though, we had good weather all the way.

–But while we were spared the disaster of having the cargo shift and the ship sink, we soon became aware of the fact that we had already suffered a more minor disaster without even knowing it, a small mishap on a similar scale to the grounding in Chesapeake Bay. Because while we were on our way to Tema, our bilge soundings revealed the fact that we were taking water in number three hold. And while the engineers pumped water out of that hold day and night, still the level continued to rise.

–Now, a person who doesn't know much about ships might think that this was a dangerous situation, but we knew better than that. We knew that a ship can stay afloat just fine with one of its holds flooded, so to us it was nothing more than an inconvenience. And what it meant was that the corn in that hold had been ruined and would have to be disposed of in the next port, after which a repair gang would have to come aboard to fix the hole in the ship—the twelve foot gash that had been torn in the side of the ship down by the waterline when we'd gently nudged the fuel dock in Dakar while docking there. And the only real danger we faced was the fact that the steel in the hull of the *Arkansas* had gotten to be so thin with age that a slight bump like that had been enough to tear a hole of that size in it.

—It wasn't long before we arrived in Tema with six holds half full of corn for discharge and one containing several hundred tons of stinking, rotten corn, and with a repair job to be done on the side of the hull. And on top of that there was the fact that, unlike in Dakar where they had used clamshells to discharge the corn, in Tema they would be using what are called evacuators, a sort of giant, overgrown vacuum cleaner. And while evacuators are safe and clean, they have one big drawback in moving corn, and that is the fact that they're slow. And they were especially slow in the case of the wet grain in number three hold which basically had to be shoveled into the mouth of the evacuator one shovel full at a time since that was the only way to get the thing to suck it out.

—So what it all came down to was the fact that our stay in Tema was going to be much longer than our stay in Dakar had been, and this in spite of the fact that we had slightly less cargo to discharge there. And though some people might have found the prospect of an extended stay in Tema to be inviting, those of us in the fantail crew soon discovered that it was a dull, unexciting little place, and especially so when compared to Dakar.

—Tema had only recently been expanded into a deepwater port, and the town consisted almost entirely of the small shacks where the longshoremen and others lived. And there was no place there for a foreigner to go except the newly built Meridian Hotel, a more-or-less modern hotel whose name reflected Tema's main claim to fame: the fact that the Greenwich Meridian ran right through the middle of town. And since the port was on one side of the meridian while the hotel was on the other side, that meant that each time we went back and forth between the two, we crossed from West to East Longitude and back again.

–Not very exciting, huh? But what else was there to do? We could always change money on the black market where we got a better exchange rate than the official one, but even dealing on the black market wasn't exciting in that town since it was all so out in the open with everyone doing it. Why, even the police would change money for you, so you had to figure that the risk factor was pretty low. And then once you'd changed your money, there was almost nothing to spend it on. There was nothing worth buying. And the only source of entertainment in town was hanging out at the Meridian each hot and humid evening, sitting out on the hotel's second-floor patio bar drinking rum-and-cokes and listening to a local band that played music straight out of a 1930's musical about Rio or something like that. Just hanging out there and fighting off the advances of the local ladies of the night…

(He looks over at Suzanne and smiles right here.)

–But you know, as boring as that place was, I don't remember ever feeling bored while I was there. And in fact, I don't remember being bored at any time during that whole trip. It was like there was always something to do, always someone to hang out with and party with. Wasn't it like that for you, too, Dave?

"Yeah, I guess." (I agree with him even though what he's saying doesn't sound right to me. Cause even if you got a lotta guys to hang out with, you're still bound to get bored sometimes, aren't you? But what the hell, why argue with him about it?)

(Suzanne doesn't agree with him, though, and she starts to argue kinda playful-like.) "And you told me you missed me so much."

–Huh?... I what?...

"You told me you couldn't stop thinking about me, don't you remember?"

–Yeah, sure I did...

"And you said you never wanted to leave me again. Do you remember that, too?"

–Yes, of course... I, uh... I missed you. I missed you a lot. It's just... Well, it's just that missing someone isn't the same as being bored, is it?

"If you say so." (She doesn't sound convinced.)

–I mean, you can miss someone and still not be bored, can't you?

(She's not answering this one.)

–Well, you can. You don't have to be bored to miss someone. You can miss them even when you're having fun...

"Okay, whatever you say. I'm sorry I butted in... Just go ahead and get back to your story." (And then kinda under her breath she mutters.) "The sooner we get it over with..."

–Yeah, the story... Where was I?... I was talking about Tema, right? I was... Let's see now, what else is there to say?... Oh I know, I'll tell about a little incident that happened in Accra, the capitol of the country, which wasn't very far away. It was a place I went to visit a couple of times during my days off...

–Oh wait a minute, I didn't tell you about my days off yet, did I? Well you see, Wild Bill and George and I worked out a system of rotating watches while we were in those African ports, a system where we'd work watch-and-watch for two days, working eight hours on and eight hours off, and then on the third day we'd have the whole day free. And so on two of my days off while we were in Tema, I went over to Accra with Victor. Do you remember Victor?

–Victor was a shore-pilot there, one of those guys who hang around ports trying to make money by acting as guides to seamen—and ripping them off more often than not. And while we'd managed to avoid shore-pilots after that first night in Dakar, we ended up letting Victor latch onto our group and stay with us the whole time we were in Tema. We made no effort to get rid of him, but instead we let him hang around with us since he was such a good guy. He was a nice kid who never asked much for his services and who always gave us more than our money's worth. And that was especially true on my two visits to Accra where he proved to be nearly invaluable because of the way he knew the city like the back of his hand. He knew all the best places to buy souvenirs and the best places to drink, and he also knew the best place to go for a smoke... You know, to smoke grass.
   –It was what he called the stone place, a place out on the edge of town where, after stopping at a little house to buy a joint, we would walk a short distance out into the jungle until we came to a clearing. And in that clearing there would be a whole bunch of Africans, thirty or more of them, all sitting around on fallen tree trunks and talking and smoking. And while I felt a bit paranoid when I first got there, what with me being the only white guy in the area, completely surrounded by Africans in an isolated spot, it wasn't long before I began to relax. Because everyone there was so laid-back and so easy-going and so friendly. I mean, how could I feel nervous when everyone was greeting me and smiling at me, smiling in such an open and spontaneous way? How could anyone feel nervous in a situation like that?
   –During my second visit to Accra, Victor and I paid another visit to the stone place, but on that day I was completely at ease from the beginning. And I greeted all the

guys hanging out there, smiling and nodding at them and saying something like, "What's happening, mon?" Oh, I was so cool back then!

—And you know, the funny thing about it is that when I was stoned, I could actually understand everything they were saying in that Pidgin English they spoke there. I mean, it was weird because normally I couldn't understand a word of it, but after just a few tokes, it was like magic. It all became perfectly intelligible to me. Every word and every phrase and every idea. And when I heard some of the guys asking Victor what he was going to get from me, whether it would be a shirt or a pair of Levi's or what, I decided to play along with them and make Victor look good. So when he asked me for a cigarette, I gave him the whole pack instead, doing my best to look like a complete sucker. Yeah, I put on a great performance out there, and it was all made possible by the fact that I was stoned.

(There's a little pause here while he looks over at Suzanne. It's like he's trying to see how she's taking all this talk about dope.)

\*　　\*　　\*　　\*　　\*

—Well, enough about drugs and enough about Tema. It was a pretty dull place and the less said about it the better. I'll just say that we finally finished the cargo there, and we finished the repairs, and then we sailed for...

—Oh, wait a minute. Before I talk about the next port, I should say something about the rumors that were flying all over that ship, the rumors about what would be our next port of call. Because you see, once you finish discharging cargo on an old tramp like the *Arkansas*, you have to go somewhere to reload, but that somewhere can be just about anywhere in the world. You never know until you actually receive the orders from the company. And those rumors had us going to all sorts of different places: to Casablanca or to Abidjan in the Ivory Coast, to South America or the Far East or just about any other place you could think of. Why, it seemed like every single day I heard the names of three or four new ports as possible destinations, and with me being the conscientious rumor-monger that I was, I duly passed them along to anyone and everyone who would listen.

—And it was really something the way those rumors… The way they added so much to the trip. The way they added to the sense of adventure or something. Because each time I listened to the name of a new port being spoken, it was like I was going there in a way. Like in my imagination or something. And afterwards, I was always left with a vague feeling of having been there. On some level.

—And you know, it was the same with all those fantastic adventures that our gang was always cooking up while hanging out in Pat's room. Those schemes to make our fortunes by smuggling dope or by recovering lost treasure or whatever. Anything adventurous. And as we would all be sitting around getting stoned and discussing the details of those undertakings, I always had a feeling deep inside as though we were actually pulling them off at the time. As though we were living out those dreams of ours and turning them into a reality of some sort. A physical reality and not just one that was in our heads. As though we were actually…

—But enough about that, okay? It's time to get back to the rumors that were floating all over the ship. And what finally happened with them was something like what happens in quantum physics when a series of probability curves collapse into a single event or reality. And in the case of our rumor-curves, they finally collapsed into the single reality of our next port which turned out to be Pointe Noire, Congo, where we were supposed to pick up a load of manganese ore bound for Montreal. That turned out to be the reality.

–Pointe Noire which in some ways was an even duller place than Tema had been, and that's saying something. It was a neat, clean little Marxist-run industrial town with even less night life than there had been in Tema at the Meridian Hotel. And while I'm sure that the Captain was relieved by the fact that it turned out to be such a well-run place, and also by the fact that we arrived there without incident—with no more groundings and no more holes in the hull—it was exactly the opposite of what those of us in the fantail crew had been hoping for. We wanted some action. We wanted another Dakar. We wanted something to happen to liven things up after all those long, quiet days in Tema. And we would have been sorely disappointed in our wishes if only it hadn't been for our good friend Wild Bill.

–Because you see, it was just around the time we reached Pointe Noire that Bill was finally coming into his own and turning into the true nutcase that we'd always felt he could be. It was then that he was finally pushing toward the extreme limits of sanity and, with Bill being Bill, he was doing so in a very entertaining way. And while he'd been getting more and more, uh… eccentric as the trip had worn on, he hadn't done anything really and truly crazy up until then.

–I mean, about the worst thing he'd done had been on an evening in Tema when he was coming back to the ship and found that his way was blocked by a rope strung across the entrance to the port. Now seeing that rope, most people would have asked why it was there and then waited for it to be removed, or if they were in a hurry, they might have tried paying off the guard to gain entry to the port area. But not old Bill. No, that wasn't his way. What he did instead was to take matters into his own hands. What he did was to reach into his pocket and pull out his trusty pocketknife and cut the rope in two. No more obstacle and no more problem. Or at least there wouldn't have been a problem if only the guards hadn't grabbed him and hauled him off to spend the night in the local jail. Good old Bill, good old Wild Bill.

—Anyway, we had to anchor outside Pointe Noire and wait there on the hook until the pilots called us on the radio to tell us that they were ready to take us in. And that meant that during our watches that night, there was nothing for us Mates to do but check the anchor bearings from time to time and listen for the call on the radio. But no sooner had Bill come to the bridge to relieve me at four o'clock in the morning than he went over to the radio and turned it off, saying, "That thing's makin' too much noise."

—"But Bill," I told him, "we have to listen to it. We have to hear the pilots when they call." And when his only reply to that statement of mine was a blank, uncomprehending look, I repeated it to him and then repeated it again. But as many times as I said it, I could see that the information I was trying to convey was bouncing right off that bald head of his. I could see that it wasn't penetrating at all, and so I finally gave up. And no sooner had I abandoned the subject than he began rushing around the bridge doing useless things. He went over to the sound-powered phone and called the engineroom to tell them that we were anchored, something that I'm sure they were well aware of. And after that, he rushed out onto the bridge wing and began blowing that little whistle he was always using to call the ordinary on his watch, the ordinary who just happened to be you, Dave. Do you remember that whistle of his?

–"Oh, yeah." (That's me. I answer his question even though I'm trying to keep quiet now. Cause while I'm sitting here listening to him, I'm getting this idea about writing up the story he's telling. And if I'm gonna write it up, I don't wanta ruin it with a bunch of comments and stuff. Know what I mean? So I'm trying not to talk, and I only talk here cause he asks me a question.)

What was he always calling you for? Do you remember?

"Just stuff. Stupid stuff most of the time. I mostly just ignored him when he called, just acted like I didn't hear."

–And what would he do then? Keep right on blowing?

"Yeah, most of the time."

–Good old Bill, always stirring things up, always up to something whether it made any sense or not. And I guess he must have kept himself pretty busy on that anchor watch, too, because according to George, it wasn't until the very end of the watch, when George had already come up to the bridge to relieve him, that he finally remembered about the pilots and turned the radio back on and began calling them. "Pointe Noire Pilots, this is the American *S. S. Arkansas*. Can you read me? I can't read you." They soon answered him and told him that they had no information for us yet, and he signed off. "Roger Amjet." But then about a minute later, he was right back on the radio calling them again to see if they had any new information. They didn't, of course, but that didn't stop him from calling them a third time shortly afterwards to ask them the exact same question once again. After that third call, though, the pilots stopped repeating their usual reply, and instead they told him to shut up and get off the radio. They told him to stop bothering them. Good old Bill.

–Well, we finally docked that afternoon, and no sooner had we rung up Finished With Engines than Bill was ready to go. He was ready to start performing. And when the stevedores pointed out the big, automated loading system they had there and said that we would be sailing the next day, he didn't believe a word they had to say. "Bullshit, we're gonna be here for a month."

(He looks over at Suzanne, but she acts like she didn't even hear the word he just used.)

–So Bill worked out a watch-rotation schedule all by himself, and then he took off to book himself a room in the best hotel in town. And he left so quickly that he was already gone before George and I had a chance to complain about his schedule which somehow had the two of us standing all the watches for the first two or three days while giving him all that time off. And I didn't get a chance to tell him that his schedule was no good—and that in any case we'd be setting sea-watches at midnight since we were going to sail the next day—until I ran into him at the hotel bar that evening. But with the way he was acting at that hotel... Well, I knew it was hopeless but still I had to try telling him.

–Our gang came into the hotel for a drink while we were making the rounds of the town, all of us except George who was on watch, and there we found Bill wandering around the bar and lobby, looking like something out of a time-warp in his Forties-style suit. And at the same time, he was making a complete spectacle of himself. I mean, first he was making these blatant attempts to pick up on some French woman right there in front of her husband and making an ass of himself in the process. And then once the two of them had gotten up and left, Bill started to get even worse. He started shouting out old union slogans from the Thirties and singing "Solidarity Forever" at the top of his lungs, and he just generally put on a complete show.

—So the group of us stayed around and watched him for a little while, long enough to have a couple of drinks, but then Pat got up and struck a salty pose and said that we should blow that place and go look for some other type of action in town besides watching Bill perform. Link agreed with Pat, and he said so over and over again, each time in a louder voice. I disagreed with them and said that we should stay there since we'd already seen enough of Pointe Noire to know that there was nothing going on anywhere, but nobody backed me up. Dave didn't seem to care one way or the other. He was just going along with the flow, like always. And Jake was too busy talking with the new friend he'd just met in the hotel bar to give an opinion either way. So that meant that it was up to me and me alone to offer resistance to Pat's salty wisdom and Link's vocal force. And given those odds, it wasn't long before the group of us left Bill and the hotel behind and went…

(Right here the tape runs out, so I flip the cassette over and tell Ken to start talking again.)

—Okay, back to the story… Well, the next morning, Bill didn't make it back for his watch at four o'clock even though I'd tried to tell him about sea-watches, and he didn't make it back for breakfast or lunch either. He wasn't back at one o'clock that afternoon, which was an hour before sailing, the time when everyone was supposed to be aboard, and he wasn't back at one-thirty when we called all hands for undocking, and he still wasn't back at two o'clock when the crew turned to. He wasn't back before we pulled up the gangway and went fore-and-aft to untie the ship, and he wasn't back before the tugs were made fast, and he wasn't even back before the crew started taking in the lines. And in fact, it wasn't until the very moment when we'd just taken in the last line and when the tugs were about to start pulling the ship away from the dock that Bill finally pulled up in a taxi.

–I was on the bridge for undocking at the time, and I remember how the Captain groaned when he saw Bill get out of the taxi and climb over the rail onto the ship. It seemed to me that the Captain had been hoping that he'd already seen the last of Bill, and he was disappointed now to find that that wasn't going to be the case. No, far from it. Because the Captain and all the rest of us were going to be seeing and hearing a lot more from him before the trip was over.

–Bill had barely missed being left behind in Pointe Noire, but that fact didn't seem to faze him in the least as no sooner had he come aboard and changed his clothes than he began calmly going about his usual business of rushing around performing useless tasks. And in doing so, he didn't even bother to go to the stern where George was filling in for him during the undocking, but instead he came directly to the bridge.

–The first thing Bill did when he reached the bridge was to go up to the pilot who was very busy at the time since he was right in the middle of turning the ship around, and he said to him, "Say Mr. Pilot, can you mail a letter for me?" The pilot glanced over quickly and nodded, trying not to let the interruption distract him from the maneuver he was performing. But Bill wasn't finished with him yet, and now acting as though he were completely unaware of what was happening around him, he blurted out, "You know what, I don't have any money with me right now. It's down in my room. So come on down with me and I'll pay you." And with that, he grabbed the pilot by the arm and began to drag him toward the ladder. And he probably would have taken the guy all the way down with him, too, if only the Captain hadn't intervened by yelling out, "Get the fuckin' money yourself!" And with that, Bill seemed to get the hint as he left the bridge without the pilot.

(Right here, Ken's getting so into the story that he doesn't seem to notice that he just used a cuss word, and he doesn't even look at Suzanne or anything.)

—A short time later, Bill returned and paid the pilot, and no sooner had he done so than he began rushing around checking the equipment on the bridge, looking for something that he could fix whether it needed fixing or not. After a brief look at the radar, he went into the chartroom where he quickly zeroed in on the course recorder and decided to check it and make sure that the heading was correct. So he yelled out to the Quartermaster, "What's your heading?" And O'Neill, who happened to be on the wheel at the time, answered him in a loud voice so that Bill could check the number against the reading on the course recorder.

—But since the heading was constantly changing with the ship being steered out through the breakwater at the time, and since Bill wanted to get it exactly right, he didn't have enough with doing it one time and instead he called out for a heading again and again and again. He called out so many times that he had poor O'Neill shouting out his heading every few seconds it seemed, and this at the same time as he was busy steering through a narrow gap and also answering rudder commands from the pilot. And it all caused so much noise and confusion in the wheelhouse that the Captain finally came in from the bridge-wing to see what all the yelling was about. And when he saw what was happening, when he saw that Bill was the culprit, he walked into the chartroom and yelled out in his lethargic way, "Get the hell off the bridge!"

—Once Bill was gone, the rest of the maneuver went smoothly. We cleared the breakwater and dropped off the pilot and began to bring the ship over to our course for

Canada. But it was just at that moment, just as we were setting our course, that Bill evidently decided that there was one more thing he should check. Because it was then that I began to hear him whistling through the voice-tube that led up from the gyro-room, giving me his signal that he wanted to check the heading on the bridge repeaters against the master gyro down below. I heard him whistle and started to walk over to the tube to answer him. But no sooner had I taken a step or two in that direction than I saw the Captain hurry over, moving faster than I'd seen him move before while muttering a curse under his breath. And the moment he reached the spot, he answered Bill's whistle by slamming the cover on the voice-tube shut.

\* \* \* \* \*

–So we sailed off into the sunset once again. We left Africa behind, taking nothing with us but memories and a few small souvenirs—that and a whole shipload of manganese ore. We began the long passage to Canada, and we soon fell back into our old routine of standing watches or doing daywork, and of hanging out in Pat's room during our free time. And by now we had plenty of African weed to smoke on our trips to the fantail as well as plenty of stories to tell. And especially in the case of Second Mate stories, we had an ever-growing abundance because of the way that Wild Bill seemed to get wilder and wilder with each passing day. And whenever we told or retold any of those stories among ourselves, they seemed so hilarious each and every one of them, so hilarious and so completely outrageous, that we laughed ourselves hysterical night after night. It was just... I don't know. But it added so much to those stories when we shared them. It made them seem so much funnier...

  –Well, the first thing Bill did after we sailed from

Africa was to get into a log-writing contest with every authority figure on the ship. He went back through the ship's Log and crossed out the entry the Chief Mate had made about him missing his morning watch in Pointe Noire, and then he wrote in, "This is an incorrect statement and so noted. WB." And after that, he went back to the page for the day before and made a long, rambling entry about a confrontation he claimed to have had with the Chief Engineer over the question of providing water for the longshoremen, a confrontation that never actually took place. Or at least it was a confrontation that never took place in Pointe Noire since Bill never stood a cargo watch while we were there. He seemed to truly believe that it had happened, though, because around the same time, he complained to both George and me about the Chief's behavior, complained and described the details of their imaginary confrontation.

—Toward the end of that first full day at sea, Bill began to run out of ammunition for his fight with authority, and it was starting to look like he might even return to normal— normal for him, that is, which was still pretty strange. But then on the second day out, there occurred an incident which was to shake things up once again aboard the *Arkansas*. It was an incident which was to provide Bill with a whole new cause.

—Because early in the morning of that second day, Link was walking down the passageway when he suddenly saw before him two young Africans. Two stowaways from Pointe Noire. They approached him, speaking in French and making signs that they wanted something to eat, and he responded to them by yelling, "What are you doing here?" And Link being Link, he didn't just yell it once. No, he yelled it over and over again, each time in a louder voice, and he soon woke up everyone who lived in that part of the after house. People came rushing in from all directions, charging out of their rooms to see what the noise was all about, and I'm afraid that they must have scared those poor stowaways half to death.

–The stowaways were a couple of young guys from Pointe Noire, one of whom the crew recognized immediately since he'd been a gangway watchman there, a watchman whose job had included the task of preventing stowaways from boarding the ship. They were well dressed in white shirts and short pants, and they looked surprisingly clean for having just spent nearly two days sweating it out in the intense heat of the stack casing which turned out to have been their hiding place. And not only were they neat looking, but they were also well prepared to emigrate to Canada or the U.S. as they set out to prove to the crew by showing them their passports and shot-cards, using sign-language to indicate that all their papers were in order.

–Now, I don't know if they really expected to be greeted with open arms into the land of freedom, but if they did, they were soon disabused of their illusions. Because when the Captain and Chief Mate arrived upon the scene, the stowaways were astonished to see that the two of them were carrying handcuffs and leg-irons. The Africans tried to explain to them in French that they were harmless and that they wouldn't cause any trouble, but their pleas fell upon deaf ears. No one on that ship could speak French and those two couldn't speak English, and on top of that the Captain already hated them for their very existence since to him, they meant nothing but trouble: fines and paperwork and lots of difficult explanations about why they hadn't been discovered before the ship sailed.

–So instead of the warm welcome that the stowaways seemed to have hoped for, they found themselves being led away to an unoccupied room that was normally used for storage. And once inside that room, the two of them were handcuffed to the bunks and basically left to rot for the entire two weeks that it would take for the ship to reach Montreal. They were kept in that room, handcuffed to the bunks all day and all night, only being released during periodic toilet calls. Left there to stew in their misery. And the only thing that alleviated that misery a little was the fact that they were quickly befriended by Jake who visited them several times each day, always bringing along snacks and cigarettes and any other small gift he could think of.

–The Captain wanted to get rid of the stowaways as soon as possible, and since the next day we would be passing near Abidjan, he sent a message to the agent there asking for permission to stop in and drop them off. Unfortunately for him, though, it happened to be a Sunday when he sent the message so he never got a reply. And as it turned out, an even more unfortunate result than that was to come from his idea of dropping off the stowaways along the African coast, and that was the fact that the idea made a deep and lasting impression upon Bill. An impression that quickly evolved into an obsession. Because once Bill had gotten hold of the idea, he couldn't drop it, not even when he was told by the Captain that the plan had been called off and that the stowaways would be riding all the way to Montreal. No, he was never able to accept that change in plans, never able to get it through his head. And instead he clung to the idea of dropping off the stowaways along the coast of Africa. He clung to the idea and clung to it. Clung until finally...

–Well, the moment of truth came around supper time the next day, our third full day at sea, while Bill was on watch. And while he'd struck me as being even odder than usual when he relieved me at four o'clock that afternoon, I really hadn't thought much about it. He always seemed strange to me, and strangeness is a hard thing to quantify. So I'd had no idea at the time that he was in the process of coming completely unraveled.

–As I was told by McGraw, the AB on watch with him at the time, one of the first things Bill did upon taking over the watch that day was to burn up the coffee pot on the bridge. What he did was he went over and, saying that he wanted to get it hot first, he plugged the thing in with no water in it. And then he walked off and left it that way until finally smoke began to pour out of it and McGraw was forced to run over and pull the plug to prevent an all-out fire.

–McGraw told me about the incident with the coffee pot when I came back up to the bridge to relieve Bill for supper at five o'clock, but even then I failed to understand the importance of it. It just seemed like another in that long string of stories that I would end up telling during our gatherings in Pat's room. And in the same way, I also failed to understand the importance of the new track line that I found laid out on the chart, a track that would take us very close to Cape Palmas, the last point in Africa we would be passing before heading out across the Atlantic.

–Bill pointed the new line out to me when I relieved him, saying that the Captain had drawn it and that he was planning on steering up near the point and dropping the anchor and then giving the stowaways over to a local fishing boat. And up where the line ended, just off the point, I could see where Bill had drawn in a little anchor symbol and written, "0731 let go stowaways." He pointed it all out to me and then asked me to double check the time of the course change and the new course and ETA while I was there for supper relief.

–Now it all sounded pretty fantastic to me, but who was I to argue? I mean, if the Captain had drawn that line and was planning on giving the stowaways to a fishing boat, then that must be what we were going to do. After all, I was on my first real ship and these were the first stowaways I'd ever had to deal with, so who was I to say? And Bill seemed so sincere about it. He was so convincing when he told me about the Captain's new plan that I swallowed the thing whole. Or at least I swallowed it for the time being since knowing that we wouldn't be passing Cape Palmas until sometime the next morning, that left plenty of time for things to sort themselves out. And little did I suspect at the time that the entire plan existed only in Bill's head.

—When Bill returned to the bridge and I went down to eat, I noticed that he'd written a message on the blackboard in the saloon, "Get rid of stowaways 7:31 tonight." But the only thing that struck me as odd about that message when I read it was the way that he'd advanced the time of our arrival at Cape Palmas by twelve hours. Because other than that, it just seemed like one more blip in the strange scenario that was being played out around those stowaways.

—And what happened on the bridge after I was gone was something that the guys in our gang were forced to piece together from various sources since none of us was a direct witness to the next string of events. Instead, what we had was the story that Dave heard from his watch-partner Rudd, the AB on watch with Bill after supper. That along with the stories that Pat heard about events in the engineroom. But given those two sources of information and given the physical evidence that George and I were able to find on the bridge, we eventually managed to come up with a pretty complete picture of exactly what took place over the next half-hour or so.

—You see, it wasn't very long after Bill had returned to the bridge and relieved me that he began to maneuver the vessel, making his approach to Cape Palmas in spite of the fact that we wouldn't be there for another fourteen hours. So telling Rudd that he saw land up ahead, he brought the ship over to the right, and then a short time later he came back to the left before turning to the right once again, weaving around and steering toward some point of land that only he could see. And evidently seeing the land getting closer and closer, he soon made a call to the engineroom to tell them to standby to maneuver.

–Now you can just imagine the Engineer's surprise when he received that call since he knew that we weren't due to arrive in Montreal for almost two weeks. So the first thing he did was to call the Chief Engineer and ask him what the hell was going on. And of course the Chief's response was to call the Captain and ask him the same question, causing the Captain to go up to the bridge in search of an answer. And when the Captain arrived there and found Bill busily maneuvering the ship toward some imaginary point of land, he immediately told him to get off the bridge. He relieved him of his duties and called up the Chief Mate to take over Bill's watch. Or as Bill wrote in the Log at the time, "Master order Wm. Burns 2/M to leave bridge & stay in room and not come back to bridge. WB."

–I ran into Bill on the maindeck a short time later, and when I asked him what he was doing there instead of being up on the bridge, he told me that the Captain had ordered the Chief Mate to standby on the bridge for the approach to land while he was out there watching for the lighthouse on Cape Palmas. Or at least that was the first story he told me before he began to ramble along and tell other stories. Stories about how he'd been relieved of his duties—for no apparent reason as far as he could see—and stories about other things as well, like about how the Captain and the Chief Mate were trying to get him out of the way so they could execute some evil plan they had. Some plan to sink the ship—or worse.

—And he went on and on in that way, babbling away in a sort of stream-of-consciousness that grew ever more bizarre until it became almost completely incoherent. And the whole time he was speaking, he was staring at me with such a wild look in his eyes, a look that radiated such craziness out through those old wire-rimmed glasses of his that I soon felt a shock go running through my body. The shock of realizing that at that moment, I was gazing directly into the face of insanity. The shock of realizing that Bill had finally gone over the line and that he was now truly and certifiably insane.

—The shock didn't last long, though, as Bill soon turned away from me and resumed his vigil for the lighthouse that wasn't there. And while the impact of that momentary insight into his true condition must have remained with me on some level—enough to where I can still feel it today—it didn't take me long to sweep the whole incident out of my conscious mind. And so by the time I reached Pat's room, I was ready to laugh at Bill as mindlessly as ever. I was ready to tell the others my latest batch of Second Mate stories: the stories of the coffee pot and the line on the chart and the 0731 get rid of stowaways and the being relieved of his duties. And as I told those stories, I laughed at them along with everyone else, the same way I laughed whenever someone else added a story of his own. I laughed at Bill as hard as I always had. Or harder even since there were so many new stories to laugh at that night.

—And then just when our gang thought that things couldn't possibly get any funnier that evening, Bill came through for us with an encore performance. Because you see, the room where the stowaways were being held was almost directly across the passageway from Pat's room, and that meant that we could clearly hear the commotion Bill caused when he came by the room—at 7:31 on the dot—to release the stowaways and take them out to a fishing boat that he was sure he'd seen waiting for them. We opened the door when we heard the noise, and then we stood looking into the spare room where we saw Bill trying to free the stowaways by breaking apart the bunks to which they were handcuffed. We soon saw how the Captain and the Chief Engineer came rushing in trying to stop him. And then as we stood there and watched the three of them running around and wrestling with each other, it all seemed so totally hilarious to us that we felt like we must be watching the Keystone Cops or something. Bill was a bit bigger than the Captain, and he was also much faster on his feet, so he was running circles around the poor, slow-moving Captain. And as far as the Chief was concerned, he was so fat and round, almost as big across as he was high, that all he could do was hang onto the bunks and try to keep from getting bowled over by Bill each time he rushed by. And the stowaways? They just sat there watching the scene with a combination of fright and incomprehension showing on their faces. And meanwhile, our gang did our best to keep from laughing out loud at the slapstick routine that we were witnessing: Bill dodging around the room, moving from bunk to bunk and easily evading the Captain's slow-motion pursuit while periodically jostling against the Chief and nearly sending him rolling across the room like a bowling ball. And we ignored the Captain's cries for help in subduing Bill because of the fact that we were all too stoned, and also because we didn't want to ruin the comic masterpiece that was unfolding before our eyes. So instead, we stood and watched and sniggered and smirked, and the only time we moved was when we got out of the way to let Bill make his escape after he finally gave up on the idea of breaking the bunks apart and instead beat a hasty retreat back to his room.

—Man, what a sight it was, and what a night. What a crazy, crazy night. One of those nights that you never forget. One where just remembering what I saw and felt at the time makes me want to laugh out loud all over again. It makes me feel young again just to think about it. Young and stupid maybe, but alive. Truly alive! The way that only the young can feel...

\*     \*     \*     \*     \*

—As you can imagine, Bill's crack-up quickly replaced the stowaways as the number one topic of conversation aboard ship, and for the next day or two, it was the only thing anyone wanted to talk about. Everyone had an opinion on the matter—everyone but Hutchins that is, since during the whole time he seemed to be so deeply preoccupied with his own endless one-man argument that I was never sure that he was even aware of what was happening with the Second Mate. But other than him, everyone you ran into on that ship had an opinion, and everyone wanted to share that opinion with anyone and everyone in sight.

—O'Neill laughed at the whole thing in his free-and-easy way, the same way he'd laughed at all the Second Mate stories I'd told him earlier in the trip. And not only did he laugh about it, but he also told me a series of sea stories of his own about crazy people on other ships he'd sailed on. The Bosun voiced an opinion about Bill, too, though whatever it was that he said, no one understood a word of it. And as for Possum, he reacted by begging people to please keep that crazy man away from him, a request that you could tell came straight from the heart because of the way his eyes would bug out and the way he'd run away each time he saw Bill coming. And if there was anyone aboard that ship who took the situation even worse than Possum, it had to be the Captain. Oh, that poor guy! Because you could just hear him groan each time he heard Bill's name mentioned.

–But though everyone talked about Bill and most of them laughed, I don't think anyone laughed as hard as we did in the fantail crew. I mean, between our being stoned and our sharing the stories and all of us laughing at things together, it would be impossible for me to describe in words just how funny it all was. And when our leader Pat told us that within all his vast experience, within his three or four years at sea, he'd never seen or heard of anyone as funny as Bill, we had to believe him. Because after all, George and Link and Jake and I were all on our first ship, so the only other guy in our gang with any sea-time at all was Dave. But he was so spaced out on all the African weed he was always smoking that he could barely remember the names of his previous ships let alone remembering any funny characters who might have been aboard. Isn't that right, Dave?

(I answer him with a little laugh.)

–And our store of Second Mate stories didn't end with Bill being relieved of his duties, either. No, far from it. If anything, it was right at that point that they really began. Because you see, Bill was sincerely convinced that the Captain was up to something. He thought he was out to wreck the ship or do something else equally horrible, and so Bill resolved to keep an eye on things and make sure that the Captain and his co-conspirators didn't get away with their evil plan, whatever it may have been.

–And since he was afraid that they might be planning on running the ship aground or stealing it and taking it to some other port besides Montreal, his first strategy was to keep track of our position by navigating from his room. Bill had a cheap little pocket compass and a pocket watch that was nearly as old as his antique sextant, and with those crude instruments, he set out to plot his own courses and fixes. And so all during my afternoon watch that next day out, I would see him step out onto the deck every fifteen or twenty minutes to check our course with his little compass. And on a couple of occasions, I saw him shoot sun-lines with his outdated sextant while using his undependable old watch as a chronometer. But since by using that watch, he was adding a huge instrument error to his already highly inaccurate sights, it inevitably turned out that when he worked out his sights, he found that he had absolutely no idea where we were.

–So for that reason, he gave up on navigating from his room after a single unsuccessful day, and on the second day after his crack-up, he adopted a whole new tactic for keeping track of where we were. He began to sneak into the chartroom from time to time to check on how things were going. With Bill being Bill, though, it wasn't enough for him to simply come up and inspect things on the bridge. No, he also had to record the results of his inspections in the Log. And so in going through the Log, not only did he go back to the entry that the Captain had made about him being relieved of his duties and cross it out and write below it, "Bullshit. WB," but he also made three or four other entries listing the various deficiencies he'd uncovered during his inspections. Entries that each ended with a phrase along the lines of, "Vessel in fine shape, personal conditions to the contrary notwithstanding. WB."

–Of course the Log entries were a dead giveaway of what Bill was up to, and when the Captain saw them that evening, he left orders for us not to allow him back onto the bridge. He wrote that if Bill came to the bridge, we were to order him to leave. And if he refused to do so, we were to call the Captain, which was exactly what I ended up having to do the next afternoon when he came up on my watch. It seemed that Bill had come to the bridge a couple of times on George's watch that morning, but when he had, George had quietly slipped him a piece of paper with the ship's position written on it and then convinced him to leave before the Captain found out that he'd been there. But when he came up on my watch to check on our noon position, I didn't use the same strategy as George. Instead, I did exactly as I'd been instructed to do. I ordered him to leave, and then when he refused, I called the Captain.

–The Captain came to the bridge, moving slowly and reluctantly toward his showdown with Bill, and when the two of them stood face to face, he spoke in a calm voice telling Bill to get off the bridge immediately. Either that or he'd be placed in irons. Bill stood firm, though, and with his head held high, he answered the order by telling the Captain, "You're a sick man."

–The Captain groaned when he heard that reply, and then he repeated his order once again in his low, droning voice, "Get off the bridge or I'll have you placed in irons."

–Bill shot back with a sense of offended honor clearly audible in his high Carolina drawl, "Why, I never heard of anything as outrageous as a Master ordering the Second Mate off the bridge and threatening to place him in irons. I never heard of it in my life. You must be crazy!" And he went on to tell the Captain that he knew that he was up to something. He knew he was working on some evil scheme, and he warned him that whatever the plan might be, he wouldn't get away with it. "Not while Bill Burns is here to stop you, you won't," he declared resolutely.

–As Bill went on and on, the Captain remained silent, doing his best to maintain an authoritative pose, and the only sound that escaped him was an occasional low groan, that and one or two clucks of the tongue. Bill kept repeating his suspicions about what the Captain was up to, the Captain and his co-conspirators on the ship who by that time may have included me given the way he glanced over at me from time to time as he spoke. And when he finally got tired of that, Bill began to throw out insults and vague threats and anything else that came into his head. But then all at once, after a long, drawling, meandering rant, he suddenly stopped in mid-sentence and, slowly drawing himself up tall and proud, he announced to the Captain and me, "I'm running for union official this year. I could borrow $10,000 right now and win." And no sooner had he made that statement than he calmly turned and walked off the bridge with all the quiet dignity of a future union official.

–Everybody laughed like hell when I described the incident to the guys that evening, and it revved us up for even more craziness from the Second Mate. But we were soon disappointed as on the next day, Bill seemed to have gone through a change. He'd toned down his behavior to the point where he'd become nearly invisible. And that was truly strange coming from Bill what with the way that he'd always been everywhere on that ship. Because now all at once, he wasn't there. He didn't come to the bridge and we hardly saw him out on deck, and even at mealtimes he was seen but not heard as for the first time since he'd been aboard, he ate his meals in silence. He ate them quickly and then left just as quickly.

–Our gang began to speculate that evening about what was going on. Had Bill given up? Had he accepted defeat? Or was there something else happening here? We talked it over and over, but we just couldn't decide. And it wasn't until George came in a bit later and told us about a conversation he'd just had with Bill that we were finally able to learn the truth.

—George told us that Bill had now come to realize that the key to foiling the Captain's evil plans didn't lie in controlling events on the bridge but rather it lay in controlling the messages that went in and out over the radio. And it was for that purpose that he'd begun work on a scheme to take over the radio shack and broadcast a plea for help to the rest of the world. And as Bill had been working out the details of his plan, he'd evidently come to the conclusion that it would take two people in order to succeed, and so it was for that reason that he'd approached George and tried to enlist his help.

—Because by then, I think that mellow George was the only person left on that ship that Bill still trusted. And while he'd long been convinced that the Chief Mate and Sparks were part of the Captain's plans, he also seemed to be having his doubts about me. After all, it was me who had called the Captain on him, wasn't it? George had never done anything like that. Instead, he'd always found ways to humor Bill and finesse him off the bridge. And now upon being approached with this radio shack plan of Bill's, George found himself being forced to finesse the guy once again. And what he did was that, once he realized that it was impossible to talk Bill out of going through with the takeover, he set out to convince him that it would be foolish for George to blow his cover by participating in it openly. He said that the best strategy in the long run would be for him to remain a hidden ally of Bill's. For Bill to go ahead and do it by himself while George remained underground, pretending to support the Captain while secretly working for Bill and awaiting the right moment to come out into the open.

—And so having swallowed that line of reasoning, Bill

was alone when he burst into the radio shack the next afternoon, shoving weak little Sparks out of the way and sitting down at the telegraph key to begin sending his plea for help to the world. But the trouble was that Bill barely knew Morse Code, and what little experience he'd had with it had been on flashing light, not on a telegraph. So whatever message it was that he attempted to send, it inevitably came out as pure gibberish. And to make matters worse, Sparks soon recovered from his initial shock and, showing a courage and fortitude that seemed out of place in his mouse-like personality, he went over to the main power switch and shut the radio off, putting an end to Bill's useless fumbling with the key. And then once the power was off, Sparks stood resolutely guarding the switch to prevent Bill from turning it back on.

—Or at least that's how Sparks described the incident to me, saying that once he'd cool-headedly shut off the radio, he'd told Bill—firmly but politely—to leave the radio shack and that Bill had complied with his order without discussion. But whatever truth there may have been in Sparks's version of the events, one thing that was clear was the fact that Bill seemed to be chastened by his latest defeat. He seemed to be adrift now, unsure of what to do with himself and unsure of how to stop the Captain's evil plan.

—He wandered around aimlessly all the next morning, and then in the afternoon, he came to the bridge on my watch once again, evidently looking for a showdown with the Captain because of the way he ignored my warnings and told me to go ahead and call the old man on him if that was what I was going to do. And it wasn't long after my call that the Captain appeared on the bridge, walking slowly toward Bill with an air of determination and authority that was seldom seen in his slow, shuffling gait. And once he reached Bill, he looked him straight in the eye, squeezing his droopy eyelids into the hardest stare he could manage, and he told him to leave the bridge immediately.

–Bill stood his ground, though, standing tall and holding his bald head erect as he gazed steadily back through his old wire-rimmed glasses, and he answered in a cool, calm voice, "No."

–The Captain didn't flinch, and he didn't even groan this time. Instead he narrowed his eyes still further, giving the hardest look he could possibly give, and then he repeated his order, "Get off the bridge. Now!"

–But Bill didn't budge, and instead he shot back, "I ain't gonna go. You gotta shoot me to get me outa here, and you're too yellow to do that. You get off the bridge!"

–At that, the Captain turned and headed below, groaning steadily and clucking his tongue, and no sooner was he gone than Bill began to strut around the bridge in triumph with a smile of satisfaction so big that it seemed to cover his entire face. He walked and pranced, and he periodically burst out into that high, idiot laughter of his. But his moment of triumph was short-lived as the Captain soon returned to the bridge carrying a pair of leg-irons, the only restraints available to him at the time since both pairs of ship's handcuffs were in use on the stowaways. And no sooner had Bill seen the Captain and what he was carrying in his hand than his entire being seemed to change in an instant. For all at once, the proud rooster became a scared little rabbit.

–Bill scurried out onto the starboard bridge wing, and the Captain shuffled along behind him. But Bill was too fast for him, and as soon as the Captain stepped onto the wing, Bill dashed around behind the bridge and over to the port wing. And as the Captain followed along behind, Bill stepped back into the wheelhouse and stood there expectantly, waiting for the Captain to enter before starting out on another round. And in that way, the two of them ran several laps around the bridge with Bill sometimes laughing as he fled with rabbit-like speed and the Captain groaning and pursuing him with tortoise-like persistence.

—And me? I just stood back and watched, stood there next to Hutchins who may not even have realized that anything was going on. I stood back and watched and laughed to myself at the comic scene that was being played out before me, and I did nothing until finally the Captain drew me into it by yelling as he trudged by for me to help him catch Bill. And so during Bill's next circuit through the wheelhouse, I made a half-hearted attempt to block his path, standing with my arms outstretched and making him dodge around me. I really didn't try to catch him, but still my actions were enough to convince him that his little game was over. So he didn't run any more laps after that, and instead he ran down to the maindeck where he knew that the Captain wouldn't follow.

—I didn't see Bill again after that until I was on my way to Pat's room that evening for our daily get-together when in passing the door to the saloon, I saw him sitting inside, hunched over at a table by himself and concentrating on the paper airplane that he was busy making. I entered and went over to apologize to him for having taken the Captain's side on the bridge that afternoon, but when I spoke, I received no reply but a blank, uncomprehending look. A look that seemed to say that he had no idea what I was talking about. So I started to explain to him what I meant. I started to remind him of that afternoon's pursuit on the bridge, but he soon interrupted me to ask if I'd seen what was written on the chalkboard. And at that, I turned and read it aloud, "Vote for Ever-Ready Burns."

—I started to laugh since I knew about his plan to run

for union official, and I supposed that this slogan must mark the kickoff of his campaign. But when I looked back at him, he wasn't laughing and he wasn't even smiling. And before I could say another word, he asked me in all sincerity, "Do you know who wrote that?" It was obviously written in his childlike scrawl, but I just shrugged my shoulders, not knowing how to answer him. And when he told me that he thought the Captain must have done it, all I could say was that I didn't know. I really didn't know. I had no idea what else to say given the deadly serious expression on his face as he spoke.

—After a moment, he returned his attention to his paper airplane which he held up and admired for some time before throwing it across the room. And then just as I was edging my way toward the door, he looked me straight in the eye and asked me point-blank, "Am I crazy?" I said no, of course you're not. It was the only response I could think of for a question like that. And then just as I was going out the door, I heard him say, "The Captain's crazy. I know that."

—My little conversation with Bill bothered me. It gave me that same uncomfortable feeling once again that maybe there was a tragedy beneath all the comedy that was Bill. But it didn't take long for me to put the tragedy out of my mind as no sooner had I arrived at Pat's room than I began to tell the guys about the great chase that had taken place on the bridge that afternoon. And as I told them the details of the story, they rolled around with laughter, picturing for themselves the comic pursuit between the Captain and Bill. They laughed and laughed, and so did I. Laughed as hard as I ever did on that ship.

—When I saw Bill the next morning, I said hello to him like always, but on this occasion he didn't answer me with words. Instead, he waved me over toward the nearest bulkhead where he reached into his pocket and pulled out a pencil which he used to write, "Hello."

—The incident seemed a little strange to me even by Bill's standards, but it wasn't until I ran into Link a short time later that I received an explanation. And what Link told me was that at breakfast that morning, Bill had suddenly gotten up and announced to all present that he was through with his efforts to take over the bridge or the radio shack. He'd said that he would no longer attempt to confront the Captain and his co-conspirators openly and that from that moment on, he would be on a strike of silence, a strike in which he wouldn't utter another word for the rest of the trip.

—Now that vow of silence must have come as good news to those who had gotten tired of hearing him rattle on endlessly in that goofy Carolina farm-boy voice of his, but I don't know that it was good news for everyone. And especially not for those who would eventually have to clean off the bulkheads. Because in the same way that Bill had been a nearly non-stop talker up to that moment, he now became a nearly non-stop bulkhead writer. He wrote anywhere and everywhere on that ship, and no sooner would he see someone coming down a passageway than he'd be getting out his pencil and beginning to converse in writing. He'd write out greetings and questions and whatever else popped into his head. He'd write simple comments or silly poems, and sometimes with George or me, he'd write out navigation problems, problems that usually turned out to be pure nonsense when we tried to work them out. And as time went on, he began to dedicate more and more of his time to writing old union slogans, old phrases that he'd chanted during the sit-down strikes of the Thirties and old-time Wobbly slogans. "Education-Organization-Emancipation" was a particular favorite of his, and he wrote it all over the ship, in big letters and small, with stars and without, circled and underlined and with exclamation points. And then at one point, he even wrote out the entire Wobbly Preamble on the bulkhead just outside the door to the saloon, wrote the whole thing from memory: "The working class and the employing class have nothing in common…"

—He wrote his slogans and his poems and all the rest of it, and then probably as a natural result of all his union sloganeering, he soon began to pour his heart into his campaign for union official. He dove into that campaign with a vengeance, writing "Vote for Burns" wherever he could find space left on the bulkheads. Especially on the bulkheads outside the Captain's office where he wrote it dozens of times. And then shortly after launching his election campaign, he made the decision to escalate it further still by getting hold of a bucket of paint—or actually two buckets of different colored paints—and really going to work.

—He took that paint and walked all over the decks painting "Vote for Burns" wherever he could find the space. He painted it on the outside bulkheads, and he painted it on the hatch-coamings, painted it on the winches and on the windlass and everywhere else he could think of. He painted and painted until the entire ship was covered with "Vote for Burns" signs. And by the time he was done, the old *Arkansas* looked like a real, true ship-of-fools. Oh it looked crazy, and I always wondered what the people who came aboard at our next ports of call must have thought. Because here was this ship with the passageway bulkheads totally covered with Bill's scribblings and with "Vote for Burns" painted everywhere you looked on the weatherdecks. And all those things stayed there, too, since the Captain wouldn't let anyone erase them or paint over them. He said they were evidence so they were still there when I paid off at the end of the trip. They were there to greet the new guy who came aboard to replace me on that floating insane asylum that they called a ship.

–Bill's campaign of silence—and his writing and painting campaign—only lasted for a couple of days, the length of time it took for him to run completely out of places to write or paint. And though it may have been nothing but coincidence, it seemed like they petered out at about the same time that the weather began to cool off. Because we were on our way to Canada and it was November, you see, so there finally came a time when we left the heat...

(Right here, you can hear how I get up and go to the door cause Pou and Nit just come in. I go over and say hello, which is "Sawaddee krub" in Thai, and right after I go, Suzanne starts to come over. But Ken tries to keep going with his story.)

–We left the heat of the tropics behind and the weather...

"Honey, Pou is here." (That's Suzanne telling him.)

–I'll be right over. I just want to finish this...

"Honey! Pou is here!" (And right after that, Ken stops the tape.)

\*　　\*　　\*　　\*　　\*

(We stand around for awhile and Suzanne tries to hold a conversation with Pou and Nit, but neither of them speaks any English and they laugh when she uses sign-language so the conversation's pretty short. But one thing Nit does is she goes over to Suzanne and touches her nose and says, "Good," then touches her own nose and says, "No good." That's cause of the way that Thai girls' noses are always real flat and they think any nose that sticks out is pretty, but you can see that Suzanne is embarrassed about the whole thing. Cause remember what I said before about her being a real good looking woman except for her nose being too big? Well, having Nit come over and touch her nose like that's too much for her to handle. But she doesn't say anything. She just stands there and grits her teeth and blushes and stuff like that while Nit does her thing.

(Anyway, the conversation doesn't last long, and we decide that the best thing to do is go out and walk around the city together. But before we go, Ken wants to finish his story. Suzanne doesn't want him to. She says she's bored. But I'm on Ken's side cause of this idea I got about writing the story out and getting it published and all that. Like what I'm doing right now. So finally Suzanne gives in and we sit back down on the mattress and turn the machine back on. And then Ken starts talking again.)

–I'll try to make this as brief as possible because I know that some people want to leave. But since I'm doing this for Dave and not for myself, I'll try not to shortchange him. I'll try to tell the whole story…

(He looks over at Suzanne while he says it, and he gets this get-on-with-it-already look, so he starts out on the story.)

–Let's see, I was just at the part where the weather began to cool off, wasn't I? Well, uh… It seemed like Bill began to cool off at about the same time, too. He started talking to people again right about then, and when he did so, he didn't sound nearly as crazy as he had before. He seemed to be back to normal, or at least as normal as he'd been at the beginning of the trip. He seemed to have forgotten all about the Captain's evil conspiracy since we never heard him mention it again. And in fact, the only time I heard him refer to the Captain at all during those days was when he asked me on a couple of occasions, "Why's the Captain picking on me?"

—So Bill cooled off along with the weather, and at the same time it seemed like our gang, the fantail crew, also began to cool off in pretty much the same way. We just... I don't know what it was. It was like the fire was starting to go out or something. And I don't know if it was because of the cold or because of the lack of new Second Mate stories or simply because we were beginning to see that the end of the voyage was fast approaching. Because while Montreal was still a foreign port, it was so close to the U.S. that it seemed inevitable that our next port would be an American one which would make it the final port for almost all of us. And that was because of the way our union rules said that George and I, being applicants rather than members, would have to get off at the first U.S. port. Jake and Link were in pretty much the same situation with their union, and at the same time, Pat's time was up since he'd already made the previous trip aboard the *Arkansas*. So what it all meant was that the only member of our gang who wouldn't be getting off as soon as we reached the States was Dave. All the rest of us were short-timers.

—And maybe it was for that reason that you could see how a definite change in attitude was beginning to take place among us as the passage across the Atlantic wore on. You could see how we were no longer looking forward to the rest of the trip and how with each passing day, we were looking more and more toward getting off the ship and getting back to our lives. I increasingly spent my time thinking about Suzanne, though I don't think I ever mentioned that fact to any of the other guys. Pat began to talk about his plans to hang out with his brother before shipping out on another ship, while Jake and Link both talked about getting back to their old neighborhoods and their old friends. And the only one among us who continued to talk about fantastic schemes and wild adventures was George, though it seemed like even he no longer believed in them. Or at least he no longer believed that any of us would ever accompany him on those adventures. And instead, he was simply talking about them for himself…

—But back to the story, okay? As we made our way north and west in the Atlantic, the temperature cooled off and the weather turned stormy, and eventually it got to be downright cold. It got so cold that the pipes leading to the forward house were constantly freezing and the engineers would have to go out and thaw them out time after time. It got so cold that my uninsulated little room out on the maindeck turned into a genuine icebox until the Chief Mate gave me a couple of portable heaters with which I was able to make the place bearable once again. Not comfortable, mind you, but bearable.

—And the storms we hit! Why, the seas would come washing right over the maindeck, making the walk from my room back to the after house for meals a dangerous little stroll—or should I say a dangerous sprint since rather than using the safety line that the crew had rigged, I always used my speed to deal with the danger. What I'd do was I'd hang out and wait for a good moment, and then I'd make a dash before jumping up onto the nearest mast-house ladder whenever I saw a big sea coming. And in that way I made it into something of a sport getting back and forth during the storms with the winner getting there with dry feet and the loser… No, it's better not to think about what would have happened if I'd ever lost.

—As we entered the Gulf of St. Lawrence, it began to snow, and I mean snow. It snowed so hard that you could barely make out the bow of the ship. And wouldn't you know it on a ship like the *Arkansas* and on a trip like that one that it was right at that moment when we couldn't see a thing that our radar decided to blow a transistor, a transistor for which we had no spares. And without the radar, we found ourselves to be in a terrible mess, running totally blind up the Gulf in a raging snowstorm. And while according to the Rules of the Road we should have slowed down or even stopped until the weather cleared up, we had a schedule we were trying to make. So instead we went for it. We charged along at full speed ahead and hoped for the best. And what the Captain did in place of a radar was to have us Mates spend a lot of time standing out on the bridge wing in the snow listening for fog signals from other ships since that was the only way we had of knowing if anyone else was around. And when it came to navigation, the only thing we had to go on was our old radio direction finder on which I took bearings every half hour or so and tried to get some general idea of where we might be.

—But then in spite of all the listening I was doing for fog signals, there came a moment when a tanker suddenly appeared just off our starboard bow, passing so close to us that I could have spit on it almost. And it was so close by the time we saw it coming that if it had been on a collision course with us instead of just missing us the way it did, there would have been nothing we could have done about it. Absolutely nothing. And in fact, the lookout on the bow might not even have had time to save himself if he'd turned and started running aft as soon as he saw the ship coming. The visibility was that bad.

—It was scary now that I think back about it, but you know at the time it just seemed like the normal thing to do. It was the way things were done on the old *Arkansas*. We left the engines full ahead and we took our chances. We played the percentages. And fortunately for us, the weather cleared up before we reached the mouth of the river, a place where we really would have had to stop and wait for the visibility to improve before proceeding upriver. And so in the end, our gamble paid off and we made it to Montreal on schedule.

—Montreal, beautiful Montreal. We pulled up to a dock where we were supposed to discharge the ore we were carrying, and no sooner had we tied up than our gang was ashore and heading for town. But you know, there was something different about the atmosphere while we were there. There was something about us. Because while we had a good time and all that, we no longer felt the same aura about ourselves that we'd felt before. It was like... It was like we were no longer this intrepid group of international adventurers or whatever it was that we'd seen ourselves as being before. Instead, we were just a bunch of guys coming ashore from a ship. We were a bunch of nobodies.

—We stayed in Montreal for a couple of days, and during that time we dropped off the stowaways with the local police. Oh how those guys shivered when they saw all that snow, and how they huddled together from cold and from fear. And they probably would have frozen to death in their short pants and shirts if only it hadn't been for Jake's efforts to scrounge up warm clothing for them. And I can't tell you what ever happened to those stowaways after they left the ship, though the last I heard, there was some local priest who had taken their side and was trying to get them political asylum based on the fact that Congo was a Marxist country. And at the same time, I heard that the priest was also helping them sue the shipping company for the mistreatment they claimed to have received aboard the *Arkansas*. And though I have no idea what came of it, they should have won their case against the company if there's any justice in the world at all. Because keeping them handcuffed to bunks for two weeks straight? I mean if that's not mistreatment then what is?

–And while the Captain was hit with both the lawsuit and the first of what would probably be several fines over the stowaways, he also received another blow when Bill refused to leave the ship on "mutual consent," a situation that could be compared to letting him resign before he was fired. Because when it was offered to him, Bill's only response was to say that he wasn't ready to get off. He said that he'd taken the job for six months and that was exactly how long he planned on staying aboard. He said, "I'm not gonna leave this ship unless they carry me off dead." And friends, he didn't leave the ship. Or at least he didn't leave it in Montreal.

–After Montreal, we stopped at a small town on the Gulf of St. Lawrence, a town named Havre St. Pierre, and there we picked up a load of titanium ore bound for Galveston. And with Galveston being a U.S. port, that meant it would be the end of the line for five out of the six of us in the fantail crew, all of us except Dave. And as far as we knew, it might even prove to be the end of the line for good old Wild Bill.

–Bill remained quiet on the trip south, as quiet as he'd been for the last week or so, but the situation within our gang turned out to be the exact opposite. Our energy level began to rise drastically once again, rising to higher and higher levels with each passing day and each mile that drew us closer to Galveston. But the energy that was rising now was far different from the one that we'd experienced earlier, because now it was no longer a group energy. Now it was nothing but a bunch of individual energies. It was nothing but channel fever, the excitement and anticipation of the end of the trip and the return to our other lives.

–We still sat around together in the evenings, though,

and we repeated the stories that we'd lived and told about during the trip. But as we told them now, there was something different about them. They were no longer vital and alive the way they'd been before, and in fact, some of them were already starting to sound pretty old and stale while others were... I don't know what they were... It was like they were kind of hollow or something. Like they'd been overrated. And as I sat there listening to them being repeated over and over again during those final days, it was sometimes hard for me to understand how I'd ever seen them as the great adventures or the great comedies that I'd taken them as being before. It was like... I mean, what were they really? Were they anything more than a collective hallucination? The product of a group high among a bunch of goofy potheads? A bunch of...

–But enough about that already! We hit Galveston and paid off, and then the whole group of us headed for the nearest bar to say our goodbyes—to say goodbye and to have one big, final blowout together. Because while it was probably impossible for us to recover the sort of magic feeling that had existed among us earlier in the trip, we were still more than capable of getting drunk together. And drunk was exactly what we got as we hit the bar sometime before noon and ended up staying there until well into the evening. We drank beer and whatever else for hours on end, and the whole time we were there, we staggered around like a bunch of drunken idiots, bumping into each other and slapping each other on the backs and howling at the moon and just generally getting crazy.

–Finally, after we'd all gotten so totally plastered that we could barely see, we decided that it was time to head back to the ship and get our gear and load it into the car that Pat had rented for the drive to the airport. But as we staggered up the gangway, we were met by O'Neill who happened to be on watch at the time, and the first thing he said to us was, "Did you hear about the Second Mate?"

–"No, what happened?"

–"Well, he barricaded himself inside his room, and he says he's not coming out. He says they'll never take him alive. And he says he's got enough food in there to last him for a month."

–And no sooner had we heard it than we all began to roar. We laughed so hard that we nearly fell down. We laughed as hard as we ever had, as hard as we used to laugh back in the good old days in Africa. "So that's why all that food's been disappearing lately," said Link, and at that we laughed even harder.

–The whole gang of us soon staggered of in the direction of the forward house, up toward Bill's room to see what was going on there, and when we arrived, we found that George had already gotten there ahead of the rest of us. We found him talking to Bill through the locked door, trying to convince him to come out without a fight. But whatever line of drunken reasoning he may have been using at the time, we immediately broke it off. Because no sooner had we entered the passageway outside Bill's room than Pat began to chant, "Vote for Burns. Vote for Burns." And all the rest of us quickly joined in, "Vote for Burns. Vote for Burns."

–We chanted loudly and drunkenly until the Captain came rushing in accompanied by the union patrolman who was aboard trying to deal with the situation, and the moment they arrived, the Captain yelled at us to shut up and get the hell out of there. And as if by magic, that lethargic voice of the Captain's cut its way through our drunken haze. That voice of the authority we'd been living under for the last few months. It hit us where we lived somehow, and our drunken chant seemed to die out in an instant. Our chant and our phony bravado which began to deflate so quickly that soon we were all slinking rather sheepishly away. Off to our rooms to gather our gear and make our exit.

—By the time we'd reassembled at the gangway, though, we were all feeling fired up once again, as drunk and fired up as we'd been a short time earlier. And when Link lost his balance while going down the gangway and dropped a box full of woodcarvings into the water between the ship and the dock, it was no time before crazy old Pat was over there climbing down a ladder on the face of the pier in an effort to retrieve it. He climbed down until his feet were in the water, and when he couldn't reach it from there, he climbed down some more. But seeing that he still couldn't reach it and that it was starting to drift away from him, he finally jumped right into the water and swam over to it, after which he somehow managed to climb back up the face of the pier with the big box in his hand.

—The rest of us were cheering him on as he made his swim, but standing next to me was the Night Mate on duty who kept muttering over and over again, "I ain't never seen nothin' like this before." Until finally I turned to him and blurted out, "That's right! This is a crazy ship! Craziest you ever saw." And you know, it's just possible that he may have believed me what with all the "Vote for Burns" signs painted everywhere you looked and with the Second Mate barricaded in his room and with an Engineer swimming around underneath the gangway. I mean, how many other ships could there possibly be like that? Not many, I'll bet. Not like the good old *Arkansas*.

—Once we reached the car, Pat revved it up and sped down the freeway like a maniac, his clothes still soaking wet and music blasting on the radio and his passengers too drunk to notice or to care, and somehow he managed to get us to the airport alive. He got us there and we stumbled inside, and then no sooner were we there than all at once it was over. The trip, the gang, everything. It was over and done with, and the only thing we had left was the goodbyes. George was the first to go, leaving to catch a plane to California, and soon after that Link was off to Philly and Jake to New York so that finally only Pat and I were left. And when the time came for him to catch his flight to Baltimore, he shook my hand and said I'll see ya maybe, and then he patted me on the shoulder.

—And all at once, I wanted to reach out and hug him. And I would have, too, if only he hadn't turned and walked away from me before I could. I swear I would have. I'd have grabbed onto him and held on if only I'd known… If I'd known just how final that moment really was. How it marked the end of so many things for me. The end of everything I'd done and everything I'd been up until then. Everything I'd been and everything I could have been, too. Because it was the end of that entire life for me. The end of my life at sea and my adventures and my… my youth! My… My… youth…

—And if only I could have grabbed on and held on. Held onto that moment and those days on the ship and those feelings I had back then and the person I was. If only I could have held on! If only I hadn't let it all go, let it…

(He stops talking right here, and it seems like I should say something, but I don't know what to say. Finally, I gotta break the silence.) "Well, you know it disappears anyway whether you hold onto it or not."

—Yes, you're right. I'm sure you are. (He stops talking again for a minute, and then he asks me a question.) So what can you add to this story for an epilogue? Is there anything you can say about any of the people from that ship? Like take Bill for instance. How did they finally get him out of that room?

"I don't remember exactly. It just seems like the patrolman talked him into coming out a little while after you guys left."

–Oh yeah, so that was it, huh? Nothing else came of it?... Well then what about the ship itself and the next trip and all that? What was it, a one-way to Vietnam?

"Yeah, we went there with a load of rice, and then we left the ship at a scrapyard in Taiwan. And if you wanta ask me, there was nothin' special happened on that trip. It was just a regular old trip…"

–Or at least as far as you can remember, huh? The final voyage of the good ship *Arkansas*… The American *S. S. Arkansas*... That fine old ship. That proud ship, sent off to Taiwan to be chopped up into razor blades. It's just… It's like… I don't know…

–And so how about the guys from the fantail crew? Did you ever see any of them again?

"It's like I was telling you before, I run into George once at the Seamen's Club in Naha a couple years back. He's still shipping out. But I never seen any of the rest of them."

–Not Pat or Link or Jake? And how about O'Neill? Or maybe Possum or Hutchins or Sparks or the Captain?

"No, none of em. I mean, I seen a couple guys around the union hall but never one of them you just mentioned, I don't think."

–No, none of them? (He doesn't say anything for awhile and neither do I, and then he says.) Well, I don't know what else I can say…

"Do you mind if I make a suggestion?" (That's Suzanne talking.)

–A suggestion?... Oh okay, you're right. The story's over and it's time for us to get out of here. So let's go.

"Thank you."
(And right here, he turns off the tape.)

\* \* \* \* \*

We hang out together in Bangkok some over the next couple days. Until it's time for him and Suzanne to fly back to the States. But we don't have that much in common what with him having a normal job and a wife and everything and me still going to sea. So it's kind of a relief when he goes. He gives me his address when we say goodbye, and I tell him I'll write him a letter someday but I never do. I don't hardly ever write letters. Maybe one or two times a year to my mother and that's about it.

But hey, look at what I just did. I went and wrote a whole book. A short one at least, and that's better than nothing. So now what I gotta do is take it down to a publisher and make some money off it. Course I'll give half the money to Ken. Or at least I will if I can remember what the hell I did with that address he gave me.

# LESSONS FROM A LIFE AT SEA

## ON THE PROPER USE OF RADAR

Being that this was a shuttle ship that came into Hong Kong nearly every week, we were used to coming in when it was foggy. And being that the radar was as old and dilapidated as the ship itself, we were used to coming in when it wasn't working. But what we weren't used to was having to deal with both those problems at the same time: with having to enter Hong Kong harbor in a fog so thick that we could barely see our own bow, and having to do so when our radar was on the blink.

    Sparks had looked at the radar earlier, as soon as it had broken down, and he'd told us then that there was actually nothing wrong with the unit itself. He'd said that the only problem was in the linkage that made the antenna turn around and that if we could only find some way to make it turn, the whole thing would work just fine. And it was based upon this bit of information that the Captain now came up with a brilliant plan to deal with the problem. He said that we should send a man up to tie lines onto the antenna, lines that could be used by two seamen standing on the flying bridge to pull it and sweep it back and forth. And in that way, we'd be able to see whatever it was that lay out ahead of us.

    It wasn't long before everything was in place, and so we began to make our cautious approach, with the Captain conning the ship and me standing by the radar screen doing my best to decipher the blips that appeared. What I saw, though, was nothing but blurs and smears running back and forth across the screen as the antenna swung, nothing but elongated and distorted targets that blended one into another. But then suddenly on one sweep, everything became crystal clear—the islands and the ships and the fishing boats—as on that particular sweep, the seamen must have pulled the antenna at just the right speed.

So braced by this initial success, we continued our plodding advance into the crowded and chaotic waters of Hong Kong harbor. We groped our way ahead, not completely blind but nearly so. Sweep—blur. Sweep—blur. Sweep—clear image! Mark the positions of those ships! Sweep—blur. Sweep—blur. Sweep—blur. Sweep—clear image! Get a range and bearing on Po Toi! Sweep—blur. Sweep—blur…

## ON THE DANGERS OF DRUGS

Having finished preparing the bridge and testing the gear, and knowing that I had nothing more to do for the next half hour or so until the ship sailed, I decided that this would be a good time for me to step out onto the wing of the bridge and try a little of that Thai-stick I'd just acquired during my shore leave in Bangkok. So I went out and stood with my back against the bulkhead in a spot where a person inside the bridge wouldn't be able to see me, pulled out the joint I'd prepared earlier, lit it up and began to toke away.

I was about three quarters of the way through the joint when I suddenly saw the Chief Mate step out onto the wing and come walking over toward me. And no sooner had I seen him than I put out the joint on the leg of my pants, my movements quick and discreet enough that there was no way he could have seen what I was doing. But then as he came right up to me and stood directly in my face and asked me a question, standing downwind and pinning me up against the bulkhead, I realized too late that in my stoned state, I'd forgotten about one other highly important precaution that I should have taken. I realized that I'd forgotten to exhale when I'd seen him coming. I realized that I was now standing there with my lungs completely full of marijuana smoke and with nowhere to exhale it but directly into his face.

What should I do? Should I blow it out all at once and get it over with? Or should I try to push my way past him before answering? No, that would never work. And since my only other option was to let it out as slowly as possible and hope that he didn't notice, that was what I ended up doing. I tried to answer him like nothing was going on. "Well, I don't know, Mate…" I said, speaking in the most strained and unnatural pot-smokin' voice you could imagine.

He never said a word to me about my voice, though, and nothing about the smell of the smoke that danced across his face. No, he just stood there with the faintest trace of a knowing grin showing on that poker-face of his. And then after awhile, he turned and walked away.

## ON CALCULATING ARRIVAL

Our Captain was finally sobering up now that we were working our way up the east coast of Africa. He'd been drunk all the way across the Atlantic, not even leaving his room for the first two weeks after sailing New Orleans, so that we'd gone days on end without knowing whether he was dead or alive. And in fact, the only signs of life he'd shown during the entire passage had been the three or four occasions on which he'd called me on the bridge in the middle of the night to ask what time it was, saying that he'd forgotten to wind his watch.

He'd finally appeared two days before our arrival at Cape Town, shaky and not altogether sober, and then he'd begun a gradual drying-out process as we'd worked our way through the various South African ports. He'd dried out until now finally as we approached the Pungoe River and the port of Beira in Mozambique, he appeared to be truly sober for the first time all voyage. But although he was sober, that didn't mean that he wasn't still capable of exhibiting strange and irresponsible behavior. Because right when we were some twenty minutes from the spot on the chart that looked to me like the pilot station, he suddenly turned to me and said, "I'm gonna go take a shower." And just like that, he left me alone on the bridge, making the approach to a port where I'd never been before.

Take a shower? Now, when we were so close to the pilot station? There wasn't time!

I began dashing about the bridge trying to get control of the situation while awaiting his return. I grabbed the binoculars and searched for any sign of a pilot boat, and I studied the chart to reconfirm the location of the pilot station. As I looked at the chart, though, I saw where another pilot station had been drawn in at a different position a little way inside the mouth of the river. And then as I looked further, I spotted still another possible pilot station a short distance upriver.

So which one was it? Which was the real pilot station? I was debating that question with myself when the sound-powered phone from the engineroom rang and the First asked me when exactly we would be taking arrival.

Arrival? How did I know? It would be somewhere between ten minutes and an hour or two from now. That was the only answer I could give him.

## ON HEAVY WEATHER

It seems that the weather-routing service our company was using had thought that it would be a good idea to send us on a straight great circle from San Francisco to Yokohama in the dead of winter, and unfortunately for us, it seems that our Captain had decided to go along with them and follow their advice. And I say unfortunately because now that we were up at the very top of the circle, up near the Aleutians though not near enough to be able to get behind them and use them for a lee, we found ourselves getting really and truly hammered.

There had been two or three big lows out ahead of us, but in the last day or so they had all gotten together and formed one giant low, a monster storm with us in its crosshairs. And while it's hard to say just how big the seas were running at the time, I can tell you that in spite of my being up on the bridge more than sixty feet above the waterline, I had to look up to see the crests of the waves each time we dropped down into a trough between them.

The seas were gigantic and, to make matters worse, they were hitting us on our quarter, right at an angle that makes ships roll heavily. And this on a roll-on/roll-off ship which, because of its strange design, had a wicked and unpredictable roll. It was a ship that didn't roll so much as it lurched from one side to the other with no real pattern to its movements. A ship that would suddenly lunge over, often when you least expected it. And while we really should have hove-to and put the seas on our bow, by now it was too late to do so since it was far too dangerous to swing our beam through the trough with the seas running as high as they were. No, the only thing we could do now was to hang on and hope for the best and try to ride it out.

And wouldn't you know it that just when it seemed like things couldn't get any worse for us, of course they did. Because it was at this point that gear began to break loose down below. First it was a bin full of lashing chains just inside the ramp on the stern and that was followed by some drums of oil. They slid and smashed around and broke other things loose, and soon objects were hitting the chains that held our seven big 20- and 30-ton forklifts in place. They hit those chains time after time, and it wasn't long before all seven of the big, heavy forklifts began to break loose one after the other.

So now we found ourselves with a real problem. We found ourselves caught on a bad course in a wicked storm with tons of steel slamming from side to side each time the ship took one of its vicious rolls. And with things going this badly for us, wouldn't you know that they were about to take yet another turn for the worse, that those big, smashed-up forklifts were about to punch their way right through a bulkhead. And as luck would have it, the bulkhead they sliced through was the very one where the cables to our steering gear were located.

The forklifts cut through the cables and we lost steering, this happening just as I was being relieved by the next watch. And with the rudder now disabled and the ship swinging out of control, there was nothing any of us standing on that bridge could do but hang on and watch. Watch as the ship swung toward its natural position in a storm like this which is bow into the wind. Watch as it swung the beam directly toward that deadly trough. The Captain stood and watched along with the rest of us, and as he did so, I heard him mutter in a low voice, "We're gonna lose this damned ship."

When I heard that, I turned to exchange glances with the AB standing next to me, and looking over, I know that a strange sort of smile must have appeared on my face. A smile like, Here we go, here's a real adventure for you. Because at that time, I was still young enough to see a sinking in just that way. But when the AB answered me with a nearly identical smile, I was surprised. What could he mean by smiling like that? He was an old guy. He couldn't possibly have the same attitude as me. So why would he smile at me in just that way?

## ON HANDLING DANGEROUS CARGO

We weren't originally scheduled to stop at Acajutla, El Salvador, but since we were on charter to the military and since we'd be passing by on our way to the Panama Canal anyway, they decided to top us off with a few hundred tons of ammunition that the local army desperately needed. This was just at the time when the insurgency in that country was reaching its highest tide, you see, a time when the newspapers were filled with talk of an imminent communist victory and a time when the signs of defeat were to be seen all over Acajutla itself. A time when many businessmen and most of the hustlers and lowlifes had already left for greener pastures, leaving parts of the town eerily vacant—and I'm especially referring to the red-light district.

The harbor was still in full working order, though, and no sooner had we tied up than the longshoremen came aboard and began discharging crates of ammunition. And being on watch, I stood beside the hatch and watched the operation, feeling a vague sense of unease that grew steadily within me. A sense of alarm at their lack of concern and the lack of respect they seemed to show for the cargo they were handling. Because far from the extreme precautions to prevent an explosion that the American longshoremen had taken in loading it, they were banging it around like it was nothing. They were acting as though there was no danger at all.

But then what really caught my attention was when I noticed the trucks over on shore that had already been loaded up with ammo, the trucks with soldiers sitting on top of the crates. Soldiers who were sitting there smoking cigarettes. Smoking!! As they sat on top of truck-loads of ammunition, they were smoking!

I noticed that, and I immediately decided to relocate myself on the ship. I decided to put some solid steel between me and those trucks.

## ON HANDLING CONTAINERS

Iran had been threatening for some time that if Iraq were to attack the oil terminal at Kharg Island, they would retaliate by blockading the Straits of Hormuz. So given that invitation, it wasn't long before our old friend and ally Saddam Hussein decided to go ahead and launch just such an attack. And as luck would have it, he did so at a moment when the container ship I was working on was transiting those very straits on its way to Dubai.

The first thing our company did was to panic, of course, thinking about what a tempting target an American merchant ship would be if the Iranians were to make good on their threat. And so it was that no sooner had we arrived in Dubai than we were told to leave again. We were told to go back out through the straits under cover of darkness and head for Fujairah, a port outside the Persian Gulf which was in the process of building a brand new container port. The only trouble with Fujairah, though, was that the port wouldn't be ready to handle ships for a few more weeks yet.

When we arrived in Fujairah, we found that all the physical structure of the new port was in place. The only thing missing was the trained longshoremen needed to handle the cargo which meant that with us being the first ship ever to call there, we would serve as the training ground for all those beginners.

The guy running the operation was a Filipino who supposedly knew what he was doing, though it wasn't long before I began to have my doubts. Like for instance with the way he had to ask me how his men were supposed to unlock the twistlocks on the top tier of containers since their poles weren't long enough to reach all the way up there. I told him that what other ports did was to put a man on top of the containers, a man who could then reach down with a pole and knock the handles over into the unlocked position from up there. My suggestion was met with an incredulous look from him, though, and when he walked away, both of us were shaking our heads at the other.

So rather than following my suggestion, he eventually decided upon a plan of his own, a plan in which he sent a man up in the spreader hanging from the crane and, while dangling that spreader somewhere in front of the twistlocks to be unlocked, he had the man swing an unlocking pole just like it was a baseball bat. He had the man swinging away trying to hit those short little handles with that long, skinny pole while standing on a swaying platform. And the platform swayed worse and worse with each swing the man took so that soon it became nearly impossible for him to keep from dropping the pole or falling down as he swung, let alone being able to connect with any of those tiny and distant targets. I'd tried to tell the guy how it was really done, but I guess he thought this was a better way.

## ON SPILLED CARGO

Each day we'd been in Monrovia, Liberia, the longshoremen had taken home little bundles of spilled rice at the end of their shifts. And as they'd seen that we hadn't said anything to them about it, each day those bundles had gotten bigger. To us it really didn't matter what they did with the spillage since as far as we were concerned, it would have been swept up and thrown away anyway if they hadn't taken it. So why not let them have as much as they wanted?

In our silence, the bundles had grown steadily larger until now, on this last day in port, this last opportunity for the longshoremen to get away with some free rice, the size of the bundles seemed to have suddenly exploded. There were guys with bundles and bags that must have contained forty or fifty pounds and you hardly saw anyone with less than ten. And as they prepared to head for home, filling and wrapping and tying their bundles, they also worked at preparing their weapons. They each took sticks and pieces of wood that they found laying around and then drove nails through them, turning those sticks into very effective instruments for warding off any and all who might try to steal their rice during the walk home.

Once the preparations were in order, the longshoremen began to heave their bundles up onto their heads and then file down the gangway one after the other, each with one hand holding the bundle in place and the other carrying a stick. They went down the gangway and along the dock in single file forming an ever-lengthening snake that went gliding away, their leader not heading directly toward the gate, though, but rather heading toward the far end of the docks. Heading toward a different gate perhaps.

I stood and watched and nodded to them as man after man headed down the gangway, bundle on head and stick in hand, the last of them still aboard ship even as the head of the procession turned behind the far warehouse and disappeared from sight. I stood and watched and wished them well. Goodbye, Africa, and good luck.

## ON TUGS AND BARGES

We were anchored in the Yangtze River near Nantong discharging heavy-lift project cargo into barges. Or at least we were supposed to be discharging cargo, though the truth of the matter was that we spent most of our time waiting for barges and only occasionally managed to move any cargo. And though we had a barge alongside on this particular day, we weren't able to work since a winter storm was blowing through the area. The wind was howling from the north and whipping up the river, making the barge surge and slam into the side of the ship over and over again, hitting us harder all the time.

We'd been calling for hours to get a tug to come out and take the barge away, but the only response we ever got was the eternal, "It's coming." Yeah, sure it was coming. I believed that as much as I believed them when they kept telling us that we'd be finished with cargo in two days. Because that's what they'd told us when we first arrived. Two days. And that's what they'd continued to tell us after each slow and unproductive day when we'd asked them how much longer it would take. Two more days. Two more days. And even now after ten days and after having discharged less than half our cargo, they were still telling us two more days. So as the guy on the radio told me once again that the tug was coming, I could finally see his statement for what it was. I could see it as another of those local myths, another of those two-days stories.

And the situation with the barge was growing critical. So critical that if we didn't get rid of it soon, it was going to do some serious damage to the ship. Fortunately for us, it was a manned barge with two men living on it, and also fortunately, the barge had an anchor. So when I yelled over to the guys on the barge and gave them a signal that I wanted to cast off their lines, they signaled back in agreement. They knew as well as I did that the barge couldn't stay where it was.

And soon my AB's and I were throwing off the lines, throwing them off and then running along the deck to watch the barge as it shot aft. We watched as it surged up near the ship, then away and then toward us again, until finally we saw how it swept just under the stern, barely missing our rudder and propeller as it went by. But a miss is as good as a mile, and so with the barge now gone and the situation resolved, I calmly made my way back to the bridge to call on the radio one last time and inform them that we wouldn't be needing a tug after all.

When asked why we wouldn't, I told the guy how we'd had to cast off the barge all by itself, and at that his voice came back to me over the radio, "But isn't that very dangerous?"

"Yes, you're right. It's very dangerous," I replied. No shit, Sherlock!

## ON THE ROMANCE OF THE SEA

Three days had been the perfect length of stay in Tamatave, Madagascar. Any longer and the place would have started to grow stale. But as it was, we could still see it as the truly refreshing place that it was. We could see it as a throwback to one of those places that the old-timers always talked about, one of those places that supposedly no longer exist.

It had become clear to us that this wasn't going to be just another port back when we'd first pulled in, back when we'd seen how the dock was covered with girls waving at us and blowing kisses as we tied up. And then when we'd gone ashore and tried to grab taxis to the nearest bar, we'd found that the local taxis were rickshaws. Real rickshaws, the type with the guy on foot. Oh, what a port it turned out to be. And what a party we had during those three days.

And now on this last day in port, I'd gone ashore and smoked a big bomber of the local weed before returning to the ship, lounging back in a rickshaw with red eyes and a smile that covered my whole face. I only smoked occasionally by this time, and so the stuff had sent me right into the stratosphere. And it was just as I was beginning my hugely mellow come-down that it came time for me to go to the bridge and take over the watch as the ship made its way up the coast of the island heading toward Dar Es Salaam.

I felt fantastic as I stood on the wing of the bridge, the warm breeze stirring my hair and caressing my body as it wrapped me in its soft and sensuous embrace. And at the same time, I gazed out at the lush green of the coast, the trees and the hills and the valleys, each with its own subtle shade of green, and they all seemed to float upon the brilliant blue of the sea that gently undulated below them. I stood there and looked at all that radiant, vibrant beauty, that beauty like some vision of heaven, while at the same time remembering all the fun I'd had during the last few days. And finally I just had to say it to myself: You know, this is the best job in the world.

## ON DOCKING A SHIP

This Captain was dangerous because of the way that, the moment he got nervous or excited, all common sense would go right out the window. Everything would dissolve into a series of screams—"Hard right," "Hard left"—with no logic behind them. Everything would dissolve into panic.

He was dangerous whenever he got nervous, and on this day when we were docking in Istanbul, he had a very good reason to get nervous. You see, the Pilot had brought the ship into the harbor area way too fast, and then he'd waited too long before backing down the engines so that it had taken an Emergency Full Astern to stop the ship and avoid hitting another ship tied up at the corner of our dock, finally missing that ship by mere feet. And so from that point on, the panic had taken over completely as we prepared to turn and back our way into the slip.

The Captain yelled over the radio for me on the stern to give a line to the line-boat that was coming alongside, and I told him that I'd do it right away. But then as I looked around, I asked myself if he could possibly be serious since our berth was all the way up inside at the far end of the slip, so far away that I could barely see it.

I told the crew to marry another line onto the one we had ready to go since one line wouldn't be nearly long enough to reach our berth, and they began to shuffle around getting ready to do so, moving as slowly as the bunch of old men in their sixties that they actually were. But meanwhile, with their preparations to marry the lines together creeping along, the Captain wanted action and he wanted it now. And he told me over and over again to give them a line. Give them a line! Give them a line!!

Okay, if that was what he wanted, then that was what I'd do. So I went over and lowered the eye on the end of our line down to the boat while the crew continued their slow-motion process of dragging another line over to marry onto the other eye. I lowered the line down and the guys in the boat grabbed it, and then no sooner had they made the eye fast than they revved up their engine and took off at full speed.

As soon as the crew saw the line start shooting out the chock, they all dropped what they were doing and stood back to watch it go. And seeing immediately that something had to be done if I didn't want to lose the entire line, meanwhile knowing that it would be useless to try to get those guys to do anything in a hurry, I finally went over myself and grabbed the eye we still had aboard ship and dropped it over one of our bits. And after that, I stood back with the rest of them and watched it go. I watched as the boat went skimming along toward the dock, and I watched as the line whipped around and shot out the chock at a tremendous speed. And I also watched as the moment came when—boing!!—the boat reached the end of the line and came bouncing back toward us just like it was on a giant rubber band.

I told the crew to get back to work while the Captain yelled over the radio to give them more line! Give them more line!! "We're workin' on it, Cap'n," I called back.

## ON UNDOCKING A SHIP

As dangerous as our Captain was on that ship, our Third Mate was perhaps even worse. He was a young guy on his first ship as mate, which is always bad enough. But on top of that, the guy was an authentic dim-bulb. He was one of those people who just don't seem to get it, and whenever he and the Captain were on the bridge together, it was a true recipe for disaster.

Like for instance there was that time when they almost took out an oil-rig that was sitting all by itself off the coast of Sicily with nothing around it but a mooring buoy for tankers about a half-mile away. What happened was that when the Captain saw that we'd be passing near the rig, he immediately panicked and began to steer toward the thing instead of going around it. And not realizing that the tanker he saw nearby was moored to the buoy loading oil, he evidently decided that his best course of action would be to cut between the tanker and the rig. And it was only when the Third Mate pointed at the symbol on the chart indicating the pipeline that ran between the rig and the buoy and asked, "What's that squiggly line there?" that the Captain finally realized his mistake. And so he managed to change course just in time to avert a tragedy.

Now as we were undocking in Tunis, though, it was the Third Mate's turn to space-out and screw-up all by himself with no help from the Captain. We had just cleared the dock and were turning the ship around when the Chief Mate on the bow called out over the radio, "We're not gonna clear this barge the way we're swingin'. You better give it some astern." And after hearing that, the Pilot ordered Dead Slow Astern to which the Third Mate responded by ringing up Dead Slow Ahead. A short time later, the Chief Mate called again causing the Pilot to order

Slow Astern and the Third Mate to space out once again and ring up Slow Ahead. By now, the Chief Mate was getting truly worked up, and I could hear as he yelled over the radio, "You gotta kick it astern! We're gonna hit this barge if you don't go astern!" In response, the Pilot ordered Half Astern and the Third Mate, true to form, rang up Half Ahead.

At about that time, I happened to look over the stern and noticed how the direction of the propeller wash indicated that the engine was going ahead rather than astern. But before I could say anything over the radio, the direction of the wash suddenly switched around and the stern began to rattle and vibrate as someone on the bridge—the Cadet as it turned out—had caught the Third Mate's mistake and they had corrected it by ringing up an Emergency Full Astern. And so with the Chief Mate on the bow yelling and screaming until he was completely hoarse, we finally managed to miss that barge by a good three or four inches.

## ON THE FUTURE OF SHIPPING

We were in Callao, Peru, discharging our usual mix of cargoes: bags of food aid and Caterpillar parts and other miscellaneous items. And once we were done with that, we were supposed to backload a number of containers to take back to the states, all of them empty containers. No loads.

While we were there, we were told that a new ship on the run would be tying up directly across from us at the dock, a foreign-flag ship as it turned out to be. You see, the company had started a containership run to the west coast of South America a few years earlier, but now that those ships had gone off to make more money—temporarily—by supporting the troops during the first Persian Gulf War, they were being replaced by other containerships. Foreign-flag ships that would take over the run and never give it back.

When the ship came in, they discharged and loaded their containers—containers with cargo in them unlike the empties we would be carrying. And the whole time they were there, we eyed each other suspiciously back and forth across the dock. We looked at them as a bunch of low-wage foreign scum who had stolen our jobs, while they looked back at us with that mixture of curiosity and pity one would naturally feel when gazing upon the last of the dinosaurs. Because to tell you the truth, that was exactly what our ship was. It was a dinosaur. In fact, it was a double dinosaur. It was an old-fashioned break-bulk freighter, and on top of that it was one that had an American flag on its stern. It was a relic. It was a museum piece. It was a ship whose time had long since passed.

# JUNGLE RUN

There's a sort of standard-issue conversation that you'll hear repeated over and over again among seamen of a certain generation, a conversation that generally begins something like this:

First Seaman: You know it's just no fun goin' to sea anymore, not like it used to be.

Second Seaman: Yeah, the good times are gone, that's for sure.

First Seaman: Cause back on those old ships, there was always somethin' goin' on. We'd go to good places, and we'd have fun and we'd get wild.

Second Seaman: Yeah, those were the days. Those were the good old days.

First Seaman: On these ships now-days, it's nothin' but boring. It's like bein' in jail or something. But I remember this one time…

The generation I'm talking about is the transitional generation, the generation that lived through the second greatest revolution in the history of the shipping industry. It's the generation of seamen who began their shipping careers in the Fifties or Sixties or even the early Seventies—in the days when the old-fashioned break-bulk freighter still dominated the general cargo branch of the industry—and then continued to ship into the Nineties and beyond, into the days that saw the final triumph of the containership and the demise of the freighter.

That second greatest revolution I just referred to is the containerization revolution, of course, a revolution whose impact upon shipping has been second only to that caused by the steam revolution, the conversion from sail- to steam-powered vessels. And while the impact of the earlier revolution has obviously been much greater upon the industry as a whole than has the second one, it's hard to say which of the two has had a greater impact upon the lives of the seamen themselves. Because while the steam revolution radically changed their lives at sea, not only creating an entirely new class of seamen known as Marine Engineers but also making it possible for the ships to follow routes and schedules that would have been unthinkable in the days of sail, it had practically no impact upon their lives in port since both types of vessels handled their cargo in very much the same way. With the containerization revolution, on the other hand, there has been virtually no impact upon seamen's lives at sea while at the same time it has radically changed their lives in port. And that is because with the ships' fast-turn-around cargo system, it has drastically reduced the amount of time the seamen spend in port. It has reduced it to such an extent as to practically eliminate port-time. It has created a world in which port stays are measured in hours rather than days, a world in which seamen only escape from their floating prisons for brief moments of freedom ashore. A world in which the seemingly endless tedium of life aboard ship is broken only by short gulps of pleasure and release.

The revolution was first launched in 1956 when a company named Pan-Atlantic—later to be renamed SeaLand—converted the first of several old T2 tankers to carry containers on deck in the U.S. coastwise trade between the East Coast and the Gulf. About a year later, the company began to convert another group of ships, a group of C2 freighters. And when it did so, it converted them to carry containers not only on deck but also below deck, something that could be said to have created the first true containerships: the first ships with hatch-covers designed to be lifted off by container cranes and the first ships with cell-guides to hold the containers in place below deck. And it was shortly after the first of those ships was launched that another company, Matson, began its own independent drive toward containerization by beginning to carry containers on deck on the West-Coast-to-Hawaii trade.

But it wasn't until 1967 that SeaLand launched the first international container trade, first on trans-Atlantic routes and later moving into the trans-Pacific trade as well. Other companies from various countries—West Germany, the UK, Japan—quickly followed SeaLand's lead, and with that the revolution jumped directly into high gear. And in fact, it all began to move so fast that within a very short span of years, the old companies that had been operating break-bulk freighters for decades suddenly found themselves faced with a very stark choice. Either they could convert their fleets and become a part of the fast-turn-around world that was growing and sprouting at a prodigious rate, or they could sit back and watch as their markets disappeared to be followed shortly by themselves. And so it was that as the Seventies wore on into the Eighties, one old-line American carrier after another was forced to make that difficult choice with some of them adapting and growing and prospering while the rest faded away and died. And with one company, United States Line, the biggest company of all, doing both those things: converting its fleet over to containerships only to run up so much debt that it crashed and burned in the mid-Eighties.

However, there was one old-line American company

that managed to survive as a break-bulk operator for years after all the others were gone—gone the way of the dinosaurs. That company was Lykes Lines out of New Orleans, LA, and while the company had acquired a sprinkling of fast-turn-around vessels during the Seventies and Eighties, the bulk of its fleet still consisted of old-fashioned freighters right into the very early Nineties. It kept those ships running for years after all the others had given up on them, and it is one of those out-dated ships from that company, one of those last-of-the-breed vessels, that serves as the setting for the sea story I am about to tell.

The ship in question was the *Alma Lykes*, a classic-looking six-hatch freighter of a design that Lykes called the Far East Clipper. She was a beautiful ship with booms and rigging that were state-of-the-art back when she was built in the mid-Sixties. And she was one of the last truly American freighters—American designed and American built—a ship that, to a seaman's eye, was a true work of art. She was a wonderful ship, and her economy and hardiness and versatility were perhaps some of the biggest reasons why Lykes Lines was able to stay afloat as a break-bulk operator for as many years as it was.

There were other...

–George, Second Mate: Excuse me, but do you mind if I say something here?

What...? What's that?

–George: I'd like to correct something you just said, if you don't mind.

You what?

–George: I'd like to correct what you just said about the Clippers, because I think you're giving people the wrong impression about those ships. Cause you see, while they were beautiful ships and a classic design and all that, they were hardly the ships that kept Lykes in business during all those years. No, that honor belongs to the Gulf Pacers, those ugly old work-horse ships. They were the ones that kept the company going all through the Eighties. They were the ships that paid the bills. And I think that fact is pretty obvious when you look at what happened when Lykes reduced the size of its fleet back in the mid-Eighties. Because what they did was they sent all their five-hatch ships to the Reserve Fleet, all the Andes Class and all the Gulf Prides, and at the same time they sent about half the Clippers. But you know, they didn't send a single Pacer to the Reserve Fleet at that time. They kept those ships running, every one of them, because those were the ships that the company depended upon.

Okay, uh… Thank you for that. I stand corrected, I suppose…

–George: And you know, while the Pacers paid lower wages to the crew and also burned less fuel than the Clippers did, they actually carried slightly more cargo. So from an economic point-of-view, the Pacers had it all over the Clippers. And the only things the Clippers had going for them were their looks and their speed. Because the Clippers were the glamour ships of the fleet while the Pacers were the working-class ships. They were the proletarians. They were…

Thank you! Thank you very much! I appreciate your contribution, but now if you don't mind…

–George: Oh what? You want me to be quiet? You want to get on with your story?

Yes I do, thank you.

–George: Well then go ahead. Don't let me stop you.

Okay then, uh… Let's see, I was… Where was I?... Oh yes, as I was saying, Lykes found a way to survive the Eighties when other companies didn't. And while one of the big reasons for its survival was the fact that its ships were relatively new and efficient and quite well-built, there were also a number of other factors that contributed to its survival. Like first and foremost, I should probably mention the government operating subsidies the company received, the subsidies for operating a number of old liner-routes out of the Gulf Coast going to Northern Europe and the Mediterranean, South and East Africa, the Far East, and the West Coast of South America. They depended heavily upon those subsidies for their survival, and so even as the economic realities of the Eighties forced them to become ever more of a tramp operation, an operation that went wherever they could find a cargo, they still made it a point to stop in at least one subsidized port on every trip they made, as in that way they kept their operating subsidies alive.

And another factor was the way that, even as the Eighties wore on and containerships took over more and more of the liner cargo, Lykes still managed to find niche markets it could serve. Like for instance, its ships would carry over-sized cargoes, cargoes that were too big to fit inside containers, or they would carry cargoes to third world ports that had yet to build container facilities, or they would especially carry food-aid cargoes, those government giveaway cargoes that were reserved for American bottoms. They would carry any type of cargo they could find, and they would carry it to anywhere in the world that it needed to go.

The cargo the *Alma Lykes* carried on the voyage I am about to describe was a typical cargo for one of those end-times voyages. It was a cargo much like the ones she usually carried during those years, a cargo that consisted of military vehicles and a small amount of ammunition, along with a few heavy-lift odds-and-ends all bound for Sattahip and Bangkok in Thailand—subsidized ports that would make the ship eligible for a government subsidy during the entire voyage—along with several thousand tons of food-aid cargo for Nepal which she would be discharging in Calcutta. And while the schedule said nothing about backloads of any sort, everyone knew it was a virtual certainty that once the discharge was finished, the *Alma* would be stopping in to load rubber and other cargoes at a number of small ports in Indonesia and Malaysia before returning to the U.S. They knew that she would be making the "jungle run."

The coastwise portion of the voyage began very slowly, giving a good indication of just how long the whole voyage was going to take as the old girl bounced around to a number of ports on the Gulf Coast and loaded food-aid cargo at each of them. And since the contracts for aid cargo at that time called for the cargo to be loaded only during a forty-hour week, with no longshore work to be done at night or on weekends, that meant she ended up spending more time sitting idle in port with no work being done than she did working cargo. And in fact, the situation even reached the rather absurd extreme where, when the longshoremen in Lake Charles, LA, finished their shift one Friday afternoon with about three or four hours of work still remaining to be done, the *Alma* actually sat idle all weekend and waited for Monday morning to roll around before finishing up the cargo and sailing on to her next port. And since Mobile, AL, was the next port, she ended up being underway not only on Monday afternoon but also all day Tuesday, losing all those additional working hours as well. And remember that this operation was taking place in what had already become the era of the containership, an era in which the loss of a few hours during cargo operations is seen as a catastrophe so that the loss of entire days is something completely unthinkable.

Because of the limits that were placed on her loading time, the *Alma* eventually took about two and a half weeks to load all her giveaway cargo and sail for the East Coast where she would be picking up the rest of her load. And she sailed with her lower holds and at least the wings of nearly all her tween decks piled high with fifty-kilo bags of rice. Her first stop on the East Coast was Charleston, SC, where she loaded the bulk of her military cargo, some forty tanks along with a few other types of vehicles that were being sold—not given away—to the Thai military. This cargo was loaded into the holds forward of the house, holds one-through-four, with first the lighter vehicles being loaded into any space that still remained in the wings of the tween decks, followed by tanks which were loaded into the squares of those decks. And then once all the forward holds were full, the rest of the tanks were loaded out on the weatherdeck so that by the time the load was finished and the ship was ready to sail from Charleston, she had her forward decks completely covered with tanks. So many tanks that she looked like she was on her way to a war zone. And not only were there tanks everywhere you looked on those decks, but there were also the chains that the longshoremen had stretched out to secure the tanks in place. There were chains everywhere, so many chains that it would have taken hours to count them all. So many chains that when a man tried to walk from the house out to the bow, he had to step over a chain with every step he took, all the way forward.

After she left Charleston, the *Alma* made a stop at Sunny Point, NC, where the longshoremen loaded a few hundred tons of ammunition into number five upper-tween-deck. And then finally she continued upriver to Wilmington where the after hatches, numbers five and six, were topped-off with heavy-lifts: a pair of airport passenger-boarding-bridges on top of number five, and some sort of railroad maintenance engine on number six.

And so with the load now complete, with the *Alma* packed with as much cargo as she could carry, it came time for her to head for the open sea, to leave Wilmington and sail for Sattahip, Thailand, her first foreign port. And to get there, she...

–George: Hey wait a minute, you forgot something. You're not supposed to tell them about where the ship went yet.

I what?... Oh, it's you again. What do you want this time?

–George: I was just saying that you left some stuff out. You left out all the part about how I laid out the routes to get there, don't you remember? I told you all about it.

Well, I didn't think it was all that interesting...

–George: Not that interesting? How can you say that? Because after all the work I put into those routes...

Yes, I know you did a lot of work, but it's just that it, uh... that I didn't...

–George: Well, if you're afraid it's too complicated, don't worry about it. I'll go ahead and explain it to the people for you so you don't have to worry about it. Because you see, it was like this. The Captain knew way ahead of time that when we left Wilmington, we'd be going to Sattahip, but with that being almost exactly halfway around the world, he didn't know which way we'd be going since the company hadn't said anything to him about it. He didn't know whether we'd be going there via the Suez Canal or the Panama Canal. And since I was the navigation officer, that meant it fell upon me to be ready for whichever of the two eventualities the company might choose. And being the competent and diligent Second Mate that I was, I proceeded to lay out both of those routes in their entirety, including not only lists of waypoints with all the courses and distances between them, but also lists of the charts we'd need to use on each route.

—First I laid out the slightly shorter of the two routes, the one that went directly across the Atlantic to the Straits of Gibraltar and then made its way through the Mediterranean until it reached the Suez Canal. From the far end of the canal, the route went out the Red Sea and then around the southern tips of India and Sri Lanka before rounding the northern tip of Sumatra and entering the Malacca Straits. And of course from there, the route went through the Singapore Straits and finally up into the Gulf of Thailand.

—Once I'd finished that route, I laid out the longer of the two, the route that cut south through the Windward Passage to the Panama Canal. And after leaving the canal, the route followed the coast of Central America until it reached a point where we could begin a great circle that would take us all the way across the Pacific, all the way to one of the passes through the islands that stretch out between Taiwan and the Philippines. And from there, the route went around the southern tip of Vietnam and finally up into the Gulf of Thailand.

—So as I say, I had both of those routes completely laid out and ready to go, and all I needed was word from the company about which canal they preferred to use. But then when the word finally came through a couple of days before sailing, I found to my surprise that they didn't want to use either of the canals. They wanted us to go via the Cape of Good Hope. And so on very short notice, I had to lay out a completely new route. I had to lay out a route that took us all the way south in the Atlantic and around the coast of South Africa, after which it crossed the southern part of the Indian Ocean to the Sunda Straits, the straits between Java and Sumatra. And after passing through those straits, the route weaved its way through the whole archipelago until it ran up into the Gulf of Thailand.

—It was a much longer route that either of the canal-routes would have been, but since that was what the company wanted, that was what the company got. And of course all my work wasn't really wasted since I kept a notebook with all my routes in it, all the routes I might need some day since you never knew where you might be going next with that company. I kept a notebook with routes for…

Okay, thank you! Thank you very much!! But that'll be enough, if you please.

—George: Oh, you mean I was… Yeah, I guess I was getting a little bit carried away there, wasn't I?

Yes, you were! But now if you don't mind, I'd like to, uh… I'd like to get back to…

—George: Of course. Feel free.

I'd like to get back to what I was saying, back to, uh… And in any case, I suppose I can always go back and erase that stuff, can't I?

—George: Oh, you wouldn't…

So let's see now, where was I?… That's right, I was talking about how the *Alma Lykes* sailed from Wilmington on a long route that took her around the Cape of Good Hope. And a very long route it was, one that ended up taking thirty-three days before she finally reached her destination.

\* \* \* \* \*

The first leg of the trip was the long, lazy passage into the South Atlantic, the passage that took the *Alma* from the mouth of the Cape Fear River to the very southern tip of

Africa, a passage that wore on for day after calm, pleasant day. The weather was beautiful as she sliced her way through the mild tropical seas, and traffic was almost non-existent in all that huge watery solitude. And so she plodded along day after night after day, traveling alone across the endless expanse of sea and sky, moving ever forward with the quiet persistence so characteristic of ships.

And as the *Alma* made her way to the south, the crew quickly fell into their daily routines at sea. The Steward's Department rose early each morning to begin their day filled with cooking and cleaning, and they didn't finish until early in the evening when they knocked off to get their rest before the start of another long day. Meanwhile, with the exception of a few dayworkers who spent their days maintaining and repairing various pieces of machinery, the Engine Department lived the life of watchstanders on a steamship during all those days at sea. They worked their four hours at a stretch down in the engineroom, their four hours of tending the machinery that kept the propeller turning throughout the passage—their four hours spent in the infernal heat of a floating steam plant in the tropics—before coming up for eight hours of rest. And as for the Deck Department, the Bosun and deck gang went out each day to perform their daily maintenance work which seemed to consist mainly of chipping and painting on some area of the deck that wasn't covered with cargo, while up on the bridge, the Mates and AB's stood their routine sea watches, their long, monotonous four hour watches. And though it was boring for them up on the bridge, at least the temperature and the scenery were far more pleasant than they were for the watchstanders down in the engineroom.

Because the fact is that there was little for them to do on that bridge besides staring out at the empty and featureless horizon. There was virtually no traffic anywhere in that big, deserted stretch of ocean, and at the same time, the seas were so consistently gentle that there was nothing to worry about in that area, either. So there was little for the men on watch to do besides looking out the windows or hanging out on the bridge wings and staring at the horizon from there. And since the radars on the *Alma* were old and not very reliable, the Mates followed the old-fashioned tradition of saving them for when they really needed them, of turning them off during the day when visibility was good. And while they ran one radar at night—they didn't follow the even older tradition of leaving them off at night as well—there was never anything for them to see on the screen even when the thing was up and running. So for that reason, the Mates tended to spend a lot of time out on the wings at night, standing outside in the warm tropical breeze, sometimes scanning the horizon in search of non-existent traffic and other times looking up at the sky and the stars. Looking at those stars that shone so brightly and in such numbers, shining unlike anything ever seen on land.

And even during the day, there was little for them to do besides shooting the occasional sun-line with their sextants or shooting the stars at twilight. But since the ship was equipped with a satellite navigator—the first type of satellite navigation system, the type that was in use before GPS—their efforts at celestial navigation were largely voluntary, something the Mates did because they wanted to maintain their skills with their sextants "just in case" or they wanted to "check" the positions the satellite navigator was giving them. Because at the time this voyage was taking place, it was only recently that celestial navigation had ceased to hold the life-or-death importance that it had held for so long, the importance it had held for centuries. It was something that was just in the process of becoming obsolete, just making its way toward the garbage heap of technological history. And while it wasn't quite there yet, not like it would be when GPS came out a year or two later, it was already well on its way.

With so little to do during the day and so little to look at besides the empty horizon, one pastime of the people on watch became that of watching sea birds in action whenever there were any present. And this was especially true after the *Alma* had made her way far enough to the south that Albatross began to appear since those birds even more than other species seemed to know all about ships. Or at least they knew how to use ships to help them procure their meals. They knew that they could coast along just above the bow of the ship, floating effortlessly in the updraft caused by the vessel's motion, while at the same time watching the water for the flying fish she was constantly scaring up and sending flying away out of her path. And what the Albatross would do was to float along until they spotted a flying fish they thought they could catch, at which point they would suddenly dive down toward the water after it. And then a short time later, they would return to their vantage point, sometimes empty-handed while other times they were still swallowing the last of their snack.

The *Alma* continued on for day after day after week, making her way through those lovely but lonely seas until she finally arrived off the Cape of Good Hope where she turned to make her way along the coast of South Africa. And as she followed that coast, she hugged the land as tightly as the crew dared to hug it, something that was especially true once she began to enter the Indian Ocean since it was only by passing very close to the coast that she was able to avoid the powerful Agulhas Current, the current that flows down the east coast of Africa before curving around toward the Atlantic. And while there is a certain danger in following this practice since much of the coast isn't very well surveyed, at least it provided the crew with a welcome change of scenery. Because for the next two days as the aging ship made her way along the coast, they were treated to one magnificent view after another, views of the points and the mountains and the fertile green South African countryside, views so beautiful as to make you think you must be gazing upon some vision of paradise.

Then at the end of two pleasant and scenic days, the *Alma* was ready to leave the coast behind and begin another long, boring crossing. She was ready to begin the crossing of the Indian Ocean. And while it is hard to believe that any stretch of ocean could be even emptier and quieter than her passage through the South Atlantic had just been, that was exactly how this new passage turned out to be. It was a passage during which the *Alma* met no traffic at all. She didn't meet a ship and she didn't meet a fishing boat. She saw nothing at all besides water.

During all the time the persistent little ship was making these long, slow passages, the crewmembers were getting to know each other, of course. They were getting to like each other in some cases, while in other cases they were merely learning to tolerate each other. Most of them were new to the ship having come aboard during the coastwise run, which was normal for the *Alma* given the length of the voyages she made, voyages that generally lasted for upwards of four months. There weren't all that many seamen around who wanted to make two trips of that length back-to-back, and at the same time, the officers' unions, the Mates' and Engineers' unions, gave their members no choice. Their shipping rules required that their members get off at an American port after having completed four months aboard, so in practice, they ended up making a complete change-out on each and every voyage.

The reason for the long trips was the "jungle run" which the Clippers made on virtually every voyage in those days, the trip to a lot of small Indonesian and Malaysian ports to backload the raw rubber that was in such demand in the United States at the beginning of the Nineties thanks to the AIDS epidemic and the resultant explosion in condom sales. Because with stories about AIDS being in the headlines day after day, the condom industry was going through a giant boom as were the suppliers of raw rubber, the rubber plantations of Southeast Asia, and also to a lesser extent the shipping companies that carried that rubber. And since Lykes's Pacers were already too old at the time to be permitted into Indonesia's ports—the Pacers were too old and the Clippers were nearly so as they fast approached the age of twenty-five—it fell upon the Clippers to serve that market. It fell upon the Clippers like the *Alma* to call at the various small rubber ports during one voyage after another.

While most of the crew were new to the *Alma Lykes* for this voyage, having signed on during the coastwise run, the vast majority of them already had considerable experience on this or similar vessels so that their adaptation to the ship was minimal. But there was one exception to the rule, that being the Chief Mate. Because while he was a veteran seaman by now and had a number of years' experience under his belt, he had never been aboard a break-bulk ship in his life. Not before he came aboard the *Alma*. So in other words, his case was the exact opposite of what would have been normal fifteen or twenty years earlier, or perhaps even as recently as ten years, when a seaman would have been boarding his first fast-turn-around vessel ever after a career spent on freighters. Because in the case of the Chief Mate, all his previous experience had been aboard fast-turn-around vessels—containerships and roll-on/roll-offs and Seabees, Lykes's barge-carrying ships—and he was now sailing on his very first freighter. His first and his last as it turned out to be.

He was a tall, handsome man, not quite middle-aged, who was more than qualified for the job he held and who soon found that his greatest problem aboard the *Alma* wouldn't be doing his job but rather it would be dealing with the slow pace and the boredom. It would be finding ways to fill his time when he had four and a half months to do the same amount of work he normally did in four or five weeks on the fast-turn-around vessels where he'd gotten his previous Chief Mate's experience. It would be finding ways to occupy himself during all those long, empty hours and days. It would be finding ways to fight the dulling sameness of those days until he could get back to the States and his one true love: the fast-turn-around ships to which he would return never to look back again.

–Chief Mate: Excuse me, but could I say something here?

You what? You… You want to interrupt me, too?

–Chief Mate: Well, you let George say what he had to say, didn't you?

Let him? It's more like he just butted in, that's what it was… But okay, go ahead and say what you want to say.

–Chief Mate: I just wanted to say that you're giving the wrong impression about me with what you've been saying just now. Cause I mean, sure I was bored a lot and all that, but there were also moments that were highly interesting and situations that called on skills you never have to use on containerships. There were situations where I had to improvise and think on my feet, situations completely unlike anything that occurs on a containership where everything pretty much follows a routine from one voyage to the next. There were moments that tested my seamanship and made me show what I could really do. So I have to say that I'm proud of what I did on that ship. And I'm very proud of the fact that I was one of the last Chief Mates ever to sail on an American break-bulk ship on a commercial voyage.

But you told me yourself that you missed the hectic pace and the intensity of fast-turn-around. And you told me that you couldn't imagine yourself spending an entire career on those old, slow-paced ships.

—Chief Mate: Yes that's true, but it doesn't change what I feel about that ship and the trip I made on it. I mean, that trip on the *Alma Lykes* was one of the highlights of my entire career, and that in spite of all the, uh... all the problems that came up, all the... you know... But when you sum up my feelings about the ship, please tell the people that I was proud of what I did. I was bored, but I was proud.

Well, okay then... But by now, I suppose the readers will already have picked up on your point, so I don't see any reason for me to repeat it, do you? No, I don't think so. I think I should just get back to the story. I should... You know, I'm not sure if it's a good idea for me to introduce another of the crewmembers at this point if they're going to keep interrupting me. Though maybe, uh... maybe I should at least introduce the Bosun right here. Because after all, he plays a major role in this story, besides which he's sort of the strong, silent type so he's not all that likely to butt in with his two cents' worth.

The Bosun was what you could call the exact polar opposite of the Chief Mate. He was an old-school seaman, one of those hard-living, hard-drinking seamen who are also hard-working when they have to be. He was a man perfectly suited for life aboard break-bulk ships, for working hard at sea and playing hard in port, and it was for that reason that he'd always made it a point not to set foot aboard a containership. He was a big man, not as tall as the Chief Mate but more muscular, and while it would be hard to describe him as handsome, he had a look that was all man. He had a look that inspired respect in other men and admiration in some women, a look that some people would describe as that of a Real Man.

And while it was probably inevitable that friction would develop between two men of such opposite types as the Bosun and the Chief Mate while being confined together aboard a ship, working closely with each other day after day, still the problems between them were minimal during the entire outbound passage. They worked together smoothly during those days as each of them concentrated upon doing his own job, and they even seemed to like each other up to a point. They liked each other, and they respected each other...

—Bosun (mumbling): Bullshit.

What? You don't agree? You didn't, uh... Well, whatever the case may have been regarding the issue of respect, at least I can tell you that there were no angry confrontations between them during that long passage and no obvious signs of friction. I can tell you that they worked together smoothly and that, to all outward appearances, the two of them got along just fine.

But enough about the crew. It's time to get back to the story of the voyage. The *Alma* finally reached the Sunda Strait, the strait that separates Sumatra and Java, after having spent nearly a month at sea. She reached the strait, and there she turned and steamed north past the deadly beauty of Krakatoa. And then no sooner had she cleared the strait than she made a sharp turn to avoid an oil-field that lay just to the north. That turn was followed over the next day or two by a whole series of additional turns to avoid other hazards, be they islands or reefs. And it wasn't until after she had run a complete obstacle course that the old girl finally came back out into open water, the open water of the South China Sea. And from there, she had a straight shot up into the Gulf of Thailand and the port of Sattahip.

\* \* \* \* \*

So at last, after thirty-three long, monotonous days at sea, the *Alma Lykes* arrived at her destination. She arrived and the crew tied her up, and immediately life aboard ship went through a sudden and complete transformation. Because first of all, sea watches were broken which meant that after all those countless days of working four hours on and eight hours off, the watchstanders now began to work eight on and sixteen off. And in an even more profound change, crewmembers were finally able to get off the ship for a few hours at a time, to go ashore and see something other than the ship and the sea. To go ashore where they could drink and carouse and chase after whores. To go ashore where they could cut loose after all those boring, repetitious days.

The heavy partiers quickly came into their own in the bars of the town—the Bosun, the Second Engineer, and a few others—while the more staid members of the crew quietly faded into the background. And while Sattahip bore no resemblance to its wild past as a U.S. base during the Vietnam War, still it was a port in Thailand and that meant that it had plenty of good seaman-type fun to offer. Seaman-type fun and seaman-type danger, too, since it was in one of Sattahip's bars that the crew was to suffer its first casualty. It was to lose its first, though not its last, member.

It happened the first day ashore when one of the ship's

First Assistant Engineers—the *Alma* was unusual in that she carried two Firsts—spent the afternoon drinking in the bar that the crew had turned into their unofficial headquarters in town. He drank there for several hours until, at a moment when everyone else from the ship had left either to shack up with a girl in one of the huts out back or to stroll the streets and see the town, the proprietors decided that it would be a good time to slip him a mickey and rob him. But their plan almost turned fatal when he had an adverse reaction to the drug they gave him so that the next thing he knew was when he woke up in a hospital on a ventilator. And though he could breathe on his own just fine once he'd regained consciousness, he soon found that breathing wasn't his only problem. He found that something had happened to his left arm while he was unconscious, something caused by the way he'd fallen or the way he'd lain, but whatever it had been, it had left his arm completely paralyzed. And when the arm didn't improve over the next day or two, when no feeling and no use returned to it, he finally had to be flown home for medical treatment.

Nothing was ever done to the people who owned the bar, of course, since they denied everything and even claimed to have found heroin on him after he'd passed out. They claimed that he'd done it to himself while at the same time ignoring any questions about where the money he'd had on him might have gone. So they suffered no legal consequences of any type, and in fact, I don't think they even lost any business from the crew.

The ship was two days in Sattahip before going... Oh wait a minute, there's another little anecdote about the arrival in Sattahip that I almost forgot about. It's a story that involves the heavy-lifts that had been loaded on the hatch-cover at number five hatch, because you see...

—George: Hello, excuse me. But is it okay if I tell this story?

Is it what? You want to...

—George: Yes, I wanta tell the story. I really wanta...

No, of course you can't! What do you think this is? This is my story, you know, and I'm the one who's telling it. Because I'm the author here and all you are is one of the characters. And you'd better remember that!

—George: Well jeez, if you're gonna be that way about it...

Yes, I am going to be that way about it! So now if you'll just be quiet and let me get back to my story, I'll uh... Let's see, I was just talking about the little incident that occurred when the *Alma* first arrived in Sattahip, the incident that actually began about a month earlier when she was sailing from North Carolina. Because no sooner had the two heavy-lifts—the two airport gates—been loaded onto the hatch-cover of number five than the Captain and Chief Mate knew that they could have a problem when it came time to unload the ammunition stowed down inside the hatch. And so they had sent a message at that time, a message telling the cargo people in Thailand about the heavy-lifts and saying that they would have to be discharged first before the ammo could come out. Then as the voyage had progressed, they had repeated their message several times, explaining that not only were the heavy-lifts in the way, but that they were also too heavy for the ship's cargo gear at that hatch so that a shore-crane would be needed to discharge them.

They had sent their messages to anyone and everyone they could think of, anyone who might need to know about the problem. But then when it finally came time and the ship arrived at Sattahip, the Captain was told to proceed directly to the ammunition pier, a pier that was not only reserved exclusively for ammunition but also one that had no shore-cranes. And no sooner had the crew tied her up than a man from the cargo office came aboard to tell the Chief Mate in an incredulous voice, "Did you know that you have heavy-lifts on hatch five?"

Well, duh! What do you think we've been trying to tell you all this time?

What finally happened was that they had to shift the ship to the city docks where the heavy-lifts could be discharged. And since the decision to shift wasn't made until after most of the crew had already gone ashore, the Captain and the Chief Mate had to scrape together anyone they could find aboard to help make the shift. They had to put together a true skeleton crew, one where cooks and oilers and everyone else went out to help with the lines.

At the end of two days, all the cargo for Sattahip was finished. All the heavy-lifts and all the ammunition were gone, and with that weight having been removed from the stern, the *Alma* was now ready to proceed up the river to Bangkok. She was sitting on an even keel, and her drafts at both bow and stern read the exact maximum draft allowable for ships entering the river. She was as deep in the water as she could possibly be and still proceed. And since she would have been too deep if she had taken on fuel in Sattahip, that meant she was now down to the very last of her reserves.

So it was in this condition that she entered the Chao Phraya River...

—George: Uh, hello...

What? What is it now?

—George: I just wanted to ask you if I could tell about how we almost ran out of fuel. About how the plant tripped out when we were at the dock that first night in Bangkok and how I thought we'd run out of fuel for real.

But... But that didn't happen at this point in the story. It happened after the ship was already tied up in Bangkok.
—George: I know that, but I just wanted to get ready.
You what?! You interrupted me so you could get ready?
—George: Yeah, I guess...
That's it! I've had it with you! I've taken all I'm going to take, so you'd better be quiet. And be quiet right now! I don't want to hear another peep out of you.
—George: Okay, so I'll wait till...
You'll wait nothing! You'll be quiet and that's all you'll do! Because if I hear one more word from you, I'll... I'll write you out of this story. That's what I'll do.
—George: Write me out? How can you write me out? I'm already in the story.
Yes, but have you ever heard of revisions?! Why, I could go back and write this whole thing over again if I wanted to. I could go back and erase you any time I wanted to!
—George: Okay, okay, I'm sorry. I'll be quiet.
Yes, you'd better be. And I mean very quiet!
—George (mumbling): Jeez, talk about a power trip...
So now if I can please get back to my story, back to the trip up the Chao Phraya River... Well, it wasn't a very long trip lasting only a few hours as it did, but what a beautiful and exotic few hours it was for those aboard. Because after so many days with nothing to see but the ocean itself, the crew suddenly found themselves plunged into a world of life and color and movement. The banks of the river were nowhere to be seen during most of the journey, so thick and abundant was the vegetation, and all the way upriver there were sights to see, sights that popped up around each and every bend. There were gaudy-looking temples and villages and rice-paddies and houses on stilts built right out

over the water. And even the river itself was filled with life, with floating vegetation and exotic-looking boats, and especially with those typical Thai long-tailed boats. There was a thriving humanity and an abundant nature all along the way. There was vitality and there was beauty. There was everything that a river in Asia is supposed to have.

The *Alma* finally reached the dock with her fuel so low that she was running on little more than fumes. And in fact, when the power plant was accidentally tripped-out while placing a strainer over the cooling-water intake, a strainer meant to prevent it from becoming clogged with the leaves and plants that constantly floated upon the river, there was at least one member of the crew who thought at the time that the last of the fuel had just run out. One member of the crew whom I won't name and who had better not…

Well, the bunker barge came alongside the next morning when controlling the draft was no longer a consideration, and so it was that the old girl never quite ran out of fuel. But even before the fuel had arrived that morning, the crew was to receive a surprising bit of news, one so unexpected as to be positively shocking though shocking in the most delightful way. Because when the cargo coordinator from the Thai military came aboard to talk with the Chief Mate that morning, it was to inform him that with this being the beginning of a three-day weekend—Monday was some sort of holiday—there would be no cargo worked until Tuesday morning. And on top of that, he said that since there were only ten trucks available for hauling the forty tanks off to their final destination, they would only be discharging ten of them each day.

So in other words, he was saying that the *Alma* would be staying in Bangkok for a whole week, something unheard of in the year 1990. And to make matters even better, the ship was tied up at the very first berth inside the gate so that all the crewmembers had to do if they wanted to go ashore was to walk around the shed and they were there. They were at the gate where formerly the Mosquito Bar had sat directly across the street. And the only disappointment for those who had been to Bangkok before was the fact that the bar was no longer there, the Mosquito Bar and in fact the whole row of seamen's dives that used to run down the block to the left. In their place was a parking lot while the only thing left for seamen in the whole neighborhood was the rather luxurious Seamen's Club that sat a short distance off to the right.

But while the wild old waterfront world of Klong Toey was gone, that didn't mean that there was nothing for the crew to do in Bangkok. Because for the mere price of a taxi, they could still find plenty of good seaman-type fun up at Pat Pong or at Soi Cowboy. They could still go off to those strange little hedonistic worlds, those worlds where the heavy partiers in the crew would have one more moment in the sun, one more chance to shine like they had in Sattahip. And since they were going to be staying in Bangkok for a whole week, that meant that this would be an opportunity for the true heavyweights in the crew to show their stuff. It would be a chance for them to weed out the middleweights and the part-timers from their ranks.

And when you talk about the heavyweights that were on that ship, of course you have to mention the Bosun right away since he was the heaviest of them all. He was a man who somehow managed to drink and carouse all night every night the ship was in port, drinking in the bars until they closed and he had to move on to the after-hours places. And then when morning would come rolling around, he would drag himself back to the ship and drag through his day's work before heading right back to town for yet another all-nighter. And the only time he spent in bed during the entire week the ship was in Bangkok was the time he spent with one bar girl or another. Because he was a man who truly seemed to have no limits.

–Jamey, Second Engineer: No limits? Is that all you're gonna say?

Excuse me…?

–Jamey: No excuse me, cause you're not tellin' this thing right. I mean, that's all you're gonna say about him is he had no limits?

Well…

–Jamey: Man, that guy was nuts! That's what he was. He was like… Well, I don't know how to say it cause I'm not that good with words. But he was like…

–Like take me, I'm a pretty heavy partier, but there's no way I could keep up with that Bosun. Cause like I'd see him up at Soi Cowboy every night with a beer in one hand and his other arm around a girl, and right away we'd start buyin' each other drinks and stuff like that and more girls would come around cause we'd be throwin' our money around like we was rich or somethin'. But I tell ya, when it came around to closin' time, I'd be headin' to bed with a girl or I'd be headin' back to the ship to get some rest. But not him, man. He'd be headin' to one-a them after-hours places, one-a them so-called coffee shops, and he'd just keep right on goin'. It was like… Like I don't know how he did it, man, cause he's gotta be made outa steel or somethin'. I mean… Isn't that right, Carter?

–Carter, AB: Who me? You're askin' me about it?

–Jamey: Yeah, cause you used to drink with him, too.

–Carter: Not like you I didn't, cause I ain't crazy. I ain't gonna go drink-for-drink with a guy who throws em down the way he does. I just… I ain't crazy.

–Jamey (jokingly): Crazy? Who you callin' crazy, huh? You hear that…?

—Bosun: What the fuck you guys lookin' at me for? I don't got nothin' to say. Cause that shit ain't nothin' but ancient history... So hey, Mr. Writer! Why don't you get back to your fuckin' story, huh?

Oh my story. Yes thank you, I certainly will. I'll, uh... I'll just... So on Tuesday morning, the Thai longshoremen finally came aboard ship and cargo operations began. And though they only came to discharge ten tanks a day along with whatever trucks and other miscellaneous vehicles became accessible in the process, those were still far from being quick and easy workdays. The tanks were so heavy that they could only be worked with the ship's jumbo boom which sat between hatches two and three where it could be flipped back-and-forth to work cargo at either hatch. But with the tanks being loaded all up and down the deck, it meant that once the first few easy ones had been discharged, the longshoremen had to deal with the rather complex problem of rigging fairleads and snaking the tanks into position, of dragging those big, heavy pieces of cargo up and down the decks one by one until they could be lifted and discharged with the jumbo. So it turned out to be a long, slow process, and at one point they even had to bring in a floating crane to discharge the tanks on the hatch cover at number four and also in the tween decks of that same hatch. But since the crane they brought wasn't big enough to reach all the way across the ship and set those tanks directly ashore, it simply became one more way of shifting the cargo around, of picking the tanks up with the floating crane and then setting them down on deck in a position where they could be picked back up with the jumbo boom. Picked up and set down again onto the waiting truck.

In the end, the cargo operations lasted the full four days that the Thais had predicted, and it wasn't until the evening of the fourth day—until the *Alma* had been in Bangkok for exactly a week—that they were finally ready to sail on to their next port. And since a lot of weight had been removed from the ship's decks and holds by this time, there was no longer anything to worry about with the draft as they were well within the required limits for descending the river. And so as evening turned into night on that final day in Bangkok, the crew went out and untied the lines, some of them sober and some of them not, and with nothing left to hold her to shore, the old girl slipped away from the dock and went quietly on her way. She turned around and sailed down that picturesque little river one more time, though this time as she went the crew saw far less than they had on the way upriver thanks to the darkness. They saw little more than shadows and village lights and the occasional apparition-like illuminated temple.

Once the *Alma* had cleared the river, she set her course for the south, running on until she was outside the Gulf of Thailand, on until she was far enough south to merge onto the maritime super-highway of the Singapore and Malacca Straits. And then once she was in those crowded shipping lanes, she followed them until she reached the point where she would merge back out again, the point where she would cut north into the nearly-deserted Bay of Bengal.

\*  \*  \*  \*  \*

So the *Alma* was back underway, and no sooner had she left the dock in Bangkok than the life of the crew returned to its old rhythm and its old routine. It returned to its four on and eight off and its monotony, and the only difference between this passage and the earlier one, other than the amount of time and distance involved in each, lay in the changes that had taken place among the crew. One of the

First Engineers was gone as I already mentioned, and a couple of other crewmembers were soon to follow. And the most important of these new casualties, at least as far as the purposes of this story are concerned, was a guy by the name of Nathan, one of the eight-to-twelve AB's. It seems that Nathan had injured his knees while using a Bosun's chair in Bangkok, and since he complained that he was unable to stand watch with his knees in the condition they were, that meant the Bosun had to take over his watches. Or at least the Bosun had to take his evening watches, spending two hours either on standby or lookout and the other two hours on the bridge with the Chief Mate. And since Nathan's knees continued to bother him—or so he claimed—he was eventually flown home from Calcutta, to be paid his "lost wages" until the voyage ended or until his knees healed, whichever came first. And what this meant was that the Bosun would have to stand his evening watches for the rest of the voyage, his two hours on the bridge each night at sea. His two hours alone with the Chief Mate.

During the first watch or two they stood together, they each made an effort to establish a normal relationship between them. They tried to engage in some sort of normal conversation. But given what completely opposite personality types the two of them were, those efforts were doomed from the beginning. And as they made their first tentative attempts at opening up and revealing themselves, they quickly came to realize that they had nothing in common. Neither of them had the least interest in the details of the other's life and they shared no interests other than the sea, so the only topic of conversation that they had available was for them to tell each other sea-stories. But even those stories had little in common given the different types of ships on which each of them had worked, so it didn't take long before they gave up their efforts altogether and lapsed into silence. They lapsed into a silence that neither of them found to be the least bit comfortable.

And it was especially uncomfortable for the Bosun who continued to make occasional efforts at conversation even after the other had long since abandoned them. He continued to tell his jokes and his sea-stories whenever the silence became too much for him to bear. But since the Mate squirmed uneasily whenever he began and never answered him at the end with more than a single sentence, or perhaps only a single word, he was finally forced to abandon even those last feeble efforts. And it was because of the discomfort he felt on the bridge that at the end of each of his two hour sessions of enforced silence, he would suddenly burst out with heartfelt enthusiasm at the sight of the AB coming to relieve him on the wheel. He would explode into life the moment he saw his watch-partner Carter on those days when the Bosun had "first wheel." He would immediately begin to laugh and joke and tell stories, and he would slap his buddy on the back. And on the days when he had "second wheel," he would do much the same at the sight of the twelve-to-four AB.

He would feel so relieved that he just had to let it out, and that was especially true at the end of each of the first few days of awkward silence when his greetings would flow directly from the heart. But then as the voyage progressed and he became more accustomed to the silence he had to endure with the Mate, there was a certain air of inauthenticity that began to creep into his outbursts. There was a loss of spontaneity. And in fact, there were days when his actions were so clearly artificial and forced that they even proved embarrassing to Carter, the man stuck in the middle between the Bosun and the Chief Mate. But still the Bosun went on day after day, breaking his two hour silences with sudden bursts of congeniality. And as he did so, he increasingly watched for the Mate's reaction. He watched the guy and hoped to see him cringe at the way his nose was being rubbed into the silence, at the way he was being shown that the silence was directed at him and no one else.

And while the Chief Mate didn't exactly cringe, it clearly grated upon his nerves each time the Bosun so demonstrably greeted Carter or one of the other AB's. It bothered him deeply to see how the Bosun changed personalities so suddenly upon the other's appearance. It bothered him almost as much as the Bosun's sea-stories had bothered him earlier on when they were still speaking to each other, those sea-stories that always sounded so much better than his own, so much saltier and with settings that were so much more exotic. It made the Chief Mate churn inside each time the Bosun laughed or even so much as spoke with the others. It aggravated him deeply. But since he knew that there was nothing he could do about it and no way for him to release his ever-growing aggravation, he had to let it simmer. He had to…

–Chief Mate: Excuse me, but could I say something here?

You what…? Oh yes, go ahead.

–Chief Mate: I just want to say that you're blowing these things all out of proportion, because it didn't bother me nearly as much as you're saying.

No…?

–Chief Mate: No, he just… He disgusted me was what he did. Cause just look at what a drunken spectacle he made of himself while we were in Bangkok. He… I mean, I lost whatever respect I might have had for him before that.

So you lost your respect for him, what? As a seaman?

–Chief Mate: No, not as a seaman, because he was

always a good seaman even when he was drunk. But he... I mean, I lost respect for him as a man and as a person. Because tell me, how could anyone respect such a drunken slob? And even though he sobered up once the ship was at sea, still I... I just couldn't get that image out of my head, that image of him returning to the ship each morning in Bangkok, bleary-eyed and sloppy and stinking of booze and who-knows-what-else. Because it was all so... so... so unprofessional!

Well okay then, I stand corrected. But now, uh... Now it's time to get back to my story, right? Back to the Bay of Bengal.

The *Alma* left the traffic lanes of the Malacca Strait once she was far enough to the west, and when she did, she headed up into the Bay of Bengal. And as she proceeded to the north, it didn't take long before it became clear to those aboard that they were entering into a world that was far different from the one where they had been up until now. They were entering into a world of nothingness, a world without life. And while they still saw the occasional ship as they went, they never saw one fishing boat in that entire bay. No boats and, more ominously, no marine life of any description: no porpoises and no flying fish and not even birds. Instead, all they saw was a sea that appeared to be dead. A dead sea in a dead world, a world that consisted of nothing but sea and sky.

Since their destination lay on the far shore of that eerie world, though, they had no choice but to continue on their way, to plow their way north through those strange and lonely waters until they reached the mouth of the Hugli River. And when the *Alma* finally arrived at that mouth, it was only to be told—in a move that was typical of the relaxed pace at which break-bulk ships operated—that she would have to anchor out for the next day or two. That she would have to swing idly at anchor until her berth became available and she could proceed up the river.

And so after two days…

–Bosun: Hey Mr. Writer, you left somethin' out!

I what…?

–Bosun: You didn't say nothin' about that steel pipe.

Steel pipe? What steel pipe?

–Wayne, AB: What? You sayin' you don't remember that? Cause I remember it real good, man. That piece-a pipe he give us when we was on anchor watch, and he says for us to use it on anybody tries to steal our lines. Says for us to kill any-a them poor suckers we catch tryin' to come aboard. Says to kill em!

–Bosun: Man, is that nuts or what? That's fuckin' psycho, that's what it is.

–Wayne: Yeah, killin' people over some fuckin' lines. That shit's sick, man!

–Chief Mate: Oh, please! You can't possibly believe what they're saying, can you? That I told them to kill people? That's ridiculous! That's… And have you noticed who it is that's making this accusation? Have you? It's the Bosun and that damned radical AB. It's the two guys I fired off that ship! So if you don't hear it from someone who's a bit more reliable, I just…

–Or you know what? On second thought, I don't think I'll even dignify their accusations by responding to them. That's what I'll do. I think I'll just…

You think you'll let me get back to my story?

–Chief Mate: Yes, by all means. Please get back to your story.

–Bosun: Yeah, let the asshole off the hook, Mr. Big-Shot Fuckin' Writer.

Well yes I will then. I'll, uh… Let's see… The *Alma* eventually heaved up her anchor and proceeded up the river, and as she went, the crew found that the scenes along the lower reaches of the river were perhaps even stranger and more eerie than the Bay of Bengal itself had been. Because wherever they looked on that lower river, things seemed so deserted and so devoid of life, and this in a country with such a huge population as India's. But along the river, the signs of life were few and far between while signs of human activity consisted of little more than a few sailing dhows and some barges being rowed with long oars—there were no motorized vessels of any sort other than the *Alma*—and the only buildings to be seen along the banks were a number of miserable little shacks. And it all looked so weird to them, so otherworldly at times, that it was hard for the crew to believe that a huge mass of humanity awaited them just a short distance ahead.

But await them it did, that enormous jumble of a city, that asphalted monument to faded glory and neglect. And while their first sight of that huge urban abyss called up a variety of emotions among the different crewmembers, there was still one more obstacle they had to pass before they would be able to go out and explore it. They had to transit the lock that lay between the river and their dock. They had to maneuver the ship into the lock that would take them up to the level of the man-made lake where the docks were located, the lake where there would be no tides or currents for them to contend with, no vagaries of nature. The lake where the tired old ship would be able to sit comfortably until she was ready to sail.

Fortunately, the passage through the lock went smoothly, and once the *Alma* was inside the lake the crew ran out long lines and used them to warp her over to her berth, over to the place where she would sit and disgorged her several thousand tons of rice. And it wasn't long after she was safely tied up alongside that the longshoremen made their first appearance and began making preparations to work cargo. To look at them, though, they seemed a very unpromising lot. They looked too old and too frail for the type of heavy work that lay before them, and at the same time their only equipment consisted of a few primitive hand-carts on the dock. So in other words, they looked like it would surely take them months to discharge all those fifty-kilo bags of rice, months or at least weeks.

But the crew's opinion of them changed quickly once they set to work and began to move cargo, and that was because of the way they worked so smoothly together, the way they coordinated their every move, wasting no effort and heaving the bags about at a prodigious rate. Moving those heavy bags much faster than a group of younger and stronger but less experienced men could ever have done. They piled the bags onto slings to lift them out of the holds, and then they piled them again onto the hand-carts before hauling them into the warehouse. And they did it all so fast and piled the bags so high on those hand-carts that with each load, it looked like they must have set a new world record. They worked that way all day long, moving cart-load after heaping cart-load and eventually working their way through all those thousands of tons of rice in a mere six days, and this in spite of the primitive methods they used.

It was an impressive performance on their part, though unfortunately it was about the only thing that most of the crew found impressive about Calcutta. Because Calcutta was no Bangkok and that was for sure. It had little to offer in the way of nightlife, and as far as the houses of ill-repute were concerned, the crew found them to be far too depressing with their rows of dingy little rooms and their patios in the middle and the girls living locked up inside like they were prisoners. The crew found them to be unpleasant, especially after what they had just seen in Bangkok, and for that reason most of them never returned to those places for a second visit.

—Jamey: Hey what are you talkin' about, man? Those places were great! The girls were cute and it was a helluva lot cheaper than Bangkok, so I had a great time there, man.

Well, uh... As I was saying, the whorehouses of Calcutta were too depressing for most of the crew, though of course it was different for a few thick-skinned individuals, for a few who had absolutely no conscience and no sense of shame...

—Jamey: What, is that supposed to be me?

Yes, for those without a conscience it was a wonderful place, though as for the rest they generally preferred to go no further than the local Seamen's Club.

—George: Hey, what about us guys who went out to the cultural sites?

You?! What are you talking for? Didn't I tell you to be quiet?

—George: Yeah, sure you did, but that was before...

Before what?!

—George: Before you started letting all these other characters talk whenever they wanted to. And I don't see you threatening any of them with that eraser of yours.

Well... That's different because I need them for the story. I mean, I can't go erasing any of the major characters, can I?

—George: No, that's true... But not all the ones who are talking are major ones, are they? Cause like look at Jamey. He's a minor character just like me.

Yes that's true, but you see the thing is that I like Jamey so it doesn't bother me when he butts in.

—George: But it does when I... So you're saying that you don't like me?

Exactly! Now you've hit the nail on the head. So shut up! You hear me? Be quiet or I'll get out my eraser.

–George (mumbling): Jeez, isn't that like discrimination or something?

So as I was saying, the Seamen's Club quickly became the one and only attraction in Calcutta for most of the crew. And just as the city of Calcutta was a far different place from their previous port, so the local Seamen's Club was far different from the club in Bangkok. Because while that earlier club with its restaurant and its gift shop and its swimming pool had resembled the lobby of a reasonably good tourist hotel, this club had absolutely nothing modern about it. Instead, it stood in the midst of an enormous slum like the final relic of a glorious colonial past. It consisted of a building or two within a walled compound, and its heavily-worn and cheaply furnished bar looked out upon a dried-up little excuse for a garden that gave the whole place a sad air of faded gentility. And while it was a place that could be described as shabby by the ungenerous, still as more than one crewmember was to remark, it wasn't all that bad when you considered what there was on the other side of that wall.

It was an enclosed little world that resembled the world of the ship in many ways, a world populated almost exclusively by seamen. But at the same time, there were important differences between the club and the ship, one of those being the fact that there was no hierarchy at the club. Instead, it was a place where the ranks mixed on equal terms. And being that it was also a world where women were few and far between, it was exactly the type of place where a woman like Starr, the Saloon Mess from the *Alma*, would become a major attraction.

She was a good looking young woman with a pretty, nineteen-year-old face and a body that had yet to lose its youthful tone. She was a woman who was right at her physical peak when she was aboard the *Alma*, a woman whose looks had yet to fade due to the ravages of weight gain and premature aging. And since on most days she was the only woman present at the Seamen's Club, she always received a great deal of attention whenever she was there, attention which she quickly came to love. And this after she had been so nearly invisible in Bangkok thanks to all those pretty Thai girls and to the fact that she had spent her time ashore visiting tourist sites, not hanging out at bars with the rest of the crew.

She had kept a low profile in Bangkok just as she had done aboard ship up to that point, feeling too timid and too vulnerable on her very first ship to have much interaction with the rest of the otherwise all male crew. She had avoided public spaces aboard ship, spaces such as the crew lounge, and instead she had spent most of her free time alone in her room. And while the others in the crew had frequently spoken about her behind her back, few of them had gotten a chance to say anything to her face besides Hello and Good morning. Few of them outside the Steward's Department that is. And even with the officers whose meals it was her job to serve, she had done little more on a social level than joke around with a few of them, joke around in a very customer/waitress sort of way. She hadn't made any real friends among them as, thanks in part to the advice she had received from her boss, the Chief Steward, she had kept herself largely aloof from everyone, both licensed and unlicensed.

The Steward had warned her repeatedly not to get involved with anyone outside their department, doing his best to convince her and encourage her in this behavior, though what he had really meant with all his advice had been for her not to get involved with anyone other than himself. Because in fact, his true motive all along had been to save her for himself. And while he had managed to keep her away from the others thanks to her innocence and her fear of the all male environment in which she found herself immersed, still he had failed so far in his own efforts to seduce her.

—Steward: Hey man, what are you sayin'? You sayin' I was tryin' to get into her pants? Is that what you're sayin'? Man, that's a lie, that's what it is. Cause I didn't want her... And she comes around there throwin' her little white pussy at me, but I just told her no.

—Starr: In your dreams!

—Steward: I told her I'm a married man. I told her I don't fool around.

—Starr: Yeah, right! Like you didn't fool around with those Thai girls, huh? And you know you're just saying all this now as an excuse, cause you couldn't get any from me back then.

—Steward: Couldn't get any? Me?! You talkin' like I wanted it, girl. You talkin' like I couldn't get it if I wanted...

—Starr: Yeah, like you couldn't!

—Steward: Shit...

Well in any case, the fact is that she had kept very much to herself during the early part of the voyage, and while she had begun to emerge slightly from her shell in the days after Bangkok, it wasn't until the ship was in Calcutta and she found herself turning into the center of attention in the strange little world of the Seamen's Club that she finally began to emerge altogether. And when she emerged, she did so with a vengeance. She went to the club each evening and sat at the bar as the men gathered around, coming over to talk with her and do things for her. And as they did so, she quickly became conscious of the power she held over them, her power as a woman. She became aware of that power and of the fact that she could get anything she wanted out of those men. And she also came to realize that she could have any of them that she might choose. That she could pick out her sugar-daddy from among the crew, pick the man who would watch out for her and take care of her for the remainder of the voyage.

So during the first few days the ship was in Calcutta, she looked the guys over and tried to decide which of them she preferred, and it wasn't until the port stay was about half over that she finally made her choice. She made that choice, and she latched onto the man she wanted, a man who turned out to be the Bosun. And while he was the same man who had acted like such a maniac while the ship was in Bangkok, now that he was in a different port, and now that he was drinking in moderation while he was at the club, it turned out that the Bosun could be a surprisingly charming and gracious man when he was only slightly inebriated. So charming in fact that he must have seemed like quite a catch to Starr as the only real problem she saw with him at the time was the fact that he was so much older than her. But she soon brushed that issue aside as well and made her decision to bestow her feminine charms upon him, to invite him to come and share her bed. She made her decision that he would be her sugar-daddy.

–Starr: Oh please, could you stop that? Because it's... I mean, it wasn't like that at all. It wasn't that... You know... It wasn't so cheap and so... It just wasn't all calculated like that. Cause what I felt for John was real, you know. It was like a connection we had, like this deep connection between us. It was like we understood each other way down deep, you know, like on some deep level. And the sexual part, well that wasn't all that important, you know. Cause we made love a few times, but that wasn't what our relationship was really about. It was... You know... It was like we had this spiritual thing going on between us or something...

—And while I'm at it, maybe I should correct a couple of other things, too. Cause you know, you said my relationship with the officers was just some waitress thing, but that's not true. It was... You know... Like I joked around with Jamey all the time cause he was always so much fun and I liked him a lot. It was kinda like he was a brother, you know. And the rest of the officers were real nice, too, or at least most of them were. Cause like except that Second Mate could be a real a-hole, you know. And then there was something about that Chief Mate, too, something like... You know, like with the way he looked at me and the way he talked to me. There was something... You know, something about that look of his that would make me feel so... so... Like it made me feel so dirty or something.

—Chief Mate: Oh, please!

What, did you think that last remark was a bit...? Yes, I guess it was a bit gratuitous when you get right down to it, wasn't it? So do you think...?

—Chief Mate: Oh, just forget about it, okay? Forget I said anything and get back to your story, will you?

Right, the story. I'll, uh... So if everyone is finished, then I'll get back to it. I'll... Well, the longshoremen worked cargo all day long during the six days the *Alma* was in Calcutta, but then each night they would go home and the docks would be deserted. And the only thing to break the shadowy solitude of those nocturnal docks would be the pigs that came out to eat the cargo that had been spilled during the day, the pigs and the occasional seaman going to or returning from the Seamen's Club.

At the end of those six days, all the bagged rice had

been discharged and, with the holds having been swept and cleaned by local cleaning gangs, the *Alma* now sat completely empty, as empty as she had been when the voyage first began. And while it might seem that at this point the voyage was virtually over, the truth is that it was just about to enter into a whole new phase. It was about to enter into the backload phase, the phase during which cargo would be loaded to take back to the United States. The phase during which the hardy little ship would bounce all around Southeast Asia, paying visits to a whole series of backload ports. A series of ports whose names had been announced to the Captain and crew in at least a provisional way during their stay in Calcutta.

Before they could begin any sort of backload, though, first they had to get the old girl out of Calcutta. They had to warp her back across the little man-made lake to the lock that would carry her back down to the level of the river. In the process, they had to run out a very long line from the stern to the lock, a line that was actually two lines married together, and then once that line was in place, they let go the lines that held her to the dock and the stern began to heave away. Unlike what had happened upon arrival, though, this time it wasn't long before things began to go wrong for them, and they went wrong thanks to a screw-up by the Second Mate on the stern.

You be quiet now! Don't you dare say a word!!

No, I'll admit it. I was just kidding when I said that. It wasn't really his fault at all. I just said it because… Because I wanted to see him… Well, I just said it, that's all.

What really happened was that the winch on the stern broke down right when the ship was in the middle of the harbor, so the crew on the bow had to drop the anchor until someone could get the thing up and running again. And while it didn't take long for the electrician to reset the breaker and get it back on line, during that time the linehandlers at the lock had taken it upon themselves to pull off the eye of the line and throw it into the water evidently assuming that it was on a reel and that the crew would have to give them a different line. But there were no reels on the *Alma*—she was much too old for that type of technology, especially being an American-built ship—and the line had simply been wrapped around a gypsy-head for heaving. And what that meant was that once the winch was back in business, the after gang had to heave the whole line back aboard, the entire double length of it, before turning around and giving it to the line boat to take right back over to where it had been.

After that little mishap, the *Alma* made it down to the river with no further problems. And once she was there, she headed back down to the Bay of Bengal where she retraced her steps toward the Malacca Strait. She headed south through that strange, dead world one more time, and it wasn't until late in the second day that the first signs of life began to appear. The first birds, the first flying fish, and finally the first fishing boats, all signs that the ship and her crew were returning to a world with which they were familiar. To the lively and crowded world of Southeast Asia.

\*     \*     \*     \*     \*

When the *Alma* reached the ship-filled lanes of the straits, she made a left turn across traffic before joining in and following the eastbound lane. And she followed that lane until she was just across from Singapore where she made another left turn across traffic and pulled into the port that would be her first stop, a port where she would stop just long enough to get a load of bunkers, as seamen call their fuel. She pulled into one of Singapore's many anchorages, and there the Chief Mate and Bosun went out to the bow and dropped the anchor after which she sat for the next few hours with a bunker-barge tied up alongside. Then once the *Alma's* double-bottoms had been filled with fuel oil, the same crewmembers went forward and heaved the anchor back up, and with that the hard-working little ship was ready to continue on her way. She was ready to head back out into the busy traffic lanes and begin the first leg of the journey to her next port. The journey to her first "jungle port," a little place in the Malaysian part of Borneo by the name of Tawau.

To get there, her first step was to rejoin the eastbound traffic lane just below Singapore, but then it wasn't long before she began to leave most of the traffic behind. Because while most of the ships turned north once they left the straits, turning toward destinations in China and Japan and other parts of the Far East, the *Alma* held onto a more easterly course, a course that would take her through the less traveled waters along the northern coast of Borneo.

She ran parallel to that coast, following it all the way to the far northeastern corner of the island, and there she passed through Balabao Strait, the largest passage between Palawan and the northern-most tip of Borneo. She passed through the strait and entered the Sulu Sea—the pirate sea as it was called by the old-time China-coasters—but no sooner was she in the Sulu Sea than she turned southeast and headed for Sibutu Passage, the main passage between the Sulu Archipelago and Borneo and the passage that would take her into the Celebes Sea. And then once she had cleared all the obstacles around that passage, she cut around and headed west-southwest until she finally arrived at her destination, the town of Tawau in the far southeastern part of Sabah state, not far from Indonesia.

As it turned out, the trip was a quiet one for the crew

since there were few other big ships poking around those waters and most of the traffic they saw consisted of fishing boats scattered about here and there. But while the passage was calm and pleasant, it was hardly what you would call a scenic one since even at those times when the old ship wasn't out in open water, even when she was passing islands or points, she generally had to pass them as far offshore as she could thanks to the many rocks and reefs that litter the area. And so it was that the most scenic part of the passage didn't come until the very end. It came as the *Alma* pulled up close to the coast just off the pretty and prosperous little town of Tawau and dropped her anchor. And then once she was anchored in that picturesque spot, she was ready to begin loading the cargo of lumber that would be lightered to her at this port, the cargo that would be brought out to her on barges.

And in much the same way that the passage from Singapore to Tawau proved to be a quiet and peaceful one, so the situation on the bridge during the eight-to-twelve watch proved to be far more peaceful than anyone might have predicted. And in fact, there even seemed to be a thaw taking place in the relationship between the Chief Mate and the Bosun during the passage, a thaw in which, though the two of them still maintained their silence throughout the two hours they spent together on the bridge, that silence began to lose some of its edge of hostility. It began to evolve from a silence between two people who despised each other into a silence between two people who simply had nothing to say.

And perhaps it was due to a sort of over-optimism about this thaw, about its depth and its future, that the two of them made the fatal mistake of deciding to go ashore together one evening while the ship was in Tawau. They made the mistake of going out to have a drink together in an attempt to truly mend fences. To...

–Chief Mate: So what? You're going to go into all that stuff right now?

Right now? Why yes, I suppose...

–Chief Mate: I mean, don't you know that there's lots of other interesting stuff you could talk about first, before you start talking about that night?

Other stuff... What do you mean?

–Chief Mate: Well like for instance, you haven't said a word about the cargo operations. So why don't you tell the people about that?

Yes you're right, of course, though I was planning on going into that a little later on...

–Chief Mate: But why later? I mean, that was some really interesting stuff the way we had to lighter that cargo. And did you know that it was the very first time I ever saw it done. Me, the one who had to supervise it.

Well, I don't know...

–Chief Mate: And then there's all the stuff about planning the load and calculating the stability, stuff I had to do all by myself. That was the first time I ever had to do any of that, too. And it was... I mean, it was nothing like working on containerships where shoreside plans everything for you and all they do is hand you the papers before you sail. Because on that ship, I was the one who had to do it all, all that old-time seaman's stuff. And I had to do it with nothing but stability tables and a little pocket calculator, cause there was no such thing as a computer on that old ship. Now don't you think that stuff's more interesting than some old... some misunderstanding?

Well, I suppose you might be right. I suppose I could talk about those things first if you really want me to. So let's see now...

When those old break-bulk ships like the *Alma Lykes*

entered into the backload phase of their voyages, it became the Chief Mate's job to plan the cargo stowage with no help from shoreside. It became his job to determine where each block of cargo should go, taking into account both the stability of the vessel and the accessibility of the cargo when it reached its destination. Because just like he didn't want to make the ship too "tender" by stowing it with the weight too high, or to make the ship "stiff" by stowing it too low, at the same time he didn't want to "over-stow" any cargo. He didn't want to stow it where a cargo that was supposed to come out at a later port was stowed on top of or in front of a cargo that had to come out at an earlier port. And so it wasn't until after he had taken all those things into consideration that he could finally tell the longshoremen exactly where to stow the cargo.

And while on this particular voyage the problem of over-stow didn't apply since all the cargo the *Alma* was taking on would eventually be coming off at the same port in the United States, the problem of stability was going to be a major concern. Or at least it was a major concern with this first block of cargo to be loaded, a cargo of lumber that would normally be stowed on deck in order to save space in the holds for the thousands of tons of rubber that were still to come in later ports. But the problem was that with Tawau being the first backload port, and with no other cargo aboard to balance out its weight, the Chief Mate couldn't possibly load all those eight or nine hundred tons of lumber out on deck. If he did so, the ship would roll over right where she sat.

So the problem for the Chief Mate became one of distributing the weight. One of loading most of the lumber in the tween decks—he still wanted to save the lower holds for rubber—and then putting just as much of it on deck as he could get away with. And the only thing he really had going for him in doing this was the fact that the ship had just taken on a full load of bunkers in Singapore, the fact that her double-bottom tanks were now full of fuel oil which added its weight to the ship's stability.

As it turned out, though, stability wasn't the only problem the Chief Mate had to contend with in Tawau, because he also had to contend with the poor quality of the longshoremen the company sent out to load the lumber. What happened was that with the shipper of this consignment being one that only occasionally had cargoes to ship, the company had no full-time longshoremen working for it. So instead, it had to go out and hire casual laborers to do the job, with the laborers in this case being mostly illegal immigrants from the Philippine island of Mindanao. They were men who would work for wages that were well below local standards, but at the same time they were also men with little or no experience as longshoremen. And to make matters even worse, when the directors of the company hired these men, they forgot to hire a supervisor or anyone else to run the gang. Instead, they sent out a leaderless, often clueless band of individuals who would have to learn on-the-job. And this while they were working for a Chief Mate who was also learning on-the-job.

Now given the fact that these under-qualified individuals were sent down to perform a task that was actually much more complicated than it might appear at first, it was hardly surprising that it ended up taking them four full days to load all the lumber from the three barges that came alongside the ship one after the other. And what complicated the job more than anything else was the fact that, once the bundles of lumber had been set down in the squares of the tween decks, they still had to be moved out into the wings as far as they could go. And since the company failed to provide their workers with forklifts or any other easy way of performing this task, they ended up having to resort to the laborious and often complex process of rigging up fairleads and using the winches on the cargo gear to snake those bundles out into the wings. And remember here that it's much more difficult to snake cargo away from the center of a hatch than it is to snake it toward it. And to have to do this with an inexperienced gang of longshoremen like the one that was provided for the *Alma Lykes?*

Well, the whole thing might have taken even longer if only the Chief Mate hadn't had the good sense to appoint a leader from among the disorganized mass of longshoremen he was given to work with, to pick out the one who seemed to have the most experience as a longshoreman. And though the man he chose turned out to be a mute, at least there were no problems with his hearing—or his understanding of English—so they soon developed a routine in which the Chief Mate would take the man aside and explain to him exactly what he wanted done at any particular time, after which the man would answer him with a series of signs and then go out and demonstrate the orders to his fellow longshoremen, walking around and pointing and making other types of signs. And in the end, it was thanks to him—and thanks to the Chief Mate's foresight in having chosen him—that the cargo was ever properly loaded and secured at all.

The loading process took four days, as I said before, days during which the crew's access to the pleasures of the town came thanks to the services of a local launch company. And though Tawau was a rather small place, still it was one that had many pleasures to offer, one whose nightlife resembled Bangkok's more than it did Calcutta's. So in other words, it was a town where the heavy partiers once again came to the fore, a town where someone like the Second Engineer found himself right back in his element.

—Jamey: Yeah man, that's me. Cause that town was like... It was a seriously happening place for such a small town. It was... I mean, like there was this one place I found called the "Call Line Club" that was like this rock-and-roll club. But all they had for music in there was these local guys playin' old Led Zeppelin and Rolling Stones and shit like that, and like they really sucked but it didn't matter cause they were gettin' into it so much. And people'd get up and take turns singin' and the girls'd dance. And when I say gettin' into it, I mean really gettin' into it, cause like the way those girls'd boogie so hard and get so down with the music that you'd... I mean, I never saw anything like it even in black clubs in the States and places like that.

So you're saying that you had a good time at that club?

—Jamey: Man, I had a good time everywhere in that town, cause like they had everything there. They had these hotel-type bars with girls in em and discos and short-time hotels with Filipino girls. So like... Man, what more could ya ask for, huh?

Yes, precisely. What more?... But while there was much for the crew to enjoy in Tawau, not all the crew enjoyed themselves and not every night on the town ended on a happy note. And that was especially the case during the first night in port when the Chief Mate and the Bosun decided to go ashore and have a drink together and do what they could to make peace with each other. Because rather than peace, it ended in quite the opposite. It ended...

I believe it was originally the Bosun's idea, wasn't it? I believe he was the one who invited the Chief Mate, though you can correct me if I'm wrong on that... Boats?

—Bosun: What? You want me to tell your fuckin' story for ya? Is that what you want?

No, not at all. I was just asking you... I just wanted to make sure...

—Bosun: Yeah, it was my stupid fuckin' idea. I'm the one who asked him.

So it was, uh... It turned out to be a bad plan, whatever the motivation behind it may have been. It turned out...

—Bosun: You wanta know what the motivation was? Well, I'll tell you what it was. It was cause this guy was so fuckin' uptight or somethin', like he was... Like if he could just loosen up a little bit and act like a man for a change, like a real person. And if he just had a few drinks in him and he started to... You know.

Well in the end, the Bosun's plan didn't work, and in fact, it backfired completely. It ended up turning a bad relationship into...

—Bosun: Ya know, if that guy was anything like them old Chief Mates, it wouldn'ta happened. Cause like with them old-timers, they were real seamen. They were men, and you could talk to em like men. They weren't like that fuckin'... That...

—I mean, with them old-timers if you got mad at em, you'd yell and scream at each other, and maybe you'd even throw a couple-a punches or somethin', but then you'd just forget about it and go back to work like nothin' happened. You didn't hold no grudges or any-a that shit, and you didn't go tryin' to fuck the guy behind his back like that asshole...

—And if you went ashore with one-a them old-timers, you'd leave all the bullshit behind. You'd just... I mean, he was just one-a the guys out there in town, ya know. And when you're drinkin', he matches you drink for drink, and you don't know who's gonna end up gettin' carried back to the ship. But with this guy... It's like you couldn't deal with him man-to-man that way cause he wasn't no man. He was… It was like you couldn't treat him like he was a man cause he was some sneaky fuckin' little… I don't know what. And on top-a he was an asshole!

Well, okay then. Thank you Bosun. Thank you for that, uh… that insight. But now back to the story.

The Chief Mate and the Bosun went ashore together on the first night the ship was in Tawau, riding over on the launch along with Starr and a few other crewmembers. And when they landed, they headed straight for what looked like the biggest and best hotel in town to have the drink they were supposed to have together. And though the Bosun was on his best behavior as the evening began, even making a few attempts at humor while they were on the launch, his jokes fell flat one after the other. They didn't amuse the Mate at all, and in fact they made him feel even more uncomfortable with the situation each time he was forced to grin or chuckle in reply. They made him feel awkward, and they made him feel like he was truly out of place.

And the Chief Mate's discomfort level did nothing but increase when several of the crewmembers from the launch decided to accompany them to the hotel, so that it was a whole group of them that finally sat down at the bar and ordered drinks. The Mate hadn't counted on this since the deal had been to have a drink with the Bosun, not with the entire crew. And while he had both dreaded and expected Starr's companionship at the bar from the moment he had first seen her get onto the launch, the presence of the others came as an unpleasant and unwelcome surprise.

The group of them sat in a line at the bar and toasted each other with their first drink, the Chief Mate pointedly tipping his glass only toward the Bosun before beginning to sip his vodka-tonic. And as for the Bosun, he immediately resumed his efforts to bring his companion out. He laughed and told stories with an air of forced amiability, and at the same time he quickly threw down his glass of scotch and ordered a second round for the group. The Mate tried to calmly desist, telling the Bosun that he had only come for one drink and didn't want to have a second, but his protest fell upon deaf ears as the Bosun continued to talk and as he drained his second drink just as quickly as he had the first before ordering still another round for the group.

The Chief Mate was feeling more and more ill-at-ease all the time, and he sat there stiffly with a weak smile on his face as the Bosun continued to rev-up his act. He sat and sipped slowly at his first drink and nursed it along as one vodka-tonic after another piled up on the bar in front of him. And meanwhile the Bosun threw down his drinks at a prodigious rate—throwing down doubles after the first couple of rounds—and with each drink he took, he became more aggressively friendly toward his companion, all the while ignoring the Mate's repeated insistence that he didn't want a second drink.

The situation deteriorated even further when the Mate, having finally finished his first drink, got up to leave only to find his path blocked by the Bosun who said, "Where you goin', Mate?" and, "You can't go yet. You got drinks on the bar." And since he said it in a tone that was hard to decipher, a tone that seemed to contain both a drunken attempt at humor and a threat of force, a threat to use any means necessary in order to prevent his companion from leaving, the Chief Mate soon backed down and agreed to have one more drink with him—one more and only one more.

So the Mate sat back down on his stool, and he began to sip on one of the five or six vodka-tonics that now sat before him. And as he did so, he resolved to wait the Bosun out, to sit and nurse that second drink along until the guy finally grew tired of the game he was playing. And so he sat and took an occasional sip, though sit as long as he might, he could see that his strategy was bringing him no nearer to making his escape than he had been before. Because with the more alcohol the Bosun drank, the more aggressive he became. He talked loudly in an overbearingly friendly way, and he even slapped the Mate on the back a couple of times, slapped him so hard that no one could ever have mistaken his gesture for a sign of friendship.

And as the Chief Mate sat and sipped his drink and watched his passive strategy come to nothing, the crewmembers seated at the bar with him watched his growing consternation with thinly disguised mirth.

–Wayne: What are you sayin'? You sayin' we was laughin' at him? Cause man, that's what we was doin'. Laughin' and watchin' the show that Bosun was puttin' on. And that Mate just takin' it, just squirmin' away like a little faggot. Man, what a trip! It was… It was crazy, man!

Well, as time went on and the Chief Mate saw that his attempt at passive resistance had failed, he finally decided to adopt a more active posture. He decided that he had to stand up and assert his authority—to remind this guy that he was the officer here—and then calmly walk out with his head held high. And so he stood up one more time, ready to stand his ground this time around. But no sooner had he done so than he was met by the Bosun once again, standing in his way in an overtly aggressive posture with his legs apart and his fists clenched and with a look on his face that showed that he meant business. And as the Bosun stood and blocked the Chief Mate's escape, he spoke in a cold, hard voice with no edge of humor to it at all, "Hey Mate, you can't go nowhere. The party's just gettin' started."

The Mate's response was to fix the man with the most authoritative and assertive stare of which he was capable, to stand as tall as he could and look down upon the man before him. But though he was a couple of inches taller than the Bosun, it proved to be the shorter man's stare that was by far the more intimidating. Because it was his stare that contained the real authority, not some theoretical authority based on positions held aboard ship but rather the true-life authority of a man who was ready to use his fists in order to have his way. And so in spite of the fact that he knew better, in spite of the fact that he knew what he would be getting himself into by doing so, it was the Chief Mate who was finally forced to back down and retake his seat. It was the Chief Mate who was forced to surrender, and this while knowing full well that in doing so, he was putting himself completely at the mercy of the Bosun. That he was subjecting himself to any and all of the Bosun's drunken whims.

But what else could he do? He couldn't get into a bar fight with a member of the crew, could he? Because where was the dignity in that? And if this guy wasn't going to let him leave without a fight, then what other choice did he have? Could he look for a chance to sneak out? Or could he look for an ally, someone to help him deal with this drunken slob?

He looked at the crewmembers seated along the bar, the crewmembers whose number kept growing as more and more of them wandered in to watch the fun. And as he looked at them with their smiles and their suppressed laughter at his expense, he saw that he could expect no help from any of them. No help from any with the possible exception of Starr. Because hadn't she already made a few small gestures aimed at calming the Bosun down and getting him back under control? So maybe she would be willing to do something. Maybe she would respond if he appealed to her for help.

He soon caught her eye and gave her an imploring look, silently but eloquently begging her to come to his aid. And the moment she saw that look, she knew exactly what she had to do. She knew that she had to step in and put an end to this thing before it got completely out of control. She knew that she had to do something to defuse the situation. And so she slid over closer to the Bosun as he sat on the barstool beside her. She slid over to him and put her arm around him, and then she whispered into his ear that the two of them should get out of there, that they should go someplace quiet, someplace romantic. She whispered that she wanted them to be alone.

But when she spoke, her words had no effect at all. They didn't penetrate the drunken haze of the Bosun's mind, and they didn't register with him as anything more than a later-tonight proposition. Because the truth is that by this time, he was already past the point of no return. He was already so far along in his state of alcohol-induced euphoria that there was no turning back. He was already too drunk—and not just on alcohol, either. He was drunk on his sense of power and on the approving laughter of his audience and on the weakness and passivity of his prey. He was drunk, and he was on his way to wherever the night might take him.

And where it took him next was to the next logical step in the progression he had just been making. It took him to the step that came after having controlled his victim and after having dominated him. It took him to the step in which he would begin to humiliate his victim. And it wasn't from any meanness of spirit that the Bosun now acted in the way he did, either. It wasn't from a hatred of his victim and it certainly wasn't from design. But rather his actions were almost involuntary as he seemed to escalate the situation out of sheer inertia, out of the need to play to the members of his audience and give them what they wanted. And if humiliation was what they wanted next, then humiliation was what they got.

They got the Bosun calling out to a prostitute who had been sitting alone at a table in the bar and signaling for her to come over. And they got him handing her several bills from his wallet and telling her to go over and make the Chief Mate happy. And they got the prostitute walking over to her new boyfriend…

—Starr: Say, while you're still talking about why he did it…

Why he did it? I'm not talking about that. I've already finished with that subject.

—Starr: No you didn't. You were just talking about it right now. And I… You know… I thought about something you should say about why he really did it, you know.

Why he really did it?

—Starr: Cause in a way, it was really about me, you know. Cause he was with me and he couldn't go with that bar girl himself, you know, so he… He got her for the Chief Mate instead cause he couldn't get her for himself, you know… Cause of me.

So you're saying that he wanted her for himself but he had to get her for the Mate instead? Is that what you're saying?

—Starr: That's right, and it was… You know, it was like some type of transference or whatever they call it.

Transference? Is that supposed to be some sort of psychological term?

—Starr: Yeah, I think so… Or isn't it? I don't know…

Well, I'm not sure about that because I've never…

—Bosun: Hey, do we gotta sit here and listen to all this bullshit? All this stupid shit about you two tryin' to analyze me?

–Starr: I'm not trying to analyze you. I'm just... You know, I'm trying to tell people why you acted the way you did and why you were such a mean drunk that night and... You know... Why you really did that stuff with the bar-girl. That's all.

–Bosun: Why I really did it? Well shit, that ain't no secret. And it's got nothin' to do with no transfer and no inertia and none-a that other horseshit you two been talkin' about.

No? So you're saying that it was...

–Bosun: It was cause-a that uptight fuckin' Mate. Cause man, if I just coulda got that asshole to loosen up a little bit. And I figured that if booze didn't do it, then maybe what he needed was to get laid.

So you're saying that it was simply to make him open up?

–Bosun: It was to make him into a man. It was to make him start actin' like a man instead-a some fuckin'...

–Starr: That and the transference, of course, cause you were feeling frustrated, you know, and you wanted to...

–Bosun: Oh shit! Can't you just drop it?!

Yes, I think the Bosun has a point there. I think we've spent more than enough time on this question and it's time to get back to the story.

–Chief Mate: Please! Let's just get this thing over with, can't we? And if you don't mind, try to make it short.

Right, I'll do that. I'll try not to drag it out. I'll... I mean, I know that this part of the story is a bit painful for certain people.

Well, what happened was that the Bosun called the prostitute over and gave her money and turned her loose on the Chief Mate. And of course, she obediently did what she was told to do—or rather what she was being paid to do. She went over to the Mate and gave him a big hug, and she even tried to kiss him and climb up onto his lap. But the Mate pushed her away and then, after telling her flatly to go away and leave him alone, he turned around on his barstool to face as far away from her as he possibly could.

The prostitute looked back at the Bosun, asking with her eyes what she should do next, and he answered by waving her on, telling for her to go ahead and try again, telling her to keep pressing her attentions upon her shy new boyfriend. And then as she moved around to the other side of the barstool, the side toward which the Mate now faced, and made one more assault upon his lap, the Bosun spoke up in a loud voice, "Hey Mate, she's for you. She's my little present." But without answering him, the Chief Mate rejected her attentions for a second time, shoving her off a bit roughly before turning back toward the other side of his stool.

The Bosun didn't like this turn of events, and his response was to get up and move closer, ready to use force if necessary in order to get the two lovers together. He walked over and nudged the girl up against her boyfriend, and as he did so, he showered the Mate with a steady stream of insults, insults which quickly escalated from, "Hey, you know what to do with one-a them, don't you?" to, "Look, if you rather have a boy, I can go look for one," to, "Now you don't wanta be no cherry boy all your life, do ya?" and finally to, "Come on, you fuckin' cherry boy!" But the breaking point didn't come until the Bosun grabbed the Chief Mate by the arm and, holding it in his powerful grip, he used it to turn the guy and shove him up against the girl. Because it was only at this point that the Mate finally realized that he had no other way out and no alternative but to match physical force with physical force. He realized that he would have to stand up and force his arm out of the

Bosun's grasp since it was only through force that he would ever be able to leave that bar that night.

So the Chief Mate stood and twisted his arm in an effort to break free only to feel the other's grip tighten still further. And as he paused and prepared himself mentally to make another attempt, he fixed the Bosun with the hardest stare he could possibly muster. He fixed him with the stare of an officer in charge. Before he could make his second attempt, though, Starr saw that this was the moment to come to his rescue. It was the moment for her to step in and do what she could to break the tension, the moment to stop this thing before it went any further. And what she did was she went over and grabbed the Bosun by his other arm and asked him to dance. And while the Bosun didn't answer her or even so much as look at her, at least the distraction was enough to make him loosen his grip on the Mate's arm. He loosened his grip and let his victim go. He let him wrench his arm free and make good his escape, let him rush out the door and into the freedom of the street. And then no sooner had his victim gotten away than the Bosun returned to his seat and ordered up yet another round of drinks for all. And as he sat and drank and talked with his remaining shipmates, he complained to them about that goddamned faggot of a Chief Mate, that goddamned cherry boy.

And as for the Mate, he walked the quiet streets for a short time before finding another hotel bar, one where he could sit undisturbed and wait until it was time for the next launch back to the ship. And as he sat alone in that bar and drank one more vodka-tonic to steady his nerves, he ran the events of the evening over and over in his head, reviewing his mistakes in dealing with the situation and trying to assess the damage done. Trying to assess the damage that had been done to his position in dealing with the crew and the damage to his dignity as an officer and a Chief Mate.

—Chief Mate: Excuse me, but do you mind if I say something here?

You? Why not? I mean, it must be your turn to interrupt my story, mustn't it? So yes certainly. Go right ahead.

—Chief Mate: I just wanted to say that I think you've painted an awfully bleak picture of that incident in Tawau, or at least a bleak one as far as my own interests are concerned. But I don't think things really turned out nearly as badly as you've just portrayed them.

—Of course, I'll admit that the whole thing was a huge mistake in judgment on my part and that I never should have accepted the Bosun's invitation in the first place. But it was just that... Well, I just thought that I should show him some appreciation for his professional abilities, I suppose. And to, uh... But then the whole thing just got so completely out of hand when he got so drunk and so...

—I mean, it was a very difficult situation for me to deal with, and it wasn't easy for me to maintain my dignity with him acting so... so... with him acting the way he was. But I think I did the best I could given the circumstances, and I don't think that I ever disgraced myself as an officer and a gentleman, if I can use those terms. I don't think I ever stooped to anything that was below my position as second-in-command of the ship. And in the end, of course, I showed him who the real boss was with the way I walked out on him. So yes, I think I can say that I handled myself pretty well in a bad situation. I think I can say that I maintained my dignity.

—Wayne: Dignity? Man, what the fuck is that guy talkin' about? You see any dignity over there?

—Mike, Oiler: No man, I don't see shit. Cause he's a

fuckin' joke.

–Wayne: He's Cherry Boy, that's who he is after that night.

–Mike: Yeah, that's what we was always callin' him. Cherry Boy!

–Wayne: Like that was his name for the rest-a the trip.

–Carter: At least that's what you guys called him behind his back. But I never once saw any of ya say it to his face. Not one of ya but the Bosun.

–Wayne: Well maybe not... But he was still Cherry Boy.

–Chief Mate: Mr. Author, please!! Can't you cut this off? It's all degenerating so badly...

Yes, you're right about that. It's time to stop the name-calling and get back to the story. So now if you'll all be quiet, I'll get back to, uh... So let's see now, where was I?...

Oh yes. There were no more incidents after that first night in Tawau. Or at least there were no major incidents, nothing but the sort of minor occurrences that you always expect when you have a shipload of seamen going out on the town. And at the same time, the cargo operations aboard ship moved along slowly but steadily with bundles of lumber being loaded and snaked into position and then secured for sea. And finally at the end of four days, all the cargo was finished and the *Alma* was ready to sail off into the sunset. She was ready to sail off to her next port, to...

–George: Hey, you forgot something.

What is this? Another interruption?

–George: I was just saying...

You!! Haven't I told you to be quiet? Haven't I already threatened you?

–George: Yes, but it's just that you left something out.

Left something out? What was that?

–George: You left out that night when your little

buddy Jamey almost killed himself. That's what you left out.

That night...? Oh yes. That's true, I did forget about that. So maybe I should digress very slightly and... But it's me who's going to tell this story, have you got that?! And all you're going to do is listen!

—George: Yeah, yeah, whatever...

Well, the night in question was the third night in port, and the whole thing began with Jamey riding back to the ship aboard the midnight launch. He had already had a great deal to drink that night, and he was coming back to the ship to sleep it off before having to turn to in the morning. But as he came staggering up to the top of the gangway, he found that his friend Chris, the Third Engineer who had just gotten off watch, was waiting to take the launch into town for a bit of late night debauchery.

Now Jamey was in no condition to head back to town at that moment, but no sooner had he seen his friend heading that way than he made the bad decision to turn around and accompany him. And so he turned and staggered back down the gangway that he'd just come up, swaying heavily as he went and leaning so hard on the railing that he nearly went right over it more than once. And when it came time for him to make the short leap from the platform at the bottom of the gangway over to the launch, that was no picnic either, though in the end, he managed to make it in one piece.

His real problem didn't come until the launch arrived at the dock in town, that moment when Jamey would have to climb from the launch up to the dock. Because you see, the launch was low and the dock was higher than you might have expected in such a small town, and the only way to get from one to the other was by climbing a rusty little steel ladder that clung to the side of the dock. It was a climb that was more difficult than it might appear at first glance, and while the Third made it up with no problem at all, poor Jamey wasn't up to the challenge. He was wobbly from the moment he first started up with his feet constantly missing in their attempts to find the rungs and his arms tiring quickly from the effort. He was obviously struggling, but there was nothing anyone could do to help him besides watch and hope for the best. Hope that he could somehow make it up. But make it he didn't as, all at once, his hands and feet slipped and he fell straight down into the water, just missing the ladder and also missing the boat as he plunged in feet first.

His heavy boots carried him deep under water, and as the two young Malays in the boat crew grabbed a boathook and a light and went over to help him, they found that he had sunk so deep that they couldn't locate him even with the help of the light. So they stood and watched and waited for him to reappear, and as the seconds ticked by, they began to chatter to each other in an increasingly excited way, evidently thinking about diving in to look for him. But then finally, just as those watching were about to give up hope, Jamey's head broke the surface and he began to gasp and sputter for air.

It only took seconds from Jamey's reappearance until the Malays had him safely aboard the boat, and once he was there, they told the Third to go on and head for town while they would take Jamey back to the ship. Back to the place he never should have left. And so it was that a special launch arrived at the ship a short time later, a launch carrying only one passenger, a very wet but hopefully somewhat wiser Second Engineer.

–Jamey: Wiser? What's that supposed to mean? Cause like, it was nothin' but an accident, that's all it was. It's just... You know: shit happens.

Yes, shit happens, I suppose. And some people never,

uh... They never learn... But enough about that. It's time to get back to the story.

*   *   *   *   *

After four days in Tawau, the *Alma Lykes* was finally ready to move on to her next port and her next adventure, and so after heaving up her anchor, she sailed out into the calm southern sea. But while the skies were blue and the sea was at peace as she went, there was no peace to be found aboard ship. Or at least there was no peace on the eight-to-twelve watch and no tranquility as the Chief Mate and the Bosun found themselves forced back into their evening routine of involuntary togetherness, and this for the first time since the uneasy truce between them had been so completely broken in that bar in Tawau. There was no peace between them and no semblance of peace as each day they teetered closer to open warfare. Because by now, they hated each other openly and neither of them made any bones about it.

But you know, that's something I'll go into later as for now I think I'd rather concentrate on the next legs of the voyage. So let's see. The *Alma* heaved up her anchor and then headed toward the south, beginning the first leg of a passage that would complete her near circumnavigation of the island of Borneo. She made her way south through the long and occasionally narrow Makassar Strait, the strait that separates Borneo from Sulawesi, and then once she had passed the southeastern corner of Borneo, she turned to the west and ran along the Java Sea. And when she reached a certain point that had been marked out on her charts, she turned to the northwest and headed toward the Bangka Strait. And while her passage in that direction might appear on the surface to have been through wide-open waters, she was actually threading her way through numerous submerged reefs and other dangers.

And once she was clear of those dangers, she...

–George: Is that all you're gonna say about that passage?

What the...? You again! Haven't I told you...

–George: Yes, it's me again! And I have something to say.

You have nothing to say if I tell you to be quiet, because remember about that eraser of mine?

–George: Yeah, yeah, you and your eraser. Well, you know what? I just don't care anymore. Because I have something to say about one of those course changes, and I'm gonna say it! And I don't care what you do with your eraser after I'm done.

You what...? You... You're serious, aren't you?

–George: Damn right I'm serious! Because I'm tired of your intimidation, and I'm gonna say what I have to say. Come hell or high water.

Well, if you're going to be that way about it, then I suppose, uh...

–George: Well thank you, your majesty.

But be brief about it, do you hear me?!

–George: Yeah sure, I'll be brief... Now what I want to talk about is the way we had to make that course change over in the western Java Sea, because I think it's such a perfect illustration of why mariners should always keep up their skills in the older arts of navigation even when they have electronic equipment aboard. It's an illustration of how those skills can save you when the electronics fail. And it was for that reason that I continued to take star positions day after day in spite of the fact that we had a satellite navigator aboard that ship. Because I just knew that someday, that old sextant of mine would save the day. I knew it...

Didn't I tell you to be brief?!!

—George: Yes, brief. Right... So I'll, uh... I'll start again. Lykes Lines was always known among seamen for carrying no more than the bare minimum of electronic equipment that was required by law. Like according to the old-timers, Lykes didn't even install radars on their ships until the law said they had to. And I know from my own personal experience that they didn't install a second, backup radar until that was required as well. And when they finally did get those radars, in both cases they went out and bought the cheapest old secondhand sets they could find.

—Well, the same thing happened when they were first required to install an electronic navigation system aboard ship. They went out and bought the cheapest old transit sat-nav they could find, and by sat-nav I'm talking about the first type of satellite navigation that came into use since this was still a year or two before GPS burst onto the scene. They bought an old sat-nav with nothing to back it up, no LORAN or anything else that they weren't required to have. They bought an old secondhand sat-nav that worked most of the time, and...

Is that what you call brief?

—George: Well, I... I was just getting to the point.

Well get to it!!

—George: Okay, okay... What I was leading up to was the fact that, since they had no air-conditioning on that old bridge, the humidity of the tropics tended to get to the sat-nav and make it trip out pretty frequently. And as luck would have it, the machine tripped out on us just a few hours before we were supposed to make our turn in the western Java Sea. This in a place where there was nothing above the surface of the sea to indicate where the many submerged dangers of those waters might be.

—So being that I was on watch at the time when we would have to make the turn, and seeing that we would be making it some fifteen or twenty minutes after evening star-time, I went out with my sextant and took some sights. Four stars just like I always did, with three to cross and allowing one to fall out, though on this occasion it turned out that I didn't need that extra help since all four lines crossed in a perfect pinwheel. Not that I'm bragging or anything. But I shot those stars and worked them out and plotted them, and I had it all done just in time for the course change. And so for that reason, we were able to make the turn from a position that was far more accurate than anything we'd ever have gotten from that old sat-nav. Not that I'm bragging.

—And you know in my whole career, that was probably my proudest moment as a navigator. It was...

Okay, thank you for that! But you're done now, aren't you?!

—George: Who me? I... Yeah, I guess I am.

So if I can please get back to my story?

—George: Yes, of course you can. Feel free... And feel free to put away that eraser of yours, too.

Don't push your luck!

So let's see now. The *Alma* was approaching the Bangka Strait, wasn't she? That is the strait between Sumatra and Bangka Island, a large island along the eastern part of Sumatra's north coast. And as she entered the strait, the trip finally became a scenic one for the crew once again. Though it wasn't nearly as scenic as it would become a short time later when, rather than steaming all the way through the strait, the ship turned and entered the Musi River on her way to the port of Palembang.

The *Alma* entered the river and as she did so, she once again entered a whole new world from that of the sea. She entered an Asian river world which turned out to have much more in common with the lively exoticism of the river leading to Bangkok than it did with the lifeless sterility of the river to Calcutta. There were tugs and very small cargo vessels plying the river wherever the crew looked, while near the mouth it was filled with motorized fishing boats. And then to add an air of exoticism to the scene, there were also a number of canoes mixed in among those fishing boats, canoes that looked like they must have come straight out of the Stone Age.

The banks of the river were low and swampy with the vegetation growing right down to the water and camouflaging those banks. But then as the *Alma* made her way upriver, rice-paddies began to appear along with a number of sawmills and rubber-processing plants. And the further upriver she went, the more the stretches of jungle along the banks gave way to large expanses of rice-paddies. At the same time, the banks were increasingly dotted with thatched huts and even entire towns built on stilts above the river, towns whose younger inhabitants would wave at the ship from their canoes, welcoming the crew and signaling for them to throw presents. Cigarettes or the like. And it wasn't until after several hours had passed that the *Alma* finally arrived at a substantial city, a city near whose banks she dropped her hook and prepared to take on a load of rubber.

This was the port of Palembang where the versatile little ship would once again have to lighter. She would have to load her cargo from barges. But in this case, unlike in Tawau, the longshoremen who came aboard to do the loading were real, professional longshoremen which meant that the work went much more smoothly than it had in the previous port. And in fact, it only took them a day and a half to load the thousand-plus tons of rubber that the *Alma* had come there to pick up.

The blocks of raw rubber they loaded were squeeze-wrapped onto pallets which the longshoremen piled into the lower holds or shoved out into the wings of the tween decks. And since rubber was the only cargo that the ship would be loading in the ports she visited in Sumatra, rubber that would eventually all be discharged at the same port in the United States, this marked the beginning of the process of filling all the below-deck space that could possibly be filled. Filling that space from the bottom up and from the wings in toward the centers in a process that would continue at later ports until it finally reached the point where it became impossible to fit one more pallet anywhere in those holds. Because as I mentioned before, this was happening at the very height of the AIDS scare and the resultant boom of the condom industry. And it was for that reason that the *Alma*, just like the other ships in the trade, was getting all the cargo she could handle, all of it and then some as she actually had to turn away cargoes for lack of space.

So the old girl was in-and-out of Palembang, or at least she was in-and-out by break-bulk standards as a day and a half would be considered a long stay for a containership. And it was because of that short stay, along with the fact that it was a very long launch ride to town, that most of the crew decided to stay aboard in this port. Only a few of the hardiest ventured ashore while the ship was there as the rest bided their time and waited for the next port, a port which would be Panjang, also located on the island of Sumatra.

Soon the *Alma* was heaving up her anchor and heading back down the Musi River, descending it until she arrived back at the Bangka Strait, and there she turned to the right, the direction from which she had come two days earlier. She turned and weaved her way back out to the southern end of the strait, but then once she had reached the Java Sea and once she had cleared all the submerged reefs and other hidden dangers that fill those waters, she turned south this time rather than returning to the east. She turned and followed the coast of Sumatra as closely as she could until, after once again dodging the oil-field that sat just north of Sunda Strait, she entered the strait and started back out in the opposite direction from which she had originally come more than a month earlier. She started to the south but then no sooner was she around the tip of Sumatra than she cut to the west and finally the northwest, entering the small bay and harbor of Panjang which sat very near the island's tip. She pulled into Panjang, and there she tied up to a dock for the first time since she left Calcutta.

It took the longshoremen two full days to load the cargo in Panjang since the ship was picking up even more rubber here than she had in the previous port. And since it was the first time in a long time that the crew had been able to walk ashore rather than having to take a launch, most of them took advantage of the opportunity to go out and stretch their legs during those two days. They walked ashore and searched out the usual sorts of seamen's bars before returning to the ship later, intoxicated and broke. A typical seaman's day ashore. And though some of them claimed to have had a good time while they were there, they all agreed that it was no Bangkok or even a Tawau for that matter.

At the end of two days, the *Alma* was on her way once again, picking her way through the many obstacles that lay between Panjang and her next port. She headed back out in the direction from which she had just come, steaming through the Sunda Strait one more time and dodging the oil-field just above that strait yet again. And from there she retraced her steps to the north, following the coast of

Sumatra and until she entered the Bangka Strait for a third time. But unlike before, this time she didn't stop at the mouth of the Musi River or anywhere else along the way and instead she continued on until she left the strait at its northern end. From there, she dodged a number of small islands off the coast of Sumatra and passed through a couple of small straits—the Berhala and Durian Straits— before finally entering the western part of Singapore strait from the south. And there she joined that maritime superhighway one more time, crossing the eastbound lane and making a left turn into the westbound lane which she followed into the Malacca Strait. And after that...

Hey, you know what? It just occurred to me as I was mentioning all those places in Indonesia that the *Alma* passed through that at the same time, I was also giving a list of the places where they have had problems with piracy over recent years. I mean, the Malacca and Singapore Straits, Bangka Strait and Durian and the Sulu Sea—and that's not to mention the various small island groups she passed. All those places have seen repeated pirate attacks on ships from the Nineties until today and all of them have appeared on lists of dangerous areas in warnings about piracy. But the thing is that, other than occasional attacks on ships in the Malacca Strait, attacks that were mainly against low-freeboard and slow-moving tankers, none of the attacks in the modern wave of boardings and hijackings had taken place yet at the time the *Alma* was making her scenic tour of the area. Because remember that this voyage was taking place in 1990 while the first of the heavily-armed modern attacks didn't occur until 1991.

Now don't go correcting me on that one, George! I can see by the look on your face that you... But don't!!

So what I was driving at was the fact that the crew thought nothing about piracy at that time, and the only precautions they took as the ship weaved her way those narrow passages at night were precautions taken against the eternal problem of thievery. Precautions against people who might come aboard with the intention of stealing anything they could get their hands on, be it lines or paint or anything else that wasn't locked up. And on those occasions when thieves boarded a ship in those waters back then, they were usually there and gone without ever being seen so that the only way anyone knew they had been there was by finding things missing. The thieves wouldn't come aboard to make the captain open the safe or to take over the whole ship, and if they were armed at all, it would be with machetes or something similar. It wouldn't be with automatic weapons. So in order to deal with a threat like that, the only precaution the crew of the *Alma* took was to lock things up at night and especially things on the stern. They didn't rig security lights and they didn't post extra lookouts. They just steamed on through like they owned the place. They steamed through without a thought of danger, something that would be unheard of today when ships are so obsessed with security. Because it was still a different world back then. It was...

Hey you know, I really should get back to my story, shouldn't I? I should get back to the part where the *Alma* was steaming west in the Malacca Strait one more time. Well, eventually she arrived at a point that had been marked out on her charts, a point where she had to make yet another left turn across oncoming traffic before arriving at her next port, a place along the northern coast of Sumatra by the name of Belawan. In this port she pulled in and tied up to a dock one more time, though the only problem with Belawan was the fact that there was very little cargo to be loaded there, not even enough to keep her at the dock for a whole day. So for that reason, the *Alma's* visit there turned out to be containership-short.

It wasn't long before she left Belawan and made a left turn in the strait, though this time rather than crossing over into the main traffic lanes, she hugged the coast as closely as she could. She stayed near Sumatra where she would be clear of most of the oncoming traffic and also where she would be able to make another left turn as soon as she reached the northwestern tip of the island, the tip of Aceh. And then once she had cleared that tip, she turned to the south and eventually the southeast, following the island's southern coast. And she followed that coast more than halfway down until she finally arrived at a certain pre-chosen gap in the string of small islands that lie just offshore along much of the coast. She reached that gap, and there she turned and threaded her way through the islands until she arrived at the port of Padang, the port that would be her last stop in Asia. Because it was here that the longshoremen would finish the job of filling her holds with pallets of raw rubber. It was here that they would stuff pallet after pallet into those holds, filling every last available spot they could find. And it was here that she would take on her biggest load and have her longest stay of all the rubber ports, a stay that would last for three full days. And as far as the crew was concerned, they had no complaints about the length of the stay, because not only did they tie up to a dock in Padang, but also in what you could call a seaman's dream-come-true, there was a bar right at the head of that dock. There was a bar they could walk to in something like two minutes.

\*　　\*　　\*　　\*　　\*

So being that Padang was the last port the *Alma* would be visiting in Asia, that meant it was also the last chance for the Chief Mate and the Bosun to get away from each other for a few days before the long, slow passage back to the United States with the load of rubber and lumber. It was their last chance to avoid each other before returning to their two hours each evening of enforced togetherness, their two hours together on a bridge that seemed to grow smaller and more stifling with each day that passed. And if the two of them didn't manage to avoid trouble during the three days the ship was in Padang, those three days when they should have barely seen each other, it wasn't necessarily their fault. Because neither of them went out looking for trouble. It was something that just seemed to happen.

But before I go into that, maybe I should say a few things about Padang, shouldn't I? Maybe I should, uh... Let's see, I should... Hey you know, it sure has been a long time since anyone has interrupted me, hasn't it? It's been like... Well I don't know. But I do know that I, uh... That I miss it in a way. Because you know, it's a lot of work having to tell this story all by myself. And it would be kind of nice if someone would help me out a little...

Not you, George! You be quiet!!

But if there's anyone else who wants to pitch in and, uh... Like say Jamey, how was Padang as a port?

–Jamey: What, you're askin' me to butt in?

Not butt in exactly. I'm asking you to, uh... to help bear some of the burden. Some of... Well yes, I suppose I am asking you to butt in. So please...

–Jamey: Ah, it was okay. I had a good time there.

It seems that you had a good time everywhere you went, didn't you?

–Jamey: Yeah, I guess I did.

And you went out on the town and all that?

–Jamey: Yeah sure, and it was good. But like we

weren't even in Padang out there at the dock. We were at some little town, and you had to take a taxi to get to the main town. And that was a good place, though only thing is you couldn't get laid there cause-a these guys they called the Moslem Police, these fanatic guys who'd be watchin' what's goin' on. And like the girls wouldn't go with you if any-a them assholes were around. Cause like there was this one time at this restaurant where a couple of us were talkin' to some girls till one-a them guys came up and said somethin' to em and they walked out on us.

–But yeah, it was a good place except for them Moslem Police assholes. I got nothin' to complain about.

Well, thank you for that. Thank you... So then the, uh... The town was... What else can I say about it before I get to that night when, uh... Say maybe I should describe the bar at the head of the dock, shouldn't I? Because after all, much of the crew never saw more of Padang than that bar, besides which it was the place where things first began to go wrong that night...

It was one of those typical dark places with loud disco music blasting away, though in one way it was different from most other bars. And that was the fact that it had no actual bar, but instead what it had was a little hole-in-the-wall like a serving kitchen which meant that instead of the crew lining up at the bar, they had to sit around at the tables that surrounded the dance floor. And of course there were girls working there, girls who seemed to be beyond the reach of the Muslim Police. Girls who were there to keep the seamen company and to satisfy their desires if you know what I mean. And it was in that dark and noisy bar that the chain of events began that last night the ship was in Padang, the chain of events that were to, uh... that were to end in...

As I was saying, it was their last night in town since the

ship was scheduled to sail during the next afternoon, and being that this would be their last chance for some shore time, a large portion of the crew was in that bar by the dock. They were there to say their goodbyes to Asia over glasses of Bintang Beer. The Bosun was there and so were most of the other heavy partiers along with just about everyone else who wasn't on watch. And all of them were drinking beers or shots or both, and they weren't thinking about tomorrow or about consequences or about all the ocean that lay ahead of them. They were only thinking about that night. They were only thinking about having one last bit of fun.

But some of them were having more fun than they really should have, as so often seems to be the case when you have a whole bar full of drunken seamen. Some of them were going too far. And that was especially the case with Starr on that particular evening, Starr who was usually such a light drinker but who got carried away with the occasion. Starr who made a huge mistake that night, a beginner's mistake among drinkers and one that could have turned out even worse than it did. Because what Starr did was to accept some pills that were offered to her by one of the Oilers, and then she mixed those pills with the beer she was drinking. So it was Starr who, uh... Starr, is there anything you want to say?

—Starr: Oh, you want me to talk about it? Is that it?... Well, I screwed up that night. I screwed up big-time. Cause I never should have taken those pills, you know. I should have... You know... Cause I never take pills. Never! But that night, it was... You know, like Mike offered them to me and I took them, and I... Well, I blew it, you know.

So then you, uh... You went and... I have to tell you right here that I'm not altogether clear about what happened that night. So if you could, uh...

—Starr: Well, it's not all that clear to me, either, cause I don't even remember most-a that night, you know. Cause I was just... I mean, I was out cold most-a the time, so I... You know... Like I remember how it was coming on so strong there at the bar, and I just like... I had to get outa there. I had to get back to the ship, you know, cause I didn't wanta... You know... I didn't wanta pass out right there in that bar. So I didn't say anything, I just... you know.

You walked back to the ship by yourself, right? And you made it with no problem?

—Starr: Yeah, I guess you could say it was no problem, cause I didn't fall down or anything like that, you know. I made it back, and I made it to my room.

—Carter: Yeah, I guess you made it okay, but you looked awful damn bad. You looked like you was really wasted, and you was staggerin' and stuff. Cause I was on gangway watch when you come back, and I says I better watch out for her, and I followed you and made sure you made it to you room.

—Starr: Well, thank you for that.

—Carter: But I didn't see nothin' else after that. I just told the Bosun about you when he come back lookin' for you, but I didn't see nothin' else that happened, not till after I heard all the shoutin' and fightin' and stuff.

—Starr: Yeah, well I don't know much after that, either. I just... I mean, it's real hazy, you know. But I just remember that I was in my room, and I was getting undressed to go to bed, and I... Like I remember that I was really thirsty, and... You know, I just had to get some water, and I musta been thinkin' about the pitcher of ice-water in the saloon, you know, cause like last thing I remember, I was walkin' down the passageway, and I... Well, I don't know, cause that's all I remember, you know, till I woke up in bed.

So you don't, uh... You can't remember anything else?... So then that means that the next step in this little drama came sometime later when the Chief Mate found her in the saloon and, uh... He, uh... Well, I suppose I should let you tell us about it, shouldn't I? So go ahead, Mate.

–Chief Mate: Who me?! You want me to tell your story for you? Is that it?

Yes, I suppose...

–Chief Mate: Why don't you tell it yourself? You're the author of this story, aren't you? So aren't you the one who's supposed to be telling it?

Yes, I am the author, but you see it's just that I'm not all that sure about... I mean, I've heard such conflicting stories about that night, and I... I... I mean does it all have to be up to me? Do I have to shoulder all the responsibility by myself with nothing but this little pencil of mine? Do I... I mean please, can't you help me out a little?

–Chief Mate: So you can't do it after all, huh? You just can't. You can get this story started, but you can't finish it.

Oh, I can finish it. It's just that I... I need a little help, that's all.

–Chief Mate: And now you come begging to me, huh?

I'm not begging, I'm just... I mean, why don't you look at it this way? I'm giving you a chance to give your version of events, so you should jump at the opportunity, shouldn't you?

–Chief Mate: My version? You call it my version? Is that what you say?! It's not like there's a my version and a someone else's version. There's just the truth, that's all there is! There's just what really happened, and then there's a bunch of lies. And that's it!

So okay then, go ahead and tell us the truth.

–Chief Mate: The truth? Well, that's very simple

because the fact is that nothing happened that night. I mean, I just... I came into the saloon that evening, and I found that little... that... I suppose I can't call her a drunken little slut here in your book, can I? But I...

–Starr: You bastard! To call me that after what you did!

Please, no name-calling...

–Chief Mate: What I did? How can she even say what I did when she was unconscious the whole time? She doesn't know.

–Starr: Oh, I know! Because I know you...

Please! Let's stop this arguing and get on with the story, can't we?

–Chief Mate: Yeah right, the story. Well, like I just said, there was nothing happened. I just... I found her passed out in the saloon, and then... Then I did what I had to do and nothing else! That's all.

–And you have to remember that I was the medical officer on that ship, so it was up to me to take care of people who needed help, and I couldn't just... I mean, I couldn't just walk away and leave her like that, could I? Because what if anything had happened to her? I mean, it was my responsibility to... you know.

So you took care of her, right?

–Chief Mate: Yes of course. I took care of her. I checked her and tried to wake her up. I shook her and stuff like that, but she didn't respond. She was really out. So then I... I picked her up and carried her to her room and laid her on the bed, and I, uh... Well, I did what I could to make sure that she was okay, and I... Because remember that I was the medical officer, so it was my duty to... You know, to make sure that she was okay.

So you just... All you did was take care of a patient, is that what you're saying?

–Chief Mate: Yes of course, because I'm a

professional, remember? And I wouldn't do anything to... I mean, no matter how great the temptation might have been, I just wouldn't have... I wouldn't do something like what I've been accused of doing. I just wouldn't!
   –Bosun: Bullshit!!
   –Chief Mate: What? Are you gonna let him...?
   –Bosun: Bullshit! I said bullshit!
   –Chief Mate: Are you gonna let him interrupt me like this?
   Well, I don't think there's much I can do...
   –Bosun: That's right. That's fuckin' right! Cause everything this asshole just said is bullshit. Everything!
   –Chief Mate: It's not! It's all true.
   –Bosun: It's all bullshit! Cause when I come in there and seen him, he was all over her. He wasn't playin' no doctor bullshit. He was gettin' ready to fuck her.
   –Chief Mate: I was not! How can you say such a thing?
   –Bosun: I can say it cause it's true.
   –Chief Mate: It's not true, it's... Please Mr. Author, can't you do something about this?
   –Bosun: No, there ain't a fuckin' thing he can do cause I'm tellin' the truth.
   –Chief Mate: Oh, please! Can't you...? I mean, this is such a horrible misinterpretation of my actions...
   –Bosun: Ain't no misinterpretation here. Cause there ain't no doctor goes feelin' her up and undressin' her the way this guy was.
   –Chief Mate: Undressing her?! She was already undressed. Or I mean mostly undressed. Because all she had on was this flimsy little silk bathrobe with nothing underneath it. Or I mean...
   –Bosun: Nothin' underneath it, huh?
   –Chief Mate: I mean, as far as I could tell there was nothing underneath it. Though I swear I never opened the

robe to look, so I really can't say for sure. But I...
   –Bosun: Oh, you lyin' son-of-a-bitch!
   –Chief Mate: I'm not a liar! I... I mean, if I was going to rape her, do you think I would have left the door open so that anyone could come walking in? Would I have done that?
   He has a pretty good point there, now doesn't he, Boats?
   –Bosun: He's just stupid, that's all. Too fuckin' stupid to lock the door.
   Well, I don't know about that...
   –Chief Mate: And I wasn't fondling her, either. I was just... I mean, I had to touch her to try to wake her up, didn't I? And to make sure that she was okay. I couldn't just...
   –Bosun: So what the fuck were your hands doin' all over her tits and everywhere else?
   –Chief Mate: They weren't! And you can't honestly say...
   –Bosun: I can say whatever the fuck I want!
   –Chief Mate: No, what I'm trying to say... What I want to say is that you can't honestly say you saw anything, because you reacted too quickly when you saw the two of us there. And you can't say that she was exposed in any way, either. I mean her... You know...
   –Bosun: Well, I don't know...
   –Crew Mess: Hey man, I sure did see it. Cause I come in there when I heard all the shoutin', and I see her layin' there with that robe wide open. Tits and cunt.
   –Chief Mate: Oh, please...
   –Second Cook: No, you got it wrong, man, cause it wasn't just open. I mean, he had her stripped down.
   –Crew Mess: Yeah you know, that's right. She didn't have no robe on. She was layin' there buck naked.

—Second Cook: Not a fuckin' thing on, man, and him feelin' her up, too. Cause he had his hands all over her.
  —Chief Mate: Oh, come on now.
  —Crew Mess: Yeah, he was workin' it, man. And like he was all ready to jump right on.
  —Second Cook: Ready, shit! He wasn't just ready, man. He was already climbin'...
  —Chief Mate: Mr. Author, please!! Can't you put a stop to this? Because they're just... They're making all this up as they go along, and you can't believe a word they say. I mean, you don't believe these two... these... these...

  What's wrong? Are you having trouble finding a word you can use in place of niggers?
  —Chief Mate: No, it's just... No! Of course not!! What are you accusing me of? Are you trying to say that I'm a racist? Is that what you're doing?

  If the shoe fits, you know...
  —Chief Mate: Well, that does it! That's all I'm gonna take from you! I'm outa here!!

  Outa here? What do you mean? You can't leave. You're...
  —Chief Mate: Oh yes I can! You just watch me. Because not only have you let these people gang up on me, but now you've even joined in yourself with this baseless accusation. So what more do I have to lose?

  To lose? Why you would lose everything. Because remember that you're a fictional character and you don't even exist outside this story. So if you walk out, you have nowhere to go. You won't exist at all and you'll never have existed.
  —Chief Mate: Well you know what? That might just be better than what you're putting me through right now. So goodbye!

  No wait! Don't be so hasty. Because I... I mean I need

you, and I... Okay, I'll admit it. I took a cheap shot at you with that one, and you really don't deserve it. So I'm sorry, okay? I take it back.

–Chief Mate: Yeah?

Yes, I know you're not a racist, and I... I really don't know why I said what I did just now. It was just... It was too easy, that's all, but I really didn't mean it and I'm sorry. I'm very, very sorry.

–Chief Mate: Well, I don't know...

So come on. Tell me what the word was that you were actually searching for. What was it that you wanted to call those two? Was it...?

–Chief Mate: What I was trying to say is that they're nothing but minor characters who don't...

–Second Cook: Hey! Who you callin' a minor character?

–Chief Mate: I mean, these characters wouldn't even have been mentioned in this story if they hadn't jumped in. And all they were doing with that talk of theirs was taking advantage of their fifteen seconds of fame by blurting out a lot of nonsense that simply wasn't true. And not only wasn't it true, but it didn't even contribute to the story.

–Second Cook (mumbling): I ain't no minor.

Yes, I see what you mean. They were just...

–Chief Mate: And especially that last part about seeing me touching her. That couldn't possibly have been true since I was on the ground by the time they got there.

–Bosun: Fuckin' right you was on the ground! Cause I come in and seen you there with your hands all over her, and I punched the shit outa you. And you know what? I think I'll do it again right now, you son-of-a-bitch!

Now take it easy there, Boats. We don't want any...

–Chief Mate: You keep him away from me, do you hear? Don't let him get near me!

—Bosun: You pussy motherfuckin'...

Bosun! Please stop!! We can't have any more of that now. We just... We're trying to tell the story and we don't want any more violence. So... So... So tell me Boats, you came in and found him there doing, uh... whatever it was that he was doing, and you punched him, what? One time?

—Bosun: Yeah, one fuckin' punch. That's all it was cause that's all that pussy could take.

One punch and he stayed down?

—Bosun: Fuckin' rights. Cause I told that asshole he better not get up. I told him he wants to get outa there, he's gotta crawl. Cause I mean... If he'da got up, I'da killed the motherfucker!

And so he left the room? He, uh... So you had to crawl out of the room, Mate?

—Chief Mate: Oh, it was all so... I mean, for an officer to have to...

—Wayne: Man, I sure wished I coulda seen that! Him crawlin' outa there and half the crew watchin'. Man, that had to be somethin'!

—Chief Mate: It was all so undignified and so...

—Wayne: And what was them names he was callin' ya?

—Chief Mate: It was so humiliating. But what could I do when he was acting so crazy? I just had to get out of there.

—Wayne: Hey Carter, you was there. So tell us about it.

—Carter: Nah, no thanks. I don't wanta say nothin' cause it was... It was ugly, man.

—Chief Mate: Yes, and you know that striking an officer is a very serious offense, don't you?

—Bosun: You asshole! Don't you know that you ain't no officer here and this ain't no ship?

—Chief Mate: Now you keep away from me! Keep him away!!

–Wayne: Get him, man!

Stop!! Please! That's enough! Do you hear me?! I said that's enough!! So calm down all of you, or I'll be forced to… Well, I don't know what I'll be forced to do. But you'd better be quiet, okay?

Or I tell you what, why don't I take over for a little while and give all of you a chance to calm down? I'll, uh… Or in fact, why don't we just drop this whole thing and move on to something else since no one has anything left to say about that incident. Or at least no one has anything constructive to say. So what I'll do instead is I'll, uh… I'll talk a little bit about the consequences of that night and then I'll get on with the story.

\* \* \* \* \*

Well, the Chief Mate felt—and rightly so—that he was in a very awkward position when it came to dealing with the incident in Padang. Because after all, he had been seen by so many crewmembers at the worst possible moment, that moment when he had left the room under what appeared to be such compromising circumstances. And while he knew that he really should have logged the Bosun and perhaps even pressed charges against him for having struck him, he didn't see how he could so when there were so many witnesses who could testify about how he had come crawling out of that room looking so shamed and so guilty. That room where, just a few minutes before, he had been alone with a scantily clad and unconscious woman. And while he may have known in his heart that he was completely innocent and that he had done nothing more than perform his duty as medical officer on the ship, he also knew that there would be far too much for him to explain. So in the end, he did the only thing he could do.

He let it drop.

Or at least he let it drop as far as the logging went. But he was hardly able to forgive and forget and neither was anyone else aboard ship. And it was for that reason that the incident quickly took on a life of its own. It became a constant subject of conversation among the crew over the next week or so, and some of the names that the Bosun had called the Chief Mate—pervert and scumbag and the rest—began to stick as nicknames among those crewmembers who disliked the Mate. And the new names soon replaced the earlier one of Cherry Boy that he had picked up in Tawau as they began to refer to him as The Pervert behind his back. Though of course, it was only the Bosun who dared to call him that openly. And while he wouldn't actually say it to his face, he frequently made reference to The Pervert when he knew that the Mate was within earshot.

And so it was that as the *Alma Lykes* sailed from Padang and began to plod her way across the Indian Ocean, as she began another of her long, slow ocean passages, there was an almost unbelievable tension on the bridge during the eight-to-twelve watch. Because while there had been a state of open warfare between the Chief Mate and the Bosun ever since the incident in Tawau, the situation now grew even worse. And in fact, the atmosphere between them had become so poisoned by this time that both of them felt the need to maintain as much physical separation as they possibly could. And what that meant was that during the Bosun's two-hour wheel watches, they would each take possession of a wing of the bridge—the Chief Mate the starboard and the Bosun the port—and whenever one of them would enter the wheelhouse to find that the other was already inside, one or both would immediately retreat to their respective wings.

It was an awful situation for both of them, and it worked very heavily on their nerves. It gnawed at them every minute they had to spend together, every second, and it was so bad that it soon came to dominate all the other twenty-two hours of their days as well. And while they each tried to brush it off or to minimize the whole thing, there was no way that either of them could truly put it behind him. So the reality was that with each passing day, they became even more obsessed with the repulsion and the hatred they felt toward each other, so much so that it soon came to color all their thoughts and all their relationships with other members of the crew, even the closest friends they had aboard.

–Starr: So do you think that's why...?

What? What's that?

–Starr: I was just asking if you think maybe that's the real reason why John changed so much in those days. The way he... You know.

John...? Oh, you mean the Bosun.

–Starr: Yes, because he started to ignore me so much in those days and, you know, I always thought it was because he blamed me for that stuff in Padang or something. But you know, now that you just said that, it made me think that like... You know, like maybe it wasn't about me after all. Maybe it was about all the stress he had with the Chief Mate. You know?

Yes, the stress could have done that, or then again maybe it was the fear.

–Starr: Fear? What fear? I never saw him...

I don't mean fear so much as I mean... Like maybe he saw you as trouble, as a source of conflict with the Chief Mate, and so he tried to avoid you. Because he didn't want any more trouble.

–Starr: Oh, I see...

And though he may have been in love with you, I'm afraid that he loved the sea even more and he didn't want to jeopardize his way of life and his...

–Bosun: Ah, cut the crap, Mr. Writer!

Cut the crap?

–Bosun: Yeah, just cut out all that analyzin' me bullshit you been pullin' and get back to your story, okay?

Cut out the... Okay, but you know it really wasn't me who started it. It was Starr...

–Bosun: And don't you go blamin' it on her, either!

Okay, I'm sorry...

–Starr: Thank you, John. Thank you for defending me.

–Bosun: Oh, shit!

Well, if we can, uh... If I can get back to the story...?

–Bosun: Get back to it!! Jesus Fuckin' Christ!

Well then, uh... As I was saying, the tension of the two hours that the Chief Mate and the Bosun had to spend together on the bridge each evening soon took control of their lives. And while it had a serious impact upon everything the Bosun did and on his relationships with his shipmates, it turned out to have an even more devastating impact upon the Chief Mate. That was partly due to the fact that he had no real friends aboard the *Alma* and no one he could confide in as all his relationships were professional ones with little of the personal thrown in. And that held true with the Captain whose favor he was constantly trying to curry as well as with those below him. At the same time, it was also partly due to his personality type, to his being a person who took things very seriously, and especially things that had to do with his profession as a seaman.

He knew that much of what had happened had been his own fault for not having asserted himself earlier and more completely, and he let his recriminations eat away at him as he relived the incident over and over again in his mind. He couldn't stop thinking about it, and he couldn't stop remembering how he had let himself be humiliated by the Bosun in front of the crew in Padang—if not earlier in Tawau. And it was that feeling of humiliation that he just couldn't put behind him. So whether he wanted to or not, he found himself spending most of his free hours searching out ways in which he could even the score, ways in which he could get back at his tormentor, ways in which he could get his revenge.

–Chief Mate: Oh come on now, you know that's not true. You know I didn't sit up nights plotting my revenge.

Well maybe not that, but you certainly were obsessed with the Bosun and with those two incidents.

–Chief Mate: Well, who wouldn't be? And especially on a ship like that where you... I mean, there was so damned much time to think about things on that ship! It was nothing like what I'm used to with fast-turn-around, because on those ships you don't have all that spare time. You just... All you do on those ships is work and sleep and not much of the latter when you're Chief Mate. But on that old ship... I mean, there was so little to do and so much time to do it in that I just... Well, I had way too much spare time and way too much time to spend thinking about those things.

And that was why it got to you?

–Chief Mate: Of course it was. Because with all that free time... I mean, a situation like that would have gotten to anybody, don't you think?

Yes, you may have a point there... But now let me get back to the story and the passage from Padang to... Hey, you know what? I forgot to mention that the *Alma* still had one more stop to make at a foreign port before she reached the States, didn't I? Because being that she was a Lykes ship and being that she would be passing by South Africa on her way home, of course the company told her to stop in at Durban and pick up cargo. And while there was no room left in her holds, stuffed with raw rubber as they were, there was no cargo on deck other than a few bundles of the lumber that had been loaded in Tawau. And remember that there were very few bundles on deck since that was all they had been able to load out there without destroying the ship's stability at that stage of the voyage. So with those nearly empty decks just begging for more cargo for the trip home, the crew was told to stop in at Durban for a final topping-off with containers bound for American ports.

At the time, the international boycott against white rule in South Africa had been in effect for a number of years, and though it was having a major impact upon the country's economy, it had done nothing to discourage Lykes from sending its ships into Durban and other South African ports on a regular basis. And that was because of the fact that the boycott had so many loopholes in it that Lykes never had a problem finding more than enough legal cargo to make the stops worthwhile. There were all the high-value ores and other types of exempted goods just waiting there for them to load, and with Durban being the main transshipment port for the southwestern Indian Ocean, there were also cargoes coming from other countries and just passing through South Africa which of course were exempt from the boycott.

So the boycott had not affected Lykes Lines to any extent and it hadn't forced any changes upon the company, but that was far from the case with the country of South Africa where the transition was by then well underway. Mandela had been released from prison a few months earlier but had yet to take power, as at the time, he was traveling the country and laying the groundwork for the black rule that everyone knew to be right around the corner. And in fact, he had just given a speech in Durban the day before the *Alma* pulled in. So things were starting to change in that country with the first black faces starting to show up at formerly all-white establishments in town and with changes taking place down at the docks as well. Because while the top bosses were still white men at that time, they were no longer the old-style apartheid screamers that had formerly been so common around there. Or at least the two white walking-bosses who showed up during the two shifts required to work the *Alma* were not screamers at all. Instead, they were both men who spoke Zulu, the language of most of the longshoremen in that port, and they were men who treated their workers with a certain amount of consideration if not actual respect.

And it was a warm, sunny African morning when the graceful little ship arrived in Durban, pulling in and tying up at the container dock where the crew had only to take a cab ride around—or a two Rand launch ride across—the harbor in order to reach the center of that beautiful little city. That city whose downtown looked like a small European city that had somehow been transplanted to the coast of Africa and whose beachfront presented the very picture of an urban paradise. And since there was no shortage of containers waiting around to be shipped thanks to the many companies that had stopped calling at Durban during those years, that meant that the longshoremen would have to squeeze as many of them as they could onto the *Alma's* decks. But being built on an old pre-container design, she had no deck sockets or anything else to make it easy for them to secure the containers in place, so it would all have to be done the old-fashioned way. The longshoremen would have to lay out dunnage to go beneath the containers, and then afterwards they would have to go around and chain them into place one-by-one.

And what this meant for the crew was that they would be staying in Durban all day and late into the night since it would take that long for all that work to be done.

It meant that the crew would have one last chance to go out and sow their wild oats before having to face the long, boring passage from Durban to Chesapeake Bay. It meant they would have one last chance to drink and blow off steam the way any good seaman would in a town like Durban. And to make things even better—at least for the whites among them—they wouldn't have to compete with crowds of European tourists for space at the bars and clubs along the beach, thanks to the boycott. Because in those days, that lovely beachfront was reserved largely for South Africans and the occasional wandering seaman.

So they went out on the town and they drank and they had a good time, and finally they returned to the ship late at night for one of those good, old-fashioned, liquored-up undockings. They returned for one of those undockings where the whole crew was falling-down drunk, most of them so drunk that they could barely function. And it's hard to say whether the serious problem that occurred on the bow during the undocking that night was caused more by the drunkenness and rowdiness of the crew—and especially of the Bosun who was the drunkest of them all—or by the sobriety of the one exception to the rule. The sobriety of the one person on the bow who hadn't gone out drinking in Durban: the Chief Mate.

The Bosun had spent the evening in the bars that line the beachfront, and while he was there, he had done his best to drown the tensions of the entire voyage in one bout of heavy drinking. He had tried to blot out his memories, and especially his memories of the last week since the ship had sailed from Padang. He drank like there was no tomorrow, or like he had forgotten that tomorrow existed, and when he returned to the ship for undocking, he was by far the drunkest member of that drunken and disorderly lot. And when that unruly gang showed up on the bow to untie the ship, the Bosun was not only drunk but he was loud. He was loud and obnoxious, and he said whatever came into his head. He just didn't care anymore. He yelled and told jokes, and he laughed with the rest of the crew. And when he got around to the subject of the Chief Mate, he insulted the guy and called him names right there in front of the crew, doing so at the top of his voice.

As for the Mate, he knew that he couldn't just stand there and take those insults, and it wasn't long before it reached the point where he had to speak up. He had to put his foot down and show those drunken bums who was the officer out there. He had to put the Bosun back in his place. But when he finally spoke, it ended up having the exact opposite effect from what he had intended. Because when he came out and told the Bosun to be quiet, told him in his most officer-like manner, it didn't quiet him down at all. Instead, it set the guy off even louder as he began to insult the Chief Mate right to his face. He began calling him a pervert and a rapist and any other name that came into his drunken mind. And then when the Mate reached the final straw and ordered the Bosun to leave the bow, the guy shot right back with, "No, you get off the bow, you asshole!"

So the Mate repeated his order for the Bosun to leave the bow. He repeated it again and again, each time in a stronger and more solemn voice. But all he ever got in reply were more insults. He got himself called one name after another, and he got told to leave the bow himself more than once. And it went on that way throughout the undocking with the Bosun refusing to budge and the Chief Mate indecisive, afraid to use force to eject a man he knew to be stronger than himself and afraid to order the other seamen to help for fear they might turn on him. So in the end, the Bosun didn't have to leave the bow until he was good and ready.

—Wayne: Hey man, is that all you gonna say about it? Cause it was like... Man, it was the funniest thing I ever saw. Ain't that right, Carter?

—Carter: Oh, I don't know...

—Wayne: I mean, the Bosun tellin' that asshole to get the fuck outa there, and that little weasel sayin', "I told you first," like he's some little kid. And he's damn near cryin' like a... like he's gonna cry if he don't get his way. Right, Carter?

—Carter: I don't know funny, cause it's kinda sad.

—Wayne: Sad...?

—Carter: Yeah, it was sad to see John doin' that to himself and gettin' himself into trouble like that.

—Wayne: Sad, shit! It was hilarious!! It was a fuckin' show! That Bosun tellin' him, "We don't need you," and, "We can get a monkey to hold that radio," and shit like that. Man, I was crackin' up. And I just wished he'da punched his lights out while I was watchin', that's all I wish... Cause you shoulda seen it, Mike.

—Mike: Yeah, man...

—Wayne: And like I didn't know it was comin' or nothin', cause I wasn't drinkin' with him. I mean, I go to them black clubs when I'm in Durban, so I didn't know shit till I come back and see him there and... Man, what a show!

So are you finished? Can I get back to...

—Bosun: Can you believe that shit?! That little fuckin'... that asshole, that... That piece-a shit that ain't even a wart on a seaman's ass! That... That... That nothin'! orderin' *me* off the bow!! Me who's like... I'm more of a seaman than he ever dreamed of bein'. I'm more seaman in my little finger than he's... well, than he's ever gonna be.

—Cause he don't know shit about bein' a real seaman. He ain't barely enough seaman to work on a box ship, and he don't know shit about real ships. He don't know how to rig cargo gear and he couldn't rig a heavy-lift to save his fuckin' ass. And a Frisco rig? Forget about it! He don't know a Frisco rig... He wouldn't know one if it come up and bit him on the ass. And you talk about that jumbo. Man, you just ask him how you flip it over to a different hatch cause he don't know. He just... And he don't know shit about cargo, either. He don't know how to set up a hold for a load of coffee 'cept he looks it up in a book or 'cept the Captain tells him how. That's all he knows about it.

—And he was always runnin' up to me sayin', "Hey Bosun, you gotta help me," cause he don't know shit. And everything he learned on that ship he learned it from me cause I'm the one... Like you remember him braggin' about loadin' that lumber and sayin' how he figured it all out on his own? Well, bullshit! Cause you know who it was taught him all about runnin' fairleads and snakin' cargo? It was me! He didn't figure out shit. It was me told him how to do it. And then that asshole turns around and orders *me* off the bow?! It's...

—And I mean I wasn't even drunk, either. I was just... You know, I was just feelin' happy, that's all. And I was actin' like a seaman.

—Cause you know what a seaman is? He's a guy who works hard and he plays hard and he's... He's like full speed ahead. Like you gotta work in all kinds-a weather and you gotta go out there any time-a day or night, hot or cold or rain or seas comin' over the deck. You gotta go out and do your job cause that's what you do. That's who you are. And then when you hit port, you go out and you have a good time and... I mean maybe you drink a little too much, but that's what seamen do. They just... That's how they live.

So, uh... Thank you, Bosun. Thank you for...

—Bosun: Cause you know, bein' a seaman ain't just a job. It's a life! That's what it is. And it's *my* life. It's what I am, and it's what I'm always gonna be. And I mean a *real* seaman, an old-time stick-ship sailor, not one-a them box-ship guys. Cause on them ships, you ain't even alive! You ain't nothin' but a piece-a machinery and you can't... You can't live like a man!

—But me, I'm a man and there ain't no way you can change that. I was born a seaman, and I'm still a seaman even if I ain't on a ship. Cause you can throw me off them ships and you can scrap em and anything else you wanta do. But you can't ever stop me from bein' a seaman, cause that's what I am. And I'm gonna die a seaman even if I don't ever see another ship.

Well thank you, Bosun. I, uh... I really don't know what to say after that. I just... I don't know. Should I, uh... Should I press on with the story?

\*   \*   \*   \*   \*

The *Alma Lykes* sailed from Durban that night amid all the yelling and screaming on the bow, and she began to make her way around the Cape of Good Hope. She began the first leg of her final passage of the voyage, the two and a half week passage that would take her to Norfolk, Virginia. And while the shouts quickly died away once the crew had left the bow, the repercussions of the incident were only just beginning. Because while the Chief Mate had tried to ignore the incident in Tawau since it had taken place ashore, and while he had done his best to minimize the incident in Padang due to certain circumstances of which readers should be well aware, this time around he went straight to the Captain without the least hesitation.

And in any case, the Captain himself had been something of a witness to the incident since he had heard bits and pieces of the Bosun's shouts coming over the Chief Mate's radio. But even without that, the Chief Mate felt confident enough to press any charges that the Captain might agree to since, unlike before, there were no extenuating circumstances in this case. There were no embarrassing details that might be brought up. There was nothing but a drunken and insubordinate seaman who had refused to leave the bow when ordered to do so by the officer in charge.

It was a firing offense, there was no doubt about that, and the only real question had to do with how far he would be able to push the case with the Coast Guard. Would he be able to convince them to suspend the Bosun's seaman's documents or to take some other action against him? He didn't know. And while things weren't nearly as serious as they would have been if only the guy had gone and hit him again, still there was a very good case to be made. It was strong and it was about as air-tight as a case can get, though somehow the Mate wasn't quite satisfied with it. Because while he could surely get the Bosun black-balled from the company and perhaps even get him to lose his papers for a short period of time, that wasn't nearly enough for him. He didn't want to give the guy a slap on the wrist. He didn't want to come up with what he saw as a halfway punishment. He wanted to end the Bosun's career and ruin his life. He wanted to destroy the guy. And his only regret was that he couldn't take him out and hang him from the yard-arm like they used to do back in the good old days.

He wanted to get something stronger against the

Bosun. He wanted to get something that would nail him once and for all, and it was for that reason that he recommended to the Captain that they search the Bosun's room for alcohol and anything else they might...

–Chief Mate: Excuse me, but you've got it wrong.

Wrong...? I've got what wrong? What do you mean?

–Chief Mate: I mean that it wasn't my idea to search his room. It was the Captain's idea to do that. He was the one who said we should confiscate his booze and make that a part of the charge.

The Captain...?

–Chief Mate: Yes, he told me that it was standard procedure in a case like this where someone was fired for being drunk. He said that you always searched their room and confiscated their booze.

Well okay then, I stand corrected on that one, I suppose. Because I always thought it was you. But okay, I'll go along with that... So it was the Captain who said they should search his room. And what happened as a result was that a group of them showed up the next morning to do precisely that: the Captain and the Chief Mate along with the Deck Department's union delegate, Carter, who was there as a witness. They showed up and then, with the Bosun standing back and looking on, they began to go through his drawers and his closet.

It was the Chief Mate who actually did most of the searching as Carter stood back with the Bosun and watched while the Captain did little more than look around in a few of the most obvious places. But the Mate put his heart and soul into the search. He looked anywhere and everywhere he could think of, pulling out drawers and looking behind them and checking up inside the vents. And while he found nothing in any of those odd and hidden places, he did come up with several bottles of alcohol in his search, bottles which had been sitting right out in plain sight the whole time. With those bottles in hand, he now had the evidence he had supposedly come for, but still he felt like his search had been a failure. He felt like there had to be something more hidden in that room, something he had missed up till now. Something! And it wasn't until he was about to give up and call the search off that he finally realized that he hadn't looked in one of the most obvious places of all. He hadn't looked in the desk drawer. And as he opened the drawer and pulled it out as far as it could go, the Bosun's face turned grim and his muscles began to tighten. The Bosun's and Carter's, too, since they both knew exactly what it was that the Chief Mate was about to find in that drawer.

The Mate's eyes lit up the moment he saw what was there, but still he took his time for dramatic effect. He rummaged around and pawed at the items in the back of the drawer, and then finally he said, "Well, look what we have here!" and held up a plastic baggy half-full of marijuana. A bag of the locally famous brand known as Durban Poison. And as he held it up, he began to gr…

–Bosun: It wasn't no Poison.

What's that? Did you say something, Boats?... Boats…? Hello…?

–Carter: He said it wasn't no Poison.

No? But I heard that it was. I heard…

–Carter: What he means is that it wasn't no real Poison, cause you can't get real Durban Poison no more. It's like Panama Red or Acapulco Gold or any-a them. It don't exist now-days and they just call everything Poison down there.

So it wasn't the real stuff?… Well okay then, I stand corrected once again and I'll just say that, uh… The Chief Mate held up a bag of something, and as he stood there and displayed it triumphantly, he burst out into the biggest and most irritating grin that you can possibly imagine. It was the grin of victory in this private little war of his. And it was that "gotcha" grin more than anything else, more than all the weeks and months of tension, even more than the knowledge that he had just been busted and that his career at sea was over. It was that grin that tore through the Bosun's nerves and sliced into his heart. It was that grin that drove him insane. It was...

    –Carter: Look at him, man. Do you see that?
    –Bosun: Yeah, yeah...
    –Carter: It's that same fuckin' smile! That sneaky fuckin'... Man, I sure would like to...
    –Bosun: Ah, forget about it. It don't do no good...
    –Carter: Yeah I know, but still man, you gotta...

You gotta try? You gotta be a man? Is that what you're trying to say?

    –Carter: Yeah, somethin' like that...

Well you should listen to the Bosun instead, because he knows by now. He knows that it does you no good and it only digs your grave deeper. That's all it does. And that's all it did for him that day when he saw that sickeningly self-satisfied grin for the first time. Because he saw it and he reacted, and he dug his own grave.

He saw it and he lost control. He let his anger and his hatred and his frustration come boiling over into a blinding rage. He saw that grin, and he launched himself forward with the speed and fury of an animal on the attack. He was upon the Chief Mate in an instant, pummeling away at him with both fists, and when the Mate tried to duck down and protect himself, the Bosun caught him with a knee that stood him right back up. And then before the guy could make another move to try to get away, the Bosun grabbed him by the throat with one hand and used his other fist to wipe away the last remnants of that infuriating smile.

The Captain stood in shocked silence for a moment before he turned and ran from the room, too old and too small to intervene, and too afraid for his own safety in any case. And as he ran down the passageway, he yelled for help at the top of his lungs, calling for everyone in earshot to come to his aid. He ran and he yelled, and he kept on going right up the stairs and all the way to his office, going to get his gun and his handcuffs and anything else he could think of.

Carter was shocked by the fury of the Bosun's attack, too, and as he stood and watched him pound away on the Chief Mate's battered and bloody face, it quickly dawned on him that it was up to him to do something about it. It was up to him to grab his friend from behind and pull him off before he killed the guy. But when he finally jumped into action, charging over and grabbing on, it was only to find that he was helpless against the Bosun's rage. And so instead of pulling anyone off, he found himself hanging there riding around on the Bosun's back like he was a shirt. And the only thing he could do from that position was to grab at his friend's arms and try to interfere with his punches, and maybe do something to break his grip on the Mate's throat.

And he must have done some good since the Mate eventually managed to break free. And when he did so, he immediately fell to the ground and curled up into a defensive position where he lay trying to protect himself while the Bosun continued to punch him and kick him wherever he could find an opening. And the Bosun did all this while carrying Carter on his back. Carter and then a second crewmember who came in response to the Captain's call for help, a second and a third and more until finally there were enough of them there to overpower the

Bosun. There were enough of them to pull him back and force him away from his victim, force him over to the far side of the room. And no sooner had they shoved him back out of range for any more punches or kicks than suddenly all the fight went out of him and he practically went limp in their arms. He stopped fighting and he stood passively in his shipmates' embrace. He stood there, and he awaited his fate.

It wasn't long before the Captain returned with his gun in one shaky hand and a pair of handcuffs in the other. And upon seeing that the fight was already over and he wouldn't be needing it, he tried nervously to tuck the pistol into his belt. He tried but failed, lacking a free hand as he did, so he finally just gave the handcuffs to the nearest seaman and told him to go ahead and put them on. And then once the Bosun had been securely shackled to the railing of his bunk, the Captain was able to turn his attention to the bloody mess on the deck that used to be his Chief Mate.

He called to the Mate and asked if he was okay, but the Mate's only response was to moan and spit blood onto the deck. So the Captain ordered a couple of those present to go get the stokes litter. And upon their return, he guided the crew as they rolled the Mate over and lifted him into the clumsy contraption and then wrestled it out into the passageway and up the stairs, nearly dropping the thing more than once before they finally reached the ship's hospital. And then with the patient safely removed from the litter and tucked into bed, the Captain spent the rest of the day rushing about trying to deal with the emergency all by himself, without the help of a Chief Mate.

He tended to his patient, cleaning him up and bandaging his wounds, and he made frequent checks on his prisoner, not only leaving him handcuffed to the bunk but also having a hasp and padlock installed on the outside of the door and even posting a guard in the passageway. And he called the Second and Third Mates to tell them that they would be working six-and-six until further notice. And between times, he made preparations to stop in at Cape Town the next day and send the Mate ashore to a real hospital if that should prove necessary.

But in the end, it wasn't necessary to stop, and even the six-and-six didn't last very long as the injuries the Chief Mate had sustained turned out to be little more than superficial. And while his face looked horrible, all cut and swollen as it was, and his body covered with bruises, still there was nothing to prevent him from making a rapid and quasi-miraculous recovery. There was nothing to prevent him from being back on his feet by the next morning or from returning to the bridge to stand his watch that evening. And so by the time the ship was clear of the South African coast, he was back on duty and ready to finish the voyage under his own power just like he had begun it. He was back to his eight-to-twelve watch and his daywork in the afternoons. And the only thing that was different now was the fact that rather than having the Bosun on the bridge with him for part of his watches—the Bosun or Nathan who had originally begun the voyage—instead he was joined by other AB's who doubled-up to cover the watches.

So everything turned out fine for the Chief Mate, his face even being back to normal by the time the ship reached Norfolk. But that was hardly the case with the Bosun who was treated like a prisoner aboard ship. Because after all, he was a man who faced very serious criminal charges when the ship reached the States, charges of assaulting an officer and perhaps even attempted murder, along with a possible drug-possession charge, though this last one was a bit problematic since in the confusion of the struggle in the Bosun's room, the drug evidence had vanished into the pocket of one of his shipmates. And since the Captain feared that he might turn violent again at any moment, he saw to it that the Bosun was kept under lock and key for the rest of the long passage to Norfolk where he would be handed over to the proper authorities. He was kept handcuffed to the rail of his bunk while at the same time the door to his room was kept padlocked with a guard posted outside. Or at least he was kept handcuffed for a day or so until the Captain decided that it was too much hassle having to come by and release him for his bathroom breaks—not to mention being too dangerous. And it also didn't take more than a couple of days for the Captain to realize that maintaining a twenty-four hour guard outside the door would ruin his overtime budget. So in the end, the decision was made that the padlock by itself would provide all the security that was needed.

And the truth is that none of those things were truly necessary, not the handcuffs and not even the padlock since the Bosun was a man who no longer had any fight left in him. He was a man who had thrown away his anger and his pride and his strength and even his will to live in that one burst of violence. He had thrown away his very life in that attack on the Chief Mate, and now he had nothing left. And so he sat in his room a broken man, a wasted man, caged like an animal but completely passive and indifferent to his fate.

He sat and he refused to speak, not answering the visitors who came by and yelled to him through the locked door and not acknowledging them in any way, neither his friends nor his lover. And he wouldn't even speak to the Crew Mess when his meals were brought—his full meals, not the bread-and-water that the Chief Mate had tried to convince the Captain to restrict him to.

–Chief Mate: Oh, come on now! Bread and water?! I never said anything about that. You're just making that up.

No, I remember that one. I specifically remember...

–Chief Mate: How could you remember it when I never said it... Or if I said it, I had to be joking or something.

Or something...?

–Chief Mate: Because you have to be taking it out of context.

Well I don't know about the context, so you might be right... But I do know about the things you said to Starr that time when she came by your cabin and tried to convince you to drop the charges. I remember what you said to her and how you teased her about her boyfriend...

–Chief Mate: You remember? How could you remember when you weren't even there? Because it was only the two of us...

Hey, I'm everywhere! I'm the author of this story, remember?

–Chief Mate: Author? You?! You're about the most pathetic, incompetent excuse for an author I've ever seen.

Incompetent? You don't really mean that, do you?

–Chief Mate: Oh yes I do. You're the most... I mean, you can't even control your characters. You let them talk back to you and bully you whenever they want to. And if they argue with you a little bit, you just cave in and change your story. So what type of author does that make you?

I don't know. Maybe an open-minded one?

–Chief Mate: Open-minded? Don't you really mean that you're a pussy?

Now I think that's a bit strong...

–Chief Mate: Do you see that? You see what I mean? You're nothing. You're letting me push you around right now. And if I were to tell you not to talk about something, then you'd just…

–Starr: Hey, what are you doing? Are you trying to stop him from talking about that day in your cabin?

–Chief Mate: Who, me…?

–Starr: Yeah! Because I was there and I remember everything. I remember exactly what you said and how you tried to humiliate me.

–Chief Mate: Me?! It wasn't me that humiliated you. You did that to yourself! You did it when you came to me wearing that tight little top with your nipples sticking right out and everything. You came in there wearing that and you said, "Isn't there anything I can do to convince you?" I mean…

–Starr: So you think that's why I went to see you? You think I went there to have sex with you? You think I went there to buy you off?

–Chief Mate: Well, I think that's pretty obvious…

–Starr: Oh, you…! You're disgusting! You're the most filthy… Why the very thought of you touching me after that… Yuck! It makes my skin crawl just to think about it.

–Chief Mate: Well you weren't acting so picky that day, not with the way you…

–Starr: I wasn't there to have sex. I was there… I just wanted to reason with you, that's all. I wanted to convince you.

–Chief Mate: Right, to reason with me. Like with that, "Isn't there anything I can do?" and looking at me that way and giving me the come-on.

–Starr: I never said that! Or at least I never said it the way you're saying it.

–Chief Mate: No, you just said it like…

–Starr: I said it like… Like it wasn't worth destroying John's life just to win your stupid little fight, and like… Like there had to be some other way, some way where you

could... where you could forgive him.
—Chief Mate: Like by having sex with you, right?
—Starr: Oh, you're so disgusting! I just... I can't even talk to you!
—Chief Mate: Okay then, don't talk! See if I care.
So does that mean that the two of you are...?
—Chief Mate: What, you again?! Are you trying to butt in?
Butt in? I don't know if I'd call it that since I am the author. So I don't think you can call it butting in...
—Chief Mate: No?... Well, I suppose you're right... So okay, go ahead, Mr. Author. Go ahead and tell your story.
Well thank you for that. And I'll just... I suppose I'll, uh... I'll skip that part about the visit to your room since the two of you seem to have covered it pretty well, and I'll, uh... I'll try to wind this thing up. I'll...
—Starr: You know, I'da done anything for him, and I mean anything.
You'd have... What's that you're saying?
—Starr: I'da done anything for John. I'da done anything to save him, cause I loved him that much.
So you're admitting that you... That you went there...
—Starr: I was crazy for him. I was crazy in love, and... You know, he was the most amazing man! So big and strong and all man, and so sure of himself. He was... I mean, he was like the picture of what a real man should be, you know. And it's like he always knew exactly who he was and what he was. And me...? I was awful young back then, and I... You know... I thought he was just about perfect.
And you say you would have...
—Starr: I'da done anything to save him. And even now, I just wish that I could somehow go back and turn him into the man he used to be. That I could... You know, that I could stop him from becoming what he is now.

Yes, I know what you mean, because ever since he lost his seaman's papers, he's turned into such a complete bum and a loser.

—Starr: Oh, please...

He's never held a job for more than a month or two, and he's bounced around working at one lowdown, low-class bar after another, drinking as much booze as he pours. And he goes home drunk every night, too drunk to remember the night before most of the time.

—Starr: Do you have to...?

And it's like ever since he lost his papers and he's no longer a seaman, he's not even a man anymore. He's become a...

—Bosun: Well who the fuck are you to talk?!

—Starr: Please, that's enough! Can't you just let it drop and talk about something else?

Something else? Yes, you're right. I should move on.

\* \* \* \* \*

So let's see... The *Alma Lykes* finally reached Norfolk more than four months after the voyage had first begun. And it was in Norfolk that all the cargo she was carrying was to be discharged, all the rubber and the lumber and even the containers which would be transshipped from there to their final ports of destination. And then once the cargo was gone, she would be heading back to the Gulf of Mexico to begin loading up for yet another voyage.

Now when a ship completes a voyage as long as the one the *Alma* had just made, there is always a major turnover among the crew once she reaches the States, and this voyage proved to be no exception to that rule. The Captain and the Chief Mate were both scheduled to get off as soon as the ship reached the Gulf, and of course the Bosun got off even sooner, being taken off in handcuffs by the police in Norfolk and locked up in the local jail. And then there was one other person who had to get off in Norfolk whether he wanted to or not, that person being Wayne who was informed a few days before arrival that he was fired. It seems that the Chief Mate had taken a disliking to him right from the beginning, and he had said more than once that he thought Wayne was some type of radical. And it was for that reason that he had kept a record of every time Wayne had slacked off on his work after partying too hard in port, with that record now serving as his justification for the firing. And while Wayne knew that the real reason behind it was the fact that he was a young black man with a goatee and an independent attitude, still the Mate's case against him looked pretty strong on paper. Because he really had slacked off in port, he and at least half the rest of the crew.

And as far as Jamey is concerned, he went out to celebrate their arrival that first night the ship was in Norfolk, he and many of the others. He went out to celebrate his first night back in the States and also his last night as a member of the crew since the next day would be his last day aboard ship. And when he went out on the town, he ended up having what you could call a typical Jamey-type evening: He got himself thrown out of one bar and he closed down another, and he finally ended up spending much of the night sleeping it off in some all-night donut shop.

Starr got off in Norfolk, too, leaving never to set foot aboard another ship. And she left much more quietly than Jamey did, practically sneaking ashore without a single goodbye. And of all the crewmembers who have been mentioned in this story, only Carter stayed on to make the next voyage, a voyage in which the ship would hit a couple of discharge ports in Asia or Africa followed by another "jungle run" on the way home. And while it might sound like that next voyage would be pretty much a repetition of the one she had just made, it actually turned out to be quite different thanks to the changes in personnel that took place between the two voyages.

–George: Hey, what about me? You didn't mention me.

Right, the Second Mate... Well his time was up by the time the ship reached Norfolk, so the union sent out another man to replace him. Goodbye and good riddance.

–George: And how about the ship? You want me to tell them what happened to the ship?

No, I'll tell them that one. You just be quiet!

–George: Ah come on, this is my last chance to say something, so I'm gonna...

She was scrapped! That's what happened. The *Alma* was scrapped a year or two later.

–George: Jeez, you're no fun.

Yes, the *Alma Lykes* was taken to India a year or two later, and there she was driven up onto a beach and cut up into scrap metal. She was cut up into razor blades as the seamen's expression goes. She was cut up after her government operating subsidy expired and she became too expensive to run, the same fate that befell all the other old Lykes ships at about that same time. They were scrapped one after the other over a very short period of time, and then once they were gone, Lykes went the way of all the other companies that had waited too long before trying to containerize. Or at least it went one of the two ways that those companies could go, because while Lykes didn't actually go all the way under, it was never able to replace anywhere near the amount of tonnage it had to scrap. And what happened was that while the company survived and continues to survive to this day, it survives only as a shadow of what the old company used to be. It survives as a small company with a very limited number of ships.

And so it is that my story ends on this sad note, with the company reduced to a shadow of itself and with the Bosun reduced to even less than a shadow. With the Bosun reduced to the wreck of a shadow if I can use that expression.

—Captain: So are you done? Is that all you have to say?

Yes, I suppose so.

—Captain: Good, because right now I have a few things that I'd like to say. I mean, I sat back and listened quietly to your slanted and prejudiced version of events, and I didn't say a word. But now that you've finished with your story, I'm finished with holding it in and I want to start setting a few things straight. I want to tell you exactly what I think.

—And what I think is that you've made a big effort in this story of yours to turn that Bosun into some kind of hero, like into a tragic hero or something... like someone out of Shakespeare. But I tell you what. There was nothing heroic about that Bosun, and whatever tragedy may have come about was strictly his own doing. And while he was a good seaman back in his day, that fast life he was living finally got to him. And it wasn't the Mate or anyone else that ruined him, either. No, it was the drinking and the drugs. Those were what did it, just like they've ruined many a better man than him. And you know, while you make it sound like everything would have turned out fine if only we hadn't busted him, the truth is that it was only a matter of time. He never could have made the transition to containerships without completely changing the way he lived, and with all the drug tests and everything we have to go through nowadays, it would only have been a matter of time before he got himself caught. Because he would have gotten caught sooner or later, there's no question about that. He never would have made it very long.

—So you see, he was far from being the hero that you tried to make him out to be. He wasn't heroic at all. And as far as that young lady is concerned, I think that the less I say about her the better, wouldn't you agree?

—Which brings me to the Chief Mate who you've gone so far out of your way to tarnish and insult. And whenever you didn't have anything bad to say about him, I heard the way you resorted to innuendo and slander, and you... The way you just did one of the biggest hatchet-jobs I've ever seen, and you did it to someone who in reality is a fine seaman and a fine human-being.

—Because the truth is that John was one of the best Chief Mates I ever sailed with. He was so good and so conscientious, and he was such a fast learner that it hardly seemed like he was working on his first break-bulk ship ever. And on top of that, he's a good man, a truly good man, one that I'm proud to call a friend. As you may know, he's been sailing as Captain on containerships for quite a few years now, and he's very well thought of in the industry. So he's been a great success at his job, and now recently I understand that he got married to a wonderful woman. So I just hope that it all works out for him this time around.

—And the one last thing I'd like to say is this: Good luck, John. God-speed and a fair wind and following seas.

# MORE LESSONS

## ON TYPHOON AVOIDANCE

More than one of us had been hinting that maybe it wasn't such a good idea to race and try to beat that typhoon, but the Captain showed no interest whatsoever in our opinions. He was sure we could make it if we just held on and shot up the east coast of Japan, so damn it that was what we were going to do. He had no time for doubts and no time for doubters like us.

But our doubts were serious, believe me, because while we might be able to make it across just in front of the storm if we were able to maintain our speed all the way, we could also find ourselves in very serious trouble if we were to lose speed because of strong headwinds and heavy swells. In fact, we could find ourselves being slowed down to the point where we ended up getting caught right in the middle of the damned thing. And since headwinds and head-swells seemed highly likely given the angle we had on the typhoon, we saw no reason at all for not playing it safe and going around to the west of Japan before cutting through the islands at Hakodate where we would be north of the storm.

It wasn't our decision to make, though, and so when the moment of truth arrived, we were on our way toward the east coast of Japan. I happened to be on watch as we passed through the small islands just off the southernmost tip of the main islands and finally cleared Tanega Shima, the last of those small islands and the last protection we would have all the way up the coast since from there on out, it would be nothing but open water.

Things looked fine as we left the lee of the island. The weather was calm and clear with no sign of the typhoon. And while it was still hundreds of miles away, I knew that we also had hundreds of miles to go before we would be safely out of its path. It was too late to worry about that now, though, as we had already committed ourselves and the only thing left to do was to hold our course and hope for the best. Hope that the Captain was right after all.

And he was right for the first half hour or so after we left the lee of the island, up until the moment when we met the first sign of the distant typhoon. Until we met a big, long, rolling swell that hit us on the starboard bow and made us bounce and pitch and slam just hard enough to raise a little spray on the bow. That swell was a bad sign, I told myself, and the Captain who happened to be standing on the bridge with me at the time must have been thinking the exact same thing. Because no sooner had the spray subsided than he told me to bring the ship about, told me to turn around and head for the west coast of Japan.

## ON THE DANGERS OF THE SEA

I knew better than to have done what I'd done, and this knowledge was far more painful to me than the physical injuries I'd just sustained. This knowledge that I'd done something so stupid and that now I was paying the price of my stupidity. This knowledge that what I'd gotten was exactly what I deserved. And it wasn't like I hadn't seen it coming, either. No, far from it. Because no sooner had I stepped out onto the deck to check lashings and read reefers that morning and seen how those big seas were building and building and threatening to come crashing over the deck at any moment than I'd said to myself, "That's death right there. Those seas are death."

But in the end, I'd ignored my own warning to myself and gone about my business as usual with my only concession to the looming danger being to stay on the lee side of the ship, the side where the danger wasn't quite as great. And I'd gotten away with it, too, or at least I had up until the very end. Because it wasn't until then, when I was on my way back toward the house, that I'd made my big mistake. It wasn't until then that, remembering how the Bosun had told me about a damaged container over on the windward side, I'd made my foolish move and gone over to check on that container.

Upon arriving there, I'd found that the maindeck was still dry on that side. That in spite of the huge seas that churned and broke just beyond the rail, not a single one of them had come washing over the deck yet. And so somehow forgetting all about the imminent peril, I'd gone down and stood on the maindeck, even daring to turn my back upon the ever-more-threatening seas as I'd stood looking up at the bottom of the container in question. And it had been while I was standing there in total oblivion, my back to the danger, that I'd suddenly heard it coming right at me. I'd heard the giant breaker as it came crashing its way over the deck, heading straight for me.

I'd turned and seen it and I'd immediately started to run, but no sooner had I taken a first step or two than it had caught up to me, and the next thing I'd known I'd been bodysurfing. I'd been completely submerged in the frigid water of the Gulf of Alaska, completely at the mercy of the unmerciful sea. But I hadn't panicked, though. I'd remained calm and thought about some old advice that someone had given me many years earlier, advice to spread out my arms and legs and thereby make it harder for the sea to carry me all the way out through the railing to what would have been my certain death. And I'd done so in spite of the fact that rather than being carried toward the railing at the time, the sea had actually been in the process of carrying me inboard, in the direction of the containers and hatch-coamings. It had been washing me and carrying me inboard until finally I'd gone smashing head-first into some steel gratings. And no sooner had I hit those gratings than I'd grabbed on and held on, held for dear life as the monster wave had continued to throw the rest of my body around at will.

The water had soon subsided, and I'd raised my head and yelled, "Help!" but my cry had sounded so feeble and so ridiculous way out there on that deserted deck, far out of earshot of anyone. So no sooner had my shout died away than I'd gone ahead and done what I had to do to get myself out of there before another wave could come over and hit me. I'd stood up in spite of the awful pain that gripped my back, and I'd made my way over to the lee side and from there back to the house.

And now finally here I was, all showered and changed and on my way to lunch. Blood still oozed slightly from the gouges in my head and sharp pains shot through my aching back as I tried to move around. But even more painful to me was the knowledge I carried around of just how badly I'd blown it, the knowledge of how I'd gone out and gotten myself injured when there was absolutely no reason for it. The knowledge of how I'd just brought this job of mine to an end. Because they'd be putting me ashore when we stopped in Dutch Harbor which meant that all my plans for the next few months would be sailing away with the ship. It meant that I wouldn't be doing any of the things I'd been hoping to do after completing this voyage and instead I'd have to dedicate the coming weeks and months to the treatment of my injuries after which I'd have to start looking for another ship.

I reached the galley and ordered hot dogs and then shuffled over and sat down at my place in the saloon. And as I sat there alone and looked at those over-cooked dogs on their stale buns, those dogs that had to be the scrawniest, most shriveled-up little wieners I'd ever seen, I was struck all at once by the profound appropriateness of this repast. I was struck by the tremendous symbolism of this meal, by the way those dried-out, wrinkled-up little wieners seemed to symbolize everything that I'd made of my life up to that moment. By the way they seemed the very embodiment of my present mood, of my overwhelming sense of failure, my sense of total and utter defeat.

## ON CARGO, BALLAST AND LIST

It must have seemed like a good plan on paper that the Singapore office came up with, the plan to load all our cargo for Hong Kong in blocks of containers on the starboard side of the ship where the cranes would have a shorter distance to move them during discharge given that we'd be tying up starboard-side-to. And to make the plan even better, they had spaced those blocks of containers out at three different hatches where they could be discharged by three cranes working at the same time.

Yes, it certainly sounded like a good plan, and it might even have worked if only it hadn't been for one or two basic laws of physics. Like for instance the law that says that if you take all the weight off one side of a ship while leaving the other side untouched, the ship will develop a list. Perhaps even a severe list. And if you do it with three cranes at once...

Well, we arrived in Hong Kong and began to discharge cargo and right away the ship went over to port. One, two, three degrees, and the Mate on watch called the duty Engineer to tell him to pump ballast over to starboard, though what exactly happened next is hard to say since I've heard conflicting reports. Some people claim that the Engineer went down and pumped the ballast just as he'd been told while others claim that he didn't. And then there are still others who claim that what he actually did was to pump the ballast in the wrong direction, to pump it over to port and thereby make the situation worse. Now I don't know which of those stories is true, but I do know that once he was done with the ballast, he didn't bother reporting back to the Mate for further instructions and instead he seemed to disappear from the face of the earth.

Meanwhile, the list kept getting worse. Seven, eight, nine degrees, and the Mate on watch searched frantically for the Engineer. Things were getting critical and we had to do something right away. Twelve, thirteen, fourteen degrees, and small systems around the ship began to fail. The lights flickered and water began to drip out of the overhead onto the maindeck passageway. The Mate finally found the Engineer but it was only to be told that by now it was too late, that due to some design flaw in the ballast system, the pump wouldn't work with the ship healed over this far. That we were helpless and there was nothing we could do to bring ourselves back.

Eighteen, nineteen degrees, and the Mate ran out on deck to tell the longshoremen to stop taking boxes off the starboard side and start putting some weight back on. He found their boss and told him that from here on out, they would have to put a box back on for every one they took off. He told him that it was the only way to prevent the list from getting even worse.

Afterwards, I mentioned to the Mate that maybe we should send a message to those cargo people in Singapore. Maybe we should explain to them about how ships lean over when you put all the weight on one side. It was something they would have to learn about sooner or later.

## ON THE ROMANCE OF THE SEA

We were coming down from Dutch Harbor with a big load of reefers—refrigerated containers—which I was in the process of checking that morning. And while it's never very pleasant in the Gulf of Alaska in the winter, the conditions seemed even worse than usual on this particular day. It was cold though not exceptionally so, but there was a brutal north wind blowing across the decks. A wind that blew at just the right angle to whip through the gaps between the rows of containers and turn those gaps into authentic wind-tunnels.

And of course those gaps between rows where the icy wind was howling were the very places I had to be in order to read the temperatures on the reefers and write them down in my book. The wind in those gaps was so powerful that I had to constantly lean over and brace myself against it, and at the same time it was so cold that my face and cheeks turned to ice. The wind seemed to go right through my pants and it frequently blew up inside my coat. And each time I took off my glove to write down a series of numbers, my fingers would immediately go numb. They would turn so cold and stiff that I could barely write with them, and putting the glove back on between jottings seemed to do nothing at all to warm the fingers back up.

I reached the end of one of the rows and there I found the Cadet who was supposed to be accompanying me on my rounds but who instead had huddled up in a spot that provided some slight shelter from the wind. And as I saw him standing there, every bit as cold and miserable as I was myself, I just had to say it to him, "You know, this is the worst job in the world."

# FWE

The world ends in the Pacific Ocean. It's there that it ends, and there it begins again. It's out into that huge expanse of water that old days go to die, and it's there that the new days are born. It's out into that greatest of all oceans that everything old goes to atrophy and to fall only to rise again and return as the new. And curiously enough, when you travel around the Pacific Ocean, you have to go west in order to reach the Far East while to reach the Far West, you go east. Because it's that great watery barrier that separates the extremes of East and West, dividing the earth in a way that nothing else ever could. No smaller ocean and no continent let alone some arbitrarily drawn line. It's the Pacific that marks the true boundaries of the world. It's that ocean which delineates the earth and shapes it. And as fate would have it, it's upon that very ocean that the gallant vessel at the heart of the story I'm about to tell lives and works and plies her trade.

Hey, what do you think about that for an opening paragraph? Pretty dramatic, I'd say. So I think I'll keep it even though it has almost nothing to do with what's going to come later in this story of mine. Because the story I'm setting out to tell you won't be some great epic of the sea filled with drama and suspense and life-altering experiences. No, it's going to be a lot less than that. It's going to be a *true* story of the sea, the story of a real voyage on a real ship. It's going to be the story of this particular voyage on this particular ship. This voyage upon which I've just embarked. And while I can't tell you how it's going to end since the events I'll be relating haven't even happened as yet, I feel pretty safe in predicting that it won't be another *Moby Dick*.

Because how could it be? How could it turn into anything dramatic or meaningful when it's going to be set in one of the most boring places on the face of the earth: a containership? A ship where every trip is just like the last one. A ship where nothing ever happens and where you can set your watch by the arrivals and departures at the various ports. The ports that are exactly the same from one trip to another to another. And in fact, it's gotten to be so bad that the joking old description of life at sea has become almost literally true when it comes to the life aboard these ships. I'm talking about that old joke where they say that life at sea is just like prison but with a chance of drowning. Because that's exactly what it's like nowadays working on these containerships.

But in spite of that, I'm still determined to write this story. I'm determined to put out the effort and finally write the sea story that I've always been meaning to write but the one that I've never quite gotten around to before. The story that I've always put off writing for one reason or another. Like with the way that back at the beginning, I was too young and too full of living to bother about writing, or like later on how I was too lazy or too... something. And like even later when I still couldn't bring myself to do it in spite of the fact that I saw how time was running out on me. Because I just couldn't make myself write about something that seemed so deadly boring to me. So lifeless.

Like for instance, what could I have written about the ships on the Alaska trade on which I've worked from time to time over recent years? The weather? The bad weather and more bad weather and still more bad weather and every once in awhile a little good weather? That's not the type of material it takes to write a great sea story or even a mediocre one. And it's not even fit for a story as weak as this one, this boring little tale that I'm setting out to tell you right now. But while the story is bound to be dull, what other choice do I have left to me now that I'm at such a very late stage in my career? Now that I'm at the beginning of what will be my last voyage ever. The last voyage I make before I retire. And since this is the last sea story I'll ever be living out, it's also the last one I'll ever have a chance to write about. It's my very last chance to say something to the world. To tell it about myself and the life I've lived. My last chance to leave something behind, some mark on the world, some record that I was here and that I mattered and that... Well, it's my last chance, okay?

This old ship I came aboard yesterday is called the *Horizon Pioneer*, or more correctly her name is the *S.S. Horizon Pioneer* with the S.S. standing for steamship since she's an old-fashioned steam-turbine job. But her name hasn't always been *Horizon Pioneer*. No, she used to be known as the *CSX Pioneer* back in the days before CSX sold her off to the Carlyle Group which changed the names of both ships and company. Even before that, though, she was known as the *SeaLand Pioneer*, a name which had to be changed when CSX got tired of milking the old SeaLand company for all it was worth, taking out all the profits and using them to subsidize their other operations while putting nothing back into the ships, and finally decided to make a real killing by destroying SeaLand altogether. By breaking it up and selling off the parts. Breaking up the classic old company that started the entire containerization revolution in the first place. And what CSX did in the process was they sold the SeaLand name along with the ships engaged in foreign trade to the Danish giant Maersk, which meant that the ships they chose not to sell at that time—the cash-cows, the Jones Act ships, the American-built ships engaged in domestic trades to Alaska, Hawaii and Puerto Rico—had to be renamed. And when CSX chose a name for that pitiful remnant of the old SeaLand giant, they chose CSX Lines, a name which later became Horizon Lines under the Carlyle Group.

But what I've told you so far doesn't take us all the way back to the beginning of the name changes for this old ship since even before she belonged to SeaLand, she was known as the *American Contender*. That was her name when she was owned and operated by United States Lines, the biggest of all the American carriers. And she went by that name until U. S. Lines went bankrupt in the mid-Eighties and the company's assets were sold off, with this particular ship going to SeaLand. But even that wasn't the first name this ship ever had since going back further still, back to the days before she was owned by U. S. Lines, she belonged to Farrell Lines which called her the *Austral Contender*. Because it was Farrell Lines which originally had her built in the Seventies for the Australia trade. Had her built back in the days when Farrell was still a big company engaged in multiple trades, before it pulled out of the Australia trade along with nearly every other trade in which it operated. Before Farrell cut back and sold off most of its ships to U. S. Lines or whoever else would have them.

She was built in the Seventies as I just said, and her design is that of a classic early containership. One built at a time when they still made containerships that actually looked like ships. Before they started building those godawful things they call ships nowadays. Those gigantic boxes with a point at one end and a second big box of a house sitting up on top of it somewhere. And that's not to mention all the boxes filled with cargo that occupy the rest of the space on deck. No, this old ship doesn't look like that at all. She looks like a real ship. She looks the way a ship is supposed to look. She has curves. She has lines. And you know, if a guy was ever in a truly generous mood, like say he had a few drinks in him or something, he might even be tempted to say that the old ship is good-looking. The old *Horizon Pioneer*. He might be tempted to say that she's pretty—in a containership sort of way.

The *Pioneer* has spent time on several different runs over the years, something that goes hand-in-hand with all the different companies that have owned her. But now for quite a few years, she's been on what could be called the mid-Pacific run, one where she stops at a couple of ports in the mid-Pacific—Honolulu and Guam—on her way to the Far East before turning around and coming back to the U.S. west coast to begin another voyage. And her first port on the west coast, the port where she begins and ends all her voyages, is Tacoma, Washington, which happens to be the place where I came aboard the old girl yesterday as Third Mate.

Yes, that's right. You heard what I said. I came aboard as Third Mate which is the exact same position I held on my first ship after graduating from the Academy all those years ago. The same job on my last ship as I held on my first one which is somehow fitting in a lifetime-of-failure sort of way, though that's not the reason why I took this particular job. No, the reason I took it was because it was the only thing available at the time. And since I really need the sea-time—I need to put in at least thirty days aboard ship—this job is just about perfect for me with the way the voyages last thirty-five days each. So I took the job and came aboard, and now what I'll do is I'll make one trip and then quit when we get back to Tacoma. Because as soon as I get in my thirty days… Though you know what? I could actually quit even before that. I could quit the minute my thirty days are up, though I doubt that I'll do so since we'll still be out in the middle of the North Pacific at the time and it's a hell of a long swim back home from there, not to mention the fact that the water is awful damned cold.

Just a joke, folks. So anyway, I'm on here until we get back to Tacoma which may seem to be a long way off right now when we're still at the very beginning of the trip. When we've only come as far as the coast of Oregon on our way to Oakland, the last stop we'll be making on the coast before we turn and head toward Honolulu. But I've spent a lot of time riding on ships by now, and I know that thirty-five days really isn't very long at all. No, it's just five weeks and that's it. Five weeks of wasted time and loneliness and boredom. Though you know what? At this point, I only have thirty-four days left. Thirty-four days and then that's it. I pull the plug. Forever!

Because this is what you could call my FWE trip, my Finished With Engines trip. It's the trip that marks the end of my career—my less-than-glorious career—in the same way that our ringing up FWE on the telegraph marks the end of a passage. The way that when we ring it up after the ship is tied up at the dock, it tells the Engineers that the passage is over and it's time for them to shut things down. Because every passage ends with an FWE command on the telegraph. And in the same way, every career ends with a final voyage. An FWE voyage. And you know what? Now that I think about it, maybe that's what I'll call this story of mine. Maybe I'll name it after that engine command: *FWE* which seems like a pretty good title right now. So that's what it'll be for the time being at least. Until I can come up with something better.

And looking at the clock now, I see that it's time for me to sign off for the day since I go on watch soon. So I'll write again later when I have another chance, okay?

* * * * *

Well here I am again. We're tied up in Oakland now after an uneventful passage south. Uneventful like always. And the only good thing I can say about it is that we had unusually good weather for this time of year, something that I hope is a sign of things to come. We rode very well on the Tacoma-to-Oakland leg which is often the worst leg of the entire voyage given the fact that we never carry much cargo on that leg, and given that half-empty containerships tend to roll like hell. Because with almost all the cargo from the Far East getting discharged in Tacoma and with the majority of the westbound cargo not being loaded until Oakland, we always have to make the run down the coast with a very light load. But we got lucky this time around. We had good weather all the way.

And now here we are in Oakland. And here I am sitting around in my room. Alone. We have Night Mates to stand the cargo watches for us here so I don't have to work tonight. I have the whole night off and I could go ashore if I wanted to, though since I have absolutely no desire to go anywhere around here... I mean, who the hell wants to go out in these places? Oakland or San Francisco? What is there for me to do? Because I can't go drinking anymore, not with the medications I'm taking. And the idea of going out and sitting around all by myself in some restaurant or going to a movie or something like that. The idea of hanging around like some Lonely Guy, that's far too depressing for me. It's something I refuse to do. And if I'm going to be alone anyway, I'd rather be locked up here in my room. I'd rather be alone in private and not out in public, all alone while surrounded by people. Alienated and isolated within the crowd. Because that type of loneliness isn't for me. It's too sad. It's too pathetic.

So instead I'm going to sit here. Just me and this piece of paper and this story I have to tell. This story of my last voyage and maybe even my last

No, I shouldn't say that and I shouldn't even think it since these aren't going to be my last days on earth no matter what that doctor may have had to say. Because I'm not dying! I'm not!! I'm sick yes, I'll admit that. Very sick. But dying? That's just one person's opinion. That's just what that doctor thinks. But he's wrong! I know he is. And I'm going to prove it, too. I'm

Oops, will you look at that? Will you look at what I just did? I went and talked about this sickness of mine which is something that I was hoping to avoid. Something I was hoping to be able to talk my way around in this story I'm writing. But I can see right now that it's not going to be possible to do that. I'm not going to be able to hide this thing that in so many ways is the true story behind the story. So instead, I'm afraid that what I'll have to do is I'll have to come clean. I'll have to tell you all about it. For the sake of the story and for posterity and whatever else. For the sake of turning this last testament of mine into something worthwhile. Something to remember.

So here goes, okay? I have cancer and that's the plain and simple truth. And it's a bad case, too, from what the doctor says. It's what he calls an aggressive cancer. And he says that... Well it doesn't really matter what else he says, does it? Because cancer is cancer. And as soon as I heard that word, I was floored. I was totally floored. I was... I don't know what expression I could use that would come anywhere near to conveying the shock that ran through my body when I heard him say that word. The Big C. And ever since then, everything has changed for me. My attitude, my outlook, my whole life. And I've even made an effort to stop just going along through life the way I always have, fat, dumb and happy, never bothering about plans for the future. Or at least nothing beyond my next ship since as far as I was concerned, I was going to live to be a hundred. But then when this thing came along, it was like, Wow! I might be mortal after all. I might be one of those guys who die, and I might even be one who dies soon. I might not have all the time in the world after all. All the time I could ever want. Because I might die young in spite of the fact that I'm already too old to do that.

And one of the first things it changed for me was my plans for retirement since I hadn't been planning on retiring for a few more years yet. But when I found out about the cancer, I went right down to the union hall and applied for my pension at the first opportunity. When I got to the hall, though, it was only to be told that for some reason or other, I wouldn't be able to start drawing it for a few more months. And to make matters worse, they told me that since it had been quite awhile since I'd shipped out, my medical benefits were going to run out on me before my pension kicked in if I didn't go out and get another ship in the very near future. They told me that I'd have a gap of a couple of months in my coverage where I'd have to foot all the medical bills myself—bills big enough to break me thanks to this goddamned cancer—and that the only way for me to avoid that gap would be to spend another thirty days aboard ship. Which of course is the deep, dark secret behind my coming aboard this ship. And it's also the secret behind my plans to quit after one trip instead of staying the four months I'm entitled to. My plans to quit as soon as I get in thirty days. Because that's the real story here. That's what this trip is all about.

So I had to get myself a ship. And do you know what

the hardest part about getting this ship was? It wasn't the part about taking the job down at the union hall. No, I'm an A-Book so there was no problem with that. The problem was getting it at a time when my symptoms were far enough in remission to where I'd be able to get a doctor to give me a Fit for Duty slip. Because not only do I have an active case of cancer, but I also look like I have it. I look like hell. I look like a walking dead man, and I can see that every time I look at myself in the mirror. And man, you should have seen the look on the Chief Mate's face when I came aboard and handed him that Fit for Duty slip. The way he looked me over, and he looked at the slip, and he turned it over in his hands like he was making sure it was real. Like he couldn't believe that anyone who looks as bad as me could possibly be fit for duty.

But you know what? Fuck him! Because I got the slip and it's real, and now I'm here and I'm gonna stay! I'm gonna do my thirty days aboard this ship and there's no way he's gonna stop me. I'm here and I'm staying.

And for all anyone knows, I might not even die from this stuff. Because even though I look like hell, that doesn't mean that I'm going there in the near future—just joking about that where-I-go-after-I-die stuff. But seriously, you can't believe everything a doctor tells you, and I really don't believe what that doctor of mine said. I don't believe it deep inside. I don't accept it. I can't accept it! Because he's got to be exaggerating. He can't be right. Not about me. Not in these days when they have so many treatments for cancer and when so many people beat it and bounce right back. People like me! Because I refuse to accept this cancer as a death sentence. I refuse to! I refuse to accept it as anything more than an inconvenience, something that I've got to work my way past. Something that I've got to overcome. Because I can beat it! I know I can. And I'm

going to beat it, too! I've got to!!
So take that, Doc.

* * * * *

Man, I can't believe those clowns in Oakland. Those clowns they call line-handlers. And I don't know where they get those guys from either, since the longshoremen around there are okay. But the line-handlers in Oakland have to be some of the stupidest people on the face of the earth. They're guys whose level of intelligence ranges anywhere from idiots to complete morons. And as luck would have it, we got a couple of the morons this time around when we were trying to undock the ship. And the worst thing about dealing with them is that you can't tell them anything when you see them screwing up, because if you do that it just makes them worse. It makes them mad. And when they get mad, they turn stubborn in their stupidity. They insist all the harder on doing things wrong.

So here's what happened yesterday afternoon when we were undocking, though maybe before I start I should explain a little bit about the situation. I should tell you that because of the long spaces between bollards on that dock and because of where they'd spotted the ship, we'd had to put all our sternlines onto the same bollard when we were tying up. And then on top of that, since the tug that came to assist us wanted to put its line up through the center-line chock on the stern, that meant that we had to take in our offshore sternline before we could take it. Because with the way this old ship is laid-out, we don't have any place to put the tug's line when that offshore line is tied up. And being that there were two wires on that bollard sitting on top of the offshore sternline—the line-handlers in Oakland have no clue how to dip a line—we had to take in both those wires first. The two wires and then the offshore sternline leaving only the one line at the bottom of the stack, the inshore sternline, to hold the ship alongside the dock while we made the tug fast.

Well, when we slacked off the top wire, there were three ways those line-handlers could have led the tag-line over to their truck. The tag-line being the small line they use to pull the big line over to the dock when tying up and also the one they can use to pull the weight off the line when they're casting it off, which is what they were trying to do with their truck at the time. There were three ways they could have led that tag-line around the horns of the bollard: there were the right way, the wrong way, and the stupid way. And as you would expect with those clowns, the first way they tried was the wrong way, after which they tried the stupid way. And then when neither of those ways worked, rather than doing the smart thing and trying the right way, they decided instead to wrap the tag-line around underneath something-or-other and then pull on it the wrong way again. After which they wrapped it around somewhere else and pulled again, and they kept doing the same thing over and over again. And so by the time they finally got around to leading the tag-line around the bollard in the right way, they had it so tangled up with all the other lines that the situation had become completely hopeless.

And the only solution they could come up with was for us to slack off more lines, the other wire and the offshore sternline, which we soon did though even that proved to be insufficient given the mess that they had created. So the next thing I knew, they were asking me to slack off the inshore sternline, too, the only line that was still holding the ship alongside the dock. I tried to talk them out of it, but it soon became apparent that if I didn't do as they requested, there was no way they were ever going to get those other lines off the bollard. So I finally did it. I slacked it off. Or at least I slacked it temporarily since it took only seconds for the line to come up tight again as our stern went swinging away from the dock. And it was only after the pilot had called the tug and told him to save the situation by going around and pushing our stern back alongside that those clowns were ever able to throw the lines off. Slowly and painfully. Able to finish the half-hour fiasco that they had created out of what should have been a simple five-minute job.

And speaking of clowns, you should see the new watch-partner of mine who came aboard in Oakland. The guy who's going to be standing watches with me for the next month. Because this guy is one of the biggest losers I've ever seen out here which is saying a lot when you consider how long I've been going to sea and how many losers I've sailed with over the years. But this guy just about takes the cake. He looks like some old wino who came here straight off skid-row, and he smells like it, too. And stupid! Man, I can't even believe how stupid the guy is. And he's not one of those quietly stupid types either. No, he's one of those types who announce their stupidity to the entire world.

Like when we were standing our first watch together last night, we'd only been on the bridge for a few minutes and we hadn't so much as said hello to each other when suddenly he opened up and started talking this whole line of nonsense to me. He started out by saying something about reincarnation and the Tibetan Book of the Dead, I think it was, though he didn't stay with that subject for long. Or at least I don't think he did since it was hard for me to tell what he was talking about given the way he wandered all over the place and mixed in so many other ideas. The way he mixed in everything from Jesus and Allah and ancient Jewish ideas about Heaven and Hell to Pluto and Siva and I don't know who else. And it was all so strange and so illogical that it probably would have been impossible for me to follow him even if I'd bothered to try, which of course I didn't. Because I had no desire to follow the line of bullshit that he was dishing out to me.

And then this morning, the same thing happened all over again while we were standing our second watch together. Because no sooner had he gotten there than he started right back in where he'd left off the night before. He started in on all that life-after-death nonsense and all that mixing-and-matching of ideas. And as it turned out, he was an even bigger pain-in-the-ass to have around in the daytime since I couldn't get away from him by simply disappearing into the chart-room for short periods of time the way I had at night. Because with the curtains being open during the day, there was no escape for me. There was nowhere I could go to get away from him. And it finally got to be so bad that I had to order him to go to work out on the wing of the bridge. I told him to go out there even though the weather wasn't good enough for him to accomplish very much. But I just couldn't take it anymore, and I had to get rid of him for a little while. I had to get a few minutes of peace and quiet. And you know, that solution worked so well that I think I'm going to keep using it whenever I can't take his presence any longer. Though I don't know what I'll be able to do on the weekends when he doesn't have to work on watch. Because those days are going to be awfully hard to take. They're going to be hell.

And in fact, I think this entire trip could turn into a hell-trip if he doesn't learn to shut up and leave me alone. I mean, a whole month of that guy? Eight hours a day locked up on that bridge together with nowhere to run and nowhere to hide? Nowhere for me to get away from him? I don't know if I can stand that. I don't know if I can keep my sanity intact throughout an ordeal like that. I just don't know. And the only thing I can say is that I hope he goes out drinking in Honolulu and gets himself fired. I hope he screws up so that I won't have to put up with him and his never-ending line of bullshit for the rest of the trip—the rest of my career.

*     *     *     *     *

Hello, this is just to let you know that I probably won't be writing very much over the next few days since this is the part of the trip where I have to perform my duties as Third Mate. It's the time when I have to go around the ship and inspect all the safety equipment. Check the equipment in the lifeboats and in the emergency gear lockers and check the condition of the fire-stations and the life-rings and all that type of stuff. So with me working all that overtime during the next few days, I won't have much time for writing.

One thing I should mention before I go out and get to work, though, is that I've found out a little more about that idiot watch-partner of mine. I've found it out whether I wanted to or not. And as it turns out, I was absolutely right about his provenance. It turns out that George really did come onto this ship straight from skid-row as he told me himself. Oh, and his name is George... No, I'm not going to write that last name of his since it's a long one with a very strange spelling. A spelling almost as strange as George himself. And besides, I already have to write it in the logbook every day, twice a day, once for each time we stand a watch together. So being forced to write that stupid last name of his so often, I don't think I'll do it now when I have a choice in the matter. And instead I'll just call him George.

So as I was saying, George came here straight from skid-row, and when he came aboard, he had a grand total of $1.43 to his name, as he told me himself. And he told me in the most open and matter-of-fact way that you can possibly imagine. He told me in a tone that revealed no sense of shame on his part whatsoever. No shame and no sense of bragging either. And instead, he told me about it like it was the most natural thing in the world. He told me in a flat, calm voice, and as he spoke he had the same stupid look on his face that's always there. The same vacant look in the eyes and the same dumb grin.

And before I go, I should also mention that I talked to Bong a little while back, Bong being the AB who was on gangway watch when George came aboard. And do you know what he had to say? He said that George's entire luggage for the voyage consisted of a single paper grocery bag. Just one. And from what Bong could tell, it didn't even look like the bag was full. Can you believe that? Here the guy is coming aboard a ship to live and work for the next several months, and all he brings with him is one half-full paper sack. That's too much. That's a real, true loser for you.

\*     \*     \*     \*     \*

We just had our first Fire and Boat Drill today which means that I only have four more to go before I get off. Because I don't know if you've ever heard of this or not, but one of the most common ways that seamen use for calculating the time they have left aboard a ship is by counting the number of weekly drills they still have left. And as I just told you, we now have the first one down, so there are four Fire and

Boat Drills to go.

* * * * *

Hey, I made the greatest discovery a little while ago. I discovered my power aboard this ship. The fact that I can get away with just about anything on here if I want to. Because what happened was that the Chief Mate came up to me to give me a hard time about the way I was doing my safety inspections. I guess he'd been watching me and had seen what a half-assed job I'm doing. He'd seen the way that I really don't give a shit about the inspections since they're the last ones I'll ever do. And so he came up to ball me out and tell me to do them right. But then as soon as he started in on me, I gave him this look like, So that's how you talk to a dying man? And I really poured it on with all that so-weak-I-can-barely-stand posture and that too-sick-to-care look on my face. And do you know what? The guy actually backed down on me. He stopped criticizing my performance and then he practically apologized for having bothered me before walking away.

And I'm talking about this Chief Mate, Chris, who happens to be one of the biggest assholes on the entire ship. He's this relief Chief Mate who's trying to make a name for himself with the company by riding the guys below him. But when he tried it on me, he ended up backing down. And when I saw that, I told myself that maybe this is a good thing after all. Maybe I can milk this situation and use it to get away with whatever I want to do. To *own* this ship even. Because now that I think about it, I can see that everyone else is giving me a kind of hands-off treatment, too. They're all going easy on me and showing a little respect for a dying man or something like that.

All of them except that idiot watch-partner of mine

that is, because that guy is so stupid that I don't think he was even aware of the fact that I'm dying until I told him about it this morning. When I told him, though, do you know what his reaction was? It wasn't to say, That's too bad, or to show me some type of sympathy. No, the only thing he said was, "We're all gonna die, Mate." Just that and nothing more. The idiot!

\* \* \* \* \*

I found out today what it was that George had in that paper sack of his when he came aboard ship. And it wasn't spare clothes since he's been wearing the exact same things ever since he came aboard. The same filthy coveralls and the same greasy coat. The coat whose pockets he's always reaching into and pulling out half-eaten apples from which he takes a few bites before returning them to the same dirty pockets. No, the thing he had in that bag was a huge pile of papers, and I know that now since he brought those papers up to the bridge with him this morning. A big stack of dirty, dog-eared papers, some of them photocopies and some apparently torn from books or magazines while the majority of them appeared to be hand-written notes that he'd made from his "studies" or his "investigations" or whatever it is that he calls them. And once he got those papers to the bridge, he started shuffling through them looking for one particular page related to a subject that he'd been talking about the night before. A subject that had something to do with some outlandish interpretation of the concept of Karma, I think it was. When I saw what he was doing, though, I yelled at him to stop and to take those papers of his down below immediately. And I told him never to bring reading material with him to the bridge again.

And him? He just smiled back at me. He gave me that same stupid grin he always gives before doing as he'd been told. Going down and then returning a minute or so later to begin spouting off once again. Spouting off with four more hours of his nonsense. Four hours of his insufferable, nonstop stupidity.

\* \* \* \* \*

Well here we are in Honolulu. It's evening now and once again I have the whole night off thanks to the Night Mates who stand the cargo watches for us here. Once again I have the opportunity to spend the evening ashore. But also once again, I'm sitting here on the ship. Sitting in my room. Alone.

Because where would I go if I were to leave the ship? What would I do? I can't go out drinking anymore thanks to the medications I'm taking, and if I can't drink then what? What can I do? And it's weird when I think about it, because back in the old days I used to spend a lot of time ashore. I used to go off every chance I got. And I had a lot of chances back then, too, working on those old freighters that would sit in port for days on end. But now after having spent so many years working on containerships, it's almost like I've forgotten how to go ashore. I've forgotten what to do and how to enjoy myself. And the only thing I still remember how to do is to go out drinking. To look for some bar where I can hang out and get drunk. But since I can't do that anymore, here I am. Just me and this piece of paper. Here I am working on my masterpiece. My so-called masterpiece.

So tell me, what do you think about it so far? Pretty dull wouldn't you say? You don't have to pull your punches with me. You can come right out and tell me what you think. You can tell me that it sucks because I know it does. It sucks big-time. Or at least it's mediocre. You have to admit that. I can see it the moment I look through what I've already written. I can see the mediocrity come shining through just like I've seen it in everything else I've ever tried to write. In every word and every sentence. In every attempted masterpiece.

Because this little story isn't really the first one I've ever tried to write. I lied to you earlier when I told you that it was. I lied because... Well, because I wanted to. And because I could. But it's not my first sea story, and it's not the second or the third one either. No, it's nothing but the latest in a long series of attempts I've made over the years. The latest and the greatest. I hope. Because maybe I can still salvage this thing somehow. Or maybe I can at least finish it which in a way would make it my first story. My first completed story. The first one I didn't grow so disgusted with that I threw it away half-finished because of its mediocrity.

And I've tried writing sea stories in any number of different ways. Like early on, I tried to write some great novel of the sea. I tried to write the type of thing that Melville or Conrad or London would write if he were alive today, the same type of classic. But then each time I tried, I inevitably reached the point where I was forced to admit to myself that I'm not one of those guys I just mentioned. The point where I would look back at what I'd written and see that there was something seriously wrong with it, though for the life of me I could never figure out what that something could be. And if I couldn't figure out what was wrong then how the hell was I going to fix it? So in the end, I'd just throw the whole damned thing away. I'd throw it away and start all over again. And as I gradually lowered my standards over the years, I even stooped to writing my sea story the way some commercial hack would write it, all sex and violence and superficiality. But do you know what? Even that I couldn't pull off. Even that stuff never rose to a level above that of pure, unadulterated mediocrity. And for that reason, I could never actually finish a book. I could never write anything that seemed like it was worth keeping.

So now in this last chance of mine, this last attempt ever at a sea story, I hope that I can finally overcome that old curse of mine. The curse of mediocrity—and failure. I hope that this story I'm writing now won't turn out to be as big a failure as everything else I've ever done or attempted to do. As big a failure as everything else in my life has been. My writing, my career, my home-life. Because not only has everything I've ever written sucked, but my career has sucked, too, when you get right down to it. It's been the career of a loser, of a guy who never made Captain and never came close. A guy who tried sailing Chief Mate for awhile but soon came to realize what a shitty job he was doing and dropped back down to the lower positions once again. Like right now when I'm making my FWE trip as Third Mate rather than Captain. When I'm right back down at the bottom of the barrel. And my home-life? Oh Jesus! It's better not to talk about that at all.

Because somehow my life has turned into this giant cliché of a seaman's life. And if you were to ask me how it got to be that way, I swear to you that I couldn't say. I couldn't point to some moment when all of a sudden it became the cliché that it is today since it didn't happen that way at all. No, it all happened so very slowly. It happened in such tiny increments from day to day as to be completely unobservable. So gradually and so subtly—but so relentlessly—that even if I'd seen it coming, I still don't know that there's anything I could have done to have prevented it. Anything to have stopped myself from devolving into one of those guys that I used to joke about when I was younger, never imagining that I could someday become one myself. One of those living, breathing clichés of a seaman's life. One of those stereotypical seamen.

But look at me! Look at my life and tell me what you see besides a stereotypical seaman's life. My wife divorced me and my kids went bad, and it's all my fault, too. It's not my wife's fault. I know that now. You can't blame her for any of it, not like I always used to do. And she was never any of the things I used to call her, either. No, she was a good woman and she held on as long as she could. Longer than she should have, perhaps, as our marriage slowly but surely deteriorated over the years. And the problems between us came mainly from me, from my being gone so much and putting everything on her. All the burden. Making her raise the kids almost single-handedly and making her take care of the house, too. And then even when I was around, the only thing I did was to increase her burden further with all the bullshit I used to pull on her. All the mind-games. Until finally there came the day when she just couldn't take it anymore. The day she decided that she'd had enough. The day she left me.

And the kids? They came out bad the way so many seamen's kids do. Or bad enough anyway. They got into drugs and all that sort of stuff, and I know whose fault it is. It's my fault for never having been there for them when they were growing up. For always being gone when they needed me most. Gone either physically or emotionally.

And now thanks to this goddamned cancer of mine, it looks like I'm going to fulfill the final stereotype of the seaman's life, the final cliché. Because it looks like I'm going to die as soon as I retire, before I've drawn more than one or two pension checks. It looks like I'm going to retire and die almost simultaneously just like a typical seaman. A typical loser. A nobody, a nothing. Gone and forgotten before my body is even in the ground. Before it's gone cold. Unmourned and unmissed and

Enough for now! It's time for me to sign off. It's time to leave you on that happy note since there's nothing more I can think of to talk about right now. Not with the mood that I've gone and worked myself into. So instead I'll just say so long. See you later. Goodbye from the tropical paradise of Honolulu.

\*   \*   \*   \*   \*

As she's done a thousand times before, the *Horizon Pioneer* casts off the lines that have bound her to shore and heads resolutely out toward the open sea. She leaves behind what has been her temporary home in port and sets out toward her real home, her spiritual home. She sets out toward the wide-open spaces of a great ocean. And as she goes, she leaves without regrets and without second thoughts. She leaves with her bow pointed unswervingly in the direction of the future. Pointed West. And on this day she is on her way toward one of the loneliest places on the face of the earth. She is on her way toward the deserted waters of the Central Pacific Ocean, a place so little-frequented by mankind that she is unlikely to encounter a single vessel during the entire weeklong passage that will take her to Guam. And rather than ships or boats or other man-made devices, her only companions on this leg of the voyage will be flying fish and the occasional school of dolphins. She will be alone, all alone as she rides gently and harmoniously along with the ever-faithful Trade Winds, slicing her way through the luminescent blue waters of the seemingly endless tropical seas.

And this is the leg during which her voyage will truly

begin. The leg during which her crew will settle into the daily routine they will be following for the rest of the voyage with only slight interruptions for the stops to be made in Guam and the Far East. The routine of the long sea passage. The routine that marks and shapes a seaman's life, the one during which

Hey wait a minute, I don't think I'm ready to go into all that stuff right now. And I don't know that you'd be interested in hearing me describe it either, would you? So maybe I'll get around to telling you about that shipboard routine stuff later on, okay? Though if I don't talk about it, I'm not sure what else there is for me to say now that we're at the beginning of this long, slow passage to Guam. This passage during which we'll see nothing and do nothing, and we'll simply live out our boring little routine from day to day. Working and eating and sleeping.

The crew will take advantage of the good weather to get lots of work done on deck with even the Engineers coming out to do welding jobs and other deck repairs. Anything to get out of the engineroom which can reach truly infernal temperatures in these warm tropical waters. And with the time changes we have to make on this leg, we'll all have plenty of spare time on our hands. Because we'll be retarding the clocks most nights during this passage, turning our days into twenty-five hour ones rather than twenty-four. So we'll all have that much more time for reading or watching movies or whatever else it is that we choose to do with our free time. And with me having so much time at my disposal, I'm going to have to come up with something to talk about, aren't I? Something to flesh-out this story of mine. Something besides this boring routine of ours, that is.

So in a situation like this, I have to stop and ask myself, What would Melville do? Would he fill up page after page with b.s.? Or would he go back and rewrite some of the stuff he's already written? Yes, that could be a good thing to do though I don't know that I'm up to it right now. Not when I still don't know that this story is going to be worth the effort. And even more so when I don't know how it's going to end so that I don't know what sort of "spin" I'll have to put on it when I do my rewrite. But rewrite it will have to be. I can see that clearly. Because so far, this story isn't turning into what I'd hoped it would be. Not at all. Instead it's coming out more like a diary than anything else, and it's never been my intention to write a diary. No, my intention is to write something good. Something worth reading and remembering. And being remembered for.

And I can only hope that as I go along, the story will somehow start to measure up. That either something noteworthy will happen aboard ship or that I'll find a way to make the dull daily routine sound interesting. A way to spice it up. And my greatest fear is that I'll find myself writing the same thing day after day with only slight variations: Today was another uneventful day in this uneventful voyage. Because I couldn't stand doing that. I couldn't finish this story if that were to be the case, and I certainly couldn't rewrite it. So let's just hope that I can do better tomorrow, okay?

\* \* \* \* \*

There was a sort of funny incident that took place on the bridge last night when I was relieving Chris, the Chief Mate. And even though it was a very minor thing, still I think I'll describe it to you since we have so few incidents on here worth talking about. What happened was that when I went up to relieve him, we had a tugboat coming the other way, something that's unusual in itself since we so rarely see anyone on this leg of the voyage. Anyway, Chris pointed it out to me and told me that it had its towing lights on after which he went into some big, long spiel about the tugs and the company they work for and the types of things they tow. And as he went on and on like some self-declared expert, I took out the binoculars and looked the tug over only to see that its towing lights were definitely not on. That it was only showing its normal running-lights. I didn't say anything about it at the time, though, and instead I pointed to the radar and told Chris that I only saw one target. Only the tug and no tow. And do you know what his response was to that? It was, "Oh, I was wondering how he could be going so fast with a tow." And then after a brief pause, he added, "But I wonder why he has his towing lights on." And me? I didn't say a thing. I didn't want to argue with him about what sorts of lights were showing, so I just shrugged my shoulders and let the whole thing drop. I made no effort to correct him.

Because Chris is ex-military, you see. He's one of those guys who came to sea after having retired from the military. And being that he learned his seamanship in the Navy, I don't expect much from him. I don't expect him to have a clue about what's going on out here since these ex-military guys never learn anything about real seamanship. All they learn is a lot of Navy nonsense. So when they come aboard these ships, they have to start learning everything over again from scratch. And not only that, but they also have to learn a whole new way of functioning out here. They have to learn to function in the do-it-yourself, jack-of-all-trades world of a merchant ship. And while some of the former enlisted men can do that, some of them can overcome their military mind-set and their orders-from-above, written and signed and in triplicate mentality and become self-sufficient merchant mariners, the former officers are hopeless cases. They're guys who can never learn to function without at least twenty or thirty swabbies hanging around to do the work while they "supervise."

Like in those old stories I used to hear about how Navy officers would take sights with their sextants, the way they'd always have to have at least three or four assistants with them, one to write down the numbers and one to spot the stars for them and one with the stopwatch and who knows what else. The way they couldn't just go out there and shoot them on their own like merchant officers have always done. But instead they needed all that backup just to shoot stars, and they couldn't

Hey wait a minute! What am I talking about? Am I talking about getting a position with a sextant? Man, I must be going senile or something, because when was the last time I used my sextant anyway? Or for that matter, when was the last time I even bothered to bring it with me aboard ship instead of leaving it sitting in the closet at home? It's been a helluva long time, that's for sure. Ever since the day GPS came onto the scene and took over the world of navigation. The day when the sextant became obsolete and at the same time, all the skill and knowledge went out of the art of navigation. Because on that day, navigation stopped being a challenge to be met by highly skilled professionals and instead it became a simple matter of pushing a button on the GPS. It became modern navigation. GPS navigation. Idiot navigation!

And you know, it's exactly the same with the cargo we carry on these modern ships, the cargo you never see anymore since all you see are a bunch of boxes. And the people on these ships no longer have to know anything about preparing a hold or stowing a cargo or securing it. No, the only thing they have to know about is stacking boxes and locking them into place. All they have to know is idiot seamanship. Seamanship so simple that any idiot can do it. Even an ex-military guy.

And these days the only vestige of real seamanship left to us is when we dock or undock the ship. Or at least we have to practice it on these old ships with their old-fashioned layout for handling lines, while on the newer ships they've managed to idiotize even that. They've installed winches designed for idiots. Winches that are extremely easy to use because of the fact that they're made to do one thing and one thing only. They're made to hold a ship alongside the dock once the tugs have pushed it into position and that's it. They're not designed to be worked, so they're perfect for seamen who know nothing about working a ship into position on a line. Perfect for modern seamen who know nothing but idiot seamanship.

And I tell you, I'm constantly amazed when I come aboard a new ship to find how few of the young seamen aboard—even the good ones—know how to work a line. How many of them I have to teach that very basic skill which I still use whenever the opportunity presents itself. That skill which is so quickly becoming a lost art. Or at least it's being lost everywhere but on the Alaska run where we still use it all the time. And in fact, it would be nearly impossible to bring one of those ships alongside in Anchorage in heavy ice without someone working the forward spring-line. But other than that, these modern ships with their modern conveniences are rapidly turning even docking and undocking into another case of idiot seamanship. They're destroying that last bastion of real seamanship and simplifying it to the point where the job can be done by idiots. Or even by trained chimps. And you wouldn't need very many chimps to do the job either, as simple and undemanding as it is to tie up a modern ship.

And I guess it's for that reason that the crews on these ships have gotten smaller and smaller over the years. Because the old-style three-man watch went out years ago. It went out with booms and kingposts. And even the two-man watch disappeared a number of years back so that now there's only one seaman left on each watch. A single AB who spends the entire four hours of the watch on the bridge with the Mate. And if you happen to get a loser of a watch-partner like I did on this voyage, you're just stuck with him, that's all. You have nothing to do but put up with him, four hours on and eight hours off, day in and day out.

And I suppose that I should mention here that I'm indeed stuck with George for the rest of this trip—and the rest of my career. He didn't get drunk in Honolulu and he didn't miss the ship, and now I'll have to put up with him for the next twenty-something days. Eight hours a day of seeing him and hearing his bullshit. And I really don't know if I can take it.

But enough about him, okay? And enough writing for today since I've lost my desire to continue now that I've brought up the subject of George. Though before I go, I have to say that I miss my first watch-partner, the old Filipino guy who got off in Oakland. Because old Henry never had a lot to say. He was a guy who kept to himself. And it was such a pleasure standing watches with him. It was so calm and peaceful on the bridge coming down the coast. So completely different from what I have to put up with now. And I'm constantly asking myself why I couldn't have gotten lucky like the other Mates did. Why I couldn't have gotten Bong, the hard-working Filipino AB on the four-to-eight watch, or maybe Mo, the quiet and competent Arab guy on the twelve-to-four. Why did I have to get George? Why me? What did I do wrong?

\* \* \* \* \*

As of today, there are three Fire and Boat Drills to go.

I think it was a mistake to have mentioned George yesterday. I should have ignored him like I did the day before. Because he's been so relatively quiet and unobtrusive after the days when I failed to mention him in my writing, while today he's been anything but unobtrusive. And though I can't say that my writing about him yesterday had anything to do with what happened on the bridge this morning, still it makes me wonder. And it also makes me wonder where he could have gotten the information he sprang on me so suddenly. Where he could have found out about my writing since I'm sure that I've never mentioned it to him. I've never said a word. I'm positive about that. But somehow he knows. Somehow he found out.

And the way he said it, too. The way that all at once, he came out of the blue and asked me, "So how is your epitaph coming along?" My epitaph?! I didn't know what the hell he was talking about at first, but then he went on. "I'm talking about that epitaph you're writing for yourself and for the Merchant Marine, too." And when he said that, I was struck speechless. I couldn't believe that he could know anything about it. And I remained speechless as he launched into a rambling discourse about writing and writers and epitaphs, saying something to the effect that all literature is epitaph, that it's always a commemoration of a fast-vanishing past, whether it's written by giants like Melville or by amateurs. Some sort of nonsense like that.

And it wasn't until after he'd gone on with that stupidity of his for several minutes that I finally regained my faculty of speech and was able to tell him to get the hell out of there and leave me alone. To go to work out on the wing of the bridge. And as I did so, I was already starting to worry about tomorrow when he won't have to work on watch so that it won't be so easy to get rid of him. I was starting to ask myself what I'll be able to do tomorrow. Like will I have to hang out on the wing myself? No, if I were to do that, he'd probably just follow me out there and keep on talking. So how about music? How about turning it on and turning it up so loud that it drowns him out? And as I pondered that last possibility, I was glad for once to be aboard a modern ship where they allow you to play music on the bridge rather than being on one of those old ships where music was a strict no-no.

And I'm going to need all the help I can get on here. I'm going to need anything I can find that will get me away from him if only for a few minutes. Anything! Though now that I stop to think about it, I really can't tell you why that is. I can't say why George gets under my skin the way he does. Why he bugs me so badly. Him and his voice and his looks and his smell! Everything about him. Because I just can't stand the guy! I can't stand being around him!!

And it's not like he's all that bad of a guy, either. He's really not. He's just a guy who likes to talk a lot—and a guy who doesn't seem to understand the meaning of phrases like shut up and leave me alone and don't talk to me. But other than that, he's actually a pretty decent guy when you get right down to it. Weird but decent. And when he talks, he doesn't do it like some know-it-all or anything like that. In fact, he's constantly admitting to me just how little he knows or understands about the things he's discussing. He talks about them like they're these great mysteries to him and he's always asking me what I think. He's always asking for my opinion which I give in one- or two-word phrases on those rare occasions when I bother to answer him at all. Because I don't want to encourage the guy, you know. I don't want to contribute to his discussions. Not with the choice of topics he makes and the way he goes on and on about all that stuff. All that pseudo-mystical stuff.

And when he talks, he seems to take his facts and his ideas from anywhere he can get them in an equal-opportunity sort of way with his subjects ranging anywhere from the Catholic church—and especially the miraculous aspects of Catholicism—to mythology to all sorts of Eastern philosophies and ideas. Ideas about enlightenment and reincarnation, karma and chakras and yoga and you name it. And the one thing that seems to remain consistent throughout his discussions is his mispronunciation of every Eastern term he uses. Like with the way he talks about the "Eye Ching" or "Ying Yang." And the way that his understanding of those terms tends to be just as far off the mark as his pronunciation. It's just as wrong. Just as irritatingly and exasperatingly wrong.

None of that seems to bother our Second Mate George, though, and he's the one guy on this ship who should know better. The one other guy who's interested in all that garbage. But each time George comes up to relieve me—George the Second that is, not George the idiot—the two of them launch right into it. They start blabbing away to each other about all their strange and silly ideas, and they do so with such energy and such excitement that it drives me right out of there. And I can't get off that bridge fast enough once George the Second is there. Because putting up with two guys like that? Two guys discussing all the bullshit that's been assailing my ears for the last four hours?

And as you may have guessed, the Second Mate is a pretty strange one himself. Not as strange as the other George perhaps, but he's still quite a piece of work. He's a guy who seems to buy into all that mystico-magical garbage, all that stuff that he and the other George are always discussing—but that I refuse to listen to. And so being that he and I have so little in common and so little to talk about, there's not very much I can tell you about him. Though the one thing I should mention right here is his collection of teas. The collection of exotic and sometimes expensive teas that he brought with him when he came aboard, herbal teas and otherwise. The teas that he's always offering to anyone and everyone who will drink them with him and that he always prepares with all the proper ceremony. And it's those teas of his that have earned him the nickname among the crew of Dr. Tea. Because that's what a lot of them call him. Though I understand that a few years back, they used to refer to him as the Wizard because of the way he would sometimes wear a cape when he went out on deck. But that's something that he hasn't done in quite some time now, so the old nickname has faded away and he's become Dr. Tea.

So as I was saying, the two Georges seem to understand each other pretty well. The two strange ones. The two "characters." And you know now that I've brought up that term, I'm starting to ask myself once again why George bugs me the way he does—George the idiot that is. I'm starting to ask myself why I don't see him as one more in the long line of "characters" that I've sailed with over the years. Someone to look at and laugh the way I've always laughed at "characters." Someone to serve as a source of future stories about the weirdoes and oddballs I've sailed with. Because he really is one of the weirdest ever. The weirdest in many years. And why I don't see him in that light, I really can't tell you. Why he's such a pain-in-the-ass to me when years ago, he wouldn't have bothered me at all. And I might even have enjoyed having him around.

Because colorful? Yes, he certainly is that. He's a good-natured old loser with lots of stories to tell whenever he takes a break from his discussions of "big ideas." Stories about his adventures on skid-row and stories about his many visits to drunk-tanks, because from what he's told me, he's been in just about every drunk-tank west of the Mississippi. And that's not to mention every skid-row. And when he talks about that stuff, he always has that same stupid grin on his face. The exact same grin he has when he talks about karma or levitation or stigmata or you name it. The same grin whether he's discussing drunk-tanks or enlightenment.

So tell me, why is it that I can't see him as the joke that he is? Why is it that something inside me wants to take him seriously? To let him get to me and bother me deep down. Because is it him, or is it me? Is there something special about him that makes him such an irritant, or is it simply the fact that I've changed? The fact that I'm no longer young. Is that it? Is it the fact that my attitudes and my thoughts and my actions are no longer those of a young seaman? That now they've become the attitudes of an old-fart!

And I can see how much I've changed over the years. I can see how I've grown old in so many ways. How not only do I no longer enjoy having "characters" with me on the ship, but how in fact I don't enjoy having anyone with me out here at all. Because over the years, I've gradually become more and more of a loner aboard ship. So much so that I've nearly become a hermit by now, and I only socialize with other seamen in the most minimal way. I only talk to them when I'm working or at meals, and during the rest of the day I sit in my room alone. I read or listen to music—or I write this story—and I have nothing to do with anyone else.

And I wasn't always like that. No, far from it. When I was young, I used to spend all my free time hanging out with the other young guys on the ship. I never used to go to my room alone except when it was time to sleep. But then as the years went by, all that changed. And it happened so very slowly. In such tiny, almost indiscernible steps. In such a slow, gradual evolution. A maturation process I guess you could call it, and one that took many years to come full cycle and create the finished product that sits here before you today: this washed-up old seaman that I've become. This old guy who spends so little time with other seamen that I can't claim to have a single friend in the world. I'm a guy whose only real friends have been his family. But now ever since the divorce, I don't have even that left. No wife, and I never see my kids who by now are old enough to hate my guts. So I have no one at all, not at home and not on the ship. And I'm nothing but a bitter old man who's going to die alone, with no one to mourn and no one to miss me. Gone and forgotten.

Hey wait a minute! What am I talking about here? And how did I get into all this depressing stuff when I started out talking about George? What is it about him that leads me so inevitably into that type of thoughts? Does it have something to do with me seeing myself in him? Is that what it is? Do I see him as some future version of myself, or some alternative version? No, that can't be it. We're far too different for that. And those comments he sometimes makes? Those comments like, "We're nothing but two copies of the same guy, you and me," or like, "The only difference between the two of us is that I'm over here and you're over there." Those comments are nonsense! They're every bit as stupid and meaningless as 99% of the other stuff he says. Because we're completely different, the two of us, and the only connection between us is the fact that we're watch-partners. Just that and nothing more. And those comments of his are simply the ramblings of an old wino who has drunk himself stupid.

No, he and I have nothing in common. We're as different as night and day. Because he's a loser! A happy and contented one maybe, but still a loser. And me? I'm not a loser, or at least I hope I'm not. And in any case, I'm far from being satisfied with who and what I am. Or what I've become. No, I'm bitter is what I am. I'm bitter as hell. I'm

Enough said, okay?

\*     \*     \*     \*     \*

Here it is two days after yesterday. Yes that's right. You heard what I said. Because yesterday was Thursday and today is Saturday since we decided not to have a Friday this week. We decided to leave it out, so here it is Saturday. Though of course we do this every trip. We always skip the Friday on the way to Guam since that's around the time we cross the International Date Line, and then on the way back, we always have two Mondays to make up for it. So in other words, it's just one of those standard things about being on a trans-Pacific run. One of those things we do every trip.

Other than that, I don't know what there is to talk about today. Though maybe I could say something about the stars since they've been so spectacular on these clear, dark nights we've been having lately. They've been so clear and so bright. And right at this time of year, too, when you can see everything down here in these waters near the Equator. When I can step out onto the bridge-wing at night and see the Big Dipper and Polaris off to the North, while if I turn and look South, there's the Southern Cross shining away for me. And if I decide that I'd rather see Orion, all I have to do is look out ahead, out toward the West where it's slowly making its way toward the horizon each night. So it's really beautiful. It's spectacular even, the number and the variety of stars that I can see.

And you know, standing out there looking at all those stars, it really takes me back sometimes. Back to my younger days. My days on the old ships when I'd have nothing to do at night but hangout on the bridge-wing and look at the empty horizon or the stars. There'd be nothing going on inside the bridge since we'd have the radar turned off whenever the visibility was good. And instead I'd spend hours standing out in the warm breeze on the wing, gazing at the stars and learning to identify them, learning the constellations. Just looking around and dreaming about

Oh who the hell cares what I used to dream about back then? Because those were such stupid dreams. They were the dreams of some young jerk-off who knew nothing about life and what really lay ahead. Nothing about loss or disillusionment or failure. And instead, all I knew back then was optimism, that stupid belief that everything will work out for the best in the end. But I was wrong, of course. I was dead wrong. Because things never work out that way in the real world. They never work out the way you imagine they will when you're young.

But enough about dreams, okay? That's not what I'm here to talk about. I'm here to talk about the stars. Those stars which used to be of such importance to us navigators way back when since they were the things we would use to find our way around the world. The stars and the sun and the moon. Just them and nothing more. They were what we would use to determine our position at sea, not some little electronic box. They were what we would use to get our fixes three times a day. Our fixes just like junkies. Because have you ever noticed the similarities between navigation terms and drug-users' terms? Like with what I just said about getting fixes, which is something that both navigators and junkies do several times a day. And do you know what we used to do in order to get a fix? We'd go out and shoot a line, that's what we'd do. We'd shoot a sun-line or a star. We'd shoot something, just like we were junkies since shooting was what gave us our fixes. Or at least that was how we used to do it long ago. While nowadays if a guy wants a fix, he doesn't bother about shooting anything, no sun-lines and no stars. No, all a navigator does anymore is push a button on the GPS, just like a trained monkey could do.

And when you look at how easy it is to navigate these days with all the modern electronics, it becomes pretty obvious why Americans and other highly-qualified merchant officers have been losing jobs so steadily over the years. It's because the shipping companies don't need highly-qualified people in order to push buttons. They can hire anyone to do that. They can hire low-wage Third World Mates to do it, guys who would be completely lost without a GPS. Guys who wouldn't know a sextant if it came up and bit them. Because in spite of the problems and inconveniences of navigating back in the old days, at least then we had a certain amount of job security. We weren't as easy to replace as we are now when we're nothing but a bunch of disposable button-pushers.

And the dependence upon GPS has gotten to be so bad so quickly, even among First World Mates these days, that if there's ever a major malfunction of the GPS system, most of the ships in the world are going to find themselves wandering around lost with no way to determine where they are until the system finally comes back online. They won't have a clue! And they won't even be able to fall back on the old pre-GPS method of navigation used by flag-of-convenience ships—monkey-flag ships—the method of calling on the radio to the ships they pass and asking them for their positions. That won't work anymore since everyone will be lost without GPS, and there won't be anyone around with the old-time skills to fall back upon. The pre-GPS skills.

I'm talking about the skills that *real* navigators have. Those skills that it took seamen centuries to build up and to perfect. And it took years for an individual navigator to acquire them, too. But now those skills have become totally obsolete—as long as GPS continues to function, that is. And those traditional skills are disappearing so fast among modern seamen that they'll be lost completely with the passing of me and my generation. They'll be unknown and unknowable to the seamen of the future. Both the big skills and the little ones. Skills like being able to get a running-fix from a group of sun-lines that you've gotten after days without a fix so that you have no idea what your position is, let alone course- and speed-made-good. When you have to improvise and figure it out from scratch. Or skills like being able to shoot stars on a cloudy evening when they're popping in-and-out of small openings in the clouds. And doing it with the wind blowing and the ship rolling. And getting an accurate fix from those stars, too.

But no. None of that stuff is needed anymore. None of those skills I worked so hard to master back in my early days. Now they're being lost. All of them! And me, I'm nothing but a repository of unnecessary skills and useless information. I'm a guy who could probably still tell you how many layers of dunnage you need to put beneath a cargo of coffee if I had to. How many layers beneath and how many up against the sweat-battens. And then once it was loaded, I could get it properly secured for you, too. I still remember all that stuff in spite of the fact that for many years now, all I've worked on have been box-ships. And navigation? Why I bet it wouldn't take very long at all for me to start getting pinwheels again when I shot the stars. Just like I used to. I still remember how. I remember the little tricks. And I still remember enough of the old navigator's shortcuts and rules-of-thumb to be able to do a lot of the calculations in my head. Without a GPS or an ARPA or a computer, and maybe even without a calculator. Because I still have all those things in my head somewhere, and it would only be a matter of calling them back up. Of going back and readapting to the old days and the old ways of doing things.

But you know what? That's not going to happen, and I know it. I know that I'm never going to need those skills again, and I'll never need to recover that old knowledge. I know that time has moved on and those skills have been left behind and lost. And the only thing they're doing now is taking up space in my brain. They're sitting in there, unneeded and unwanted, and they're waiting for me to die so that they can die along with me. Because here we are, the old skills and the old salt, shriveling up and dying together. Useless and abandoned and forgotten.

Hey, will you look at that? Will you look at how today's writing session is ending up? Today's session which started out on a pretty light note but is now ending up in bitter territory once again. Just like yesterday. And that without my ever having mentioned old you-know-who in my writing today.

\*  \*  \*  \*  \*

So let's see, what is there to talk about today? What can I talk about without getting into all that depressing stuff? Like how about the weather? I could talk about that, couldn't I? There's nothing depressing about that.

No, the weather has been great so far. Though of

course it's always good on this part of the trip. Good but hot since on this leg we run along with the Trade Winds. We go the same direction they do and the same speed, so there's almost no wind across the deck at all. It's like we're in a complete calm out there. And with the way the tropical sun beats down on us in the daytime, it can get awful hot out there for the guys who have to work on deck. Those guys of whom I'm not one since the only work I do at sea is to stand my watches on the bridge. My four hours of standing around looking at the scenery, followed by eight hours off.

And as I look at the weather up ahead, it appears that we may get lucky this time around. That the good weather could continue indefinitely. Because by now we're far enough to the West to be able to pick up Japanese weather maps, the best ones for spotting future typhoons. And when I look at those maps, I don't see a thing to worry about. I don't see anything that might bother us in the coming days as we make our way to Guam and then from there to Hong Kong. Right up the heart of typhoon alley. I don't see a single baby typhoon anywhere in sight.

It's not like I was expecting one, though, since this isn't typhoon season. But out here you never know. These typhoons aren't purely seasonal the way the hurricanes in the Atlantic are. No, typhoons can develop at any time of the year, and it's just that there are a whole lot more of them during the season than there are out-of-season. They come along one after the other during the season while off-season they only show up from time to time. But they never disappear altogether, not out here where they have this full-sized ocean to brew themselves up in, rather than some mini-ocean like the Atlantic.

So as I was saying, it looks like we have a straight shot to Guam, and we'll be arriving there in two more days.

We'll be pulling into port and breaking this at-sea routine that we've fallen into as we switch over to an in-port routine for a day or so. A routine where I won't be standing my watches on the bridge, but instead I'll be standing them on deck. I'll be walking around the decks keeping an eye on the lines and the cargo operations and all that. And with the way things work these days, I'll also be dealing with some "security" bullshit. Some of the bullshit that's been foisted on us over the last few years. And while common sense may have won out over some of the most outrageous proposals that were made by the security-nazis, still we take more than enough silly and unnecessary precautions to make me feel like a complete idiot for implementing them. And especially so in a quiet little port like Guam, a place where everyone working there knows everyone else, and probably knew their parents and grandparents, too. When we pull in there, though, we'll be locking everything down like we were entering some terrorist stronghold when in fact we'll be in one of the safest ports in the world.

But the security-nazis tell us that we have to do it, so that's what we do. We take a lot of useless precautions that are mainly there to justify the jobs of a bunch of assholes, a bunch of bureaucrats who have nothing to do all day long but come up with new and "improved" regulations. Because to tell you the truth, I don't see what purpose most of this stuff serves other than that of job-justification for bureaucrats. Though I suppose that there's also the petty little power-trips that so many of those people are obviously on. The sick thrill they get out of ordering us around and making our lives as miserable as possible. Because between the security-nazis and the bean-counters who run the shipping companies these days, it's like there's a real, concerted effort going on to make life at sea as unlivable as possible. A conspiracy almost. A conspiracy to make this life into one that no sane person would ever consider for a moment.

And there are times when it makes me so mad. Times when I get this urge to run out and do something crazy. Something that would scream into those guys' faces: Hey! Wake up!! And look around you! Try to get back in touch with reality and look out for the *real* threats. And stop fucking with us!!

I'd love to do something like that. I'd love to rattle the security-nazis' cages and shake up that narrow little world of theirs with some act of open rebellion. Some futile and meaningless gesture performed in the cause of freedom. I'd love to do that even though I know that I never will. Not now when they've already won. When they've already imposed their system. Even their mentality. And the aging freedom-fighters like myself have long since lost. Because the old free-and-easy days of shipping are gone forever, and there's no way we'll ever be able to bring them back. And gestures? What gesture could I possibly make out here, anyway? What *effective* gesture? None that I can think of.

And the only outrageous thing I can think to do would be to go out and score some weed and then blow it into the faces of the drug-test-nazis. Those assholes whose only "safety" concern is to give drug tests to anyone and everyone they can find. And it's reached the point these days where if someone gets seriously injured on the ship and you manage to save him in spite of your very limited resources and your own limited training, the only thing the Coast Guard will have to say to you afterwards is, Why didn't you drug test him? Why is it that when you found that guy lying on the deck half-dead, you didn't say to him, I'll perform CPR on you in a minute, but first please pee into this bottle? Why didn't you do that? Why did you save his life instead of drug testing him?

Oh, the stupidity of it all! And I'm just glad that I won't be at it much longer. I'm glad that I won't be dealing with the security-nazis and the drug-test-nazis for more than another few weeks. I'm glad that I'll finally be getting out of this industry and this life.

And as far as empty gestures are concerned, I could probably get away with just about anything on this ship if I wanted to. Anything that didn't go big-time. Because with the way I have the guys on here so spooked and so scared of offending a dying man, there's no telling what I could get away with. And especially now that we're past Honolulu so that if they were to fire me, they'd have to fly someone else out to relieve me. Someone to relieve a dying man who is being fired before he can renew his medical benefits. Oh, the guilt-trips I could put them through.

But you know, the trouble is that the guys on the ship aren't the problem. Not at all. The Captain is a real decent guy, and even Chris is okay for being ex-military. No, the people I really want to offend are somewhere else out there. Somewhere far beyond my reach. Out in that nameless, faceless bureaucracy. Out where they can never be touched by *real* people like me, either physically or emotionally. Instead they live in their insulated little world where any gesture on my part would be lost. Where it would be seen as nothing but a curiosity. Nothing but an amusing anecdote to be told around the office. Nothing but

Oh, it's hopeless!

\* \* \* \* \*

We had a little incident on the bridge this morning. An incident that illustrates just how deluded George is with all that mystico-magical bullshit of his. The way he can convince himself to believe anything about his so-called "powers."

What happened is that we've been having problems with our 3cm radar for some time now until finally this morning, the thing stopped working altogether. It went completely dead on us. And when George heard about that, he walked right up to the radar and, after looking it over for a few moments, he put his hands on it and closed his eyes and began to chant something very quietly. Almost to himself. He chanted away for a minute or two, and then he turned to me and said in a confident tone, "It's okay now, Mate." Just like that. He told me that it was fixed.

Well, I tried the thing out a little while later, figuring that all it had needed was a little rest, and as it turned out, I was right. Because when I turned it back on, I found that it had started working again on its own, working as well as it ever had. I found that my rest-cure had worked. But when George saw that, he immediately began to take credit for the whole thing himself, and he couldn't stop talking about it for the rest of the watch. He went on and on like he really believed that he'd fixed that radar with his laying-on-of-hands bullshit. Like he couldn't understand that it had simply been the rest that had "cured" it. And with the way he was talking, I could see that there was no way I'd ever be able to convince him otherwise, even if I'd bothered to try. Which of course I didn't since I see no point in arguing with an old wino burnout like him. So instead, I let him talk away. I left him to his little world of delusion.

And the crazy things he had to say when he got onto the subject of his "powers!" Like the things he said about this incident they had in the engineroom a couple of days back, this incident where a steam-leak broke out and barely missed one of the Engineers. Where it burst out just after he'd walked past it. And do you know what George had to say about that? He said that he was the one who saved the

Engineer that day. That it was he who held things back until after the guy was out of range. George! He claimed that he did it through mental-telepathy or something like that. Through concentrating the powers of that alcohol-soaked brain of his. And it was so ridiculous to hear him say that stuff that I just had to burst out laughing. I had to laugh right in his face. I couldn't help myself.

But somehow it didn't faze him a bit when I laughed at him that way, and it did nothing to wipe off that eternal stupid grin of his either. And if anything, it seemed like my laughter made him insist all the more stubbornly on what he had to say, repeating over and over again his nonsense about the power of laying-on-hands—among other things. Rattling on and on about how a person can learn to channel positive energy through his hands, and about the things he can accomplish when he does so. The things he can do and the things he can cure. And I remember that there came a moment when he kind of paused and then, staring me straight in the eye, he said in his most forceful voice, "You know Mate, that laying-on-hands can even cure *some* cancers." And with the way he said it, he was obviously referring to my own cancer, though by putting so much emphasis on the word some, I couldn't tell what he was trying to say. Whether he was implying that he could cure me or that he couldn't. Though of course it really doesn't matter what he meant by that statement since whatever it was, it was just another of his delusions. Another of his mystico-fantasies. And it was something that no one else but he could ever believe.

No one with the least bit of common sense, that is. No one but George the Second since when he came to the bridge to relieve me and heard what George the idiot had to say, he immediately swallowed the story whole. Hook, line and sinker. And the only questions I heard him ask were about the details of how it had been done. They weren't about whether or not such a thing is possible. No, all he wanted to know were things like where exactly the idiot had placed his hands and what mantra he had used when he'd done it. Things like that. And as I listened to the two of them going on in that way, I had to stop and ask myself several times which of the two was the real idiot. Which was the goofier ball in that pair of goof-balls? Which was the real clown among clowns? Questions which I still can't answer.

And while I'm on the subject of George the Second, maybe I should mention the fact that he's been getting on my nerves more and more with each passing day. Still not as much as the other George, of course, and not for the same reasons since with him it has nothing to do with endless blabbing. No, with him it's that eternal goddamned tranquility of his that gets under my skin. That imperturbability. And I've tried any number of times to get a rise out of him without the least success. Like I've tried mixing up his teas or hiding them, and I've thrown out comments meant to offend him when we run into each other at meals, but nothing I've done has bothered him. Nothing has made him mad, and the only reaction I've ever managed to get out of him has been a benevolent smile. That and maybe some mild comment.

It's been easy with some of the other guys, though. Like take Chris for instance. It's so easy to rile him up that it's not even fun anymore. Especially not with the way that he never lets it out. The way he swallows his anger so as not to offend me. And a couple of the Engineers are exactly the same way. It's easy to get them mad, but then they won't say a word back. They'll just sit there and take it while they boil inside. And it's only George the Second who never shows the least sign of anger. It's only he who answers all my provocations with a mellow smile. And it's been so frustrating! I've gotta find some way to get to that guy. I've gotta make him burn the way I do with everyone else. I've just got to.

But enough about that and enough for today. Enough until after Guam since we'll be docking there during writing-time tomorrow while who knows about the next day. Who knows when I'll have another chance to write. And who knows what I'll have to say when I do.

\* \* \* \* \*

What is it about walking the deck of a ship in a tropical port that brings so much back to me? So many memories and so many emotions. What is it that makes me think of my youth again? Think of it and feel it even. A bit of it anyway. Because it wasn't like I was entering some time-machine standing that cargo watch in Guam. It wasn't like I was really going back into the past. No, it was just that I could see that past somewhere off in the distance. I could see it and I could feel it, those old emotions rising up once again somewhere deep within. Those feelings of youth and vigor and adventure. Those feelings that I'd thought to have died so long ago.

Because in spite of everything, I still love this life. I love ships—even containerships—and I love going to sea. I love the whole atmosphere of ships and docks and cargo. Of loading up and sailing away, or of entering port and tying up. I love it as I would some former happy home, the place where I spent the best days of my youth and the place where much of my heart still lives. And even though the strong emotions of my youth have long since left me—the thrill of entering a new port that I've never visited before, a new place to go off and explore, or the cleansing feeling that comes with a return to sea after a long port stay—still there's something that remains. Some residue of those old emotions. It's something that's stronger and more real than simple memory. Something more vital. And it's something that can still be called up from time to time when the circumstances are right. Like when I walk around on deck in a tropical port. Like yesterday in Guam.

And when I stop to think about that feeling, I can see now that it's not about any one specific thing. It's not about the old ships I used to work on all those years ago, and it's not about the exotic ports they used to visit, and it's not even about being young and alive and grasping at life with both hands the way that only the young can. No, it's not about any of those things. It's about the entire way of life. It's about living the seaman's life. And if today that means living it on containerships rather than freighters, then so be it. And to tell you the truth, I've become so accustomed to containerships by now with their short trips and their predictability that I probably wouldn't return to the old ships even if I had the opportunity. Those old ships with their long trips to Third World ports, trips where you never knew where you were going next or when you would get there or what problems you'd encounter in trying to contact home once you were there.

No, those ships aren't for me anymore. Not when I've become so adapted to this other life—and when I've left my youth so far behind. Because now I'm an old-guy and I know it. And I have old-guy attitudes toward life aboard ship. Attitudes where I don't want adventure anymore, and I don't want excitement, and I don't much care about variety either. No, all I want now is the old-guy stuff. I want peace and quiet, and I want predictability. I want to know what lies ahead of me on this voyage, and I want to know exactly when it will end. I don't want that open-ended stuff anymore.

And when I think back to the old ships now, I finally know why it was that so many of the old guys aboard would moan and say, "Oh no," whenever something went wrong. Why they wouldn't see it as an adventure the way I did, as an opportunity to shake up their lives and live again—really live—rather than as a mere inconvenience. Because now that I'm old myself, I can finally see their point-of-view. And I know that if anything were to really happen on this ship, anything to ruin our quiet routine, I'd probably be the first to moan and say, "Oh no." I'd be the oldest of the old-guys. And I'd be the last in line for adventure.

I came to that realization while standing cargo watch in Guam yesterday, that realization and the others I just mentioned. I thought about all those things as I wandered the decks. And I had plenty of time to think about them, too, since I covered part of Chris's watch for him—the Second Mate and I covered it—so that he could go to town. Off to the old hangouts from his military days. But he was very hesitant when he first brought up the possibility of my taking his watch. He had a look of doubt in his eyes as he spoke and as he looked me over trying to assess my condition. But I quickly assured him that I could handle it. I told him that I feel much better than I look—something which might actually be true—and in the end, he chose to believe me. He chose to let me work overtime while he headed out to visit places where he could relive what for him must have been the good-old-days.

And I made it through the watches just fine. I made it in and out of Guam in one piece. And now as I sit here writing, we're on the first whole day of our last westbound leg. The first day of the passage that will take us to Hong Kong, our furthest point from home since when we leave there, we'll be turning back toward the East. We'll be steaming over to make a quick stop at Kaohsiung in southern Taiwan, and then from there we'll be setting our course for home. We'll be heading toward Tacoma and the end of this voyage. The end of my career, too, since when we reach Tacoma, I'll be ringing up FWE for the very last time.

\*   \*   \*   \*   \*

It's not much further now, and it won't be long before we pass the line of small islands that stretch between Taiwan and the Philippines, at which point we'll be leaving behind the tranquility of open waters and entering the chaotic world of the South China Sea. That world so full of ships traveling every which way and fleets of fishing boats that stretch as far as the eye can see. That super-populated world of the Far East which is so different from the other side of the Pacific that it's hard to believe that they're two sides of the same ocean.

And it's a world that brings back lots of memories for me. Memories of my younger and wilder self. That young guy who used to love coming over here to these countries. The Philippines, Thailand, Vietnam. Those were great places for a young seaman to go. Places to drink and carouse and have fun. And places to get laid, too. And I took full advantage of it back in the day. I certainly did. Like on this shuttle ship I worked on years ago where we used to stop at Manila every week, and we'd stay there for a day-and-a-half or so. And me? I was young and single back then, and a little bit crazy, too, and I used to eat it up. I'd never sleep when we were in Manila, not unless I was with a girl, and I'd only go back to the ship when I had to stand watch. But then I'd go right back ashore again the minute my watch was over, and it didn't matter what time of the day or night it was since I was having way too much fun to spend time hanging around in my room on the ship. And I'd catch up on my sleep while we were at sea on our way back to Hong Kong.

And when I think about those days and the shipmates I had back then, the guys I used to hang out with ashore. Man, it was great! We had such good times together and so much camaraderie. And of course we had our little inside jokes, too. Like I remember how each time we'd pull into Manila, I'd tell Steve, one of the ABs on my watch and my number-one drinking buddy, "I think this time I'm gonna go look for a girl who's… short with dark hair and dark eyes." A standing joke between us since all the girls in the Philippines fit that description.

And Vietnam? It was good though I didn't care too much for that whole industrial-scale, mass-produced sex thing, the type of thing you find whenever there's lots of military around. Instead, I had more fun in places that catered to seamen, like in Manila or like during that first time I was ever in Bangkok. And I'm not talking about Sattahip here. I'm talking about Bangkok itself. The big city. Because that first time I went there, I had the most amazing experience with a bar-girl ever. She was so enthusiastic!

It was in one of those seamen's bars in Klong Toey, one of those places where the girls would take turns dancing on the stage while wearing bikinis. And the moment I looked at her dancing up there, I knew that she was the one for me with the way that something electric seemed to pass between us as our eyes met. And so when Mama-san came over and asked me if I liked any of the girls, I pointed straight at her. Straight at… Oh, I can't remember her name anymore, though that's probably the only thing I've ever forgotten about her. And what happened was that as soon as her turn to dance was over, she came charging down off the stage and jumped into my lap and started kissing me. And she never let up all evening. In the bar, in the room. She wanted more and more and more. And when it came time for me to go back to the ship, she cried. She didn't want me to leave.

Well, I tried to find her again the next time we were in Bangkok, but by then she wasn't working there anymore. And when I asked Mama-san about her, all she wanted to do was to set me up with another girl. One who looked something like the one I was looking for. So I was never able to find her again. And in the end, I did what any self-respecting seaman would have done. I went with another girl. Another one and then another. The story of a seaman's life.

Though unlike so many other seamen, I stopped playing around the minute I got married. I stopped going with the girls completely, and I was always faithful to my wife. Always! I never cheated on her once—for all the good it did me since she ended up leaving me anyway. She dumped me like an old piece of garbage. And why it was that I didn't take up with the girls again after the divorce, I really can't tell you. I must have lost the urge, I suppose. Or maybe the habit. And by this time, it's been so long since I've gotten laid in one of these ports that for all I know, I may have forgotten how. I may not be able to do it even if I were to try.

And try? I don't know. It looks like we'll have enough time in Hong Kong for me to go out and do my stuff there. Probably not Kaohsiung since we're usually just in-and-out of that port. But Hong Kong? It's not the best port over here for that sort of thing, but then again it's not the worst. And given how easy it is to reach town these days ever since they built that subway. Nothing like it was back in my "glory days" when it could be an adventure in itself just getting to town and back from way out there in Kwai Chung. But now, all you have to do is hop onto the subway and you're there. So why not? Why not take advantage of it? My last chance ever to go ashore in a foreign port. My last chance to go out and give the Far East a real send-off. A real seaman's goodbye. And since I can't drink these days, then what else is there for me to do during my time ashore? Go sight-seeing or go shopping? Or go over to Wan Chai and get myself a girl?

Which should it be for a guy like me? A guy who no longer has a wife to be faithful to and nothing else to lose. Nothing to be afraid of. Because AIDS? Who cares about that when I'm already dying of cancer? When I'll be dead long before the AIDS can do anything to me. So maybe I will. Maybe I'll go out and sow whatever I still have left in the way of wild oats. Maybe I'll go say goodbye to Asia in a way that's proper for an old salt like me. Who knows?

And by the way, there are only two Fire and Boat Drills to go.

\*     \*     \*     \*     \*

What is it about George? How is it that he knows exactly what I'm writing each day almost as though he were sneaking into my room and reading it? Because there I was yesterday afternoon writing about the girls in the Far East, and then there he was last night asking me about them. And asking like he knew all about it, too. Asking me about Manila and even about my first time in Bangkok. And he kept going on and on even though I refused to answer him or so much as acknowledge that I'd heard what he was saying. Because I won't discuss my personal life with that old wino. That loser. I won't tell him a thing about myself.

Not even the least private parts like those old stories from my wild days which I've shared with any number of watch-partners over the years. But with him, I refuse to talk about it. I absolutely refuse.

And it wasn't like he was pulling some dirty-old-man stuff on me or anything like that. No, he was just asking me about those days and those girls. And the problem was the way that he wouldn't take a hint from my silence and let it go. But instead he kept coming back to it in his rambling discourse until finally it reached the point where I couldn't take it anymore, and I had to try to make him stop. I had to speak up and say what's probably the longest phrase that I've spoken to him since the day he came aboard. I told him, "You know, you should watch it with those dirty thoughts of yours, cause God'll get you for it."

But do you know what he said back to me? He said, "Well, you should know about that, Mate, since it looks like he sure got you." And he said it in such a calm and off-handed way. Not like he was trying to insult me and not like it was a come-back either. No, he just said it like he was stating a fact. And even though it was dark at the time, I could see from the glow of the radars that he still had that same old stupid grin on his face. That same irritating look. And I was so mad when I heard him say that—and especially with the way he said it—that the only thing I could think to do was to turn up the music as loud as it would go. To turn it up and drown out whatever else he might have to say.

The strange part about it, though, is that in a certain way he was actually right in what he said. Far more right than he could have imagined at the time. Because when I woke up this morning, I felt terrible. I felt like God might actually be out to get me. I felt like my cancer was relapsing on me or something, and I've been feeling that way all day long. I hurt all over, and I'm almost too weak to stand, and I can hardly keep my food down. I feel the worst I have in a long, long time. I feel as bad as I look even. Worse if that's possible.

I was barely able to drag myself through this morning's watch, and when I think about the one that awaits me tonight, I wonder how I'll be able to handle it. Tonight when there will be so much traffic and so many fishing boats to deal with. Fishing boats that can get so thick out here that I swear there are days when a person could walk all the way from China to Taiwan simply by stepping from one fishing boat to the next. And if I can somehow make it through that watch, I'll still have to face the arrival and docking in Hong Kong tomorrow morning followed by a cargo watch there. A cargo watch during which things will be moving fast and I'll have to be all over the ship. Three, four, five cranes? Who knows? All I know is that it'll be a real challenge for someone feeling as sick and weak as I am. It'll be hell!

And then after a little rest that afternoon, I'll have to be right back in the grinder that evening. Back for the hardest cargo watch of all when the longshoremen will be finishing things up and doing all the lashings and when I'll have to be climbing around everywhere to check on them. That followed by the undocking followed by a bit of sleep followed by more traffic. Lots of traffic and another port coming up.

Oh God! I hope I can make it!! I hope I can survive the next couple of days.

\* \* \* \* \*

Well, I made it through the battle of Hong Kong. Just barely. But I didn't make it ashore there feeling as badly as I do. Instead I spent my free time resting. I spent what should have been my last shore leave ever in a foreign port lying in my bed. Going nowhere and doing nothing and feeling way too sick to even think about shore. And all that stuff about girls and wild oats and blowing off steam? None of it came to pass.

And now here we are on our way to Kaohsiung where we'll be tying up at some godawful hour in the middle of the night and then sailing a few hours later. Sailing by dawn. The perfect timing to ruin any chance I have of getting a little rest tonight before we start the long passage back to Tacoma. And while I know that I should be resting now instead of writing, there's a bit of breaking news that I'd like to tell you about before I lay down. News that I heard while we were in Hong Kong and that confirms a rumor that's been floating around the company for quite some time now. News that the company will soon be replacing the old ships on this run with a group of new ships. Ships that they'll be building very soon from what they say.

The thing about the new ships, though, is that they'll be just like all the other ships that are being built these days. They'll be built to "international standards" which is another word for low-quality. And while they may have a good design and they may have state-of-the-art electronics on the bridge since the Third World Mates they're designed for would be completely lost without them, the construction itself will be cheap. Maybe even shoddy. And the living conditions will be strictly Third World. They'll be built with low-grade steel protected with low-grade paint, and given the quality of those materials, the ships won't last very long at all. Not like the old *Pioneer* has lasted. And there's no way that those new ships will still be floating when they reach the age of this ship now. They'll have rusted out quickly and been scrapped years before. They won't last the way this old American-built workhorse has lasted. This classic old Cadillac. Because what the company will be doing is it'll be trading in this well-worn Caddie for a brand new Hyundai. For a ship whose only improvement upon the old one will be the fact that it's new.

But they won't be scrapping these old ships once the new ones come online. No, they're much too valuable for that since so few ships have been built in the US in recent decades, and since cargoes to Hawaii and similar places are restricted to US-built ships only. So the new ships won't be able to carry that cargo. They'll only be carrying the Guam cargo westbound, and these old ships will have to continue in service on the Hawaii trade. Hawaii and Alaska and Puerto Rico. That's where they'll be spending their twilight years. The years during which they'll slowly but surely rust away to nothing. The years during which they'll be run until they die completely the way SeaLand has always done with its ships. Forty years, forty-five. Who knows? As long as there's enough steel left in the hull, they can keep patching up everything else.

And as I stop to think about those new ships, it opens up a certain new perspective for me about the true nature of this run that we're on. Because this ship has been running here for something like twenty years now, and all during that time, people have come and gone. They've come aboard and made two, three, four trips only to get off again and be replaced by someone else. And that's been going on with all the positions aboard. There's been a constant rotation of people while the ship itself has gone on and on, one trip after another during all these years. But now with a new ship coming out to replace it, I can see that the truly "eternal" thing in the equation hasn't been the ship at all. No, it's been the run. And just like with people, the ships can be replaced while the run itself will go on.

Forever. It'll outlast everything and everyone.

Especially someone in as bad shape as I am right now.

\*　　\*　　\*　　\*　　\*

I'm just barely dragging along these days. I couldn't write the first afternoon out of Kaohsiung since I needed all the rest I could get after the terrible night we spent there. And now a day-and-a-half out, I'm feeling only slightly better. Just good enough to be able to write a few lines.

And the way I look? It must be terrible given the worried expression that comes over Chris's face each time I show up on the bridge to relieve him. The way he looks at me as though he's not sure that I can make it through the next four hours. Because as bad as I'm feeling, there's no way for me to cover anything up anymore. There's no way that I can put on a happy face and pretend that I'm okay. And whatever the source of Chris's concern, whether it's for me and my well-being or whether it's out of fear that he as the medical officer will soon be dealing with a dying man, he's definitely worried about my deteriorating condition. I can see that written all over his face.

Even George seems to be worried about me lately, and he keeps telling me that he can help me if only I'd let him lay-on his hands. Let him use his so-called "powers" on me. And I've caught him a couple of times trying to sneak up from behind and get his hands on me in spite of the fact that I've repeatedly told him no. I've caught him, and I've stopped him cold. Because letting him touch me? Him with those filthy hands of his. Those hands that he's never washed. I wouldn't let him touch me to save my life. And I certainly won't let him touch me for those stupid reasons he gives, those claims about miracle-cures. I'd rather suffer than let him do that. I'd rather die. So every time he tries to get his hands on me, I order him away.

And it looks like I'll have to be dodging him for quite awhile given all the ocean that lies between here and Tacoma. All those days of steaming and all the watches that we'll be standing on the bridge together. Because with us being only a day-and-a-half out of Kaohsiung, we're still in the Far East right now. We're following the Kuroshio Current as best we can from the east coast of Taiwan up toward Japan. And then once we've worked our way clear of Japan, we'll still have the entire North Pacific Ocean stretching out ahead of us.

So we have days and days of steaming ahead—days of dodging George and his hands. And we're likely to encounter bad weather along the way which will only add to the sleep-deprivation we'll soon be suffering from the time changes we have to make before we reach Tacoma. The nine hours of sleep that we'll have to lose in order to make up for all the extra sleep we had on the way over. And the first short night we'll have will be tonight, our first advance-the-clocks night. So it's going to be a tough passage back feeling the way I do. And the only thing I can say about it is something that I've already said before: I hope I can make it.

\*    \*    \*    \*    \*

The strangest thing happened on the bridge last night. And I'm not sure that I can explain it to you since I don't know what it was myself. Not exactly. I don't know if it was something real or if it was an illusion, a hallucination brought on by my weakened physical condition. But whatever the reality behind it may have been, I'll tell you as much as I know.

What happened was that George finally succeeded in

laying his hands on me last night while we were on watch together. He snuck up behind me in the dark and grabbed me, one hand on my head and the other near my heart. And the moment his hands touched me, I felt this tremendous jolt run through my body. A jolt that came from I-don't-know-where. Not from his hands, I'm sure of that. It came from some other place. From somewhere deep within me, I think. And while part of the jolt came from the shock of being grabbed like that in the dark, there had to be more to it than that, as powerful as it was. And the only thing I can tell you for sure is that it didn't last very long, only a second or two. Only as long as it took for me to shake off George's unwelcomed embrace. And then the moment I'd broken free, I started to shout at him at the top of my lungs.

I yelled and screamed for the next ten minutes, maybe twenty, and in the process I vented everything that I've been holding inside all trip. All the anger that I've been storing up, all the hatred and the resentment. And I told him exactly what I think of him, repeating it over and over again while at the same time warning him never to touch me again. But the whole time I was yelling, he stood there with that same old stupid expression on his face, that same dumb grin. I could see it in the dim quarter-moonlight that filled the bridge. And I could also see that he was completely unfazed by my tirade. That my words were having no effect upon him whatsoever. And when I'd finally finished with all my shouting and given him a chance to speak, his only response was to say to me, "There you go, Mate," said in a tone like, You're welcome. Like all my screaming had been my way of thanking him for what he'd just done. And then after he'd said it, he didn't say another word for the rest of the watch. He stood there in complete silence for the first time since he's been aboard.

But do you know what the funniest thing about the whole situation is? It's the fact that when I woke up this morning, I felt great. I felt the best I have in a long time. Since before this cancer even. And all day long, I've been asking myself what could possibly have led to this cure. Was it just a coincidence that the bad days I've been having lately came to an end right after George pulled his laying-on-of-hands bullshit? Or was it because of the cleaning-out I gave myself with all that yelling the night before? The way I unloaded so much anger and frustration after he touched me? Letting it go instead of holding it inside the way I've been doing for far too long. Because I know that releasing pent-up anger can do wonders for a person's physical condition. It can cure many ills. And I find that to be a much more credible explanation for my "miracle-cure" than the idea of George having worked some sort of magic with his touch. The idea that he cured me with his hands.

Whatever the source of the cure may have been, though, it seems to be the real thing. And while I'm sure that I still have the cancer, the symptoms have disappeared almost completely. The nausea is gone now and so are most of the aches and pains. Most but not all. And I know that I look a whole lot better today than I did before, better than I have in days or weeks. Maybe even better than the day I first came aboard the *Horizon Pioneer*. And I can see the change not only when I look at myself in the mirror, but I also saw it in the expression on Chris's face when I relieved him on the bridge this morning. And I heard about it, too, when the first thing he said to me was, "Wow, you look great today!"

I was glad to hear him say that, though since George was already present on the bridge at the time, my other first reaction was to say to myself, Oh no, here we go again. Here's the ammunition George needs to regale me with four more hours of talk about powers and laying-on-hands and who knows what else. Four hours of continuous bullshit. But to my amazement, George did nothing to take advantage of the opportunity. And in fact, he didn't talk to me at all beyond saying good morning and making a few in-the-line-of-business comments while otherwise holding his silence just like he had the night before—after the "miracle-cure" that is. And while he was evidently leaving it up to me to begin the day's conversation, that's something I'll never do with him. Never. And instead, I reveled in all the new-found peace and quiet. I enjoyed it while I could get it, though as time went on, it seemed like his silence was somehow drawing my attention toward him far more surely than his talking had ever done. And soon I found myself asking if this person on the bridge with me could possibly be the same guy I'd been standing watches with for the last two or three weeks. And if it hadn't been for the fact that he still wore the same old dirty clothes and still had the same stupid expression on his face, I might have mistaken him for someone else. Because as strange as he'd always appeared to me, now with this sudden change in personality of his, he seemed to have become stranger still. He seemed to have become a complete cipher.

As we stood that watch together in silence, my thoughts were being drawn ever more strongly toward him. And I asked myself over and over again who this strange person could be in reality. Who and what. And the more I thought about it, the more weird and outlandish ideas there were that came popping into my head. Extraordinary explanations about what might lie beneath that deceptively bland surface of his. Like could he be an angel or a saint? Or a devil? Or in a less Christian vein, could he be a master of the esoteric arts? And could the wino that I see before me be nothing but a clever disguise?

I didn't know what to make of him anymore, and I couldn't tell if there was anything at all hidden beneath that shabby exterior. If there was anything more to him than the fool he appeared to be. And as I went on thinking about him, the words that kept coming back to me were the expression holy fool. Could he be a holy fool? I asked myself. He was a fool, of that I was certain. But a holy one? The idea was hard to swallow. Because look at him! Look at those filthy clothes and the coat with the half-eaten apples in the pockets. And look at the stupidity written all over his face. Those vacant eyes and that eternal dumb grin. That can't be the face of a holy fool. It's too… I don't know what. It's too foolish!

And speaking of fools. When the other George came up to relieve me at noon, he immediately noticed the improvement in my condition, but rather than saying anything to me about it, he spoke instead to my watch-partner. He said, "So I see it worked." And with that for an opening comment, the two of them launched into one of their discussions, a discussion of the type that I'd been dreading all morning. And as they went on and on about the intricacies of laying-on-hands, I couldn't get off that bridge fast enough. So I shouted out the course to my relief and headed straight for the stairs. And then all the way down, I shook my head as I once again pondered the old question about which of the two Georges is actually the greater fool. Holy or otherwise. Which of them is the fool among fools? And as I stop to reconsider that question now, I still can't give you an answer. I still can't tell you which of them it is.

\* \* \* \* \*

I don't know why it was, but for some reason I was feeling

open and even a bit friendly toward George during our watch last night. It may have had to do with the fact that a few hours earlier we had passed Miyake Jima, the small Japanese island that will be the last piece of land we'll see for a long time since after Miyake, there's nothing ahead but open water. And if we don't pass near enough to the Aleutians to be able to see them, our next landfall won't come until we're all the way over on the far side of the Pacific. It'll be either Vancouver Island or Cape Flattery, the northwestern corner of Washington State, depending upon our exact angle of approach and the visibility on the day we arrive.

So maybe it was the open water combined with the good weather that appears to lay ahead during the crossing. Because now as we start out across the ocean, it looks like we may have gotten lucky with the weather once again. The weather maps show that we're right in the middle of a high as we begin the crossing, and since everything will be traveling with us as we make the passage, we should be able to ride the thing all the way home. We should have this good weather throughout the passage. A small mercy to a dying man.

Whatever it may have been, though, the good weather or the wide-open waters, I felt a vague desire to open myself up a bit during that boring, uneventful night watch. A desire to engage in conversation with George, though a normal conversation. One about normal, everyday things rather than the weird stuff that he usually likes to talk about. So before the watch had advanced very far, I decided to break the silence which by then had filled the bridge during our watches for nearly an entire day. I decided to ask George about his life ashore. And he immediately responded to my question by rattling off a story about his adventures on skid row. A story which was followed by another and another and still another. And while many of them were stories that I may have heard before, I can't say for certain since I hadn't paid attention to him during the earlier recountings. And as I listened to the stories now, the one thing they seemed to have in common was the fact that they all began with the phrase, "I was so drunk that I don't remember what happened exactly, but..."

He went on and on with his stories, and he even told me about his lost childhood in Omaha, but then after awhile he began to turn the tables on me by asking about my own past. And given the mood I was in at the time, I willingly obliged him. I told him about my life. Parts of it anyway. I told him about the good days, the ones that I like to remember as being good days. Those days when my wife still loved me and the kids were small and cute. Because even in the most screwed-up, unhappy family there can still be happy memories. There can be moments worth treasuring. And my unhappy family life was no exception to that rule. We had our happy days and months, maybe even happy years as I think back to them now with my selective memory. And I didn't hesitate to talk about those days, only pulling back when George began to probe into more recent years. The unhappy years.

I didn't want to talk about that at all. About how badly my family life has ended up and with what bitterness on all sides. So whenever he started to get into that area, I immediately changed the subject. I took the conversation back to the good days or back to his life. And I did so in spite of the fact that, by the way George framed his questions, he seemed to know all about my problems already without my ever having mentioned them. He knew about them in the same way that he'd known about my writing without having been told. But whether he knew all there was to know or not, still I refused to discuss my problems with him. Because they're private. They're things that I keep to myself, and I don't go discussing them with watch-partners or anyone else.

So given my reticence to talk about the finer details of my life, and given the repetitiveness of George's stories about his life, it wasn't long before the two of us were forced to fall back upon the old device that seamen always use to sustain a conversation when they reach the point where they have nothing else left to discuss. We began to tell each other sea stories. We told stories about accidents and arguments and funny incidents, and of course we told about the "characters" we'd sailed with over the years. But as the two of us took turns telling our stories, I seemed to notice a pattern emerging in the ones that George was telling me. A pattern in which, whatever type of story I might tell him, he'd answer me with one that was similar to mine but better. Like if I were to tell him about a funny character I'd known, he'd tell me about a funnier one. And if I told him about an incident that took place in some exotic port, he'd tell about one from an even more exotic port. And as the conversation went on and on like that, he began to get on my nerves. Because I didn't like being constantly one-upped in that way, and it bothered me deeply even though there was no sign in his demeanor or his tone of voice to indicate that that was what he was trying to do. Instead, he told his stories in the most casual and matter-of-fact way that you can imagine. And maybe it was that very nonchalance of his more than anything else that got to me, the way he kept beating me without even trying. And when it finally reached the point where I couldn't take it anymore, I disappeared into the chartroom, staying there for a long time. And upon reemerging, I refused to talk with him anymore that night.

By this morning, though, I was ready to take him on once again since his more-or-less victory in our sea story contest of the night before had been eating at me all night long. I was ready to tell him a sea story that he wouldn't be able to top. But in order to do that, I had to cheat a little bit. I had to tell him a secondhand story, one which I'd heard from another guy I sailed with a few years back rather than telling one which I'd lived out myself. Though when I told it to him, I did so as though it were a first-person experience. What I told him was a story about being on a ship in Mogadishu at the time of the Black Hawk Down incident. And as I talked, I really laid it on thick, telling him everything I could remember having heard from the guy who was actually there and embellishing upon it from my imagination whenever memory failed me. I told him about the snipers across the harbor who made it impossible to go onto the offshore side of the ship, and I told him about the military coming around and asking for volunteers from among the crew to man the barricades around the base, and about spending time on those barricades while most of the soldiers were away on their rescue mission. I told him about how at first we all took it as a sort of lark—or at least how the seaman who was really there did—up until the humvees started returning to the base filled with dead and wounded. And I told him how from that point on, things took on a much grimmer tone.

George listened to my story quietly and attentively, nodding his head from time to time. But then rather than conceding once I was done with a statement like, "Wow, that's quite a story, Mate," what George did instead was to launch into a story of his own. And the story he told me this morning was a real doozy. So good that I just have to outline it here while it's still fresh in my mind. I have to include it in this book of mine. Somewhere.

It was about being aboard an old C-4 named the *Trans Colorado* in 1975 during the last big offensive against South Vietnam. He told me how they were ordered to go from Saigon up to Da Nang to evacuate military vehicles, but how Da Nang fell to the communists before they got there, and how after a short wait they were ordered to look instead for three barges filled with some five thousand refugees each which had been towed out of Da Nang and then cut loose and abandoned by the tug that had been towing them. And he told me how they found the barges after they'd been adrift for five days with only the small amount of water that the people had brought with them, and he went into all sorts of details about the sufferings of the people aboard, most of them soldiers and their families. He told about people who had been drinking seawater, mothers even giving it to their kids, and about the piles of dead people on the barges. The bodies that kept piling up even after they were aboard ship since the *Trans Colorado* carried nowhere near enough water for fifteen thousand thirsty people. The bodies were stacked up on the stern, he told me, and they were buried at sea until the crew ran out of old scraps of metal for use in weighing them down. And one other thing he told me about was how there were so many pregnant women among the refugees that seven babies were born the first day they were aboard ship.

Well, the ship was ordered to Cam Ranh where they were supposed to pick up three hundred "high priority" refugees, embassy employees who had come overland from Da Nang. And once they were there, everyone went ashore to join the half-million other refugees living on the beach, so many of them that the Red Cross could only help the mothers and newborns while the old people were left to die. And George swore to me that in the piles of dead bodies on the beach, some of them were still moving. It wasn't long before they were told to reload with refugees and head for a small island off the Mekong. But since many of the Vietnamese soldiers were convinced that Saigon would hold out and that the country would simply be re-divided further south, they insisted that they wanted to be taken to Vung Tao, a jumping-off point for Saigon. And being that the US commanders wanted to avoid a repetition of the incident in which the *Greenville Victory* had been hijacked and beached at Vung Tao by the soldiers aboard, they soon told the Captain to proceed there, which he did. And it wasn't long after the ship had dropped its anchor that several of the soldiers swam ashore to get help, returning later with barges and fishing boats that soon took everyone away never to be seen by the crew again. And so it was that when the ship finally sailed from Vietnam, it sailed empty.

It was quite a story that he had to tell, and I felt deeply moved by the air of heart-felt tragedy with which he told it. So moved that as he neared the end, all the negative and competitive thoughts which had previously filled my mind had long since vanished. Only to return with a vengeance when he closed his presentation with a quick little, "That's one I heard from a guy I sailed with, too. Just like your story."

And I was so angry when I heard him say that! To find out that he'd been leading me on all that time just to hit me with that wise-ass remark of his. And the way he said it, too. So calmly and casually and with that same old stupid grin on his face. I could have killed him right then! I swear I could have. And for the rest of the watch, I refused to say another word to him no matter what he said to me or how hard he tried to restart our conversation. Because I won't speak with someone who would pull a stunt like that. Not with him! Not for the rest of the trip. I won't say a word unless it's an order I give him in the line of business. I refuse to speak to him as though he were a human being, not after the way he's behaved toward me. I absolutely refuse!

One last thing I should mention before I go today is that tonight we'll be making a four hour time change, so I don't know what sort of condition I'll be in come writing time tomorrow. I don't know if I'll be able to write or not. But this Captain has decided that with the eight hours we still have to advance the clocks, it would be better to make two big, four-hour changes spaced out a few days apart rather than changing one hour every night all the way back to Tacoma. He seems to think that it's better that way where we suffer through two twenty-hour days during the passage rather than having all our days be twenty-three hour ones. And me? I don't know which of the two is worse since they both suck. Either the two big whammies or the continuous drain day after day. Both of them are terrible, and I just hope that I can handle this first whammy coming up tonight and tomorrow.

Oh, and one other last thing. There's only one more Fire and Boat Drill to go.

\* \* \* \* \*

I can't believe the email I got today! I read it, and I still can't believe it. I read it on the bridge computer during watch this morning, and it's the most beautiful thing I've ever read. Beautiful and completely unexpected.

It's from my daughter who I sent an email to when I first came aboard. But when I wrote to her, I never expected to hear anything back knowing how much she hates me. I only wrote so that she could contact me in case of an emergency, like if someone was suing me or my wife's lawyer wanted more money or something like that. Some type of bad news. And I never expected her to write with anything good to say. Certainly nothing like the email that came today, all these weeks later. Because it came right out of the blue. And when I first started to read it, I was filled with apprehension. I was bracing myself for her to finish the build-up and break the bad news. But to my surprise, the bad news never came. Not a word of it. There was nothing but happiness and light in what she had to say. And the more I read, the better it became. And the better I began to feel, too. The younger. The more alive.

She started off by talking about the old days. About her childhood and some of the things we used to do together when she was small. Back when we were happy more-or-less. And after each incident she described, she ended by telling me how much she loved me back then. How much she looked up to me and how much she enjoyed being with me. And as I read those words of hers, so many things were coming back to me. So many good things. Like memories of the way she used to get so excited whenever I got back from sea. The way she'd give me such big, enthusiastic hugs the minute I walked through the door. And even when I wasn't fresh off a ship, her face would still light up the minute she saw me. Back when she was small that is. Before everything fell apart.

So she went on for awhile about the old days and about her feelings for me, and then all at once, she came right out and told me that she still loves me. She said that she's never stopped loving me. Not really. She said that it was only anger that made her say the things she did, not hatred. And she said that she forgives me for everything, and she wants to see me again. And do you know what else she had to say? She said that I'm a grandfather, that's what she said. She said that I have a grandson I'd never known about, one born since the last time I heard anything personal from her a few years back. And when she talked about the little guy, Joshua, she said that she'd like me to come over and meet him when I get off the ship. She wants us to get together and try to heal whatever there is left of our family. She wants everything to be forgiven. And she wants me back in her life. Hers and my grandson's.

So just call me grandpa! Joshua's grandpa. And it's funny how emotional I'm getting now as I write these words. I'm getting all worked up, and I can barely wait to go over there and see them. I want to go right now. I want to meet my little heir. And that mixed race stuff? It doesn't bother me a bit since he's still my grandson no matter what he looks like. And even if he doesn't resemble me in any way, still he's carrying around my genes. He's carrying around lots of me inside him.

And I was so ecstatic when I finished reading that email of my daughter's. I was so happy and so excited that I don't know what it was that came over me, because before I knew what was happening, there I was talking with George again. I was talking with the very guy I'd so recently sworn never to speak to again, and I was doing it as though we were old friends. As though everything was forgiven. And I was even starting to let out a few of the family secrets, though I swear that he congratulated me on being a grandfather before I ever mentioned that bit of news to him. But I was so elated at the time that I just didn't care anymore. And there was nothing I wouldn't have told him right then, absolutely nothing. I was way beyond holding back secrets. And if George had wanted to, he probably could have gotten a lot of things out of me during that watch. But he seemed to have no interest in doing that, and instead all his comments and questions had an air of supportiveness to them. He wasn't probing me and he wasn't expounding, but rather he was helping me in some strange sort of way. He was helping me to work my way through all the thoughts and emotions that had come flooding into my head and heart and being. And one of the few strange statements that I remember hearing from him this morning was when he said something like, "It just goes to show you that eventually, everyone can be helped. Even the hard-cases."

And speaking of strange statements from him, there are a couple of other things that he's said to me over the last few days that now in hindsight I can almost interpret as having been premonitions about the arrival of this email. Almost but not quite since in reality they were nothing but vague statements that had something to do with my receiving good news from home in the near future. And it's only now as I look back and reinterpret them in light of today's events—and when I take them out of the context in which they were spoken—that they begin to look like premonitions.

And besides, if he's truly able to predict the future then why would he have gone and made such a ridiculous statement as the one he made toward the end of the watch this morning? The statement where he asked me if I'd only received one email so far, with so much emphasis being placed on the words so far as to imply that I'm about to receive another one soon. Implying that lightning is about to strike twice! And with the second strike being even more improbable than this first one has been. Because if anyone hates me even more than my daughter has over recent years, it's my wife and son, in no particular order. They both hate me so much that it would be impossible to quantify. So the idea that he's predicting a reconciliation with one or both of them? How ridiculous! How utterly absurd!

Before I go today, I should mention the fact that I'm feeling fine after that four-hour time change last night. I feel great. As good as I have in years. Though in spite of that, I'm still going to knock off a bit early today. We grandpas need our rest, you know.

\* \* \* \* \*

Lightning has struck twice! I can't believe it. My son actually wrote to me today. My son who's hated me so much for so long—and with such good reason. Because I was a bad father to him. I was a real asshole and I'll admit it. Not so much when he was young, but as he got older. Definitely. And I can't tell you why it was that I did the things I did. Why I treated him the way I did and why I said all those things. Because it wasn't like I thought they were the right things to do and say. Not for a minute. But they were things that I felt like I had to do at the time. Like I was compelled to do them somehow. Those things I did to keep him in his place or whatever you'd call it. Things to knock him back down a notch or two whenever it seemed like he was getting to be too big. And I knocked him down so many times. I can't remember how many. Knocked him down hard, too. Emotionally or physically. I knocked him down as hard as I could. And now as I look back at it, I can see that I went way too far with the things I did. That I knocked him down too many times without ever building him back up between times. Because it's pretty obvious from the way he's turned out. The way he's so permanently knocked down by life and everything in it. The way he just can't seem to make it. Can't make his way in the world and can't make anything of himself.

But in the email he sent me today—the one he must have gotten the address for from his sister—he didn't mention any of that bad stuff. Like it was all gone and forgotten, and the email was full of good news. Hopeful news. He said that he's got a job now, a good job, and he said that he's off the drugs, too. And he's even got a new girlfriend who's not a doper so maybe she can help him to stay straight. And while his message was short and not very articulate, still the thing hit me like a ton of bricks. It hit me where I live. And I could barely hold back the tears when he called me his childhood hero and said that I was always the guy he wanted to be like when he grew up. That really got to me. But then when I saw the way he signed the thing, the way he called himself Glenn, Jr., that was when I broke down completely.

Because that's a name he stopped using years ago, even before the first time he told me that he hates my guts. Back in the days when the worst thing he'd ever said to me was that he didn't want to be me, and especially not a junior me. But there it was in his email, written in black-and-white, the name I gave him all those years ago rather than his middle name. And seeing it brought on such a flood of emotions in me, confusing and conflicting emotions. Like the love and pride of a father, and the disappointment and the resentment and especially the shame. The shame about the way I treated him. They all came to me in a jumble, those emotions and so many more. So many of them that they overpowered me completely, and I had to let them out in tears. I had to but I couldn't. I didn't know how anymore after so many years of having held them inside. They'd become stuck somewhere deep within. They'd become embedded in my very soul. And the pain was almost unbearable as they forced their way irresistibly toward the surface, ripping and tearing themselves free one by one and tearing me apart in the process. Shredding everything that had been me for so many years now. Decades even. The pain in my guts and my throat and my eyes where the tears made their excruciating appearance. A few of them at first, then more and more, and finally a flood.

I cried and heaved and sobbed uncontrollably for I don't know how long. For minutes or hours. And the whole time I cried, George stood by me calmly and reassuringly, giving me the silence and solitude I needed at that moment. He didn't blab away with any of his nonsense, and he didn't ask questions either. And the few things he had to say during that time were the exact right things. They were the things I needed to hear. He was so tactful, so delicate even, that it's hard for me to believe that it was actually him.

But me, I was anything but tactful with the way I couldn't stop myself from crying. And I went on and on. I cried and moaned and whimpered until finally I'd purged myself of everything. The tears, the pain, the guilt. And the next thing I knew, some strange new emotion was flowing into me to fill the void that my being had so suddenly become. Some emotion that I'd never felt before. Something fresh and clean. Something filled with hope and the possibility of salvation, filled with the reassurance that all is not necessarily lost and that things can actually work out in the end. And as I felt that sense of hope rising steadily within me, still I was unable to speak right away. Not coherently. Not after the emotional roller-coaster that I'd just been on. And it was only sometime later that I was finally able to formulate phrases once again.

And when I did speak, the first thing I wanted to do was to ask George how he could possibly have predicted all this. How he could have known that my kids were going to write to me the way his statements from the last few days seemed to indicate. But when he answered me, his words turned out to be just as strange as so many of the other things he's said to me over the past few weeks, because what he said was, "Oh, knowing about it's the easy part." What? I wanted to know. What was he talking about? "I mean, it's easy to know that stuff. The hard part is making it happen, and especially with someone as hardheaded as you. Someone who makes it so hard to help them." And with the way he said it, he almost had me believing that it had actually been him who

No I'm sorry, but I don't think I can go on today. I feel too drained by what's happened and way too confused. So I think I'd better call it quits until tomorrow, okay?

\*   \*   \*   \*   \*

There's so much I want to talk about today that I don't know where to begin. But I suppose I'll start with the weather since it's become such a factor lately with the way it's been going downhill so fast over the last twenty-four hours or so. It looks like we've been caught from behind by a fast-moving low or maybe a newly-developing one. It's hard to say what it is since nothing shows up on the weather maps. Or at least nothing that looks anywhere near as severe as what we've got. And what that means is that either the maps are wrong or else we're dealing with some sort of localized disturbance, though if it's local, it's been going on for an awful long time by now. And with the weather maps being of no help, the Captain has no idea how to deal with this stuff and get us out of it, whether to head north toward the Bering Sea or to go south or what. And so instead, all we've been doing is riding it out and hoping for the best.

It's gotten to be pretty ugly, though, with strong winds and building seas, and the ship is bouncing around in a way that it hasn't done all trip. In a way it probably hasn't done in years. It's moving around so violently now that I can't sit at my desk anymore. It's too hard to hold on when I sit there, and in any case I've had to wedge the desk chair into a corner where it won't slide around and smash into things each time the ship takes a big roll. So now as I write, I've got myself braced up in the little padded armchair that serves as an easy-chair in my room, sitting sideways on it with my back against the bulkhead and my feet propped up on the edge of the bed. Not a very convenient way to write, that's for sure. And being in weather like this can be depressing with the way it makes it so hard for a person to sleep. Hard to do anything at all since you're always having to hang on. But for some reason, I don't find this weather today to be a bit depressing. I find it exhilarating in fact. I find it rejuvenating. And so in spite of the inconvenience, I still feel like writing my little heart out. And I'll just have to stop and grab on each time the ship takes a big roll.

There's something that's been bothering me over the last couple of days, something besides the weather, and that's the whole question of George and his premonitions. Because how could he have known about those emails before I even got them? And I leave aside any claims of his about having caused them to be sent since that's so clearly impossible. It goes against all the laws of nature, not to mention all logic and all common sense. I mean the idea that someone can patch-up relationships through telepathy? Give me a break! That can't be done any more than a person can cure people by laying-on-hands. And if there was anything that caused the kids to write to me now when they did, it was probably the fact that they just heard that I'm dying and they feel a little sympathy toward me. And they want to reconcile with me before it's too late. That's an explanation that makes a little sense. And it's one that doesn't involve any "powers."

And while I'm on the subject of powers, why was it that George didn't get my wife back for me too if he can cause all this stuff? Remarried or not. I'll tell you why he didn't. It's because he can't, that's why. He can't do it, and he didn't do any of the other things that he's tried to take credit for either. And his predictions? They were probably just a few stray statements of his that I latched onto and blew out of all proportion. Stray statements within his endless stream of nonsense which only seem like premonitions when I take them out of context and ignore all the meaningless bullshit that accompanied them. So in reality, he didn't predict a thing. No more than George the Second did when he asked me each of those last two days if I'd gotten good news from home. Asked before he'd been told anything about the emails—though not until after having seen the expression on my face. And at least he didn't try to take credit for them the way my watch-partner George did. No, his only response upon being answered in the affirmative had been a quiet, "That's good."

Still it bothers me, though, and I can hardly wait until I get another chance to see George on the bridge tonight and ask him more questions. And as I write these words just now, I can't believe what I see myself saying. That I'm actually looking forward to seeing George? It seems impossible though somehow it's true. I want to talk to him, and I want to hear what he has to say. And I only hope that I can hear him since that's become such a problem of late with the way the wind has been howling around the bridge and the snow-pellets have been striking the windows and bulkheads so loudly that it sounds like the place is being sandblasted. So it's been almost impossible to hear what he's had to say to me during the last couple of watches. The very watches during which I wanted so much to hear him.

At the end of the watch this morning, he handed me a

folded-up piece of paper. He gave it to me without a word. And it was with a certain amount of excitement that I stopped in at my room to look at it before continuing on my way to lunch. When I unfolded it, though, all I found was a grubby old piece of paper with the words, "Dying ain't an If, it's a When," written on it. Just that and nothing more, written in big, child-like letters. And when I saw that, I couldn't help but say, "What an idiot!" out loud as I wadded up the paper and threw it away. And then all the way down to eat, I cursed him lightly for the joke he'd played on me, for the way he'd built up my hopes for nothing. For that meaningless little phrase.

Well, I took a little nap after lunch. I've been going to sea long enough by now to know a few of the tricks, and what I did was I stuffed my lifejacket and my survival suit under one side of the mattress so that I could lay down in the little valley between there and the bulkhead. And in that way, I actually got a little sleep. Not much but a little. When I woke up from the nap, though, it was like all of a sudden things were starting to make sense to me. They were starting to fall into place. And as I search for the key to all this new-found enlightenment of mine, it seems to lie right there in that phrase of George's. The one about death being a when.

Because what I realize now is that during all these years, I've been treating death as though it were an if. Not consciously perhaps, but on a deeper level. I've been treating it as though it were something that can be avoided. And I've been living under the illusion that if I could just overcome some particular danger, like say this cancer that I have right now, then somehow I'd go on to live forever, never having to face death again. And by treating it in that way, all I've really succeeded in doing is to turn it into something to be feared and fought against. But now as I begin to accept my death as a when, as an inevitability, I'm finally starting to make my peace with it and to lose my fear and resentment. And in fact, I think I'm even beginning to look forward to it in a certain way. I'm beginning to feel happy and contented with my death. And I can feel a readiness rising up deep in my guts. A readiness to be off on my last and possibly my greatest adventure.

And now as I look ahead toward my death, my inevitable death, the sensation that comes over me is no longer one of fear or self-pity or any of the other emotions that I used to feel. No, what I feel is a strange stirring within me. Something very much like the way I used to feel years ago when I'd go aboard a new ship, especially one bound for exciting and exotic places. A feeling like, Here I go, off on an adventure. Off to see new places and do new things. It's a feeling of expectation, one of excitement even. It's a tightening in the breast as though I long to be off. And as I look ahead now, I ask myself, What greater adventure could any of us face than that of dying? What journey of exploration could we make into a land more unknown? Into a frontier more final.

Because death is the last great mystery. It's the eternal mystery and the eternal frontier. It's a place from which no explorer has ever returned to tell us what he's found. A blank spot on the map that each of us must fill-in for himself when the time comes. And me, I can hardly wait to see what's there. To see if there's some sort of fairy-tale land like the one the Christians talk about, or if it's the great blackness of the atheists, or if it's simply a road back to another rebirth. I want to see what's there for myself. I want to know the truth.

So yes, I'm prepared to die, though I also hope that my death won't come too soon. Not before I've had a chance to see my kids one last time, Sarah and Glenn, Jr., and little

Joshua, too. To see them and try to make up for a few things. Or to apologize to them at least. To tell them how sorry I am for everything. Because I don't know that it's possible to do anything more than that. To change the hatred back into the love that was once there—or that I like to think was there. Long ago. But I want to try. And I want to talk to them, too. I want to tell them all the things I've learned over these last few days. I want to tell them about death and also about life. About love and change and reform and redemption. About making up for past mistakes and setting them right. And about the possibility that with time, love may actually be able to conquer all. Even hatred.

I want to tell them all those things, and I want to discuss them with George on the bridge tonight, too. I want to discuss them if the wind and snow will let us, that is. Tonight Monday and then again tomorrow on Monday morning, this being the day we have to repeat in order to make up for the Friday we skipped on the way over. And by the way, today is also my thirtieth day aboard ship. It's the day when I become a real, true short-timer. I've made my thirty days now, and all I have to do is reach the dock at which point my job—and my career—will be over. When I mentioned that fact to George this morning, though, he came back with some vague statement about both of us being short-timers. Something to imply that he'll be quitting when we reach the West Coast I suppose. It was too hard to tell what he meant since I could barely hear him when he spoke.

\*　　\*　　\*　　\*　　\*

The strangest thing happened on watch tonight. And while I know that I've used that phrase before, this time it's really true. It was something so strange that I'm almost afraid to tell you about it since you may not believe me. But I assure you that I'm not lying. Everything happened exactly the way I'm about to say. And it happened just a few hours ago since it's still the middle of the night as I write these words. It's a time when I should be sound asleep, though I'm far too wound up over the evening's events to be able to sleep. And instead, here I sit with this piece of paper, trying to make sense of things for myself and for you. And as I tell you about the watch I just stood, I'll try to tell everything in order, the way it actually happened.

When I took over the watch, the ship was practically hove-to. We were getting beat to hell, and I could see one of the Aleutian Islands, Amchitka, on the radar less than twenty miles away, but it was impossible to see the island itself given the visibility we had. The walls of spray that pounded the bridge one after the other, each time the ship smashed into another monster wave, and the almost uninterrupted flurries of snow-pellets blowing horizontally. And on top of that it was pitch-dark since the clouds covered the sky so thickly that they blocked out virtually all the light coming from the full moon. And standing up there on that dark and heaving and trembling bridge, George hardly moved a muscle all watch. Instead he stood propped up in one spot behind the wheel while I moved slowly and carefully about, moving during the lulls between violent pitches and heavy rolls. And I went from one handhold straight to another, from the radars to the chartroom to a position near the wheel where I was able to talk with George.

He was unusually subdued on tonight's watch, though. Even more so than he has been on the previous couple of watches. And it's almost like the more the weather has deteriorated, the darker his mood has become and the less he's had to say. He already gave up that endless blathering of his days ago, back on the day of the so-called miracle-cure, and he never resumed it again even after I began to talk back to him, either telling sea stories or later when I began to speak from the heart. And then as the weather turned bad over the last day-and-a-half, George came to restrict his speech even further, doing little more than answering my questions or throwing out the occasional odd little statement. Until by now on this watch tonight, he'd reached the point where he was saying almost nothing. He was listening to me while I unburdened myself, but then he'd answer with a single word if he bothered to answer at all, just like what I used to do with him earlier in the voyage. Though what those words of his may have been tonight, I really can't tell you since all of them were lost to me in the scream of the wind.

As time went on, I started to ask myself what had happened to George. Why had he changed so much? Was it only the weather or was there something more to it? What had become of the lovable old loser that I'd come to know? Where had he gone? Because as I looked at George from time to time during the watch, the only thing that remained the same was that eternal stupid grin of his, while the person behind the grin seemed to have changed completely. And I couldn't understand how it was that this guy who had spoken to me endlessly and uninterruptedly for nearly a month by now had so suddenly become the virtual mute that stood before me. And during the entire four hours that we were together on watch, there was only one phrase that I actually heard come out of his mouth. A phrase he spoke directly into my ear after having grabbed my arm and pulled me over to him. He said, "I don't think I can help you anymore, Mate. I think I already stuck around too long." Just that and nothing more. No explanation.

But it wasn't until the end of the watch that things

took a turn for the truly bizarre. It wasn't until then that the inexplicable somehow became reality. And I can't tell you how it happened exactly. All I can talk about is what I saw and what I heard. And the first thing I noticed was the way that, while I was in the chartroom filling out my log for the watch, the weather went through a sudden and dramatic change, one as dramatic as any I've seen in my career at sea. More so perhaps. As the storm seemed to blow itself out all at once, and the winds and seas died down within a matter of minutes—or seconds. And while at first I took the change for a simple lull between waves and wind gusts, I soon came to realize that there was something more to it as the moon popped out from behind the clouds and illuminated the night. It lit up both the chartroom and the rapidly-dying seas outside. And as I gazed out the windows in amazement at the scene, Amchitka Island loomed ghost-like on the suddenly crystal-clear horizon, the moonlight reflecting eerily off its snow-covered mountains.

Eventually returning to the task at hand, I began to debate with myself on what to do about the log entries I'd just made, whether I should cross out the force eleven wind I'd written down and replace it with a three, when I heard the door at the bottom of the stairs open and close. I heard my relief, George the Second, making his way to the bridge. He didn't stop when he reached the top of the stairs, though. He didn't say hello to me and he didn't look at the chart, but instead he walked directly toward the curtain leading to the wheelhouse. And he did so as though he were on a mission. He walked straight through the curtain, and then a few seconds later, he called out for me to join him. And when I stepped through the curtain myself, I immediately saw in the moonlight how George—my watch-partner George—lay stretched out on the deck while the Second knelt down beside him. Before I could say a word, though, the Second Mate spoke to me. "He's dead," he said in a calm, matter-of-fact voice. Dead? I couldn't believe what he was telling me. "And he's cold, too," the Second continued. "It looks like he's been dead for hours. Maybe even days." Hours? Days!? What was he talking about? How could he be dead that long when I'd just spoken to him a few minutes ago? And when he'd spoken to me, what? Twenty minutes ago? Half an hour? So how could he have done that if he was already dead? He couldn't have. It's impossible!

I wanted to see for myself. I wanted to check and see if his body temperature was really as low as all that. But as I walked over and started to bend down, I all at once noticed the moonlight shining directly into his face, and at the sight I froze in my tracks. Because that face of his! There was something about it though I didn't know what. There was something about the expression on it. And it had nothing to do with the way the eyes stared sightlessly ahead. No, it had to do with that grin of his, that grin which was still there even in death. Still there and still the same though somehow it was completely different as it had lost its comical aspects and its air of stupidity, and instead it had taken on a distinctly new air. An air of peace and harmony. Of saintliness almost. Like the calm grin of a Buddha gone to his reward. And seeing that grin, I was completely incapable of touching him. I couldn't lay a hand on him or even a finger.

George the Second and I soon called up the Captain and Chris, the medical officer, and with their arrival the group of us began to perform a seldom-used shipboard ritual. The Captain called on the satellite-phone to get medical advice and to make reports, and then once it had become clear that George was far beyond being revived, we set about removing his body. We, along with the Bosun and

Mo, George's relief, and another seaman that Chris had called out, placed George in a litter, and then we wrestled him down to the ship's hospital, a place where his body will be properly prepared and taken for longer-term storage in the morning.

And all the while we were performing those tasks, we tried to come up with a good, logical explanation for what appeared to be the super-rapid cooling of George's body. Or at least the Captain and Chris and I worked on it, along with the Chief Engineer who the Captain had wanted to have in on events. We discussed the dark night and the way George had been propped up behind the wheel, making the exact time of death uncertain. And we also discussed the ravages of alcohol on his body caused by so many years of heavy drinking. And in the end, I think we all came away satisfied. All of us but George the Second that is, since he still seems to believe that some sort of miracle occurred on the bridge tonight. That a dead man actually walked and talked. Only he refuses to accept the fact that nothing "magical" has ever happened on this ship, either tonight or in days past. Nothing! Everything that's happened here can be explained. Every incident and every coincidence. All of them. Without exception.

Even without miracles, though, I'd say that the events that have taken place aboard the *Horizon Pioneer* during this voyage have provided a very rich food for thought. There have been a number of eye-opening occurrences. And especially in my own case where the last few days have proven to be a watershed. Life-altering even. And as I look back upon these days during the short life that still lies ahead of me, I'm sure that I won't forget these experiences or the man who shared them with me. George—George Altschaffl, my watch-partner during my last voyage ever. My FWE voyage. I'm truly grateful to him for the small role he played in the great self-awakening that I've experienced aboard this ship. I'm grateful for the way he listened to me when I needed someone to listen and for the piece of paper that, by chance, he happened to hand me right at the time when I needed to read those words. I'm grateful for that, and I'll always be grateful to him for the way he was there for me. The way he supported me.

And I've learned so much over these last few days. So much that now as I sit here and look at this piece of paper on the desk before me, I fail to see any good reason to finish this little story of mine. Any reason to rewrite it or even to save it for that matter. Because what is this story that I've been writing but a paper monument to myself? And the futility of epitaphs and monuments has by now become so very clear to me. The waste of time and energy that they represent, these memorials to ourselves that we try so desperately to leave behind as though they were something of value. When in reality the only thing that monuments are good for is gathering dust—or pigeon droppings. And I can see now that the only true monument that any of us can leave behind is the ongoing consequences of our thoughts and our actions. It's the love and happiness that we leave in the hearts of those we knew, those who were close to us. That's our only monument. And it's the one that I hope to be able to repair somehow before it's too late. It's the epitaph which I'll have to devote all my future energies toward rewriting. Not this silly little stack of paper.